Yankee Girl in Dixie

Theresa Schimmel

Theresa Schimmel

PUBLISHER'S INFORMATION

Author contact: terryschimmel@yahoo.com

Website: www.tamstales.net

To request permission, contact Theresa Schimmel: terryschimmel@yahoo.com

Printed in the United States of America
First Printing, 2022
ISBN 978-0-9912998-4-3

Published by Theresa Schimmel: www.tamstales.net

DEDICATION

This book is dedicated to all those who strive to bring the truth of our shameful past to light and ensure equal rights for all. The struggle is far from over.

"When the bicentennial – and perhaps the tercentenary- of the Civil War occurs years from now, there will be those who will rear up and posit that the war was all about something called "states rights" and barely at all about slavery. They will say that the Confederate flag is just a banner for those who identify with Southern culture, no less benign than a high school mascot, not nearly a symbol of a society that believed people of one skin color were so far inferior to those of another that they should only have been chattel.

Were they able, though, to transport themselves back to the early 1860's, they would find that the only state that any Southern secession document talked about was related to the institution of slavery, and that short of the accent of their English and the sauces of their food, the only thing that separated the bulk of the people in each section of the country was their laws concerning slavery."

*- Excerpt from Chapter Eight of **Worst President Ever** by historian and author, Robert Strauss*

ACKNOWLEDGEMENTS

I would like to thank the many people who have helped and supported me in the process of writing and publishing *Yankee Girl in Dixie*. My writing group, I. Michael Grossman, Yvette Nachmias-Baeu, Eugene Kincaid, Eugene McKee, Enid Flaherty, Camilla Lee, Jane McCarthy, and Bill Seymour, all provided valuable critiques, guidance, and edits. Bibliophile volunteer readers, Carolyn Hansen, Bob Stiepock, Ehren Schimmel, and Judi Scott gave useful advice and feedback. In the latter stages of revision, my editor, Jeff Ayers offered very helpful suggestions.

I'm grateful for the expert guidance and review of legal content by Patrick McKinney and Dr. Eugene McKee's review of medical content. I thank Robert Strauss for granting permission to use the quote from his book.

And, as always, I appreciate the support and encouragement of my husband, Steve, and sons, Carl and Ehren.

CHAPTER ONE

September, 1972

Fielding Elementary School was on a dusty road, a two-story red brick building with a large, mostly dirt playground shaded by four stately live oak trees draped with Spanish moss. A few other teachers were arriving as Cassie pulled into the parking lot. She was the only new hire, assigned to teach the 'Educable Mentally Retarded' primary class of eight children, mostly boys. She'd read their files, some of which were sparse. The youngest child was six, the oldest nine. Most came from either the nearby low-income projects or the surrounding neighborhood of small wooden houses on cinderblocks with sagging front porches alongside dirt alleyways. Unlike Cassie's quiet neighborhood of air-conditioned homes and manicured lawns, the area brimmed with life. Neighbors chatted with each other on front stoops or fanned themselves on porch rocking chairs while children jumped rope or rode bikes. They stared at her when she drove by, her white face a novelty.

Wanting to make a good first impression on teacher orientation day, Cassie had chosen her outfit carefully. Dressed in a blue cotton blouse and tan pencil skirt hemmed modestly at the knees, she entered the school library. The faces staring back at her from the right were all white, and those on the left were all black. She didn't want to upset the paradigm, but every fiber in her being screamed that she should veer to the left, strike out against this self-made segregation.

"Mrs. Cunningham?"

Cassie turned at the sound of her name. A short, older black woman reached out her hand. "I'm Maise Washburn. I teach kindergarten right across the hall from you. The kids call me Mrs. W. Come with me. I'll find you a seat." Easing her wide hips around the tables and chairs, she escorted Cassie to a round table on the right where two women were busy conversing. She then returned to her seat at the front table alongside Mr. Horace, the principal.

Two standing fans barely stirred the sticky air as the teachers fanned themselves with the folders from the tables. Mr. Horace pushed back his chair and stood to address his staff. With his dark grinning face, gray beard, and portly build, Cassie half-expected him to break out singing *Zip-a-de-doo-dah, zip-a-dee-day.* . . Instead, he droned on, his words slow and soporific, interrupted only occasionally by Mrs. W's comments, usually corrections. Cassie's head began to nod as last night's limited hours of sleep caught up with her.

"I'd like to welcome a new member of our teaching staff, Cassie Cunningham."

With a jolt, Cassie's eyes opened and she blinked as everyone turned towards her.

Mr. Horace smiled. "Will you please stand, Mrs. Cunningham, and tell everyone a little bit about yourself?"

Rising, she brushed a curl behind her ear and took a deep breath. "Hello, I'm Cassie, and will be teaching the Primary Special Education class. I'm new to Pensacola as we moved here just last year. I transferred from the University of Connecticut to the University of West Florida to finish my Special Education degree while my husband was completing flight training at the naval air station. I'm excited to begin my teaching career here at Fielding and look forward to meeting and working with all of you."

"Thank you, Mrs. Cunningham. Now, Mrs. Washburn has a few more things to go over before we break for lunch. I'll be in my office if anyone needs me."

Mrs. Washburn directed everyone to open their folders and take a look at the enclosed papers: staff list, class rosters, daily schedules, phone numbers for various offices and agencies, and school handbook. After answering a few questions, she announced it was time for lunch and herded them into the cafeteria. They were given plastic-wrapped sandwiches, chips, and soft drinks, before taking their seats. Again, the teachers sat in division, as if some invisible line existed. The two women at her table nodded at her before returning to their private conversation.

"You read your class roster, yet?", one of them asked the other.

"Yeah, I've got Malcom Jenkins again! Can you believe it? I retained him 'cause he didn't learn a lick last year, but thought sure they'd give him to one of the other second grade teachers, but no, I'm stuck with him again. And you know what that means, another year of banging my head against the wall. This time I'm not going to take no for an answer on getting him tested. He should be in that EMR class for sure." She blushed slightly and turned toward Cassie. "Aw, what is it you're teaching again. I . ."

"Primary Special Education Classroom. My name's Cassie Cunningham. I don't believe we've met."

"Oh, right. I'm Mary Jordan. Teach second grade."

"And I'm Sheila Withers. First grade."

"Nice to meet you. Have you taught here long?" Cassie opened the bag of chips and munched while waiting for a response.

They looked at each other, and Mary answered. "We got sent here when the courts told us to come."

"The courts?"

Mary lowered her voice. "You know – from all that desegregation flap. Negro kids got to have some white teachers now. That started back in 1962. I got sent here in '63. Thought about applying over at the local Christian Academy, but the pay's not as good, and I got kids going to college. What are you going to do, right Sheila?"

Sheila shrugged in reply. "Some of them aren't so bad. Had me a girl last year that was smart as a whip. She was my pride and joy."

Mary snorted. "Yeah, but they all end up the same. Don't matter whether they're smart or not. At least with your kids, Cassie, you don't expect much."

Cassie bristled. "Excuse me?"

"Your kids. They're retarded, so you just have to keep them in line, ya know?"

Sheila laughed. "Yeah, and that's not easy. You got some hell-raisers in there. I don't want to scare you none, but the last teacher ended up with a nervous breakdown, or at least that's the rumor." She took a bite of sandwich. "You'd think we could at least have a change of sandwich. Another year of bologna and cheese, and barbecued chips."

Mary reached into her purse and took out a plastic fan. "Yeah, lousy food and insufferable heat. I'm sweating already and it isn't even noon yet."

CHAPTER TWO

Cassie slammed the alarm button. Her body moved robotically from the bed to the shower. As the tepid water trickled down her face, she reached for the soap and began to lather. Again, she hadn't slept well. That wasn't unusual, but the added anxiety of first day jitters made sleep even more fitful. Wrapped in a towel, she padded to her bedroom, closed the curtains, and sat on the edge of the bed. She picked up the silver-framed wedding photograph. "What am I doing here, Jack? Alone. It wasn't supposed to be like this." The groom smiled back at her, tall and proud in his Navy whites, arm coiled around his bride's waist. "You know how anxious I was to start my teaching career, but how can I do this without you?" A tear fell on the glass as she stared at her image. Red-gold ringlets framed a delicate round face and smoke gray eyes. Inhaling deeply, she said, "Enough self-pity. I can do this. I've got a classroom of children waiting for me."

***

Her classroom was at the end of the hall. Cassie got busy, re-propping the books in the book nook, aligning the desks once more, with frequent glances at the clock. She saw the door's

Welcome sign fall from the door, grabbed the tape dispenser from her desk, and knelt to re-tape it.

"It's the humidity. Nothing stays on the walls or door for long."

Cassie looked up to see a tall, grey-haired woman, wearing a loose print blouse over elastic-waist pants and orthopedic shoes. Creases formed around pale blue eyes as the woman spoke in a raspy voice.

"You must be Mrs. Cunningham. I'm Mrs. Hicks, your classroom aide."

Cassie stood and extended her hand. "How nice to meet you. I'm so pleased to have an aide. Have you been at Fielding School very long?"

Mrs. Hicks chuckled, "You could say that. Longer than I can keep track of. Seen lots of babies come and go. Some new ones in here this year, I understand. But a couple of 'um from last year."

"Can we chat a bit before the children arrive?"

"Well, I'd love to, Mrs. Cunningham, but I got bus duty, and I see them coming now. You'll see me soon enough."

Cassie picked up a piece of chalk to write her name on the blackboard. She sensed someone at her door again. Wide as she was tall, black hair etched with gray and beads of perspiration, Mrs. Washburn waddled over to Cassie and held out a round board with a handle. "Mrs. Cunningham. You'll be needing this."

"What's this?"

"Your paddle. Read your handbook. It will tell you how many swats you can give 'em. And believe me, your babies will need it. They're darlings, don't get me wrong, but too slow to learn much without some persuading. I knows most of them, so you just holler if you need any help, okay?"

Cassie nodded, as the paddle was thrust into her hand. *A paddle? Really?*

Twenty minutes later Mrs. Hicks reappeared, this time with eight children lined up behind her. Two boys shoved each other as they entered the room. "Hey, none of that. Get in there and mind your new teacher. I'll be back soon."

Cassie addressed her incoming students. "Please, take your seats, children. Your names are on your desks."

The children entered warily, looking for their names as directed.

One of the boys who'd been pushing, stood in the doorway, not moving. Cassie stepped towards him. "Come in. What's your name?"

He didn't answer, and instead, shrunk into the doorway. Another boy yelled out, "That's Weldon. You gonna whoop him, Teacher?"

"Whoop him?"

"Yes, Ma'am. With the paddle."

Suddenly Cassie realized that she still held the paddle in her hand. "Oh, no..." She set the paddle on the chalk tray, walked to the door, and knelt before the thin dark boy, seeing his eyes widen with fear. She spoke softly, "Weldon, I'm your new teacher, Mrs. Cunningham. You're not in trouble. Please, come in and take a seat."

He darted past her to the back of the room, and sat on the floor. The children all watched as Cassie walked over, stretched out her hand, and said, "Come, Weldon. I'll show you your desk." Tentatively, he took her hand as Cassie led him to his seat.

She walked to the front of the room and smiled broadly. "My name is Mrs. Cunningham. I'm your teacher for this year. When I come to you, I'd like you to tell me your name and how old you are." When she approached the fourth boy, a small sandy haired child with more freckles than she, he dropped his head. "And your name?"

A barely discernible muffled reply, "Jeff".

"Jeff what?

"Jeff W-w-wayd-don." There were loud snickers. The boy looked up and glared at his classmates, his face red.

Cassie looked at her class list. "You must be Jeff Rayturn."

"Yes'm". His head dropped again.

"And how old are you, Jeff?" He shrugged his shoulders.

The boy to his left spoke, "He's eight like me. He just looks like he's six. Little pipsqueak ain't grown an inch in two years and he can't talk right."

Jeff leaped from his seat, fists drawn, and took a swing at the tease, who first ducked and then shoved Jeff back into his desk. Jeff rose up again, hollering, "Gonna g-g-get you, Lewis!" The children all jumped up, some standing on their desks, and yelled, "Fight, fight, fight!"

Cassie grabbed Jeff before he could take another swing. "Lewis, take your seat."

Lewis answered with a big grin. "Sure teacher. Don't wanna hurts the little runt."

She tightened her grip on Jeff, as he scowled at his tormentor. "That's enough. Here, Jeff, why don't you take this desk?" She led him to an empty desk in the front corner of the room.

"Whap, whap, whap." Cassie jumped at the sound. Behind her, stood Mrs. Hicks, yardstick in hand, cracking it on the teacher's desk. The children all scurried to their seats.

"Sorry I was late getting back to the room, Mrs. Cunningham. Some of the buses were late this morning. I'll just set in back 'till you tell me what you's want me to do. Mrs. Hicks strode slowly to the back of the room, her eyes boring into each child's as she went. She took a wooden chair from the back, pulled it up directly behind Lewis, and laid the yardstick across her lap.

Eight pairs of eyes stared at the new teacher. The altercation had thrown her. She needed to get this right, their beginning.

"Hey, teach, why's you got a couch and a rug in here.?" It was Lewis again. "You gonna sleep in here, or something?" A couple of students snickered.

"No, Lewis, but I'm glad you asked that question, because I chose those two items for a very specific reason. Would you all follow me to the back of the room, please?" At Cassie's request, Mrs. Hicks assigned a specific place on the rug for each child. Cassie sat on the couch and looked at the upturned faces. *These children will be my family now, for this year, at least. I need to choose just the right words.* "This is where we will gather every morning to start our day. Even though you're all different ages and not doing the same work, it's important that we come to know each other and work together as a group. We will use this area also for story time and sometimes I may ask individual students to come here for quiet."

"You mean if we be bad, teacher?"

Cassie smiled at the rosy-cheeked girl sitting directly in front of her. "I hope not, Ruby, but that too is a good question because everyone needs to understand how to act in our classroom, right?" Heads nodded. "This morning we had a fight in class. I think we can all agree that fighting in school is not a good thing."

Again, Ruby piped up. "The boys always fightin', 'specially Lewis."

"Shut up, Ruby. You fight too."

"Only when's I'm picked on."

Lewis jumped up, only to feel Mrs. Hicks firm hand on his shoulder. He sat back down.

Cassie pulled out a chart from behind the couch. "I wrote some rules for our classroom. Let's take a look at them and talk about what each one means." She read.

1. Be kind to one another.

2. Listen to the teacher and each other.

3. Try our best.

"Ain't no rule there 'bout fightin' Teacher."

"Well, Lewis, let's read that first rule again as a group." The children all repeated *Be kind to one another.* "Maybe we should put some other sentences there to be clear we all understand what KIND does and doesn't mean. Is it kind to fight?" They all shook their heads. Cassie wrote under the first rule NO FIGHTING. They continued with the discussion as Cassie added to the chart, using their words.

1. Be kind to one another:

   NO FIGHTING. NO PUSHING. NO HITTING. NO NAME-CALLING. NO STEALING STUFF.

2. Listen to the teacher and one another.

   DO WHAT TEACHER SAYS. ONLY ONE PERSON CAN TALK AT A TIME.

3. Try your best.

   DO YOUR WORK. ASK FOR HELP IF YOU'RE STUCK. DON'T TEAR UP YOUR PAPERS.

"Nice job, children. We've agreed on the rules, so I'll post them in the front of the room. Please return to your seats now. Each of you has a folder on your desk with worksheets for you to do today. If you need help, be sure to ask me or Mrs. Hicks."

Somehow Cassie got through the morning, moving from desk to desk, guiding them in the paperwork she'd prepared based on what she knew of their skills. Some labored over each pencil stroke, eyes beseeching her for help.

Mrs. Hicks cajoled many of the children with frequent terms of endearment. "Now, Sweetie, you know how to do that. You just forgot over the summer. Take your time. That's it." Then on to the next. "Here, Teddie dear, hold out your hand, and I'll trace the letter for you. Feel it? Now you try. See. You can do it!" Then she gave him a squeeze. But she never turned her back on Lewis, who had finished his work before all the others. Cassie allowed him to take a game from the back shelf. When the first lunch bell rang, Mrs. Hicks rose and said she had to go help in the cafeteria. "Our class has second lunch, then recess. After that, I'll be by so you can take a break, Mrs. Cunningham."

"Thank you, Mrs. Hicks."

Mrs. Hicks walked to the front of the room, turned around, and slapping the yardstick in her hand, raised her voice, "Children, you b'have ya'selves. Remember, I'll be back. You got ya'selves a nice teacher, now, and you do as she tells you." Then she set the yardstick in the corner and headed down the hall.

With Mrs. Hicks gone, Cassie took a deep breath. She was on her own now. The children looked at her expectantly. She collected the finished work, read a short story, and then with as firm a tone as she could muster, directed them to line up at the door for lunch.

Orange and green lunch trays were stacked at the end of the cafeteria line. Cassie took one and inched forward with the children. She watched as the lunch ladies ladled food onto each child's platter.

"Excuse me, but what is that?" She pointed to the container of small round-shaped tan things swimming in thick sauce.

A thick-waisted woman of indeterminate age paused, her metallic spoon in mid-air.

"Whad'u mean, what's that?" With her hairnet pulled tight across her brow, the lunch lady frowned at Cassie.

"Those brown things." Cassie pointed.

"Why, those be butter beans, lady. Ya' never seen butter beans before?"

"No, I guess not." The woman shook her head, muttered under her breath, and plopped a peanut butter sandwich next to the beans.

In the past, Cassie's observations of school lunch rooms were ones of constant din and chatter. Here, the only sound was the scraping of forks and spoons against metallic trays. She stared down the table at her class. Almost in unison, they scooped up the beans, tore large chunks of peanut butter sandwiches to chew, and then used the crusts to mop up the remaining butter bean sauce. They gulped chocolate milk from cartons and ate orange wedges, some even devouring the skins. Finished with their food, the children stared at her half-full tray.

"Ain't you gonna eat your orange, Teacher?"

It was Ruby. Her brown eyes, half-hidden with stringy greasy hair, hungrily stared at her teacher's tray. Cassie answered, "Oh, well, did you want . .?"

"Thank you, Ma'am." Her hand reached across the table greedily, and the orange wedge quickly disappeared. The other children glared at Ruby's engorged cheeks as her eyes twinkled in triumph and the juice dribbled down her chin.

After lunch, Cassie led the children to recess. They tore onto the playground like a swarm of insects. With a mixture of high-pitched squeals, bellows, giggles, and chatter, they were in constant motion. A few teachers clustered by the monkey bars. Cassie sauntered to the trees, shading her eyes from the bright sun.

"Hey, Teacher!" Cassie looked up to see Ruby hanging upside down with legs draped over an expansive oak limb, like the Spanish moss that adorned it.

"Ruby! Get down there from there! You could fall!"

Ruby laughed.

"She don't never fall Teacher." Cassie looked down at Angie, a pretty, butternut-skinned girl with narrow face and braided hair who sat in the first row. "Ruby can do anything."

"Well, that may be so Angie, but she might fall. Don't the other teachers ever make her get down?"

Angie shrugged. "No Ma'am. Sometimes the boys come 'round and peek at her panties, but I stand guard and throw sticks at them. They don't mess with her much anymore."

Cassie tried to picture this wisp of a child chasing off some brutish boys. "Don't you ever want to climb the trees too?" She fondly recalled her own tree scrambles.

"Can't"

"Oh, but I'm sure..."

Angie rolled up her left pant leg to show a metal brace encasing her leg from ankle to knee.

"I see."

Cassie tried to recollect what she'd read on Angela Williams. She was quite sure that there was no mention of a physical handicap.

"Mrs. Cunningham, isn't it?" Cassie turned to see a tall angular woman, face reddened from the heat, with strands of mouse-brown hair poking out of a thick bun wrapped on top of her head. Her hand gripped Weldon by the arm. "This is one of yours, I believe?"

"Yes, Weldon is in . ."

"Well, you need to keep a better eye on him. I just pulled him off of one of my boys. Fist-fight, and ten to one, this one started it." She shoved Weldon towards Cassie.

"I'm so sorry. I didn't see.."

"I know you didn't see. That's what I'm telling you. Watch him. In case you haven't figured it out yet, this one's a troublemaker."

Cassie squatted down. "Weldon, look at me. Tell me what happened." He shrugged. She repeated. "Weldon, tell me what happened." She waited. Weldon's fists tightened as he stared at the ground. "I didn't do nothin."

The other teacher crossed her arms. "Say what, boy? You know darn well you started that fight."

"Did not! They was pickin on me!"

"Are you yelling at me? I can march you up to the office right now, if that's what you want."

Cassie stood. "Again, I'm so sorry about this, Mrs.?"

"Miss. Miss Webster. First grade. You need to straighten this boy...,"

"Thank you for bringing it to my attention. I'll speak to Weldon."

"He needs more than that. He needs..."

"Thank you, Miss Webster."

At the sound of the bell, Miss Webster stomped off as swarms of children ran to their teachers, creating pockets of life amid the red clay. Cassie was bumped and pushed as the children jostled for position in a semi-straight line. She called for Teddie, who took his place as assigned line leader, his large saucer-like eyes looking up at her. She placed her hand on his shoulder, smiled, and began to count those behind him. Like over-wound clocks they jiggled and twisted, trying to bring their bodies back to stillness. She walked backwards, turning occasionally to check the remaining distance, while calling out names in reprimand for the occasional shove. At the entrance to the school door, she spoke to them.

"Remember now, children, recess is over. Calm yourselves as we go down the hallway."

"Can we have a drink, Teacher?"

"Yes, we'll stop for a drink, but a quick one. Then I want you to go immediately to your desk and put your head down to rest." Watching them line up at the water fountain, she smiled. It was a good beginning. She could do this. Tonight, she would write all about it in a letter to Jack.

CHAPTER THREE

She opened a beer from the refrigerator, took a big gulp, and collapsed on the couch in front of the fan. The air conditioning was on the fritz again and the repair man wouldn't be by until Saturday. By then, she'd look like wilted lettuce. She thought back on her first day and smiled, the children's' faces flashing like images in a View Master. Oh, the stories she could already tell Jack! She reached for stationery and pen, her eyes already watering at the thought of him. No, not today. She'd told herself no more tears.

Dear Jack,

I made it through my first day with the kids! Guess I better tell you right out. You've got competition. I'm in love. It took only one day, but I already love every one of those children. At first, I was overwhelmed. They seemed so far behind, but some of them are definitely bright. I'm not sure why they are classified "educable mentally retarded". I've read their files and honestly expected them to be much slower. Mrs. Hicks said she was 'right impressed' with how well I did with the kids. She's my classroom aide. Comes on like a female drill sergeant at first, swinging her yardstick, and barking at the children. My first thought was "Oh, no. How am I going to tolerate that? But all you have to do is watch her with those kids. I swear she's like an old mother hen, clucking to keep them in line, but watching over them with care. They're all a little afraid of her. Maybe that's not such a bad thing. Some of them are pretty rough around the edges, if you know what I mean. Remember you telling me about some of the guys in training? Like "Boots" and what was the big guy's name? Oh, yeah, Luke, I believe. Well, Weldon and Lewis, are cut from the same cloth. Fists ready to fly at the slightest provocation. Lewis is outspoken - ready to challenge me at every turn. Weldon, more reserved, strikes me as troubled with something. I hope I can find out what. Zebedia, nicknamed Zebbie, a large, soft- spoken boy, seems eager to please. Two of the boys, Trevor and Teddie, are brothers. The older one, Trevor, is very protective of Teddie, who adores his brother. Only two girls in the class right now; Ruby, who's white, and Angela, who's black. Their smiles are sweet, but they are toughies inside. Have to be, I guess, to put up with all those boys. Then there is Jeff, the only white boy in the class. He has a significant stutter and is small for his age, which – you guessed it- means he's a prime candidate for bullying. So, as you can see, I've got my work cut out for me.

I was so busy today that for once, Jack, I didn't think constantly of you. And I didn't cry either! It doesn't mean I don't miss you though. It was you last night Jack, wasn't it? Your soft breath blowing on the back of my neck. Remember how you would tenderly lift up my curls to do that? I used to elbow you and say, "I'm sleeping, Jack." But you'd do it again anyway, and start to kiss my neck. Come again to me, Jack, please?

Your darling,

Cassie

She slipped the letter into the envelope, and wrote his name on the front before placing it on the stack of unsent letters. Pouring her now warm beer down the kitchen sink, she looked out the window and saw AdaMae cutting flowers. She marveled at how her neighbor could toil in the garden in such heat. No doubt she was picking flowers to set out for Cassie's visit.

AdaMae Lee was the first person she and Jack met when they moved into their new home. They were in the yard, planting some newly acquired azalea plants when Cassie looked up to see a white-haired woman holding a glass pitcher of lemonade in one hand and plastic tumblers in the other. A retired florist and experienced gardener herself, AdaMae became a reliable resource for Cassie's novice gardening.

Cassie now had a standing invitation for Wednesday dinner. It was the one night that she ate properly. Cooking had never been her forte. Her offerings were simple routine fare; spaghetti, hot dogs, Hamburger Helper. When Jack was home, he'd often order pizza or pick up fried chicken, but once he was deployed to Vietnam, Cassie rarely bothered to cook. She ate mostly sandwiches, tossed a salad, or skipped meals entirely, and had lost weight. AdaMae was on a mission to fatten her up. Cassie's mouth watered just thinking of the home-made biscuits sure to be served at AdaMae's tonight. She'd best shower and get dressed.

Pulling a spring green summer sundress over her head, she rummaged through the pile of shoes for her sandals. It was one thing that annoyed Jack, her shoes tossed everywhere. His shoes were still lined up neatly on the left side of the closet, next to the box of letters.

There were only two beers left in the six-pack. That should be enough. They rarely had more than a beer apiece. She grabbed them from the refrigerator and headed out the door. An old van with **Can-Do Handyman** lettered on the side was parked behind AdaMae's Buick sedan. Maybe AdaMae was finally getting that patio door fixed. Her knocking elicited a deep bark. It couldn't be Rufford, AdaMae's terrier mix, who rarely barked. The door opened to a massive furry creature pawing at the screen. From the living room, a voice commanded, "Alice, get down." The creature obeyed as a hand pulled on its collar and then pushed open the screen door.

AdaMae called out from the kitchen, "I'll be right there, Cassie."

"Sorry about that. She won't hurt you. Just likes to say hello."

Cassie looked up to see a tall young man holding the dog's collar. She judged him to be older than she by a few years, perhaps in his late twenties. Following him to the living room, she lifted AdaMae's Persian cat Magnolia off the wicker chair and brushed white hairs from the cushion before sitting down. The grandfather clock chimed five times, Rufford's cue to push through the patio door doggie window and settle on the carpet.

AdaMae entered, loose strands of hair falling from her bun. "Hi, Cassie. Did you meet my grandson?"

"No, only made Alice's acquaintance."

AdaMae laughed. "Well, Alice isn't one to be shy, are you?" She bent to scratch Alice's mottled fur and gave Rufford a pat as well.

The young man stretched out his hand. "Sorry, should have introduced myself. Grant. Grant Lee."

She shook his hand. "Hi. Cassie Cunningham. Pleased to meet you."

He smiled in return, the left side of his mouth sliding up slightly higher than the right, revealing bright, perfect teeth.

She watched him sit cross-legged on the carpet, one hand on his dog, the other pushing shoulder length brown hair from his face, revealing chestnut eyes flecked with green. Despite the dark color, there was a luminescence about them that made Cassie feel as if she was gazing into a deep dark pond. Tanned, muscular arms extended from a tie-dyed t-shirt. Bare feet protruding from tattered jeans rubbed against the shag carpet.

"Don't let my grandson's hippy look deceive you, honey. He's as straight an arrow as they come." AdaMae kissed the top of her grandson's head, and sat on the couch behind him. "Dinner will be ready in a minute."

"Oh, almost forgot. I brought some beer." Cassie handed the beers dangling from the plastic ring to AdaMae. "Sorry there's only two. I didn't know you had other company."

"No worries. Grant, you want to pour us some brews?" She handed him the two beers. "There's another six-pack in the refrigerator."

"Sure, Grams."

Cassie watched his long legs untwist with ease before he strode into the kitchen.

AdaMae wiped her hands on the dishtowel in her lap. "I hope you don't mind, dear, but Grant's missed the past couple Sunday dinners with me, so I asked him over tonight."

"Of course."

Grant returned with the beers and handed one to Cassie.

"Thanks." She sipped the frothy head and licked her upper lip.

Grant was back on the floor, his mug between his legs. He looked up at her and said, "I usually never miss a chance to chow down on Grams' cooking, but the past couple of weekends have been filled with school prep."

"You're a teacher?"

"I teach history at Escambia High. I understand that you're a teacher too. What school?"

"Fielding Elementary."

"I know the area. You like it?"

"Only just started, but I think I will. I expect it will be a challenge, but I love the kids."

"The kids are what make teaching worthwhile, don't you think?"

She nodded, and then turned to AdaMae. "Are you getting that door fixed? I saw a work van outside."

"Oh, that's Grant's van."

She looked back at Grant. "But I thought you were a teacher?"

"I am, but you know what a teacher's salary pays. 'Sides, I need a second job in the summer. Handyman jobs fill in the gap, and working with my hands is a nice change from preparing lesson plans."

"So, what kind of jobs do you do?"

"Pretty much anything. I get more jobs than I can handle, really."

AdaMae stood and stepped around the sleeping dogs. "Mr. Lee taught Grant everything he knew. That's actually Mr. Lee's van outside. I keep telling Grant he should get a new one. That thing is thirty years old."

"Gramps left it in good condition. It's got plenty of miles left, Grams, just like you."

She snapped the dishtowel at him. "I've got to pop some biscuits in the oven and check on the chicken."

Cassie stood. "I can help. Do you want me to set the table?"

"Already set. We're eating on the patio. Jes' you set down and chat some more with Grant. I'll call ya'll when supper's ready and we'll carry it out."

Cassie sat back on the paisley print cushion and reached for her beer. She crossed her legs, tugged at the hem of her dress, and gazed at the dust particles floating in on the light shafts from the patio door louvres, trying to avoid his gaze.

"Grams has told me a lot about you."

Cassie turned in her chair to face him. "She has?"

"It's been awful nice of you to spend so much time with her. She stays busy with her gardening but I know she's been lonely ever since Gramps passed away."

"Me? It's her that's been nice. She's been a godsend to me ever since..." She stopped midsentence.

He set his beer down and inched forward, arms draped over his knees. "I'm sorry about your husband." Something in his voice told her that he understood.

She nodded. "Thank you."

Just then, Alice lifted her head from the rug, sniffed the air, rose and lumbered into the kitchen, followed by Rufford. Grant laughed. "Chicken must be done."

She liked his deep yet soft laugh. "Alice is a big girl. Can't make out her breed."

"Heinz 57 as best I can tell, but some collie in her for sure."

"Thought so. Hope you don't mind me asking, but why did you name her Alice? Doesn't seem to quite fit."

He laughed again. "When I got her as a puppy at the pound, I had no idea she would grow to be so huge. I'm a Woody Guthrie fan. Named her after his song."

"Song?"

"You know. *Alice's Restaurant.*"

"I guess I don't know it."

"You've never heard *Alice's Restaurant?*"

She shook her head. She was mostly a Beatles fan, and Jack didn't pay much attention to music, although he did have a collection of 45's stuck in a box along with service medals and ribbons. They'd come a few weeks after his death, along with Jack's flight manual and a photo of him in his helicopter. With his earphones, helmet, and tinted goggles, he was barely recognizable as her husband. She stuck the box in the bedroom closet and hadn't opened it since its arrival.

AdaMae called from the kitchen. "Supper's ready! Come help me take food out to the patio."

The temperature had dropped to a more comfortable eighty-five degrees. The round teak table was set with quilted placemats and cloth napkins. Sprigs of yellow coreopsis and marigolds sat in a center vase. A welcome breeze blew across the patio as Grant and Cassie carried out bowls of fried chicken, collard greens, butter beans and cheese grits. AdaMae brought out hot biscuits and butter.

"You've really outdone yourself, AdaMae." Cassie pushed the salt and pepper aside to make room for the grits. Cassie had once made the mistake of telling AdaMae of her distaste of grits.

Her neighbor's horrified reaction was, "How could anyone not like grits?" Since then, dinners had included all kinds of grit fare. Sausage and grits, bacon and grits, shrimp and grits. Cassie was acquiring a taste for grits.

Grant passed the collard greens to Cassie. "Have you tried Grams' collards? It might taste a little strange to your Yankee palette. I didn't like them at first when I moved here."

She took the bowl from him and scooped a small portion of the dark greens onto her plate. "You didn't always live in Pensacola?"

He shook his head. "Moved here from New York to live with my grandparents, after my parents died."

She looked over at AdaMae with surprise. *Why hadn't she told her this*?

"I think we could use some ice tea." AdaMae grabbed the pewter pitcher and abruptly left the table to get a refill.

Cassie turned to Grant. "Did I say something wrong?"

"No, it's just hard for Grams, even after all these years. My parents died in a car crash when I was twelve. My father was her only son."

Cassie gulped, unsure what to say. She knew about words for the grieving. How they bounced off of you. Was that still true after years had passed? What must it have been like for a boy to lose both his parents so suddenly? Yet he appeared very well-adjusted, very content.

"I didn't know. I'm …. I'm so …"

"It's okay. It's been almost sixteen years. Every once in a while, Grams will take out pictures and we talk, but …well, memories can be both good and bad."

"Yes. I know." She blushed as his eyes locked on hers. She decided to change the subject. "Your name, Grant Lee. Kind of…ah..."

He laughed. "Kind of an oxymoron of nomenclature, isn't it? The famous General Lee is actually a distant relative."

"Really?"

"And my mother, being from the north, thought my name should be balanced out."

"Your mother was from New York, then?"

"Yes. My father met her while attending Columbia University. Grams said she was deathly afraid of her son going up there and turning all 'Yankee' on them."

"She calls me that sometime -Yankee, like I was some kind of foreigner."

"Well, to many here, you are. My grandfather told me that when he and Grams went to my parents wedding, they were shocked that there were so many woods, pastures, and farms up north."

"What did they expect?"

"Parking lots and skyscrapers."

AdaMae returned and poured refills of the iced tea. "Are ya'll talking about me?"

"All good stuff, Grams." Grant winked at his grandmother.

She smirked in reply. "Thought sure you'd be into 'teacher talk' by now. Grant talks about 'his kids' non-stop if you let him."

Cassie asked, "How long have you been teaching?"

"This is my fourth year at Escambia High School. First year was the roughest."

"I suppose all teachers find the first year hard."

"I suppose. But there were additional challenges."

"Challenges?"

He grabbed a drumstick, took a big bite, chewed and swallowed before responding. "First year of integration."

This was the fall of 1972. She quickly did the math. "So, 1969 was the first year for blacks and whites in your school?" She shook her head. Growing up in a suburban northern town, she followed the passage of the Civil Rights movement, saw the demonstrations on television, but it was all quite distant to her. There were only a handful of black students in her elementary and high school, and a few in her dormitory at college.

AdaMae smeared butter on her biscuit. "Grant was in the thick of it, that's for sure. I was so proud of him, trying to get through to some of those blockhead administrators about doing what's right. I thought sure he'd be fired for speaking out on behalf of those colored kids. They sure was picked on, poor things."

Grant corrected his grandmother. "Black, remember Grams."

She waved her hand in dismissal. "I know, I know, so you keep telling me."

Cassie thought of Fielding Elementary, technically integrated, but there were far more blacks than whites. "So have things improved?"

"Yes and no. I mean there is a certain tolerance now, less overt acts of racism, but socially there is little to no integration still. I push the envelope in my classroom. It's gotten me in hot water with some of the parents."

"Push the envelope? Explain."

"I have assigned seating. Without it one side of the room would be white, the other black. I also pair them up for projects, putting black and white students together."

"Your own little social experiment?"

"You might say that."

"Any progress?"

"Subtle, but I think so. I've even seen a couple of friendships develop. Some jocular exchanges in class. Outside of class it's still strained. There are social norms to maintain."

"I think I know what you mean. I can't believe how segregated our staff is at school. It makes me really uncomfortable at faculty meetings."

"You can't be afraid to shake things up a bit, Cassie. Take the first step. Sit in the black section."

"You think so?" She wasn't sure she had the courage.

"Now who wants pie for dessert?" AdaMae stood to clear the plates.

"Pie too? You shouldn't have baked in this heat." It was a little cooler today but by Cassie's gauge, 85 degrees was still plenty hot.

"I didn't bake. Grant made the pie. I can only take credit for teaching him to make the flakiest pie crust you'll ever taste." She smiled lovingly at her grandson.

Grant stood to help his grandmother clear the dishes. "I hope you like key lime pie. It's Grams favorite."

"I don't think I've ever had it."

He shook his head. "Grams, you were right, she is a Yankee Girl."

CHAPTER FOUR

Cassie let her head fall to the stack of papers on her desk. It had been a long day, mostly tamping down one crisis after another. Angela was in tears again from the misfit of her brace. Ruby had lice, which meant every child had to be checked. And of course, there were the usual scraps. What was she going to do about Weldon? He'd been in a fight again today. Fourth one this week. And when he wasn't fighting, he was sleeping at his desk. The child obviously wasn't getting enough sleep at home.

Many of the children were beginning to respond to the behavior rewards program she'd set up. Each child had a booklet taped to their desk. Cassie put stickers in them for work completion, kind deeds, following the rules, etc. At the end of the week, the children could 'cash in' their stickers to retrieve a prize from the prize box. Cassie made regular trips to K-Mart to replenish the small trinkets and toys. Despite her efforts to reward Weldon whenever possible, his sticker collection was sparse. He had an excuse for every fight. It was always the other kid's fault. Today Lewis had bumped Weldon's desk on his way to the reading corner in the back of the room. He'd pounced like a coiled rattlesnake ready to bite. It took all her effort to pull them apart. She had sent notes home, hoping for a response, but so far there'd been none.

Pulling Weldon's file from her desk drawer, she reread its contents. Though his test scores were borderline, she suspected his ability was much higher. Quick to complete math equations and answer comprehension questions, he still struggled to sound out words. The phonics-based material she hoped would work had not been approved by the administration. She ordered it anyway. What better way to spend her money? The list price in the catalog was half her weekly salary, but it looked promising and may be effective with other students too. This was Weldon's second year in a self-contained special education classroom. She'd talked to Mrs. Hicks about him, whose response was, "That boy's got more than a chip on his shoulder. More like a boulder." That about sized it up. But why?

The social history was sketchy. He lived with his grandmother. No siblings. Normal birth. Parents no longer in the picture. Like with many of the children's files, no phone number was listed. Then she noted the address: 110 Fielding Street. Right down the road. She'd already made a couple of visits to other children's homes. Maybe it was time to make another; visit Weldon's grandmother in person.

She stood, pushed back her chair, and went out into the corridor. The school was almost deserted. She'd stayed late preparing tomorrow's lessons and cutting out some stenciled letters for the bulletin board. Stepping outside, she was momentarily blinded by the bright sun. The hot air shimmered over the blacktop. Putting on sunglasses, she started walking down the street, checking each house number. Perched on cinderblocks, the houses sat on dusty lots, pock-marked with weeds. Dogs dozed under the porch pilings or scratched persistent fleas. Jacked-up junk cars littered a few empty lots along the road. A cat jumped from the hood of one and scampered underneath.

110 Fielding was a two-story tired clapboard building on a dead-end street. A battered grey pick-up was parked in front and a faded sign hung above the door: *Two-Spot Bar. Weldon lives here?* Cassie heard laughter from inside. Taking a deep breath, she walked up the wooden porch steps strewn with broken bottles and peeked through the open door. The room was dark, hazy with smoke. Flies buzzed in and out of the open windows. She heard the smack of colliding pool balls as her eyes adjusted to the dim light, and she spotted two men at a pool table.

Tentatively, she stepped inside, her voice cracking when she spoke. "Could you tell me where I might find Mrs. Roosevelt?"

One man, pool cue in hand, asked, "Who you be?"

She heard the menacing tone and tried to reply with a steady voice. "I'm Weldon Roosevelt's teacher. I was hoping to speak with his grandmother."

"She done gone to town."

Cassie hesitated only a moment. "Would you please tell her Mrs. Cunningham stopped by? I'd appreciate it."

Conscious of cold stares on her back, she retreated. Sweat trickled down her armpits. She glanced back, but no one followed. A small figure moved in the shadow of the upstairs window. Was that Weldon? No wonder he was always tired. She could only imagine what it must be like for a child to live above a bar. The only time she'd seen him smile was petting some mangy dog that occasionally followed him to school. At least he had a canine friend.

The school parking lot was empty save her maroon Toyota. Unnerved by her brief visit to the bar, she shakily pulled on the school's front door. It was locked. How could that be? Where was the custodian? She looked at her watch. 4:00 p.m. Normally, he would still be here. Her car keys sat at the bottom of the purse left in the classroom closet. Now what? She walked around the school, peering into each window, hoping to spy Mr. Ramsey, the custodian, but there was no sign of him. Sitting on the front steps like a lost child, Cassie pondered her predicament. The nearest store was at least three miles away and she wasn't even sure if it had a pay phone. And who would she call? Guess it would have to be a cab.

Five minutes passed, then ten. A green sedan pulled into the lot. A car door slammed. An extremely tall, black woman strode towards her, brushing red clay dust from the side of her fashionable beige bell bottom trousers. She stopped in front of Cassie. "Hello. You waiting for someone?"

Cassie stood. "No. It appears I'm locked out."

"The custodian's not here?"

"No sign of him."

"Hmm. He's usually still here. I was going to get a few of my files."

Cassie pushed her sunglasses back and squinted into the dark, regal-like face. "You work here?"

"Yes. I was about to ask you the same question. I thought I knew the whole staff. Are you new?"

"Ah-ha. Cassie Cunningham. I teach Primary Special Education."

The woman smiled. "Ah, yes, I was planning on stopping by your room soon." She extended her hand. "Lareina Gooden. Most people call me Reina."

Cassie shook her hand. "Nice to meet you. I'm afraid I don't remember you from any of the staff meetings, but you do look familiar."

"You've probably seen me in the hallways. I've stopped in to talk to some of the teachers but haven't made any of the faculty meetings. Unfortunately, I'm assigned to three different elementary schools as the social worker, and I can't make all the meetings."

Cassie nodded in appreciation. Juggling the work load of three schools had to be demanding, yet there was something about Reina - the way she spoke and carried herself - that implied confident competence.

"I guess we'll both have to call it a night and head home. It will be a treat to get home before five o'clock for once." She turned back toward her car.

Cassie hesitated a moment, and then called out, "Reina!"

Reina turned abruptly, her low heels kicking up dry dust.

"Sorry, Reina, but I'm *really* locked out. I left my purse in the classroom."

"You need a lift then? Where?"

"If you take me to a pay phone, I can call a taxi."

"Nonsense. I'll take you home." She walked briskly to her car and opened the door. "Hop in. Better hurry, thunderstorm's coming."

Cassie glanced up at the darkening sky. A few drops began to fall just as she slid into the passenger seat.

Reina put the key in the ignition and started the engine. "Where to?"

"Bluffs Drive- off of Bayshore Boulevard. Do you know where that is? It's about a twenty-minute drive I'm afraid. I'll pay you for the gas."

"Don't be silly. Happy to help." As they pulled out of the parking lot, they heard rumblings of thunder. Reina's gold bracelets jangled as she turned on the wipers. She glanced at Cassie and asked, "How is it you got locked out?" She listened attentively as Cassie shared her frustration with Weldon's classroom behavior and the failed attempt to contact his grandmother at the *Two Spot* bar.

Reina had to raise her voice to be heard over the pounding of the rain. "You went to the *Two Spot*?" Cassie nodded sheepishly, sensing some disapproval. "Cassie, how long have you lived in Pensacola?"

"We moved here a little over a year ago."

"From up north, I presume?"

"Connecticut."

"In case you hadn't noticed, things are a little different down here. I take it you've never heard of the *Two Spot* bar?"

"No. I didn't even know that was where Weldon lived until I got there."

"It's not my place to lecture you, but the *Two Spot* has a reputation. Not a good one. I wouldn't advise you going there again. Even I wouldn't go there, and I'm not lily-white."

Cassie blushed. "I just, I mean, I thought maybe talking to the grandmother would help. I've been trying to get to know the families of all the kids. I've made other home visits." She looked over at Reina, whose eyebrows were slightly raised and lips pursed, as if she were about to say something. For some reason, it was important to Cassie for this woman to understand her motivation. Surely a social worker would agree that the teacher and parents must work together. Why then, did she suddenly feel like a child who had just misbehaved?

By the time they pulled onto Cassie's street the rain was torrential. Gullies of water rushed alongside the car. Reina turned on the radio just in time to catch an emergency warning of flash flooding and an advisory for motorists to get off the roads.

"My goodness. I've never seen rain like this!" said Cassie.

"Welcome to the Panhandle."

"My house is the one on the corner, brick with white shutters." Cassie pointed.

As Reina drove into the driveway, Cassie asked, "Please, won't you come in?"

"Won't your husband mind?"

"No." Something stopped her from telling Reina about Jack.

"If you're sure. It might be awhile before the roads in my neighborhood are passable. There's one road under a bridge that always washes out in these downpours." She put her hand on the door handle. "Well, you ready to run? You do have a house key, don't you?"

"Yes, a spare one hidden under the mailbox."

They lifted their respective door handles at the same time and made a mad dash along the stone pathway. Cassie fumbled for the key under the mailbox, unlocked the front door, and entered the foyer. Reina stepped in behind her, stomped her feet on the rug and shook. Droplets spewed from her thick Afro hair.

Cassie shuddered. "We're soaked. Let me get you a towel to dry off. Better yet, why don't you let me put your clothes in the dryer? I'll get you a robe you can wear while they're drying. I think I'm going to get something drier myself."

"If you don't mind. Yes, that would be great."

Cassie walked to the bedroom, quickly unzipped her skirt, and kicked off her shoes. Changing into a t-shirt and shorts, she headed to the bathroom to grab her robe for Reina, then realized that it would be way too small. She grabbed Jack's blue robe hanging next to hers.

Reina was still standing in the foyer. Cassie handed her the robe. "Here. You can change in the hall bathroom. There are fresh towels there to dry off."

"Thanks."

Cassie grabbed a towel for herself and headed to the kitchen, where she leaned forward to towel-dry her hair.

"That's some head of curls you got there."

Cassie flipped back her hair and looked up to see Reina standing in Jack's robe, the one she gave him for his birthday, that he only got to wear once. "I hope you don't mind- the robe- that is. It's my husband's. I didn't think mine would fit you."

Reina laughed, the kind of laugh that warmed you like a swig of bourbon. "Not at all. Petite, I'm not."

"Oh, but you have a lovely full figure, I mean. . ."

"Yeah, I got curves in all the right places, or so I've been told. You said this was your husband's robe? You sure he doesn't mind? Will he be home soon?"

Cassie ignored the questions, stood, and opened the refrigerator. "You want something to drink?"

"Whad-ya got?"

"The usual, or I can put on some tea."

Reina came from behind and pulled the refrigerator door wider. "You saving that beer for your hubby?"

"No. I'm the beer drinker, not Jack. Usually have one every day after work, especially since I moved to Florida."

"Well, I don't want you to change your routine on my account." Reina grabbed two beers from the refrigerator and set them on the table. They each popped open a can, took a swig, and looked at each other in awkward silence.

Cassie spoke first. "Maybe the rain will end the heat wave."

"Heat wave? Is that what y'all think? It's just plain hot here, and the rain just raises the humidity level from 90% to 100%. I never minded much as a girl, but after I went up north for college, I found I liked the cooler air. My family says I'm crazy. They can't imagine why I would like the cold."

"You went north to college? Where?"

"Yale."

Cassie gagged on her beer. "I'm from Connecticut." She looked at Reina with new appreciation. It took real brains to get into Yale. "I went to the University of Connecticut. My husband did too."

"Navy ROTC, right?"

"How'd you know?"

"Saw his picture in the living room."

Cassie took another long swig of beer. "How 'bout something to go with that beer? I think I've got some crackers and Cheez Whiz." She stood and opened up a kitchen cabinet, reaching for both.

"Crackers and Cheez Whiz? How'd you guess? My favorite. Like old dorm days. My roommate and I pigged out on that something fierce."

"Yeah. I introduced the gourmet fare to Jack. He got hooked on it too, much to his mother's chagrin."

"Hmm, let me guess. Only Momma's home-made cooking good enough for her boy."

Cassie laughed. "Not exactly. His folks had a cook, a gourmet one at that. I didn't even try to compete."

"Wise decision."

"Reina, you said you liked it up north. Why didn't you look for a job there when you graduated from college?"

"I did. Worked one year at a social service agency. But I missed my family, and knew I was needed more here."

"I see."

"No, you don't."

"Excuse me?"

"Sorry, but you've only lived here a year, right? Although, even if you lived here all your life, you still couldn't possibly understand."

Cassie shrunk back into her chair. "You mean because I'm white, right?"

"Look, Cassie, I can tell you're a good person. You want to make a difference in the lives of those kids, don't you?" Cassie nodded. "And I bet you're thinking some of these parents just don't care or else they'd be coming to the open house and anxious to meet you, right?"

"I wouldn't say they didn't care. I just want to talk with them, that's all. To tell you the truth, Reina, I'm not sure many should even be in Special Education. I mean, little Angie has a brace on her leg because of cerebral palsy but I don't think there's a damn thing wrong with her intellect. And Ruby. I've seen her talk her way out of more scraps with her tales than anyone can imagine. She's not dumb. Trevor is the sweetest boy I've ever met. He does all his work, never misbehaves, and seems on grade level. But when I asked Mrs. Washburn about him, she just said, 'Of course he's a sweetheart. But he and his brother Teddie are Hawkins. Learned a long time ago that Special Education class was the best thing for those Hawkins kids.' Can you believe that? A whole family is relegated to Special Education! And Lewis. What can I say about Lewis? He walks in every day with this big grin and you just know, just *know* that he's already planning trouble. If he spent half as much time on his schoolwork as he did scheming and fighting, he'd be a genius. He and Weldon clash constantly. Weldon is the firewood, and Lewis the lighter fluid. Thank goodness for Mrs. Hicks. She has a way with them."

Reina chuckled. "Aw, Mrs. Hicks. Bless her soul. She only appears tough. You know that, don't you?"

"Yes, but she seems to have the kids at least partially fooled."

"That's her secret. Love them to death, but keep them off balance."

Cassie laughed. "That's it, exactly."

"Cassie, don't get too down on the parents. Lots of them haven't had the best of experiences in schools. They know their kids need education, but they're not too anxious to interact with any school officials or teachers. Most of them went to segregated schools. Not that there's been much change, even after Brown vs. Board."

Cassie thought of all the white children in her neighborhood, lined up each morning at bus stops waiting for the Christian Academy school bus. "Yeah, I've noticed."

"I commend your efforts to connect with the parents. I'm not always available, but I'll help when I can. Call me if you need help contacting a parent. Okay? Your jaunt to *Two Spot* - not a good move."

"Okay. I'll remember that."

Reina walked to the kitchen window. "I don't want to overstay my welcome, but it's still coming down in torrents out there. You mind if I use your phone? I'd like to call my neighbor and see how the roads are there."

"Sure, use the one in the living room on the end table."

Cassie cleared the table and followed into the living room, both beer cans in hand.

Reina hung up the phone. "My neighbor says our road is impassable. I'm sorry. Looks like you're stuck with me a little longer."

"Sorry? I love the company. Why don't you plan on staying for dinner?"

"Thanks, I'd like that. Are my clothes dry yet? I'd like to look more presentable when your husband gets home."

"Right." Cassie left to retrieve the clothes from the dryer. Why was she hesitant to tell Reina about Jack? She'd grown tired of the sad looks, the pat comments of sympathy. She wanted Reina to like her for who she was, not because she was the object of pity. She liked Reina, saw her as a potential friend. No one else at work had made any friendly overtures. Not that they had treated her poorly. But she was the new girl on the block. Most of them were veteran teachers and there was a clear racial divide. The white teachers grumbled about their "assignment" there. The black teachers smiled, but kept to themselves. Even the teacher's room was voluntarily segregated. She never saw a black teacher and white teacher in there at the same time. She decided to ask Reina about that.

"Clothes will be dry in a few minutes." Cassie looked at Reina stretched out on the couch; her full Afro pressed against a throw pillow. "Reina, can I ask you something?"

"Shoot."

"I know the schools are, for all intents and purposes, still segregated. Didn't take me long to figure that one out. But the staff? It's like they were two totally different entities. The first staff meeting was really unsettling, with all the black teachers on one side, and the whites on the other. Why is it like that?"

"This is 1972, eighteen years since *Brown vs. The Board of Education*. You see how "integrated" the schools are." Reina gestured quotation marks. "Segregation may not be legal but it is alive and well here. If you haven't discovered that yet, you soon will."

"So, attitudes haven't changed much?"

Reina laughed. "Glacial progress."

"So how do I deal with it?"

Reina swung her legs off the couch and set her beer can on the coffee table. "Look, Cassie. Things aren't ever going to change without a little rocking of the boat. I know you want to fit it, but just be yourself. Do what seems right to you, not what others are doing. Some people will take notice. If they hate you for it, you don't want them for friends anyway, right?"

"No. I guess you're right."

"You probably have already shaken things up in this neighborhood."

"What do you mean?"

"Having me here. Blacks just don't make social calls in too many of these neighborhoods. Despite the rain, you probably had a few curtains pulled aside checking out the darkie running across your lawn earlier. When I leave, you want me to saunter slowly to my car in case anyone missed me the first time?"

Cassie chuckled. She liked Reina's sense of humor. "Let me see what there is to eat. I was planning on ordering a pizza but I doubt they're delivering. I'm not much of a cook, so it will be simple fare."

Reina set down her beer can and followed Cassie into the kitchen. "I'll help."

Cassie stared into the open refrigerator. "There's a couple of pieces of left-over chicken. Not much else."

"Let me see." Cassie stepped aside as Reina pulled open veggie drawers and took out scallions and carrots. Opening the cupboard, Reina found a can of peas and some Bisquick.

Cassie said, "Look's like you've got a plan. What can I do to help?"

"Open these cans for me, would you? You got milk or cream?"

"Both. In the frig."

Reina grabbed the milk carton and asked for a pan and cutting board.

Cassie got them out. "Okay, now what?"

"Put some music on. I like to dance while I cook."

"I'll see what I can do." The radio was sure to have limited offerings. She opened the stereo console and flipped through her album collection. "Any requests?" she yelled from the living room.

"As long as it's not country!"

Cassie pulled out a Supremes album and placed it on the turntable, setting the needle on the record and turning up the volume. Coming into the kitchen, she joined Reina in a hip grind to the rhythmic strains of "Baby Love". She chopped carrots while Reina mixed up biscuit dough, marveling at Reina's ability to mix, chop, stir, dance, and sing along, as if all in one motion.

"Anything else you want me to do, Chef?"

"Have a seat. I've got this. Might want to open another beer though."

"You got it." Cassie took out a couple more beers and began setting the kitchen table. Soon the air was filled with the aroma of chicken pot pie. The timer beeped just as they finished putting their hands up in the air to dramatize "*Stop in the Name of Love.*"

"Diana Ross is through performing. You ready to eat?" Reina stopped swinging her hips, grabbed the dishtowel off the rack, and opened the oven to pull out her home-made chicken pot pie.

"Smells delicious." Cassie said.

"Normally I'd make the biscuits from scratch. But it would've taken too long."

After one bite, Cassie pronounced it scrumptious. "Where'd you learn how to cook?"

"My Mama, of course."

"Does she live here in Pensacola?"

"She did. We lost her about a year ago. Daddy's been having a tough time. But I go over as much as I can, mix him up a big batch of ham hocks, collards and corn pudding, his favorite. That keeps his stomach smiling anyway."

"Oh, I'm so sorry, Reina. About your mother, that is."

"Thanks. I do really miss her. We did squabble some, mostly about my choice of boyfriends, but I swear I can still hear her giving her opinion of everyone I meet. She was hoping I'd have found myself a husband by now. Speaking of husbands, I forgot to ask if you wanted me to hold up supper for your husband. He coming home soon?"

Cassie swallowed her last bite of chicken. She couldn't avoid the subject any longer. "No, he's not coming home. My husband passed away a few months ago."

Reina gagged. "Cassie! You should have told me. I- I had no idea. And here I am sitting in his robe. This is his robe, right?"

"Yeah. I gave it to him for his birthday, but it wasn't long before he shipped out to 'Nam, so he didn't get to wear it much." Cassie set her fork down and took a deep breath, trying to hold back the tears, but her eyes puddled and slowly, they came. "I'm sorry, I didn't mean to cry."

Reina walked around the table and wrapped her arms around Cassie. Her gold loop earrings flicked Cassie's ears. "It's okay, Honey. Go ahead and cry."

Cassie grabbed a napkin from the table, wiped her face, and blew her nose. "No, I'm all right now. Really I am."

Reina stood, squeezed Cassie's shoulder, and then returned to her chair. "Tell me more, Cass."

"We met in college. I knew immediately he was ROTC. You know, buzz haircut and all. Despite the attraction, I told myself that I didn't want to date someone in the military. At least not in these times. He'd asked me out a couple of times and I'd said no. But Jack was persistent. We were paired up as lab partners in chemistry. Jack likes to tell that if it weren't for his hard head, we never would have ended up together."

"There's obviously a story there. Hard head?"

Cassie smiled. "Clumsy me dropped a beaker and we both bent over to pick it up at the same time, bumping heads. I felt dizzy and went to the rest room. He followed."

"Into the rest room?"

"Yep. Hollered through the door first, asking if I was okay, but when I didn't answer he came in. I was pretty woozy, but I remember the intensity of his blue eyes, the warmth of his hands when he touched my forehead, and his concern about me. I lost all defenses. We started dating after that, got engaged 6 months later, and married in June of '71, when Jack finished college and boot camp. I still had another year to go, so when Jack was sent here for his aviation training at the naval base, I transferred my credits to the University of West Florida so I could be with him. We knew there was a good chance he'd get ordered to Vietnam. He was a helicopter pilot. How could he not? But I was hoping that it would be later, that the war might be over, but …."

"Jesus, Cassie, a helicopter pilot? I've read about their casualty numbers. My kid brother just got drafted. I'm hoping for an assignment that keeps him away from 'Nam."

"Yeah, I know what you mean. But Jack loved what he did. If you read his letters, it's sometimes hard to tell who he loved more, me or 'Gigi'. That's what he named his helicopter, after his grandmother. He was proud of what he did, some troop drops, but mostly medevacs. He didn't write much about the missions. I suspect he didn't want to worry me. His letters were often about the men in his squad. They got close, all of them, but he wrote most about his crew chief, Earl. Jack said he was fearless; didn't even flinch when they took fire. Instead, joked that it was a piece of cake after facing down the Ku Klux Klan."

"Earl was black?"

"Yeah, came from Louisiana, I think."

Reina reached across the table for Cassie's hands. She held them in silence, knowing when words weren't enough. "How long has it been, exactly?"

"They came on May 18th. I'll never forget the date. I'd just written Jack to tell him about landing the teaching job."

"They?"

"The officers. There were two of them. It was a night just like this one. When the doorbell rang, I couldn't imagine who it could be out in such a storm; thought it might be the air conditioner repair man. Then I opened the door and saw them, hats tucked under their arms, water dripping off their shoulder boards. At first, they were in silhouette - the sky was so dark, but then lightning flashed and I could see their faces… and I knew."

"What did they say?"

"They came in - sat in these same kitchen chairs we're in now. I kept apologizing to them for the AC being out. Their shoes were so shiny- kept squeaking on the linoleum floor. I remember staring at their stripes -tried to remember what Jack taught me about rank. It was so damn hot; my thighs were sticking to the chair. I made coffee, poured them both a cup. Set out cookies."

"But what did they *say*, Cassie?"

What DID they say? The words seemed to float over her, like drifting dandelion seeds. 'Too many wounded. The Huey is equipped for seven. Crash…his body …So sorry, Mrs. Cunningham. So sorry…so sorry…'

"Do the exact words matter? His helicopter crashed. He's dead. They left phone numbers to call. They're in a drawer somewhere."

"Numbers to call?"

"Should I need to talk to someone."

Reina watched Cassie clear the dishes. "*Do* you need to talk to someone, Cassie?"

Cassie didn't respond. Instead, she turned away and set the dishes in the sink.

"Cassie?"

She turned and leaned against the sink. "I'm doing all right. It's been four months, almost. Went home for most of the summer. My family begged me to stay, but my home and my job is here now." Then she stepped toward the window. "You hear that?"

"What?"

"No rain pounding on the roof. It's stopped."

Reina followed Cassie to the window and looked out. "You're right. I suppose I should be on my way." She turned to Cassie. "How are you getting to work tomorrow?"

"I forgot about that. Take a taxi, I guess."

"Look, Cassie, I don't want to presume, but if I stay over, I can drive you in the morning. I know some of the roads going to my place won't be passable 'till then anyway."

"I'd love that! We have a spare bedroom."

"Thanks. Let's get these dishes done. You have some coffee?"

"I'll start a pot. AdaMae brought over some chocolate cake yesterday. Want some?"

"Sure. Who's AdaMae?"

"My neighbor. I'll tell you all about her over coffee."

Cassie curled up her feet on one end of the couch and sipped coffee as Reina did the same on the other end. The television was never turned on. Conversation filled the hours until she noted Reina yawning.

"Goodness. Did you realize it was 11 o'clock? I've got to get up by six. I'll go make up that spare bed for you."

"Thanks."

Cassie took sheets out of the linen closet, and began making the bed while Reina was in the bathroom. "There's a new packaged toothbrush in the medicine cabinet," she yelled. Despite the late hour, Cassie lay awake thinking back on the laughter and conversation of the evening. It was the first time in months that her last thoughts before sleep were not of Jack.

CHAPTER FIVE

The thunderstorm left air steamy and as thick as wet cotton. As usual, Cassie was exhausted at the end of the day. She was pleased with Weldon today, though. He'd not been in a single fight, even when Lewis had done his best to provoke him. Lewis's day, however, had been another story. Unlike Weldon, who often scowled, Lewis's Cheshire cat grin was not necessarily a good thing. The wider the smile, the more likely he was to be scheming his next attack. The happy face strips, stickers, and weekly rewards for good behavior weren't working with Lewis. Nor were the many talks she'd had with him in the hallway. Mrs. Hicks' threats occasionally reigned him in but not much. Sending him to the principal's office was a waste of time. Mr. Horace lazily chatted with the perpetrator, gave him a nickel, and sent him back to the classroom. Hence, the teachers' nickname for him, "Mr. Nickels".

Today was the last straw with Lewis. Seeing that Weldon was steering clear of him and focused on schoolwork, he went after Jeff instead, an easy target. Cassie found this especially galling since Lewis was twice Jeff's size. Before she could stop him, Lewis had reached behind Jeff's back in the cafeteria and speared a slab of ham from his lunch tray. Jeff jumped up and started swinging. Lewis straight-armed him, laughing and chewing all the while, Bits of ham spewed from the corners of his mouth. Fortunately, Mrs. Hicks showed up, grabbed Lewis, and marched him back to the classroom. Calming Jeff down took some effort on Cassie's part. Giving him the slice of ham from her tray assuaged his anger.

Lewis stayed inside for recess. Mrs. Hicks sat across from him, with the yardstick on her lap, glaring at him the whole time. Once the children came in and put their heads on their desks for their daily rest period, Cassie directed Lewis to come out into the hall. He stood with his back against the wall, eyes toward the ceiling.

"Look at me, Lewis." He looked at his teacher, the corners of his mouth beginning to turn upward. "Don't you give me that smile, Lewis, not after what you did!" She shook her head. What could she say that she hadn't already said? "What am I going to do with you, Lewis? I've tried everything to get you to listen to me. What's it going to take to get you to behave?"

A defiant grin appeared on his face. "I ain't goin' to do nothin' you say 'less'n you whoop me like my Mama does."

Just then, Mrs. Hicks came out to the hallway ready to go on her break.

"Give me that yardstick, Mrs. Hicks. Turn around Lewis." Cassie whacked Lewis one swat on his rump. "Now go in there and behave yourself!" Lewis turned around and said, "Yes, Ma'am."

She handed the yardstick back. "I can't believe I just did that. What is wrong with me?"

Mrs. Hicks clucked, "Now, don't go frettin' over it. Took you longer than most."

Remorse had persisted throughout the day, despite an afternoon of improved behavior from Lewis. How could she have ever paddled a child? It was against everything she believed. She knew it wouldn't really change a child's behavior. She needed to reach them some other way. She vowed right then and there that no matter how angry she felt, no matter what the child's transgression, she'd never again hit another child in her classroom.

She was reaching some of them. She was sure of it. Even Mrs. Hicks had said so. "Ain't never seen these kids work so hard before. You doin' a fine job with these young'uns, Cassie." Ruby was now reading at a second-grade level. Angela was getting the therapy she needed, thanks to Cassie's relentless harangue. Teddie knew the alphabet and was memorizing sight words. Zebbie was reading independently. Trevor had mastered a whole year of math in less than two months. Even Jeff occasionally smiled at her, especially when he got stickers for finishing his daily work. His stutter was a little less pronounced. She just had to find the magic that would work with Lewis. Despite his improved behavior in the afternoon after the paddling, corporal punishment was not it. Suddenly she thought of Grant. What would he do? From previous talks, she knew he faced some tough kids at the high school. Was he able to just stare them down with those deep-set eyes and towering height? Or did he have some tricks of the trade he could share? She would have to talk with him about Lewis.

From Weldon's improved behavior, she wondered if a corner had been turned as a result of her visit to the bar. He must have been the one peeking out at her from that upstairs window of the *Two Spot* Lounge. But what about the grandmother? Did she know of the visit? Today, Cassie had told him how proud she was of him, had given him stickers to earn something from the "prize bin." Weekly trips to the dime store to purchase the various awards ate into her meager paycheck, but it was well worth it.

At the sound of heavy footsteps approaching, Cassie stopped ruminating and turned to see an imposing but matronly looking woman standing at the door. Rising from her chair, Cassie stepped towards her visitor. "May I help you? "As she peered at the gray-haired woman, she saw the resemblance. The ebony cheeks were fuller, but the same deep-set eyes and definitive scowl, the pursed thin lips, and pointed chin told her this must be Weldon's grandmother.

"You Mrs. Cunningham?"

"Yes, I am."

"Weldon's teacher?"

"Yes. You must be Mrs. Roosevelt. How nice to meet...."

"Don't be comin' to my bar any more, you hear!"

"I'm sorry. I did try to call first but couldn't reach you. I wanted to talk to you about Weldon."

"What for? What's that boy been doin' now?"

"I've been concerned about him. He gets into a lot of fights at school."

"Well, you got a paddle, don't you?"

"Yes, but. . ."

"Well, *use* it." She turned on her heels and marched down the hall, leaving Cassie standing in the doorway, mouth agape. At the end of the hall she almost bumped into Reina, who was headed toward Cassie's classroom.

Reina stopped short, side-glanced Cassie, and then greeted Mrs. Roosevelt.

Cassie could hear snippets of conversation, but didn't dare move to hear more. Initially, the grandmother stood with crossed arms and a scowl, occasionally glancing back at Cassie. Reina's soft alto voice echoed in the empty hall. Cassie heard her name more than once. After a few minutes, Mrs. Roosevelt nodded and shook Reina's hand.

Cassie eagerly awaited Reina's arrival to hear what had transpired. "What did you say to her?"

"That she needed to work with you to help her grandson."

"And she agreed? But she seemed so hostile toward me."

"What did you expect? Look, Cassie, like I told you before. This community has seen its share of discrimination, indifference, you name it. Why should Mrs. Roosevelt trust some new teacher traipsing to her place of business, who is probably going to lay blame on her for her grandkid's problems?"

"Then why did she talk to you and agree to help?" Cassie waited a moment but Reina didn't answer. "It's because you're black, isn't it?"

"Not entirely. I'm sure it helped. But you've probably already learned that white or black, some teachers don't give a damn. I told her *you* did. Told her you were the best teacher her grandson probably ever had or will have and that he needed to get on track this year if he was going to make it."

"You said all that?"

"I sure did. Told her to get her grandson into bed on time, get him some earplugs if need be to block out the noise from the bar. Also told her you'd be sending notes home to keep her up to speed on how he's doing. That okay with you?"

Cassie smiled, still glowing from her friend's praise. "Of course, it is!" She touched Reina's arm. "Thanks, Reina. You're amazing."

"I can't take all the credit. Helps to have the name Gooden."

"What do you mean?"

"Dr. Gooden has probably treated almost everyone in this community. People trust my dad."

"Your father is a doctor?"

"He is. I'm headed over there now actually. Why don't you join me? I'd like you to meet him, and excuse me for saying so, but you look beat. Pretty rough day, huh?"

"How can you tell?"

Reina laughed. "I can tell. C'mon. Follow me to my dad's house."

"If you're sure he won't mind."

"Dad loves company."

It wasn't a long drive, but as she pulled into Dr. Gooden's driveway behind Reina's car, Cassie noted subtle changes in the neighborhood. The houses were still small and modest, but there were lawns in the front, paved driveways, some with garages. As in the other black neighborhoods, there was a fair amount of activity; kids shooting baskets at the end of the street, some girls double-dutching on the sidewalk, adults sitting on their porch fronts. Dr. Gooden was one of them. He stood as Reina slammed the car door, and Cassie followed.

Reina embraced her father and pecked him on the cheek, before turning to introduce Cassie. "Daddy, this is Cassie Cunningham. She teaches Special Education over at Fielding Elementary."

Cassie extended her hand, which Reina's father immediately clasped in his two massive hands.

"It's a pleasure to meet you. Reina doesn't bring many friends by. You must be special."

Cassie blushed. "Thank you, Sir. It's nice of you to welcome me to your home."

He motioned for her to follow him inside.

Light filtered through the living room's swag lace curtains, draped on either side of a worn leather couch. In the corner was a wing-backed brocade chair and standing lamp with fringe-trimmed shade. A multi-colored braided rug covered most of the wood flooring. An overflowing bookcase lined one wall. The opposite wall was covered with school photographs, mostly of Reina and what Cassie guessed to be her brother. But the center black and white photo was of two men shaking hands. Cassie walked closer to get a better look. It was of Dr. Gooden and Dr. Martin Luther King. She turned slightly, but he answered her question before she could ask.

"Yes, I met him in the flesh."

Dr. Gooden was smiling in the picture. He was a handsome man, tall like Reina, with the same high cheek bones and broad shoulders, and even now with shoulders stooped and hair tinged with gray, he was striking. It was hard to judge his present age. Reina had said she was twenty-seven, and that her parents had her late in life, so Cassie judged the man to be in his late sixties.

"Did you know him well?"

"Me? No, just met him that once. But it was an honor, for sure. It was 1964. I was attending a gathering of alumni from Meharry Medical College. Dr. Robert Hayling, a fellow alumnus, active in the Southern Christian Leadership Conference, had invited Dr. King to come to St. Augustine to help push for integration there. He introduced us."

"I remember reading something about Dr. King being in St. Augustine. Wasn't he jailed?"

Dr. Gooden nodded. "That he was. He only spent the one night, though. It was a key time in the movement. The Civil Rights Act was passed later that year. I would have to say Dr. Hayling was very instrumental in its passage. He'd learned not to accept false promises from politicians, and persisted with demonstrations and sit-ins despite President's Johnson's pleas to cease. It was a stroke of genius getting the wife of the Massachusetts governor to join him at the Ponce de Leon Motor Lodge to demand service. Got lots of press coverage when the two of them were arrested."

"So, Dr. Hayling was a close friend of yours?"

"No. He graduated long after me, then served four years in the Air Force before going on to dental school. I was too old for the service during World War II. But Robert Hayling was a persistent man, someone I admire. Anyone who is kidnapped by the Ku Klux Klan, beaten half to death, and still keeps fighting is a profile in courage. The movement had many such heroes. Still does."

"Who wants a beer?" Reina stood behind them holding two cans of beer. She handed one to Cassie, and offered the other to her father.

"No thanks. Aggravates my heartburn. You can fix me a bourbon and milk, though."

Cassie choked on her first swig of beer. "Did I hear you right? Did you say bourbon and milk?"

"That I did."

Reina interjected. "Daddy, Cassie's from Connecticut. I doubt that unique beverage concoction has made its way north."

Dr. Gooden laughed. "Don't know what they're missing."

"Dad thinks the bourbon helps his heart and the milk helps his ulcer." Reina popped open the other beer, took a swig, and walked back to the kitchen to fix her father's drink.

They sat across from each other, Cassie at the end of the couch, and Ralph Gooden in the corner chair. Like his daughter, Dr.

Gooden exuded a confident, yet unassuming air. A framed family photograph on the table caught her eye. Reina must have been ten or so, her brother just a baby. Dr. Gooden, dressed in suit and tie, stood behind his wife.

"That was taken not long after Clay was born. I wish I had a more recent family photograph. Other than that portrait, I only have snapshots of my wife."

"She was a beautiful woman. Reina told me of her passing. I'm so sorry for your loss, Dr. Gooden. You must miss her very much."

He sighed. "I do. It's been a year now, and they say time heals all wounds, but I'm not so sure."

She nodded empathetically, breathed in deeply, and changed the subject. "Your practice must keep you busy."

"Too busy. I've cut back on my appointment hours. Had to. My wife used to handle all the appointments, records, and bookkeeping. Now, I'm having trouble keeping up."

Reina walked in, handed her father his drink, and set a tray of crackers and cheese on the coffee table. "I've told you before, Daddy - hire someone."

"I can't afford an office assistant. Besides, who would I hire?"

"Maybe one of those women who keep dropping by."

Dr. Gooden frowned. "You must be joking. It's bad enough they come in with all these fake ailments that I have to pretend to treat. Have one of them in my office every day, fawning over me? I don't think so."

Reina laughed. "Daddy is now the most eligible bachelor in town, at least among the older widows, and even some of the young ones."

Cassie wedged a piece of cheese between two crackers. "I'm not surprised. A doctor is a prize catch for most women. I meant to ask, what made you want to be a doctor?"

"My big sister."

"She encouraged you to go into medicine?"

"Not exactly. She was a few years older than me, married, and pregnant with her first child. When her delivery time came, there were complications. The mid-wife knew she needed emergency care and drove her to the hospital, but they refused to admit her."

Cassie took a bite of her cracker and cheese. "But why?"

Reina took a seat on the couch next to Cassie. She answered the question. "Because she was black. There were no hospitals in town that admitted black people back then."

Cassie choked on her cracker.

Reina slapped Cassie on the back. "You okay?"

She nodded, catching sprayed cracker crumbs in her hand. "But I don't understand. How did they get medical care?"

Dr. Gooden leaned forward in his chair, his hands on his knees. "Exactly. There were midwives, and some with medical knowledge or just plain home remedies, liberally applied, but Pensacola needed a doctor, someone who would serve the black population. I was determined to be that someone. Been doing it now for thirty-five years."

"Your sister? What happened?"

In a soft, measured tone, Dr. Gooden answered. "Her uterine membranes ruptured. The labor was obstructed. The baby died from asphyxiation. My sister died three days later from sepsis."

Cassie's face blanched. She couldn't speak. What could she say to this man whose face, even after all these years, reflected the pain of that memory? She would have liked to offer a comforting embrace. Instead, she reached for Reina's hand and squeezed it.

Dr. Gooden stood, set his drink on the coffee table, and asked, "Would you like to see my office?"

"Is it nearby?"

"Right on the other side of this wall. Built an addition onto the house."

Cassie followed him into the kitchen and out a side door, which opened up to his office. They entered the examining room first, which was like so many Cassie had seen before. The raised table and stool, cabinets on the wall, and sink underneath. There was a sliding door, which he opened and behind that was the waiting room. Unlike the very sterile looking examining room, the walls were vividly colored and plastered with photos of children and families. Bins of magazines and toys were interspersed between the chairs. An aquarium full of colorful fish stood against a side wall.

"Daddy's first patient gave him a photo of her family and asked if he would put it on his wall. Since then, he's asked for other patients to do the same." Reina gestured to the right. "As you can see, that wall is covered."

Cassie walked over to admire the photos, and then commented on the lush hanging ivy plant in the bay window dressed with floral print curtains. "Everything is lovely, very welcoming."

"Mom decorated the interior, but most of the construction was done by men in the community. The bank refused to give my father a loan so he bartered labor for medical care. I think half of Daddy's clients still pay him with bartered items or service, which explains why his bank account is still so meager." She turned toward her father. "That's a thought, Daddy. Isn't there someone who would do your books in exchange for medical care? I'm sure one of those widows would do it, and who knows, maybe something more?" She side-winked at Cassie.

"Enough of that, young lady. I already had the love of my life. Lillian was the only one for me. Good thing she taught her daughter how to cook. You are planning to cook tonight, aren't you Reina?"

"Of course, Daddy."

"Well, let's get to it then! And you'll join us, won't you Cassie?"

Cassie gladly accepted. While waiting for Reina to prepare dinner, Cassie listened to Dr. Gooden relay stories of his wife, how they met, and their early years together. With the mention of his wife's name, his face radiated. She couldn't help but think how less than an hour ago, that same face had been contorted in pain from the memory of his sister's death.

As she sat at their kitchen table, enjoying red beans and rice and buttered cornpone, she continued to be haunted by the story of his sister. She knew about the Jim Crow laws, but Dr. Gooden and his family had lived it. She wanted to know more, and somehow wanted to express her sense of shame, sympathy, whatever it was that she was feeling.

"Dr. Gooden?"

He looked at her.

"I'm so sorry about your sister. I should have expressed my sympathy earlier. It was just... I was kind of shocked."

He put up his hand. "No need to say more. It was the way life was for us in those times. I'm hoping it will be better for my children and grandchildren." He nodded towards Reina. "She can try on clothes in the department store now if she wants. My wife never could."

"I still get the looks, though."

"The looks?" Cassie asked.

"The ones that say they don't want your brown ass touching anything that might end up on a white person." Reina cut another slice of the cornpone. "At least I've never been kicked out of places. Clay has, even now. Last week, he was home on leave and was in uniform. The usher at the Bay Theater told him he still had to sit in the 'nigger' section in the balcony."

Dr. Gooden frowned. "He didn't tell me that. Did he tell anyone else? The local NAACP office?"

"You really think he wants to be labeled as a troublemaker, Daddy? He finishes boot camp in a week, and then finds out where he'll be assigned. You know me, Dad. I'll fight injustice at the drop of a hat. But I don't want Clay sticking his neck out right now, not when someone might be inclined to stamp 'Vietnam' on his orders. He might end up dead, like Cassie's husband."

Now it was Dr. Gooden's turn to be shocked. He set his fork down. "How come no one mentioned this to me?" He looked at Cassie, his eyes holding hers, sending such a strong message of empathetic grief that she had to turn away or the tears would come once more.

***

A different kind of exhaustion gripped Cassie when she entered her home. The classroom trials were forgotten, replaced with anguished thoughts from the evening's conversation. She knew that she would never really know the anger and humiliation that Dr. Gooden and his family must have experienced but she appreciated that they opened up to her.

Flicking on the bedroom light, she glanced at the clock. Already 8:30. She needed him now, needed his touch, his comfort. She pulled out the box of Jack's letters, choosing one dated just before his death.

My dear Cassie,

I only have a minute. Earl and I are scheduled to go out on another mission soon. Can you believe we are 9000 miles apart? In my heart, you are here, with me. I have so many pictures of you in the room and helicopter that the guys call me 'Love-smitten Jack.' I don't mind. It fits. I'll never stop loving you. You won't forget me, will you? Write soon, my love,

Jack

Like Dr. Gooden, she had known the one true love in her life. He was gone. She would never get him back, and yet the thought of never again feeling the warm embrace of a man's arms or knowing the exhilaration of a lover's kiss left her aching.

CHAPTER SIX

The halls were silent, as they usually were when Grant arrived at Escambia High School. He liked to get in early, sip coffee at his desk, and review his prepared lessons. The text book was too dry and too inaccurate to rely on as his only source of material. Covering the Civil War, or, as most southerners liked to call it, "The War of Northern Aggression" was always a bit tricky. More than once he'd gotten in trouble for his assertion that slavery was the root cause, and then going beyond the syllabus to include the post war era of Jim Crow and segregation.

Today, they would be debating the arguments that led up to the Missouri Compromise. He hoped the students had done the assigned reading, and that the two debating students were prepared. Senator Rufus King from New York, aka Aaron Mitchell, would argue that Congress had the power to prohibit slavery in a new state and Senator William Pinkney from Maryland, aka Leroy White, would argue that new states had the same freedom of action as the original thirteen and were free to choose slavery. It took some serious arm-twisting on his part to convince Leroy, a popular black running back on the football team, to play the role of a southern white Senator. Leroy's teammates razzed him about it, but Leroy was one of those rare self-assured adolescents, who could laugh at criticism and remain popular. Should be an interesting day. He took a last sip of coffee, pushed back his chair, and turned to write on the blackboard.

Her perfume preceded her. Amy Nilehouse, Home Economics teacher, Rm. 104, who he had mentally nicknamed "Bloodhound", had yet to give up the hunt. Approaching thirty, she was desperate to avoid "Old Maid" status. Grant had initially fallen for her charms, or rather, his lust overruled his judgment. After only a few dates, he knew better than to succumb further. She was the classic man-eater, and he refused to be her prey. He moved behind his desk as she approached.

"Grant, I knew I'd find you here. You put the rest of us to shame. You know that, don't you? Remember – 'All work and no play makes for a dull boy.' Can you make it for drinks tonight? Some of us are going to Sully's after work." She stepped closer, brushed back loose strands of black hair, and ogled him like he was a big fat pork chop.

With a plastered smile he responded. "Sorry, Amy. My grandmother needs help with her car. Promised her I'd come by right after work."

"That won't take you long. You're such a whiz at fixing things. Drop by afterwards, okay?"

He could give further excuses. His grandmother expected him for dinner, etc. But he knew no excuses would deter her.

"If I can. Thanks for the reminder. Gotta' get this stuff on the board before the horde arrives."

"Sure, see you later." She sashayed out the door. Guiltily, he stared at the nice round derriere tightly wrapped in a fuchsia mini-skirt. Too bad the personality wasn't as appealing.

He grabbed his coffee cup at the sound of the first locker slamming. Soon the halls were filled with the familiar sound of shuffling feet, chatter, giggling girls, and the occasional boisterous expletive. Time to step into the hallway. He knew who to keep his eye on. Despite his efforts to recognize potential in each of the students, some of them came with the tag, 'troublemaker' and did their best to live up to it. Fred Crowley was one of those. Crossing his long legs, Grant leaned against the door frame and swallowed the last of his coffee. He glanced down the hall toward Fred's locker. The bulked up six footer's arms pressed against his neighbor's locker. At first, he couldn't make out the victim's identity. Fred's biceps blocked his view. A hand reached out from under, and Fred quickly slapped it back. "What's your hurry, twerp? We're just getting to know each other." His victim was the new kid in his first period class, a transfer from St. Paul's Christian Academy. Don't get too many of those. What was the administration thinking, assigning him a locker next to such a notorious bully?

Grant strode toward Fred. At six foot three, he was able to look down at the red-haired junior. With crossed arms and furrowed brow, he spoke in his usual calm but deep voice.

"Mr. Crowley. Good to see you made it on time today. Better get a move-on. The first bell is about to ring."

Fred's arms dropped as he mumbled something under his breath. He yanked a book from his locker, slammed the door, and shoved his way down the hall in the other direction. Grant would have the pleasure of his company fourth period, along with some of his ex-football cronies. Ever since Escambia High had integrated, some of the players seemed to have one big collective chip on their shoulders. Didn't take a rocket scientist to figure it out. The team was now fifty percent black. Competition to be on the team was fiercer than ever. Fred hadn't made the cut.

The bell rang, precipitating the mass rush to first period classrooms. He spotted Leroy coming towards him. "You ready, Senator Pinkney?" Leroy flashed a grin. "Yes, sir." Probably the first time a black man ever argued for the expansion of slavery. His adrenaline started pumping. Yes, it should be an interesting day.

CHAPTER SEVEN

The end of the work week brought both relief and dread. Weekends for Cassie meant a chance to sleep in and vary her routine. It also brought increased loneliness. From Monday through Friday, teaching consumed her, leaving little time for memories. At least now, sleep was coming sooner than it had in those early grief-drenched months.

Pulling into the driveway, she grabbed her school bag, stepped from the oven-like car, and pondered how to fill the weekend hours. How she wished she could share her teaching experiences with Jack. She hadn't written to him all week. Just writing his name used to bring solace. Now, it seemed to re-open a wound. She still read his letters, pictured him far away, sitting on his bunk as he wrote, not gone forever. Dropping her school bag, she hurried to the bedroom to pull the shoebox of letters from the closet. She opened the one on top, the one she knew by heart.

Dearest Cassie,

I'd like to come back here someday. That may sound strange but it's a beautiful country. Take away what the war has done to the place and it's a country of picturesque beaches, lush tropical jungles, and vast rice fields. The units on the ground are leery of the rice paddies, though.

Not only are there leeches and snakes, but our guys have been ambushed in them. I'm lucky to be up in the air. We go out on missions almost every day. I know you hate this war, Cass, but I'm doing mostly rescue missions, bringing guys back to be patched up. Don't worry about me. My co-pilot, Earl, says I'm the luckiest dude ever. Already have flown fifteen missions and haven't been shot at yet!

I know how you love flowers, Cass. You'd flip over all the ones here. I don't know the names of most of them, but there are so many different orchids. I wish I could pick them and send you a bouquet. How's the garden coming? Do you remember the day we put it in together? I do, or at least the post-garden party!

The sunset last night was this exquisite reddish-gold, reminding me of your hair. I miss the touch of you, Cassie. I miss you. But I'll be home before you know it.

Love,

Jack

The memory of their gardening debut brought a smile to her face. It had been her dream to have a garden. After much research, she'd made a list of the flowers and plants that would thrive in northern Florida and began ordering the various bulbs and seeds; shooting star with their dainty purple flowers, rose periwinkle, black-eyed susans, and wine lilies. As soon as the bulbs and seeds arrived, she started preparing the flower bed at the side of the house. That's where Jack found her and helped with the digging before turning the garden hose on her, leaving her soaking wet.

"Yes, I remember the post-garden party, Jack. How could I forget? - the way you carried me into the house, how you said you couldn't resist a girl in a wet t-shirt." She wanted to remain sitting on her bed reminiscing, but knew it would only bring more tears. Instead, she folded the letter, placed it back in the box, and quickly changed into denim shorts and t-shirt. "Time to weed that garden of ours, Jack."

Setting a small transistor radio on the lawn, she turned the dial to her favorite station. Engrossed in the mindless rhythm of tugging and pulling, she didn't hear his footsteps.

"Hi. Grams told me to bring you this."

Startled, she fell back onto the grass, tossing a clump of weeds into the air.

"Sorry, I didn't mean to scare you."

She couldn't see him at first. Blinded by the bright sun, she shaded her eyes. It took a moment to recognize him. Dressed in tattered jeans and a grease-stained t-shirt, he was even dirtier than she.

She blinked a few times. "Grant? Is that you?"

"Yeah, sorry for the grunge look, but Grams insisted I come over with cold lemonade when she saw you slaving in the heat."

She stood, brushing hands on her shorts, before reaching for the lemonade.

"Thanks. That was thoughtful of AdaMae." She took a long gulp and exhaled. "I guess I was thirsty. Probably not the best time of day to be weeding. Do you want to go inside? It's cooler."

"No. I'm fine. But if you don't mind, I could use a breather from working on Grams Chevy. Can we sit in the shade?"

They found a spot under the magnolia tree. Cassie pushed

a limp curl behind her ear. "I probably should at least go in and wash. I must look a sight."

Grant sat cross-legged; long arms stretched over his knees. "No more than me. Here, you want this?" He pulled a bandana from his pocket and offered it to Cassie.

She took it, rubbed the dirt and sweat from her face, and hoped she looked more presentable. "Thanks."

"Where's your faithful companion, Alice?"

"Romping with Rufford in Gram's backyard, or at least I hope that's all she's doing. Gram's trying to break her habit of digging in the garden.

"And how will she do that?"

"Chili pepper; sprinkle it on the ground in her digging area."

Cassie shook her head. "Your grandmother is a wonder. She seems to know a little bit about everything."

"Just about, although she'll be the first to admit that she's no mechanic or handyman."

"She's got you for that."

"Uh-huh. Great way to spend my Friday evening."

"Sounds like you're complaining."

He laughed, a deep baritone laugh that Cassie found appealing.

"Naw. I love coming over and helping Grams, but have to admit I'm ready to unwind a bit after this week. I imagine you feel the same?"

"Teaching is exhausting, for sure, and my class especially challenging. Sometimes I question if I'm doing things right."

He leaned forward. "Challenging how?"

She told him about her students, her struggles in reaching them, the seemingly laissez-faire attitude of much of the staff. He listened, eyes never wavering.

"The poverty is bad enough, but what most upsets me is the way these kids are 'written off' by so many - just because they're in a special education class. I'm not even sure why some of them are in there. Sure, all of them are behind some, but with most, it's not by much, and I *know* they can learn. They just need a chance and more people to believe in them. You know?"

He nodded. "They have you, Cassie. You believe in them. That's something."

"I guess. But I wish I could do more. And their lives are so limited. Most have never been out of their neighborhood, never mind outside of Pensacola." She paused, suddenly realizing that she had monopolized the conversation. "I'm sorry. Guess I talk too much."

"Don't apologize. You're passionate. You care. I like that. Look, Cassie. I've taught at the high school for four years. Lots of my kids come from the same neighborhoods. I know what you're saying."

It felt good to talk to someone who understood. "Today when we went outside and read books under the big oak tree, I told the kids about the free tickets the teachers were given for them to go to the Pensacola Fair, and you know what they said?"

"Let me guess. Most had never been, right?"

"Right. Either their parents didn't have cars or couldn't afford the rides or had to work on the weekend. It breaks my heart. I wish I could just put them all in my car and take them." She began plucking at the grass.

"Why don't you?"

She straightened. "What? But how could I? I only have a Toyota compact. What if they all say yes?"

"When would you go?"

"Next Saturday, I guess."

"I have the van. When I take out all my tools, and put in the seats, it seats twelve. Would that be enough?"

"You mean drive your van? Is it automatic?"

"Naw. But I'd drive."

"You'd go with me?"

"Sure. Be fun. I haven't been to the fair in years."

"You would do that? I mean it would be giving up your whole Saturday."

"What else do I have to do? Gives me a good excuse to ditch Gram's chore list – and eat cotton candy. Did I tell you I have a sweet tooth?" He grinned.

She smiled in response. "I don't know what to say. That's so generous of you. I can't wait to tell the kids! I'll send permission slips to the parents on Monday and see what kind of response I get. Do you want me to call you when I know for sure that we're going?"

"Yeah. Can you remember my number or do you want me to write it down?"

"Better write it down." She stood, brushing grass off her thighs. "Come on in. I'll write it next to my phone."

He stepped inside but told her he'd stay in the entranceway, given his grimy condition.

Cassie rummaged through the kitchen drawer for paper and pen, and was about to ask for Grant's phone number when she saw him staring at the large wedding photo on the wall. Jack in his crisp Navy whites. Cassie in the ivory silk wedding dress she'd so painstakingly sewn.

Grant heard her approach. "Nice wedding picture."

"Thanks. I think so. Would have been a year this past June 6th."

Grant remained focused on the picture. "He was a commissioned officer, right?"

"Yes. Second Lieutenant."

There was a long pause before Grant spoke again. "So, he must have known 'Nam was a likely destination?"

"You're wondering why he joined?"

He nodded. "I'm sorry. None of my business, really. Just have a hard time wrapping my head around it. He must have believed we belonged over there."

"I can't say he did or didn't. We talked about it, and he told me it was a family thing."

"A family thing? Not sure I follow."

"His father, his grandfather, even his great grandfather. They all served. He wanted to follow in their footsteps."

Grant looked intently at Cassie. "And you? What do you think? I suppose you have to believe it was all worth it, given the sacrifice."

She shook her head. "If you're asking me if I believe in the war, the answer is no. Never did. And no, I don't think any of their deaths are worth it." She tried to gauge the reaction on his face.

Surprise? Anger? No, not that, troubled seemed more apt. He was staring again at the picture. "Grant, what's your number?"

"It was low, my draft number. Not sure what I'd done if I'd been called up."

"Grant, I was asking for your phone number – for the field trip, remember?"

CHAPTER EIGHT

The seats were all in place. The van hadn't looked this spotless in months. Since she'd called on Wednesday, Grant found his thoughts frequently drifting to Cassie. He knew it wasn't a date. He was just helping her out. Just a driver and chaperone, that's all.

He pulled into Gram's driveway and grabbed the thermos from under the seat. As expected, Grams had a full pot of coffee on the stove. He poured most of it into his thermos as she sat out on her patio reading the morning paper.

"What's this about some trouble at your high school?" She pointed to an article on the back-news page.

He screwed the top of the thermos and bent over her shoulder to read the piece.

"I thought things had settled down there. What's going on? You're not involved, I hope."

It had been a dicey week. Two parents had complained to Principal Frye about the debates in class. Wouldn't be the first time, nor would it be the last. Fortunately, Frye had learned over his thirty-year tenure how to smooth feathers. He'd reassured the parents that his staff diligently followed the prescribed curriculum at Escambia High. Later, Grant got the usual lecture in Frye's office. He would stick to the curriculum for a couple of weeks before detouring again. It was a little dance they did every year. But the newspaper article was about the recent walkout. Black students were protesting the school's use of the Confederate flag, the playing of "Dixie" and school mascot name of "Rebels". Most of the teachers were unsympathetic, complaining the students were making a big stink about nothing. They saw the symbols as representative of everyone and as tradition. Grant thought otherwise. He knew some of those who walked out; knew they'd presented a signed petition to the administration. Their grievances had been ignored. The walkout was not a rash, impulsive action, as was reported in the newspaper. Black students legitimately saw the flag, song, and mascot as symbols of racism. He told his grandmother all this and of his concern for those involved, especially Leroy, the leader of the protest. There were rumors of suspension, maybe even expulsion.

Grams folded the paper and placed it on the table. "They won't expel them, will they, Grant? Why, that goes on their school record."

"I know. I've been advising Leroy on some possible college applications. This won't help any. Although, that may be the least of his worries."

"What do you mean?"

"After the walkout, he got threats."

"What kind of threats?"

"Physical threats."

Grams shook her head. "That's terrible. Seems to me those students are just exercising their right to free speech."

"I wish everyone felt that way."

The creaking patio door interrupted their conversation. Cassie approached, wearing a bright yellow sundress and hair clipped back from her neck.

Putting the newspaper aside, AdaMae said, "My, aren't you a sunny picture! Ya'll look like you just sprung from my zinnia patch."

Cassie smiled back. "You ready to go, Grant? I already threw my bag into your van,"

He realized he was staring at her and took a moment to respond. "Bag? You mean purse?"

"No. Money and ID are in my pocket. The bag has first aid items, kids' emergency contact info, etc. You know, the 'just in case' stuff."

"Aw. Must have been a Girl Scout."

"Actually, I was."

Grant grabbed the thermos and kissed his grandmother on the cheek. "Bye, Grams. See you later."

"You two have fun. Don't forget to count heads before leaving the fair."

He smiled. No matter what the occasion, his grandmother had to give some cautionary advice. He placed the coffee thermos behind his seat before starting the ignition and backing out of the driveway. He glanced at Cassie, whose head was turned toward the passenger window. The anticipation of this day had helped him get through the past week. More than anything, he wanted it to go well. And he wanted to get to know this young lady sitting in his van.

CHAPTER NINE

Daydreaming, Cassie didn't hear Grant's question at first. "So, how many of your little 'challenges' are we picking up today?"

"Seven. Two of them will be waiting for us at the school parking lot, but all the others have to be picked up at home."

"Where first?"

"Jeff's house. It's on Chase St. Let me check the map." She opened and spread the map on her lap. "Go up G St. and take a left. His house is 119."

They almost passed it. Chase St. was a dirt road with only a few houses, each one more decrepit than the last. A bent mailbox with the numbers 119 stood on a patch of dirt with sleeping hound dogs. Grant parked in front of the clapboard house with sagging porch. He turned to Cassie. "You want me to go in with you?"

"No. I'll just be a minute. His grandfather is expecting me." She opened the van door. One dog wearily rose and loped toward her. She patted him on the head. "Hey, boy." Flies buzzed around the ripped screen door. Jeff emerged. His freckled face had been scrubbed pink, his blond hair slicked down, and he was grinning from ear to ear.

"Hi, T-t-teacher." He jumped down the steps. Behind him, holding the door, was Jeff's grandfather. With the white stubble on his chin and a gimp in his walk, Jeff's grandfather was a slimmer, toothless version of Walter Brennan. Even the high-pitched voice sounded like the well-known actor.

"Mornin', Ma'am. Jeff's a'jumpin out of his britches to go. Mighty nice of you to do this." Two younger boys peeked shyly from behind him. "I ain't been to the fair since I was a young'un. Still remember it though." He yelled after Jeff, now climbing into the van. "You mind your manners now, Jeffry. Do what the teacher says, ya hear me, boy?"

Jeff yelled back. "Yes'n Pappy."

"I'll take good care of him, Mr. Rayturn. We should be back sometime this afternoon. Not sure of the exact time. Is that okay?"

The younger brothers wrapped skinny arms around their grandfather's legs, as he responded. "No rush, Ma'am. I'll be busy enough with these other two." Cassie knew that was all too true. The grandfather had told her that his daughter left the children with him two years ago and he hadn't seen her since. A widower on Social Security, he was doing his best.

The van kicked up a cloud of dust as Jeff waved goodbye from the window.

Cassie turned around in her seat. "You were the first one we picked up, Jeff. Still have get the others. You look very nice today."

Jeff beamed. "Who is c-c-coming?"

"Weldon and Angela are waiting for us at the school. We have to swing by Ruby's house next and then the projects to get Teddie, Trevor, and Lewis." At the mention of Lewis' name, Jeff's smile disappeared. The only one Lewis tormented more than Weldon was Jeff. She'd have to do her best to keep them apart.

Ruby's house was just as dilapidated as Jeff's, but instead of hound dogs the front patch of dirt was crowded with assorted junk appliances. Bouncing atop one of the washing machines was Ruby. The girl was never still. At school, Cassie tried keeping Ruby's boundless energy in check by giving her assorted chores.

Visiting the Tillingly house was like being transported into the nursery rhyme, 'There Was an Old Woman Who Lived in a Shoe.' Mrs. Tillingly sat in a caned rocker with a diapered baby on her chest. Another, somewhat older baby chewed on the railing of the adjacent playpen. Two toddlers, their big round eyes ringed with dirt, stood munching from a shared potato chip bag. Swinging on a tire hung from the large oak tree at the side of the yard was a boy of about five, whom Cassie had seen getting off the bus with Ruby each morning.

"Ruby, your teacher's here." Mrs. Tillingly juggled the baby under one arm and slowly rose from the chair. All the children had her round moonbeam face and dark eyes. "Sorry she ain't more spruced up, Teacher. Done told her to wash, but she don't pay me much mind."

"Hey, Teacher." Ruby skipped over to Cassie and took her hand. "What we goin' to see at the fair? Can I git me some cotton candy?" She rushed to the van and peered inside. "Hey, Jeff." She looked over at Grant. "What's your name?"

"Grant. What's yours?"

"Ruby. You Teacher's boyfriend?"

Grant smiled. "Just helping out today. You ready to go?"

Before Ruby could answer, Cassie said, "Ruby, I think you need to wear some shoes to go to the fair."

Ruby ran back to the washing machine, crawled behind it, and pulled out a pair of purple flip flops. "I'm ready. Bye, Mama." She waved to her mother with one hand while clutching the flip flops with the other. "Move over, Jeff. I want to sit by the window." Jeff did as he was told.

Cassie spoke briefly with Ruby's mother before getting in the van.

Grant turned towards her, "She has her hands full."

"You could say that."

"Next stop?"

"The projects, and then the school."

"Do you know which apartment units?"

"Yes. I've been to visit most of the parents. Teddie and Trevor are brothers. Their mother is a sweetheart, but very young, and struggling, like they all are. And then there's Lewis."

"Ah yes, Lewis."

"I've met his mother. She doesn't take any guff from him. I'm sure she'll have him ready."

Teddie and Trevor stood clutching their mother's hands in front of their ground floor apartment complex. Cassie was again struck by the mother's youth and beauty. With doe-like eyes, café au lait skin, and soft smile, she was striking. She'd visited before and assumed that she was a single mother, as no mention of the father was ever made. But one day while watching the children at recess, she saw Teddie and Trevor walk over to the fence and yell "Hey, Daddy!" to a young man passing by. Confused, she'd asked Mrs. Hicks about it.

"Yeah, that's their Daddy all right. He works at a gas station near here. Has a room overhead."

"Why doesn't he live with his family?"

"Couldn't do that."

"What do you mean, couldn't do that? Shouldn't those boys have a father in the home?"

"I suspect he's there more than not, but if he were to live there permanently, his wife would lose her welfare check."

"But why?"

Mrs. Hicks sighed. "Cassie, do you think that young man, actually not much more than a boy himself, makes enough money pumping gas to support a family?"

"No, I suppose not. But why can't he live with his family?"

"The welfare worker would report it. The income would have to be claimed, and they'd lose the welfare check and probably their low-rent housing."

"But that's not right!"

"No, but that's the way it works. A lot of the fathers have to sneak around 'cuz of them stupid rules. Damn shame if you ask me."

Cassie recalled that conversation as she stepped from the van and thought how much she still had to learn about the lives of her students. The young mother walked toward Cassie, holding her sons' hands, speaking in a soft whisper. "Good morning, Mrs. Cunningham."

"Good morning, Mrs. Hawkins. Are the boys ready to go?

"Oh yes. They're so excited. They each have a dollar in their pocket to spend. Is that enough?"

Cassie smiled. "More than enough. Don't worry. I'll take good care of them."

Grant stepped out of the driver's seat, and walked toward Cassie.

"This is my driver and friend, Grant Lee. He owns the van and will help out with the kids today."

"Nice to meet you, Ma'am." Grant nodded in Mrs. Hawkins' direction.

The mother smiled, nodded back, and then bent down to kiss each son on the cheek. "You be good now. Mind your teacher, and thank her for taking you to the fair."

"Yes'm." They hugged their mother and followed Grant and Cassie to the van, climbing over Ruby and Jeff to get to the back seat.

Lewis was waiting on the front porch. Cassie had met the mother once before at parent - teacher conferences. Like Weldon's grandmother, she made it clear that she believed that sparing the rod spoiled the child. Cassie had no doubt that switching Lewis' backside, as the mother had recommended, was a regular occurrence in their household. Gripping Lewis by the shoulder, the mother marched up the sidewalk and greeted Cassie. "Mornin', Mrs. Cunningham." Lewis was a big boy, but his mother was bigger. She used her ample size to her advantage as she swung Lewis around and glared at him. "You remember what I told you. Behave yourself, or you know what's comin." Pushing him toward Cassie, she said, "He's all yours now, Mrs. Cunningham. Don't let him get away with nothin', you hear?"

"Yes, Ma'am. I'm sure he'll be good, won't you Lewis?" She tried to match the mother's stern tone, knowing full well that she could never compete in intimidation. Grinning, Lewis stepped into the van and took a seat next to Trevor.

Cassie shut the van door. "Just one more stop and we'll have them all. You know where the school is?"

"Ah-huh." It took only a few minutes to arrive at the school. Angie and Weldon were waiting for them in the parking lot with Angie's mother, with whom she spoke briefly before telling them to climb into the far back seat of the van.

Grant then drove to Interstate 10 before exiting onto Mobile Highway for the fairgrounds. Once in the parking lot, the children sprang from the van and followed Cassie to the admission booth, where she handed over the entry tickets. As they darted through the gate, she called out, "Hold on a minute! I need you all to listen carefully." She looked at each of them, making sure they were giving her their full attention. Lewis' eyes were already drifting away. "Lewis, are you listening to me?"

"Yes, Ma'am."

"You are each to stay with your assigned adult. Lewis, Teddie, and Trevor, you will stay with Mr. Lee at all times. Ruby, Angie, Weldon, and Jeff will stay with me. Got it? We'll meet back here at noon to get something to eat."

The sky was a milky white, still muggy, but at least she didn't have to worry about the scorching sun. Even so, she had covered her fair face with sunscreen. She scanned the already packed fairgrounds, and rose her voice to be heard above the din of carnival barkers and tinny music of amusement rides. "Where should we go first, kids?"

Practically in unison, they replied, "The rides!" She went to the ticket counter and bought three strips of ride tickets, enough for each of them to choose three rides. Grant headed toward the roller coaster, while Ruby and Angie tugged her arm, shouting,

"C'mon Teacher. Let's go to the ferris wheel." She was able to squeeze between Jeff and Weldon in the bucket behind Angie and Ruby. More than once she had to yell at Ruby to keep her hands on the bar and not lean over. Stepping off the ferris wheel, they ran to the adjacent bumper cars, each dashing to the car they wanted. Cassie paired up with Angie and did her best to maneuver away from Ruby, Weldon, and Jeff, who spent most of their time crashing into each other.

"Okay, kids, just one more ride. What will it be?"

Ruby yelled out, "The roller coaster!"

"Are you sure, Ruby? You won't get sick?"

"Naw."

Cassie turned to the others. "Is that what you all want?"

Angie shook her head and pointed to the carousel. "I want to ride on the merry-go-round, Teacher."

"And you boys?" Jeff looked at Weldon. Cassie remembered the time Jeff vomited after being spun too fast on the playground spinner. But if Weldon chose the roller coaster, Jeff would too. To her surprise, Weldon replied, "I like that black horse on the merry-go-round."

"Merry-go-round, it is." Cassie began walking in that direction.

Ruby stamped her foot. "But *I* want the roller coaster! *Please*, Teacher."

"I'm not too good on roller coasters, myself, Ruby. And I don't think you should go alone. If you wait, maybe Mr. Lee will take you later. Okay?"

Ruby beamed and followed the others to the merry-go-round. Cassie handed over the tickets and watched the boys rush to the horses they wanted. Struggling to lift her braced leg up onto the carousel, Angie turned to Cassie. "Will you ride with me, Teacher?"

"Ruby, stay right outside the fence here until we get off, you hear me?" Ruby nodded while Cassie lifted Angie onto her chosen white jeweled horse. Soon children straddled the brightly painted horses and spectators surrounded the carousel. As the music played and the horses pumped up and down, Cassie placed a hand on Angie's back. Glancing to the left, she saw her reflection in the inside mirrors and for a moment it was she on the jeweled white horse. With his hand wrapped around her waist, Jack had squeezed her tight as the horse rose and stole a kiss as it descended. With eyes closed, she inhaled deeply, savoring the memory of that date at the Big E in Springfield.

"Teacher, the ride stopped." Angie tugged on Cassie's sleeve.

She blinked at the sound of her name. Lifting Angie from the horse, she spotted Jeff and Weldon hopping off the carousel. "Wait up, boys!"

She pushed through the crowd but Ruby wasn't there. Frantically, Cassie ran around the carousel, calling for her. Why hadn't she paid closer attention? It had only been about five minutes. Panicked, she recalled Mrs. Washburn's rebuke. "Y'all crazy? Takin' those wild kids to the fair. I been teachin' lot more years than you. They goin' to be fightin' or runnin' off. No telling what might happen."

"Is Ruby lost, teacher?" Angie asked.

She took a deep breath before answering. "I'm sure she didn't go far. Let's all look together, okay? Stay close now."

They walked past a couple more rides and assorted food vendors. Cassie checked all the lines, desperately hoping to catch a glimpse of the seven-year-old with the dirty red dress and long stringy brown hair. Should she find a police officer? Report Ruby missing? She needed to stay calm, especially in front of the children, but fears of what might have happened gripped her. Then she spotted Ruby's purple flip flops lying outside the livestock tent. She picked them up and told the children to follow her inside. Upon entry, she was immediately struck with the pungent aroma and cacophony of assorted farm animals.

"Phew. It stinks in here." Weldon stopped in his tracks and held his nose.

Jeff waved him forward. "C'mon. It's just m-m-manure."

Cassie didn't know where to begin. The place was huge, with sections marked off for every kind of barnyard creature. They passed the hogs first, each seemingly more rotund than the last, some with colored prize ribbons already attached to their individual pens. Where would Ruby go? Then she saw Angie's mouth open and her eyes grow big. She was pointing toward the cattle pens. "What, what is it, Angie?" She looked in the direction Angie was pointing but at first didn't see anything. Angie began to whimper. Then Weldon started running. She looked again, and this time it was Cassie's mouth that opened in horror. Ruby was perched on one of the corral fences. Inside, stood a huge bull. She saw the girl tumble forward, red dress splayed in the dirt, fifteen feet from the snorting creature. He raised his horned head and stared at the intruder. Cassie didn't remember screaming, but onlookers said that it was indeed her scream that brought everyone running, including Grant and the other boys, who'd seen them and followed into the tent. They saw it all; the bull charging, Ruby frozen in place, Weldon crawling under the fence, grabbing Ruby and pulling her back to safety.

It was all Lewis could talk about the rest of the day, even as he munched his hot dog and slurped his slushy. Grant treated them all to cotton candy. Lewis wrapped his arm around Weldon's shoulder. "You be my hero, Weldon. You sure is brave. You want some of my cotton candy?" Weldon pulled off a sticky wad of pink confection, stuffed it in his mouth, licked his lips, and stuck out his chest.

Grant leaned over to Cassie and whispered. "Kind of reminds you of a cocky rooster, doesn't he?"

Cassie chuckled and poked him with her elbow. "Oh, let him have his moment of glory. He deserves it." She watched the boys laughing together and shook her head, muttering, "Who would have thought?

CHAPTER TEN

Escambia High teachers were told to double their hall patrol time. Grant could feel the tension and was on edge himself. Rumor had it that suspensions would be handed down at the end of the day. Confederate flag decals were pasted on many of the white kids' books. Black kids avoided walking alone. There had already been incidents out in the parking lot and on one of the buses. Fortunately, each time an adult had intervened before anyone was hurt. He thought of Cassie's students, especially Angie and Ruby, as they giggled together and shared French fries at the Fair. He wondered if their friendship would withstand the social pressure of racism as they grew older. He'd seen a few last over the years, but not many.

He entered the teacher's room, grabbed his paper bag lunch from the refrigerator, and checked his mailbox. A folded note with his name scrawled on it was wedged in the corner. He read it silently and then cursed under his breath.

"I heard that, Grant. Old man Frye harassing you again?" Amy's voice startled him and he almost backed into her. "That's Mel Higgins handwriting."

How did she know what the football coach's handwriting looked like? Maybe those rumors about the two of them were true.

"Since when does the football coach write notes to the history teacher?" She plucked the thin white paper from his hands before he could answer. He tried to yank it back but she'd already spun away from his reach. She backed into the corner near the staff bathroom. "Jesus, Grant. Is he serious?"

"Maybe. I don't know."

"What does he mean about you stirring up trouble? That if any of his players are suspended, he'll make you pay?"

He shrugged. It was true that a number of the black players on the football team had been involved in the walkout, encouraged mainly by Leroy. Also true, he hadn't deterred Leroy from the walkout when he'd come to him for advice; perhaps even encouraged him. He was having second thoughts about that now. Not because of this threatening note but because of the students' probable suspension.

"Are you going to report this threat, Grant?"

He shook his head. The less interaction he had with Frye the better. "Naw, Mel's just blowing off steam." He grabbed the paper from Amy, tore it up, and dropped the pieces into the trashcan.

Amy tugged on his arm, half-pulling him into the corridor. Her voice lowered to a whisper. "Mel doesn't make idle threats. I should know."

He was tempted to ask her what she meant by that, but he didn't. The last thing he wanted was to become Amy's confidante. He glanced at the hand still holding his shirt sleeve. The red-painted fingernails were perfectly manicured, fingers adorned with assorted gold jewelry, but not the adornment she most craved, a diamond.

"Don't worry Amy. I'm sure it's nothing. I'm more concerned about the students. They don't deserve punishment for acting on principle. Isn't that what we're trying to teach them?"

She dropped her hand and scoffed, "I swear Grant Lee, I sometimes wonder about you." She turned on her heels and sauntered down the corridor, trailing an exotic scent.

The suspension notices came at the end of the day. Leroy stormed into his classroom. "Ten days suspension, Mr. Lee! Everyone who was in the walkout. They think it's over, but it's not. We're not going to stop 'till that Confederate flag comes down, the Rebel mascot is gone, and the band stops playing Dixie!"

This time Grant was more cautionary. "Leroy, you might want to rethink that. Another infraction and you could be expelled."

Leroy frowned. "But you said we were right. We have to fight for what is right, don't we, Mr. Lee?"

Was it right to give this boy any encouragement? Had he, as Mel Higgins said, *stirred up trouble*? But how could he tell this young bright idealistic student to back down or apologize like they demanded. Leroy was a natural born leader, fighting for what he believed to be a just cause.

"Do what you think is best, Leroy. But be careful. And remember what Martin Luther King taught. No violence."

CHAPTER ELEVEN

Cassie poured another cup of coffee, cinched her bathrobe, and retrieved Saturday's newspaper from the front porch. Glancing at her neighbor's driveway, she saw Grant's van parked behind AdaMae's Ford clunker. Bent at the waist, his head buried under the car's hood, Grant couldn't see her. She smiled, recalling her last image of him - striding through the fairgrounds, Weldon atop his shoulders with children following like he was a Pied Piper. Her students, especially Weldon, had been asking if Grant could go on another trip with them. She'd been meaning to ask if he'd take them to a pumpkin farm. Maybe now would be a good time to ask him. But then she spotted the stain on her robe, fingered the tangles in her hair, and heard her stomach growl, giving notice that she needed food with coffee.

Crunching the first bite of toast slathered with peanut butter she unfolded the *Pensacola News Journal* and read ESCAMBIA STUDENTS SUSPENDED FOR WALKOUT; TENSIONS RISE. AdaMae had told her of the walkout. It had made the headlines of the front page. She read further. *Eighty-eight students have been suspended for participating in a walk-out from classes to protest the high school's use of the Confederate flag, the Confederate Rebel mascot, and the school song, Dixie. A petition requesting change was submitted to the school principal, Mr. Harold Frye, who said, "I have discussed the petition with the School Board and they agree that there is no reason to make any changes. It is unfortunate that some of our student body takes offense at these honored school symbols."* She immediately thought of Grant. No doubt some of his students were involved. She was anxious to hear his reaction.

Finishing the last of the toast, she carried her coffee to the bedroom and fished a pair of jeans from the dresser drawer. The phone rang as she was pulling a UConn t-shirt over her head. She rushed to the kitchen and grabbed the phone on the fourth ring.

"Hey, Cassie."

She was pleased to hear Reina's voice. With a new love interest in her life, Reina had been somewhat scarce, and Cassie was beginning to think she was going to fall into that 'forgotten friend' role. "Reina, was wondering when I'd hear from you."

"Yeah, I know. Been a while since I've called. Sorry about that. But I really want you to meet Bill. We're going to the high school football game tonight. You want to join us?"

"Football? Really? I didn't think you were into it."

"I'm not. But Bill is. Played all through high school and college. He's anxious to check out the local talent. If TV football is any indication, he'll be too absorbed in the game to talk much, but we can go out afterwards. You in?"

"Are you talking about the Escambia High game?"

"Yes."

"Haven't you seen the news?"

"About what? Remember, I was out of town at a social workers' conference all week."

Cassie filled her in on the walkout. "You and Bill still want to go?"

"Knowing Bill, yes. The only thing he loves more than football is politics, especially local politics. Did I tell you he wants to run for County Commissioner? I may be his campaign manager. This news will get him juiced for sure. But I'll check in with you later today, okay?"

"Okay. I may be going over to AdaMae's house. Grant is there. He may have a better idea of what's going on and what to expect at the game tonight."

"Ah, the mysterious guy you keep talking about that I've yet to meet."

"I don't keep talking about him."

"If you say so. Why don't you ask him to join us? I've been saying I want to meet him, especially with a name like Grant Lee."

Cassie hung up the phone, aware of a sudden annoyance with her friend. She hadn't talked that much about Grant, had she? It's true that Reina had shown some curiosity about him, even hinted that Cassie should ask him out. How could she suggest such a thing? Reina was the one person with whom she'd shared her grief. What made her think she could ever love someone other than Jack? Determined to push irritation aside, she snapped the front of her jeans and headed out the front door.

AdaMae answered her knock. "Cassie, I was hoping you'd swing by. Grant's here. He's already asked after you."

Cassie was again nettled. AdaMae was starting to throw out hints too. She lingered in the living room, avoiding asking for Grant. "Everything okay with your car now, AdaMae?"

"Right as rain. Grant installed the part it needed. You got time for coffee? I put a fresh pot on."

"No thanks. Already had more than my share."

"Well, if you don't mind, I'm going to have a warm-up. I do have to leave in a bit for a hair appointment. Normally I avoid the beauty parlor on Saturday mornings, but I had to postpone my appointment because of the car. Have a seat. I'll be right back."

Cassie sat on the couch and was soon joined by Rufford, who pushed through the doggie door and jumped into her lap. "Hey, boy." She scratched behind his ears and he rolled over for the requisite tummy rub. Loud barking ensued, followed by Alice, who bounded into the room, circled three times, and sprawled out on the carpet, her large paws covering Cassie's Keds. The front door slammed, and she smelled his scent first, a pleasing mix of male sweat, earth, and motor oil.

"Cassie."

At the sound of his voice, the hair on the back of her neck rose. She took a calming breath and tried to sound nonchalant. "Hi. Been working on AdaMae's car, I see."

"Yeah. Let me wash up. Don't go away."

He returned just as AdaMae stepped from the kitchen and gave him a warm smile. "Thanks for fixing the car and preparing that new perennial bed for me, Grant. I can plant my bulbs now."

Cassie raised her eyebrows. "Wow! You did all that this morning?"

"What can I say? I'm an early riser." He took a seat next to Cassie on the couch. "If you ever need any yard help, be happy to give you a hand."

As he spread one arm over the back of the couch, his fingertips brushed her shoulder. She tightened. "Appreciate it, but I think your grandmother's list keeps you plenty busy."

AdaMae laughed. "Yeah, I guess you could say that. But I'd be happy to share him."

This time it was Grant who laughed. "Subcontracted indentured servant, am I?"

Cassie had forgotten how much she liked his laugh. Conscious of his body just inches from hers, she changed the subject. "I read about the suspensions. What's happening?"

His smile disappeared. "It's a mess, that's for sure."

AdaMae pushed against the chair's arms and rose.

"Well, I've heard all this before. Good timing for my exit." She turned toward Grant. "Remember I'm going to be gone for a few days."

Cassie looked up. "Oh, where?"

"My sister, Vivian, has been begging me to come for a visit for ages now. She lives over in Tallahassee. Her husband passed a couple years back and she doesn't have kids. Nothing but her two cats to keep her company, which is why I have to leave Rufford with Grant." She turned to her grandson. "Don't forget to walk him."

Grant stood to kiss his grandmother goodbye. "I won't. Tell Auntie Vivian I said hello."

"I'll do more than that. I'll give her a big kiss that has your name on it."

Cassie started to stand, but AdaMae pressed her shoulder.

"Don't get up, dear." She then patted Rufford. "Be a good fellow."

Grant walked his grandmother to the door before sitting back on the couch.

Cassie said, "So, fill me in."

"It's been a tough week. I think I told you about Leroy, right?"
She nodded. "Well, he was one of those suspended."

"Didn't you also say he was on the football team?"

"Yeah, and he's not the only one."

"Football players you mean?"

"About a third of the starting team won't be on the field
tonight. Coach Higgins blames me."

"You? But why?"

"I'm a history teacher, and it hasn't gone unnoticed that I
detour from the textbook often. I kind of fill in the blanks about
the whole "fighting for states' rights" mantra of the Confederacy;
teach the truth. Coach says I'm giving the kids ideas, making his
niggers 'uppity'."

"No! He actually said that?"

Grant nodded. "He was waiting for me in the parking lot yesterday
when I left work. Says if they lose tonight, he'll make me pay."

"Oh my God. You have to report this."

"To whom? The cops? Some of them are his former players.
And believe me they have no sympathy for the suspended students,
especially the football players. Most think they've betrayed the
Coach and the school."

"But you don't think that."

"Of course not."

"So, what are you going to do?"

"Nothing. Just keep an eye on Leroy and the others. Do what I
can to keep them out of trouble. They have the most to lose."

"You think they'll be at the game tonight?"

"Not supposed to be, but there are rumors they plan to make a showing. If I see Leroy or any of the others, I plan to waltz them right out of there – if I can."

"So, you're going to the game?"

He took a sip of coffee before replying. "Yes."

"You think that's wise, what with the Coach's threats and all?"

"Pshaw. He's just blowing off steam. He'll be too busy pumping up his second-string players to have time for me."

"Reina invited me to the game tonight. She wants me to meet her new boyfriend, Bill."

"You going?"

"Think so."

"Might be trouble there, Cassie."

"You're going. You must think it'll be okay. Why don't you sit with us?"

He brushed the hair from his eyes, leaned closer, and gazed at her. "I'd like that."

She stood. "I better get home. I've got lots to do. I'll meet you at the game, okay?"

"Right."

As she entered her house, she realized that she'd forgotten to ask Grant about the pumpkin farm. She didn't dare go back. Why was she shaking? Leaning against the wall to steady herself, her shoulder bumped Jack's picture. It fell to the floor. Quickly she bent down, centered it back on the hook, relieved to see that the glass hadn't cracked.

CHAPTER TWELVE

Grant spotted Cassie waving in the stands near the forty-yard line. He zig-zagged up the bleachers to join her, leaned over, and whispered, "Would have got here sooner but I wanted to check out the parking lot, see if Leroy was there."

"And?"

He shook his head. "No sign of him yet."

Cassie then made the introductions.

"Nice to meet you both." He reached past Cassie to shake Reina and Bill's hands. Both tall and broad-shouldered, the pair made a handsome looking match. "Cassie talks a lot about you, Reina. Grew up around here, I understand. Where'd you go to high school?"

"Booker T. Washburn. Pre-integration years."

He nodded. "Y'know I did some tutoring there the summer after high school."

Reina raised her eyebrows. "Really? Did you like that?"

"It was a learning experience."

Reina smiled knowingly. "I bet it was."

Grant turned to Bill. "And you Bill, not from around here?"

"Close enough. Mobile, Alabama."

"Ah, yes, Wallace country."

Bill laughed. "Not in my neck of the woods."

Grant heard the laugh but also saw that look of wariness. He'd seen it all too many times. Whites weren't to be trusted, not until they proved their stripes. He got it. "Not popular in my book either, but GW got a lot of votes in this county. 'Course he's out of the picture now."

Bill nodded. "That was one crazy redneck who shot him. Good thing it wasn't some black guy. Would have started a second Civil War around here."

Grant had never thought of that before, but knew Bill was right. "Well, we've got our own Civil War brewing right here at Escambia High."

"So I hear. Your football team must be hurting."

"You could say that. I know a number of the suspended players. A little worried that they might show up."

"And that could spell trouble."

Grant nodded. "More than a little, I suspect."

Grant perused the stands, looking for Leroy. He saw the usual roving troops of boys eyeing the cliques of giggling girls. Was it Grant's imagination or were there more Confederate flags than normal being waved in the crowd? Chords of *Dixie* blasted through the stadium as the band strutted onto the field, followed by the school football team. The crowd cheered.

Escambia lined up to receive the kick-off from the crimson and grey clad Tate players. They didn't have the ball long. A third down fumble led to Tate's first touchdown. At the end of the first half, Escambia had yet to score. Tate plowed through their defense, scoring two touchdowns and two field goals for a score of 20-0.

The half-time buzzer sounded just as Grant spotted them. Wearing their orange and blue football jerseys, a group of black students climbed the bleachers to the top of the stands and stood in the back row, their arms crossed. All eyes turned towards them, ignoring the school band marching onto the field. Grant counted seven players, including Leroy.

"Excuse me." Grant began weaving his way up the bleachers. He knew it was only a matter of time. Maybe he could talk them into leaving before anything happened, convince them that just making a brief appearance was enough of a statement. He didn't see Fred Crowley coming from the other direction, and Fred wasn't alone. About ten guys gruffly pushed people aside as they climbed.

Grant arrived just as Fred planted his feet in front of Leroy and barked, "You don't belong here, boy." Leroy glared back. Fred shoved Leroy in the chest, who fell back against the top railing. Grant stepped between them.

"Get out of my way, Teach. These boys need a lesson and we plan to give it to them."

"Nothing to be gained by that, Fred. I suggest you all go back to your seats."

Grant furtively scanned the area below, looking for a police officer. Instead, he saw the school mascot, a student dressed in a Rebel uniform, running out onto the field waving the Confederate flag as the band struck up the first notes of 'Dixie'. He never knew who swung that first punch. Nor did he see much of the ensuing brawl. The fist that landed on his jaw knocked him backwards. He tumbled over fans, feeling his ankle twist under the seats before hitting his head on one of the metal bleachers. He didn't remember the ambulance ride to the hospital.

CHAPTER THIRTEEN

Cassie sat at the kitchen table preparing her lesson plans for the week, listening for any sounds from the bedroom. The doctor said that Grant shouldn't be left alone, not after suffering a concussion. With AdaMae out of town, Cassie insisted he come home with her. Groggy from pain killers, Grant was in no shape to argue. The spare bedroom was strewn with boxes, so she settled him into her bed with Bill's help. After Reina and Bill had left, she curled up on the couch with her mother's hand crocheted afghan and drifted off to sleep.

The hospital room was dark. The only sound was the beep of the bedside monitor. She stood alone in the doorway, afraid to approach. "You may not recognize him. There are extensive burns from the crash. Little chance..." She didn't listen to the rest. She crept closer to the bed. Jack's eyes were closed, the skin was blotchy and taut. His close-cropped hair was matted with blood. She touched his forehead, and the eyes opened. "Cassie, I've been waiting. Finally, you've come." He reached for her hand.

She awoke abruptly, rubbing her hand, hoping to retain his touch. She'd not dreamed of Jack in weeks. Why now? Then she remembered the recent hours at the hospital with Grant, bedside hours she never had with her husband. She knew nothing of his final hours, other than his helicopter crashed. Did he die on impact? Had he called for her at the end? Why hadn't she sensed it? But there had been no intuitive sense, no telepathic message. Only now, in her dreams, did she hear him call for her. She never had the chance to tell him one more time how much she loved him. There had been no goodbye.

Sometimes, she still thought he would walk through the door, press her against his crisp Navy whites and hold on forever. Exhausted, she fell back into a fitful sleep with Rufford at her feet, only to be disturbed again, this time by a distant moan coming from the bedroom.

The bruise around Grant's right eye looked garish in the morning light. His jaw was swollen. Five dark stitches closed the gash that had splayed blood on the shirt, now tossed in the bathtub. His head was partially shaved, leaving a white trail along the stitch line.

His eyes fluttered open. Cassie?"

She stepped forward. "Do you need anything?"

He stuck his tongue out and drew it back in. "Mouth is dry; feels like fuzz."

"It's the medicine." She picked up a pill bottle from the bed stand. "Pain killer. You're due for another. I'll get you some water."

Upon returning, she propped two pillows behind his back and helped him to sit up. Handing him the glass of water with a pill, she said, "Take these if you're feeling pain."

He shook his head. "Not yet. Where am I?"

"My house. You have a nasty cut on your head and the doctor said you suffered a mild concussion. Do you remember what happened?"

"Some. I remember the punch. Was it Fred?"

"I really don't know. I went with you in the ambulance and Reina and Bill came later. They said the fight spread and got pretty ugly. You weren't the only casualty last night. A matter of fact the doctor said normally they would have kept you longer but they needed the bed for other patients."

Grant pushed himself higher in the bed, winced, and grabbed his head. "Wow."

"You should try not to move."

"Have I been here long?"

"A few hours. I was told not to let you sleep too much. Have to make sure you don't have any complications from the concussion."

"Guess that explains the headache and why my brain feels like sludge."

Sunlight poured through the open blinds, exposing dust and clutter. A pink bra hung from the open dresser drawer. An emptied beer can lay on the end table along with an open bag of chips. Her slovenly habits had been a source of marital stress with Jack. Now, she no longer tried to be tidy. Hastily, she picked up the scattered clothing strewn on the floor, tucked them under her arm, and asked, "Are you hungry? Do you think you could eat something? How about some toast?"

"Maybe in a bit. But first, tell me what happened after the scuffle with Fred's gang."

"I don't know the whole story. As I said, I left with the ambulance, but fists were flying everywhere. Details might be in today's paper, which is probably in the driveway. I'll get it."

Grant inched his way out of bed, trying to stand, but quickly realized it was a bad idea. He fell back against the pillows.

Cassie returned with the newspaper. "Made the front page."

He stared at the headlines: **Riot Erupts at Escambia High Football Game**.

"Jesus. They're calling it a full-scale riot."

Cassie asked, "Any mention of you in there?"

He scanned the article. "No, thank God. Just the number of people injured, and arrests made." He folded the paper, took a deep breath, and closed his eyes.

"You in a lot of pain?"

"Not sure which throbs more, my head or my ankle, … I'll be okay." He glanced over at the crutches propped against the wall in the corner. "Ankle's not broken, is it?"

"Sprained, but you'll need crutches for a few days." She reached under the sheet and retrieved a water-filled icepack. "Let me get a fresh ice pack now that you're awake." She returned with the ice pack and a plate of toast.

"Sorry you have to play Florence Nightingale."

She set down the toast, lifted the sheet, and carefully placed the ice pack on his ankle. "I'm not complaining, but you might. Haven't played nursemaid since my mom and brother both came down with the flu. Somehow, Dad and I escaped it."

"You never told me you had a brother."

"I didn't? How could I not tell you about Jeremy? You probably aren't up for conversation right now, though."

"Sure I am. Need to turn my mind to something else. Tell me about Jeremy."

"You sure you're up to talking?"

"Absolutely. Headache is already getting better."

She sat gingerly at the edge of the bed. "My parents thought I was going to be their one and only, even though Mom told me they'd wanted lots of kids. Ten years after I was born, she got pregnant. Jeremy was the result. I adore him. I think it's the hardest thing about being away from home, not seeing him."

"He must miss you too."

"So he says. We talk every week on the phone. Sometimes it's a little hard to understand him, but Mom fills me in on stuff I missed."

"But he must be what, twelve? Does he have a speech problem?"

"Kind of. Jeremy's the reason I went into Special Education. He's a Down Syndrome child." She paused, wondering how Grant would react, but he just waited for Cassie to continue.

"Mom said the pediatrician recommended putting him in an institution. She and Dad would have none of that. It was pretty tough for them the first couple of years. Trouble feeding him, heart issues requiring surgeries, and of course he was quite delayed. He didn't take his first step until two and a half. Mom cried when he did, and I think even Dad shed a tear or two. Jeremy was a roly-poly thing, full of smiles, and laughed at just about everything I did. How could I not adore him?"

"Sounds like the feeling is mutual."

Cassie blushed. "Yeah, he's my biggest admirer. Handsome bugger too. I've got a picture of him in my wallet. I'll show you." She reached for her purse.

Grant took the picture as Cassie sat back on the bed. The photo showed a somewhat pudgy boy with a thick thatch of corn colored hair and deep blue eyes with the tell-tale slant. He was holding a basketball and grinning from ear to ear.

"Likes basketball, does he?"

"Loves it. He belongs to a special needs recreation league."

"Basketball was my game too."

"Really? With your height I bet you were good at it." She could feel the tip of his toes against her thigh; felt a sudden rush of warmth.

Grant told of his playing years in junior high and high school after moving in with his grandparents. "Really kept me sane that first year and helped me make friends. Tough to be the newcomer, a Yankee, no less. I was an easy target for bullies, until I grew four inches in one year and just kept on growing."

"So, you were a basketball star?"

"I don't know about being a star, but my popularity grew when I broke a record on number of points scored by a player in one game."

"Jeremy would be impressed. Did you play in college at all?"

"I was offered a basketball scholarship, but by then I had decided there was more to life than basketball, and besides, I didn't want to leave my grandparents. Gramps health was already failing. I didn't know how many more years he had. Decided to go to the University of West Florida, right here in Pensacola. Even with that, I was still considered an outsider by the other kids, since I was born in New York."

"I forget sometimes that you weren't born here, but now that I think about it, your accent is only on a few words."

"I have an accent?"

Cassie laughed. "Of course you do."

"Not as much as you."

Cassie laughed again. "Yeah, the kids at school have already pointed that out."

"Ah, yes, your little 'challenges'. How's everything going at school?"

"Well, in the classroom, things are really improving. Believe it or not, ever since the fair, Weldon and Lewis have become best buds, and they kind of keep the others in line. They're constantly saying, 'Don't you be messin' with Teacher.' Mrs. Hicks is amazed. She thinks I've performed some kind of miracle."

Grant took a bite of toast. "You kind of have, Mrs. Cunningham."

Hearing her married name threw Cassie off guard. She fingered her wedding ring and glanced toward the shoe box of Jack's letters in the open closet. She hadn't read any in over a week, nor had she written a letter. A part of her said it was good and right to begin to let go, but a certain smell or touch kept bringing back memories. Last night was the first night she hadn't clutched Jack's pillow trying to breathe in his long-lost scent. Yet she had dreamed of him.

She edged off the bed. "I think I need to get back to lesson planning and you probably need to rest. Don't forget the pain pill if you need it."

"You don't have to leave. I'm not that tired, really."

It was a plea-filled request, and she felt guilty leaving, but she could not stay. That would only bring a different kind of guilt.

"I'll check back soon." She walked to the door, aware that his eyes were on her.

CHAPTER FOURTEEN

On the way home from work Cassie decided to stop at the Piggly Wiggly and pick up some chicken for supper. After all those meals AdaMae had cooked for her, the least she could do is cook for her grandson. She'd try her mother's skillet lemon chicken recipe. It looked easy enough. She pushed the cart through the produce section first, trying to decide on a vegetable. So many were still unfamiliar, especially all those strange greens: collards, mustard greens, chard. She'd stick with what she knew best, grabbed a bag of carrots and began looking for the lemons. As she reached for the lemons, she overheard the conversation of two women nearby.

"The whole thing is so ridiculous. Ever since they put *them* in our schools there's been nothing but trouble. Thank goodness I enrolled my kids in the Christian Academy."

The other woman nodded. "My Melanie is starting high school next year. She wants to go to Escambia High, but after this fiasco, there's no way. Getting rid of the Confederate Flag! It's downright unpatriotic if you ask me. Where's their pride, for God's sake?"

Cassie was unaware that she was staring at them with her mouth open, or that she was squeezing the lemons much too hard, until the two women turned, looked at her, and pushed their carts away. Unsettled by the store conversation, she almost took a wrong turn on the way home. Did they really equate displaying the Confederate flag with patriotism?

Kicking her shoes off, she walked into the kitchen, set the grocery bags on the table, and was about to check on Grant when she spotted the note between the salt and pepper shakers.

Dear Cassie,

Thanks for taking such good care of me. I really appreciate it. Called my Aunt Vivian and spoke with Grams, who wanted to cut her vacation short and come take care of me. I insisted she finish her visit, but asked if I could stay at her house, since it's all one floor. Hope you'll swing by for a visit.

Thanks again,

Grant

How, she wondered, did he manage to make it to his grandmother's house? Cassie stuck the chicken in the refrigerator before heading to her bedroom. The bedspread was pulled up. The water glass was empty; the pill bottle gone. He'd awoken when she tiptoed into the room earlier that morning. She'd apologized for intruding and for the mess, but he only mumbled incoherently. She should check up on him, let him know about supper plans.

She tapped lightly on AdeMae's front door, afraid he might be asleep.

"Come in!" Stretched on the couch reading the newspaper, Grant didn't even look up when she entered. "Damn!" He slammed the paper down and pounded the wall with his fist. The dogs lifted their heads at his outburst and then trotted to Cassie, who patted them and said, "Are you okay?"

"Sorry. I can't help it. You haven't read today's paper yet, have you?"

"No. A lot about the riot?"

"Yeah. One-sided if you ask me. You should read the paper's editorial. You'd think the Confederacy was some kind of saintly brotherhood fighting for freedom and democracy. Doesn't anyone know history around here?"

"Maybe they read the wrong history books."

"Touche'. If anyone should know that, it's me. I've seen plenty of them."

Cassie had never seen him angry. "I suppose history is seen differently in the hearts and minds of those conquered."

"So I've been told, but there is such a thing as truth."

"I think I'm seeing another side of you, Grant Lee."

"The self-righteous bastard?"

She laughed. "I didn't say that. I get a little perturbed at ignorance myself." She told him about the conversation in the grocery store.

"No surprise there. When integration became mandated, most white parents enrolled their kids in private schools. You probably already figured that out."

Cassie thought of all the uniformed school children waiting for the Christian Academy bus in her neighborhood. "Yes, I know, but their racist comments still shocked me. Speaking of which, have you heard any more about what happened?"

"Only that I've been suspended indefinitely."

She dropped into the chair across from him. "Suspended? No! Why?"

"There'll be an investigation. Just have to hope the truth comes out. I doubt my version of events is going to line up with Fred's or some of the others."

"Are you going to get a lawyer?"

"Lawyer? Hadn't thought of that. Times like this I sure wish we had a teacher's union, but the district squelched that idea a few years back."

"Do you have any idea how long their investigation will take?"

"Nope, but I suspect longer than the sick days I planned on taking off this week."

"How are you doing today? And how did you manage to get over here?"

"It wasn't too hard. Just took my time. My head isn't throbbing."

"Well, Florence Nightingale is coming to the rescue again. I'm going to make you dinner."

"You don't need to do that. I can scramble up some eggs or something."

Cassie shook her head. "Already bought the ingredients, although I can't make any promises. Cooking has never been my forte, but I have a recipe from my mother that I've been meaning to try."

"And you want me to be your guinea pig?"

Cassie chuckled. "That's the plan. 6 o'clock okay? I'll bring it over. See you then."

***

Her mother said that it took about an hour to prep and cook. But it seemed to take almost that long to gather all the ingredients and get the chicken started in the pan. The recipe called for lemon zest. What the heck was that? It was only a tablespoon. Couldn't be that important, could it? She managed to get the chicken and all the other ingredients into the pan by 5:30. If she needed it done by 6, then perhaps she should turn the heat to high. Her mother would die at her choice of instant mashed potatoes, but it seemed the safest and quickest option. Every time she'd tried cooking rice it had burned, and she didn't want to heat up the house by putting potatoes in the oven. She peeled and chopped the carrots, placed them in a pan to cook, and headed to the bathroom to take a shower.

As she turned the faucet to cold and stood under the pulsing spray, she thought of home. The leaves would be turning color, the air would be crisp. Summer clothes would be packed away and dresser drawers filled with sweaters. She loved taking long walks in autumn woods, hearing the sound of leaves crunching under her feet, the scurry of squirrels scampering for acorns.

A couple of times, before going off to college, she had taken Jeremy camping. She taught him how to pitch a tent and make a fire. They would sit out under the stars and she'd point out some of the constellations. After that, he always named them in the night sky when he could find them. The doctors were wrong about Jeremy. He'd proven how capable he was. Her parents' love and caring teachers made all the difference. She was determined to be one of those teachers, one who made a difference.

She stepped out of the shower and stood naked in front of the fogged mirror. At twenty-two, she had all the curves of womanhood, but the sparse diet was beginning to show. She'd lost weight since Jack's passing. Perhaps a double serving of mashed potatoes tonight? And maybe of chicken too? *The chicken! Was that a burning smell?*

She ran to the kitchen and lifted the cover off the pan. "Oh, no!" The chicken broth had evaporated, leaving only a sticky brown sauce that smelled of scorched lemon. She slid the pan off the burner and poured in some water. Burnt-scented steam rose into the kitchen. How could she make it right? She turned the chicken pieces over and began scraping charred black bits off each piece, added more chicken broth, along with the juice of another lemon. That should do it. She placed the chicken, potatoes, and carrots in separate serving dishes, put them in a shopping bag, and dressed quickly. At the last minute, she grabbed the half gallon of ice cream from the freezer, and tossed it in the bag too. She hoped he liked strawberry.

When he opened the door, she noted the dress button-down shirt and fresh scent of Lifebuoy.

"Hey."

She smiled, suddenly conscious of her old jeans and sleeveless tee. "You look… ah, nice. I mean, I guess I should've dressed up a bit."

"You look super. Thought it was time I washed up and got out of my bathrobe."

"I'll bring the food into the kitchen. It's still warm. After I set the table, we can eat."

Hobbling on crutches, Grant followed Cassie into the kitchen, almost bumping into her as she abruptly stopped and stared at the blue-checked tablecloth on a table set for two with a white tapered candle decorously placed in the center. Not sure what to say, she unloaded the food onto the counter. She didn't dare turn around to look at him. What was he expecting?

"Is everything all right?"

"Everything's great," she said, hoping he didn't hear the tension in her voice as she put the ice cream in the freezer.

"So, what's for dinner? I'm starving. He propped his crutches against one end of the table and hopped to his seat.

Cassie set the serving dishes on the table. "Lemon chicken, potatoes, and carrots."

Grant lit the candle. "A little candlelight to celebrate."

"What are we celebrating?"

Grant smiled. "My return home. Your delicious meal. My suspension. Take your pick."

"Sarcasm. Another personality trait I've not seen before." As she scooped the potatoes onto her plate, she noted the liquid runoff. She'd been distracted when reading the box. Was it two cups of water, not three?

They cut into the chicken at the same time. Most of the blackened skin had been scraped off. Hopefully the inside wasn't burned too. As the knife slit open the chicken leg, a trickle of pink oozed onto the plate. How could it be both burnt and raw at the same time? She looked across the table at Grant, whose fork was poised mid-air. With forced smile, he put the chicken piece into his mouth and chewed. She didn't dare do the same. Instead, she poked one of the carrots, only to see it fly off the plate onto the floor. The carrots were still hard. Had she forgotten to boil the water? Setting her fork down, she gazed at the plate of watery potatoes, raw blackened chicken, and hard carrots. *She refused to cry.* Instead, she took a deep breath, looked at Grant and said, "Well, I guess we can safely say we aren't celebrating my delicious meal."

Grant erupted with laughter, spewing the last bits of chicken onto his plate. He grabbed a napkin to wipe his face. "Oh, I don't know. I've never had sushi chicken before."

Cassie chortled. "I'm sorry. I did warn you that cooking was not my thing."

"That you did. Didn't I see you put some ice cream into the freezer?"

"For dessert, yes."

"Haven't you heard the adage, 'Life's short; Eat dessert first'?"

Cassie stood and began clearing the dishes. "I'll get the bowls and spoons."

"And I'll get the ice cream. How about Gram's whoopee pies to go with it? There's some in the frig."

Cassie spooned generous portions of ice cream into each bowl. "Hope you like strawberry."

"Second only to Rocky Road." He placed a large whoopee pie in each bowl. "C'mon, let's eat on the couch. Do you like *Mission Impossible*? It's about to come on."

"Love it. Lead the way." She picked up the bowls of ice cream, blew out the candle, and followed Grant into the living room, silently promising to clean up the mess later. Despite her disastrous dinner attempt, there was also a sense of relief. Eating ice cream while watching television should be safer than sharing a candlelit meal with Grant. It was getting harder to avoid the mutual attraction, but she needed to make sure it stayed as friends only. What would Jack think?

CHAPTER FIFTEEN

School started as usual, greeting the children, getting them settled into their morning paperwork before gathering for a story, the children's favorite part of the day. Cassie had chosen *The Giant Jam Sandwich*. It was a good choice. They were enthralled by the story and loved the silly names of the characters, especially Mayor Muddlenut.

"Teacher, someone's here." Weldon was pointing to the door, where Reina stood with her hand on the shoulder of a young girl.

Upon Cassie's approach, Reina said, "Mrs. Cunningham, you have a new student. This is Sharelle."

Cassie bent down trying to look into the girl's face. Sharelle's chin rested on her chest. "Hi, Sharelle. Welcome to our classroom. I'm Mrs. Cunningham, your new teacher." She stood and spoke to Reina. "Surprised to see you here. Didn't know you hand delivered new students."

"Sharelle is a special case. I'll fill you in later after school, if you're going to be around."

"Sure, I'll be here." She turned her attention back to the quiet child standing next to her. "Come with me, Sharelle. I'll introduce you to your new classmates. We were just finishing up our story time for today."

Sharelle's Afroed head stayed down throughout the introductions. She didn't speak all day, despite Cassie's efforts, as well as Ruby's, who was quite excited about having another girl in the classroom. As soon as the last child was dismissed, Cassie went to the front office to retrieve the transfer records of Sharelle McKnight. It was a skimpy folder with outdated information that told her little, other than Sharelle's age and former school, with a very spotty attendance record. Cassie found Reina waiting in the classroom when she returned. Holding up the folder, she said, "I hope you have more information than what I found in here."

"Some. I know she lives with a mother and younger sibling. That's about it for family information."

"She doesn't strike me as a behavior problem. Quite shy. Didn't say a word all day."

"That's why she's here."

"What do you mean? Since when did shyness qualify a child for special education?"

"Cassie, it isn't just today that she hasn't spoken. I contacted her former teacher and Sharelle has yet to speak in school."

"You mean not *ever*?"

"Not ever."

"Has her hearing been checked?"

"Of course."

"And?"

"As far as the audiologist could determine, her ears are fine."

"And educational testing? What does that show?"

"Pretty hard to test a kid that won't talk."

"But she's nine years old!"

"I know, and we have very little in her school records. That's why I called the previous school, but they couldn't tell us much, as she'd only come to school a few days and there were no previous school records."

"Do you suppose she hadn't been in school prior to that?"

"Possibly. I'm going to try to get out to the home when I can, but it might not be for a while. I'm really backed up in my paperwork, and there are some other home visits that have been penciled in for quite some time now. And with the coursework that I'm taking at the University three days a week after school, I've got less time."

Cassie nodded. "Well, I appreciate your stopping by to tell me. Have you and Bill recovered from all the excitement at the game?"

"Bill's pretty shook up about it. He's been away too long. I think he forgot how entrenched the racist attitudes are here. How's Grant doing?"

"Better. He's staying at his grandmother's house. He's been suspended though."

"Suspended? But he tried to prevent the fight!"

"We know that, but the school authorities are investigating the whole incident."

Reina shook her head.

"You think he'll get his job back, right? Once they learn the truth."

"I don't know, Cassie. I hope so. Depends."

"Depends on what?"

"Whose version of the truth they believe. And perhaps more importantly, what they want to believe. I only met Grant once, but

I get the impression that he's rocked the boat some at Escambia before this."

"He told me about some problems he's had with parents and the administration for veering from the prescribed curriculum, and for covering current events too much, but that doesn't have anything to do with this."

"Maybe, maybe not."

"But, Reina, he didn't do anything wrong! They *have* to give him his job back!"

Reina squinted at the heightened pitch of Cassie's voice. "I hope so." She touched Cassie's arm. "You have to forgive me. I'm a bit of a cynic. It'll probably all turn out fine." She stepped toward the door. "Have to run. Call me when you get a chance, okay?"

"Sure."

Why had she reacted to Reina with such distress? Maybe because she'd seen Grant every night this past week. At first, she told herself it was just to check in on him, but the half-hour visits turned into an hour, then dinner, and then talking way past her bedtime. The late-night hours were beginning to catch up with her.

Driving home, she thought of their conversations. She learned that Grant loved to camp, but usually did so in the wilderness, far away from official campgrounds. He hoped to hike the Appalachian Trail someday. She discovered that he loved bluegrass music and could play the harmonica. He had a sweet tooth, which is why he loved to bake. Despite his sprained ankle, he managed to bake a fantastic chocolate cake yesterday and gave her half of it. But it was when he spoke about his students or the subject of history that he became most passionate. He was convinced that if more young people understood history, especially American history, they would be more engaged citizens. Even more, she loved the way he listened, his dark eyes always gazing at her intensely.

When she pulled into the driveway, she was surprised to see Grant suddenly appear by her car door. "Goodness. You startled me. How did you get over here so fast on crutches?"

He shrugged. "What can I say? I'm practically sprinting with these things. Doc says I need them for another week or so though. How about you come over for pizza tonight? Maybe watch *Mission Impossible* again together."

"I thought your grandmother was coming home tonight?"

"Tomorrow."

"Oh, right. Well, I guess I could. Kind of need to crash for a bit though. You know how it is for teachers on Friday nights."

"Yeah. Take your time. What do you want on your pizza?

"Peppers and mushrooms. See you in a couple of hours."

"Great. I'll order the pizza for 6:30 then."

She nodded and walked up the driveway. Flipping open the mailbox, she stuck the mail between her teeth while retrieving the house keys from her pocketbook. Kicking off her shoes, she dropped the mail on the end table by the couch and turned the air conditioner on high. She stretched out on the couch and let the window unit blast full strength. Within minutes she'd fallen asleep as envelopes scattered.

CHAPTER SIXTEEN

Grant stacked the books on the table and straightened scattered papers. He'd decided to use the convalescent time for research. A colleague had dropped off the requested library books. He finally was making a dent in what he'd long wanted to do, write a book on the Reconstruction era. But it was only that, a dent. He needed to get to the university library to research articles on microfiche. His former university professor kept encouraging him to seek admission into the doctoral program. That required both time and money, in short supply for a teacher. He was anxious to get Cassie's opinion. He found he could talk with her about almost anything. She had a practical wisdom that belied her youth. He also found that he couldn't stop thinking about her; what it would be like to kiss her. But he could not compete with a dead husband, especially a handsome war hero.

He heard a car drive up. Was the pizza boy here already? He'd just called. There was a quick knock on the door and then it opened before he could even grab his crutches. Alice jumped off the couch and ran to the door, with Rufford right behind.

"Yoo-hoo! Grant!"

"Amy?" Grant hobbled forward.

Alice was now mixing assorted growls with a steady stream of barking. Rufford followed suit. Amy stood frozen in the doorway, scowling in return. "Go away!"

Grant whistled for the dogs and they trotted back to his side. "Amy, why are you here?"

"Don't look so surprised. Why wouldn't I come to see a dear friend in need?" She held up a bottle of wine. "Thought we'd share a few glasses of wine. You're injured and probably bored out of your mind, and I'm beat. It's been a long week." She kissed his cheek and strutted to the kitchen. "Where's your corkscrew and glasses?"

"Amy, it's really not a good time. How did you even find me?"

"I have my sources. What do you mean, it's not a good time? When is it ever a bad time to have some wine? It's pretty good stuff too. I splurged. A name brand Italian Pinot Noir. I hope you like red."

He could hear her opening and closing cabinet doors.

"Found some glasses. Where do you keep the corkscrew?" she yelled from the kitchen. Alice rose again, emitting a low growl.

"Sit, Alice." The dog lay back down on her haunches. Grant picked up his crutches and gimped into the kitchen. "Amy, this is really very sweet of you, but really, as I said, it's not a good time."

"But of course it is. You must be feeling so low, after all that's happened. Everyone's talking about you."

"About me?"

"Do you know anyone else on suspension?"

"What are they saying?" As much as he wanted her to leave, she'd piqued his curiosity.

"Depends. Most of the teachers think you're being framed. The kids are split. A lot of your favorites are defending you. But the general anti-walkout crowd thinks you were in cahoots with the coloreds."

He winced at the put-down. Like many of the teachers, Amy wasn't thrilled when the school had integrated.

"Ah, found it." She pulled a corkscrew from a drawer and began twisting it into the cork on the bottle. Filling both glasses to the rim, she handed one to Grant and lifted her own. "Here's to your recovery." She took a swig, then glanced over the rim of her glass. "Why aren't you drinking? It's good. You on meds or something? A little wine won't hurt you. When I broke my leg a couple of years ago, I always washed down my pain meds with wine. Made them take effect faster." Amy pulled out a kitchen chair and took a seat. "Take a load off, Grant, and fill me in. I want to hear all about that night. Is it true you took a swing at Fred?"

Grant sat across from Amy. His nose twitched from the scent of her perfume. He leaned his crutches against the table. "Is that what he's saying?"

She took another sip of wine and nodded. "Yep. Says you got all in his face, mad as a hornet 'cause they told the colored boys to go home. Said they were just trying to avoid trouble."

"Fred? Avoid trouble? That's laughable. No one believes him, do they?"

"People believe what they want to believe, Grant. And before this even happened the lines were drawn as to who was on what side. You're not with the majority opinion. I guess you know that."

"But aren't they investigating the facts?"

"Which are?"

"I saw Fred and his boys going up to Leroy and friends and walked over there to talk to them to avoid a confrontation. Then before I knew it a fist was in my face."

"Fred's?"

"I think so, but it all happened so fast, to tell you the truth, I'm not sure whose it was. But it came from Fred's gang. I know that. Leroy and his friends were behind me."

Amy drew her chair closer to Grant and crossed her legs, her black pencil skirt rising to mid-thigh. "Well, of course, *I* believe you. Did you tell Frye all this?"

"Sure I did. Told the superintendent too. But I haven't heard anything more about coming back."

"Hmm. Well, maybe they're waiting for the dust to settle. Things are pretty dicey right now. Lots of kids still out. Fights breaking out every day. Racist graffiti popping up in the bathrooms like garden weeds. I took a sick day myself this past week 'cause I was so stressed out. You should be glad you're not there."

"Maybe, but I *want* to be there. And I want my name cleared. Judging from the newspaper articles and editorials it doesn't look like the "dust is settling", as you say. He shook his head. "Did you read today's editorial? You'd think the Confederate flag was God Almighty himself."

"It is for some folks." She stood and clasped Grant's hand. "How about we go into the living room and talk about something more pleasant?" The doorbell rang. "You expecting company?"

Grant grabbed his crutches. "Actually, yes. That's what I was trying to tell you." He opened the front door as Alice and Rufford raced to greet Cassie, who ruffled their fur and said, "How you doing guys?" She let them lick her hand and asked, "Did the pizza arrive yet?" She held up a paper bag. "I brought my usual six-pack." Before Grant could answer, Amy stepped into view.

"And who might this be, *my dear*?" Amy circled both hands around Grant's arm.

Cassie didn't know if it was the abrasive tone of voice or the way the woman clutched Grant's arm like a vice grip; she knew a coy territorial claim when she saw it. He had never mentioned a girlfriend. But then she had never asked. How stupid of her. Of course he had a girlfriend. He was smart, good-looking, twenty-eight years old. Why wouldn't he have a girlfriend? And why should she care? She stuck out her hand. "Hi, I'm Cassie Cunningham. I live next door."

Grant threw back his shoulder to loosen Amy's grip. "Cassie, this is Amy Nilehouse. She teaches at the high school. She was just leaving. Weren't you Amy?"

Amy released Grant's arm and replied in a pout, "I guess I am." Ignoring Cassie's outstretched hand, she brushed past her and turned to Grant, "Don't forget - You can't afford to lose any friends right now. You know what I mean?" She turned on her heels, opened the door of her turquoise Cadillac, threw it into reverse, and peeled out the driveway.

"I'm sorry. Did I show up at a bad time?"

"No, *she* did."

"But she seemed upset. I mean...I didn't mean to interrupt anything between you and ..."

Grant scowled. "There's nothing to interrupt. Amy is a colleague. That's all."

"I'll put the beer in the refrigerator." Cassie walked to the kitchen, the two dogs padding after her. Grant followed. With her hand still on the fridge door, she asked, "How's the ankle today?"

"I thought I'd be off these damn crutches by now, but still can't put any weight on my foot."

"The doctor said it was a pretty bad sprain." She looked over at the table and spotted the wine and two glasses, one of them still full. She picked up the bottle to read the label.

Grant leaned against the kitchen door frame. "You know much about wine? 'Fraid I'm no wine connoisseur."

"Me neither. Gift from Amy?"

He nodded. "Would you like a glass?"

"Sure, but I'll get it. Go sit in the living room. I'll be out in a minute"

Cassie returned with a plate of cheese and crackers along with the wine. Grant had already settled onto the couch and had his foot propped on a hassock. He patted the spot next to him. "Here, have a seat. Tell me about your week."

She sipped at the wine. "Hmm. Nice." Kicking off her shoes, she leaned back, head resting on the cushion.

"Rough week?"

"Not too bad. But I do have a rather perplexing new student." She told him about Sharelle.

"Have you talked to Reina about her?"

"Yes, she's the one who brought her to the classroom. Says she plans to make a home visit soon, which should give me more information. But it won't be for a while." She turned towards him. "And you? Heard any more about your suspension?"

"No, but Amy seems to think the lines are already drawn and it has more to do with this whole Confederate flag controversy than me."

Cassie shook her head. "I still don't get it. I've been reading the paper all week, and I've yet to read one editorial supporting the students who staged the walkout. Why don't people understand? Certainly, if I were black, I wouldn't want to look at that flag every day, reminding me of a war to keep my people enslaved."

"That's not what Southern whites were taught. To them it's a sacred symbol. And God knows, they'll swear to their dying day that slavery wasn't the cause of the war. To them, it's all about 'states' rights.' But you have a point. It's high time someone did write an editorial with the other point of view. I've got time on my hands. Don't know if they'll print it, but it's worth a shot."

"Are you sure that's wise under the circumstances?"

He smiled. "No, but caution be damned. Nothing's ever going to change if people don't face the truth. 'Sides, I want to stand up for those kids. They deserve better than this." At the sound of knocking, Rufford and Alice ran to the door once again. Grant reached for his crutches.

"Don't get up, Grant. I'll get it." Cassie set her wine on the coffee table.

"Take the money from my wallet. It's on the kitchen table."

She took the pizza from the delivery boy and set the box on the coffee table. "Still piping hot. You want a beer, or stick to the wine?"

"I'm kind of enjoying the wine. How about you?"

"Usually would choose beer, but have to admit this wine is good. Your friend Amy has good taste. Kind of feel guilty drinking it."

"Why?"

"I think it was meant for you to share with her, not me. It seems to be expensive stuff."

"Pff. She can afford it."

"Yeah, that Cadillac of hers looked brand new. I didn't think anyone could afford a car like that on a teacher's salary."

"They can't. Her father gave it to her. He's a big-time lawyer."

"Money and good looks, and a father who's a lawyer might not be a bad thing right now. Maybe you should have let her stay and sent me home."

Grant grabbed the wine bottle and refilled her glass. "No, thank you. I'm quite happy with my chosen dinner companion." He reached over and fingered the curls around her temple. "Have I told you how much I love your hair?"

Cassie blushed. "I'll get some plates for the pizza. Ought to eat while it's hot."

"Right." Did he overstep? The way she was looking at him, he'd hoped it was the right moment. Now, as he watched her retreat into the kitchen, he knew that moment might be gone.

He took the plates she offered, emptied the wine bottle, and raised his glass, "Here's to you, Cassie, my Florence Nightingale." He swigged the last of his wine, trying to work up the courage to say more, to tell her how he couldn't stop thinking about her, to say that when she left each evening this past week, it was all he could do not to beg her to stay. Instead, he tapped his empty glass nervously and said, "Grams will be home tomorrow."

"Oh right. I'm sure you'll be happy to have her back."

He nodded. He wanted to see his grandmother, but knew it would also mean alone time with Cassie would end. Somehow, it seemed that if he didn't tell her tonight how he felt or kiss her tonight, that it would never happen. He set down his wine glass and leaned towards her, but she moved away, reaching over to pick up their plates on the coffee table.

"Well, I'd better clean up and get home. I'm kind of ragged from the week."

He touched her arm. "Do you have to go so early? I thought we were going to watch Mission *Impossible*."

"I know. I'm sorry. I'd probably fall asleep. You'll have to tell me what happens."

His eyes followed her as she picked up the pizza box and plates and walked to the kitchen. This might be his only chance. Her hands were pressed against the sink as hot water ran over the dishes. She startled at his touch, but quickly turned around. He pulled her close, letting his crutches drop to the floor. Her lips were warm and soft, but suddenly he stumbled.

She reached out, easing him onto a chair. "You're without crutches. Doesn't it hurt?

"Was worth the pain." He took her hand. "Don't go."

She bit her lip. It would be so easy to stay, to feel once again a man's embrace, to let his kisses consume her. She shook her head. "No. I can't. I … I really can't." Tenderly, she brushed the hair from his eyes. "I'll come by tomorrow, okay?"

He nodded and dropped her hand. He was afraid of this. It was too soon. He'd scared her away. "Sure." He watched her walk out the door.

CHAPTER SEVENTEEN

Despite wine-induced drowsiness, she knew sleep would not be possible. She didn't want to think about what just happened. Even on the short walk home, the questions raced through her mind. Could she possibly be in love? Or was she just lonely? How could anyone take the place of Jack? She hadn't written him all week. No one else knew about the letter writing. They'd call her crazy, perhaps even delusional. She suppressed the urge to reread Jack's letters for the umpteenth time. It would only bring tears and guilt. Instead, she flipped on the television and plopped on the couch.

"Today, the White House reported that a preliminary peace treaty was drafted at the negotiations in Paris. Secretary Kissinger will be meeting with President Thieu of South Vietnam to review the details. After over 56,000 American casualties, the war's end may soon be at hand."

Cassie closed her eyes. The war's end. The war that took Jack's life only a few short months ago. Maybe there would be no more widows. But it didn't change the fact that her Jack was gone. Curled into the corner of the couch, she finally drifted to sleep.

She was walking in a dense forest, pushing the foliage aside when she heard it; cries of children in the distance. Then she saw them running towards her, their arms outstretched with frightened faces, both Vietnamese and Black. They touched her clothing and pressed against her. Someone tugged on her hand. She looked down. Sharelle was pulling her forward. Together they retreated from the jungle and stepped out into a grassy meadow. There was a loud whirring noise above. She looked up to see a helicopter slowly descending and then land a few yards in front of her. A uniformed figure jumped out in a crouched position, his hand outstretched. She reached for it and then saw his face, Jack's face. She climbed aboard with him. The helicopter began to rise and she turned to smile at the children squeezed into the back of the helicopter. She leaned against Jack's shoulder. High above, they flew, over winding rivers, thatched huts, and lush rice fields. As a small airbase came into view and Jack set the helicopter down, he shouted over the noise of the helicopter. "You're safe now, Cassie."

She flung her arms around his neck. "Come with us, Jack, please."

"I gotta go back." One by one, the children were being lifted from the helicopter. "Go with them, Cassie."

"Not without you." Tears streamed down her face. He took her hands from his neck as someone tugged at her waist as she too was lifted off the helicopter before it once again rose into the bright sun.

"He had to go, Cassie." Arms tightened around her. The embrace was warm, comforting. Her soft tears erupted into a wail and her body went limp. Aware that she was now cradled in someone's arms, she opened her eyes and beheld Grant's face.

She awoke trembling, covered in sweat. Staring at the revolving ceiling fan, she heard voices. The living room television still blared. She sat up, rubbed her neck and then walked to the television set to turn it off. She'd dreamed of Jack before, but never in Vietnam and never in his helicopter. And never was it so real.

She was too unnerved to sleep, even though it was now one a.m. She went into the kitchen to fix herself a mug of warm milk. Carrying it into the bathroom, she ran water into the tub. Her hands were still shaking. What did it all mean? Why had Grant been in her dream? It was his kiss. It had unnerved her. How was she going to face him tomorrow? She settled into the hot water and tried to clear her mind, but couldn't stop the questions.

Craving dreamless sleep, she crawled into bed, and didn't wake until she heard the sound of barking at the front door.

"Cassie!" She pulled the pillow over her head. Who was knocking at the door at this hour? She opened one eye to check the time on the bedside clock. Eleven in the morning! Oh my God! How could she have slept so late? She rolled out of bed, grabbed her robe, and went to answer the door. AdaMae, holding a wicker basket, stood on the porch step with Rufford. "Brought over some of my biscuits and home-made jam you like so much. The least I could do for you taking such good care of my grandson."

"AdaMae! Come in. I'm so sorry for looking the way I do. I overslept." AdaMae set the basket on the coffee table while Rufford pawed at Cassie's robe. She nuzzled against his fur. "Let me get you some coffee." She scooped the grounds and poured the water. "Will just take a few minutes. Do you mind waiting while I put some clothes on?"

"Not at all. Take your time. I know where your coffee mugs are. I'll get them out."

She pulled on her jeans and grabbed the first sweatshirt she could find. Splashing water on her face in the bathroom, she dried it quickly upon hearing AdaMae's raised voice from the living room.

"Rufford! Get down from there!"

Cassie laughed at the sight of Rufford sitting on the coffee table, his tail wagging, his nose sniffing the basket. AdaMae pulled him off the table.

"Sorry about that."

"No need to apologize. I'm sure there's enough for Rufford." She hugged AdaMae. "Welcome home. Let me get you that coffee now, two sugars and cream, just the way you like it."

"Thank you dear. Shall we have biscuits with our coffee? They're still warm."

"Absolutely." Cassie took two small plates from the cupboard and a knife from the silverware drawer for the jam. They took their first bites together as Rufford, looking shamed, settled on the floor. Cassie slipped him a piece of her biscuit.

"As I was saying, I want to thank you for taking care of Grant."

"You don't have to thank me. Just did what any friend would do."

AdaMae nodded. "Well, he certainly is lucky to have you for a friend. I understand you even cooked some?"

Cassie laughed. "Do I detect a note of sarcasm?"

AdaMae smiled. "Cooking isn't usually your strong suit, dear."

"Still isn't. But necessity is the mother of invention. Grant was nice enough not to compare my cooking to yours." She paused before adding, "How is he this morning?"

"He slept rather late too. I did unwrap the bandages to look at his ankle."

"And?"

"Still swollen some and quite black and blue, but not as bad as that gash at his temple. Can't get used to how he looks with that shaven patch on his head. But he says it's starting to fill in some. He's always had such a thick head of hair." She set her coffee cup down and leaned back in her chair. "Cassie, can I ask you something?"

Oh, no. He didn't tell her, did he? He was close to his grandmother, but surely he hadn't told her about the kiss. "What is it?"

"Well, Grant told me how he got hurt and about the suspension. He made it sound like it wasn't that big a deal; that it would all blow over soon and he'd be back to work. You were at the game. You saw what happened. I'm assuming you've followed the local news. What do you think?"

Cassie sighed, relieved that the question was not about her. Grant, no doubt, was trying to calm his grandmother's anxiety, but from reading the newspaper AdaMae must know it *was* a big deal and suspected that Grant's job might be in jeopardy. "Yes. I was there. I think he did the courageous thing, facing those hoodlums, trying to prevent violence. Whether the school board sees it that way, I can't say. Are the school board members the ones who will decide about his suspension?"

"Yes. That worries me. They're all elected officials, apt to swing with popular opinion. Not sure if that will help or hurt. The students love Grant, I know. Do you think that will help?"

She nodded. "Of course." She wanted to reassure AdaMae, but remembered the virulent letters to the editor attacking the suspended students. Students didn't vote in elections. The people who wrote those letters did. "When is the board meeting?"

"I'm not sure. I don't think Grant knows yet." She stirred her coffee and took a sip. "Of course he hasn't healed enough to go back yet anyway. At least not in my opinion."

Cassie took another bite of her biscuit and watched Rufford lick the fallen crumbs. Should she go over to see Grant today? She would have to face him at some point. She stared out the picture window and saw shaggy Alice dart out AdaMae's back door, followed by Grant on his crutches. She couldn't make out his face as his hair hid it from view. Had his sleep been plagued by dreams too? Were they of her?

AdaMae glanced out the window. "Oh, Alice must have needed to go out. I'd better get on home and see if Grant needs anything. Will you come by?"

"Maybe. But I have a lot of school work to do. Perhaps later in the week?"

"Wednesday, at least. I'll make something special for supper, okay?"

She nodded. "I'll be there." She walked AdaMae to the door. Maybe by Wednesday, she and Grant could return to the way things were.

CHAPTER EIGHTEEN

Sharelle arrived late Monday morning holding a fried red snapper wrapped in newspaper. Setting it on her desk, she unwrapped the paper and began gnawing on the scaly pink fish.

Lewis held his nose. "Pfew! Teacher, make her put that fish away. It stinks."

Cassie said, "If it bothers you Lewis, you can work at the front of the room."

Lewis gave Sharelle a sideways scowl before shoving his chair back and going to the designated table. Cassie squatted by Sharelle's desk. "That's a very nutritious breakfast, Sharelle. When you finish, come sit with me on the couch. I've got some pictures to share with you." Ten minutes later Sharelle threw the greasy newspaper and fish bones into the trashcan and took a seat next to Cassie. With the custodian's help, Cassie had hauled the couch into the classroom, hoping it would provide a cozy spot for the children to read books, calm down when angry, or just relax. It had done all three on many occasions.

Cassie opened a large book of photographs. "I thought you might like these pictures." Turning the pages, she pointed to colorful photos of African villages and wildlife. The nine-year-old girl's eyes grew big at the sight of a child pulling in a fish on a fishing line. Sharelle grinned and pointed to the fish. Cassie responded, "Yes. Look at that. He caught a fish just like yours! I wonder if he'll cook it for breakfast too."

Sharelle smiled and then began to turn the pages herself. She pointed to a hippopotamus wading in the river.

Cassie said, "Hippopotamus. It's a very big animal that lives in Africa."

Sharelle turned to another page.

Cassie said, "Those are flamingoes. Aren't they a pretty color pink?"

Sharelle continued turning the glossy pages, each time pointing, then cocking her head, waiting for Cassie to name what was in the picture.

With the child now pressed against her, Cassie couldn't help but note how Sharelle's tangled, bushy Afro was thick with grease and her body reeked of urine. She hoped Reina would make that home visit soon.

Before long, they were joined by Ruby bouncing on the couch. "I finished all my work, Teacher. Can I look at the book too?"

"Sure you can. Just a few minutes before lunch though, so I'd better check on the others' work. Why don't you and Sharelle look at the pictures together?" As she slid the book off her lap and handed it to the girls, Mrs. Hicks approached. "Now there's a pair. Ruby might just be the ticket she needs."

Cassie glanced at the two girls huddled together. "Hmm. You may be right. If it's more language that Sharelle needs, Ruby's energetic babble will fill that gap nicely." She turned back toward Mrs. Hicks. "Have you checked the children's morning work?"

"Yes. You should see Zebbie's math paper today. He's really doing great. He might even be above grade level."

"I know. I just wish his reading would catch up. I have another conference with his parents this week. They're concerned about him."

At the sound of the lunch bell, the children rushed to the doorway. Despite Cassie's admonitions, they continued to push and shove in line, each anxious to be the first one to get to the cafeteria and grab a lunch tray. She stood in front of them. "We won't move until everyone has their arms at their side. No shoving, remember? Zebbie is the line leader today. Everyone should be in a single line behind him." The shoving stopped and a somewhat crooked line of children began weaving its way down the hall to the cafeteria.

Lunchtime was not Cassie's favorite part of day. The cafeteria was like a three-ring circus with teachers cajoling and reprimanding, some with smiles on their faces, but many with paddles in their hands. Once lunch was served and children seated the talking stopped, as students shoveled in their food. Today's meal was a rare treat; fried chicken, rice with gravy, and butter beans. But the teachers knew they had to keep a close watch. Someone might grab a drumstick from a classmate's plate resulting in a howling racket, or the even more serious occurrence of choking, as some child tried to chew the chicken bones.

As usual, cafeteria worker Mrs. Jenkins gave Cassie a broad smile, heaping generous portions onto her tray, including two large pieces of fried chicken. "Still pipin hot, Mrs. Cunningham. 'Jes made 'em this mornin.'"

"Thank you, Mrs. Jenkins." Cassie smiled back, remembering the overheard conversation between Mrs. Jenkins and the cafeteria supervisor the previous afternoon.

"I don't care what the rules say. She done give mor'n half her food to those chilluns. So she goin' to git more. 'Sides, she need to put some meat on those bones of hers. So that the way it goin' to be." Nobody argued for very long with Mrs. Jenkins.

Cassie sat in the middle of the long bench. The only sounds were the scraping of silverware on melamine trays and the gulping of milk. In a matter of minutes, the trays would be empty. She now announced in advance who'd be getting her extra portion and, following her example, a few of the less impoverished children occasionally shared their food.

She looked over at Zebbie as he stripped a piece of white meat from his chicken breast and handed it to Ruby. How could he not be her favorite? A gentle giant if there ever was one, he never treated a classmate with anything but kindness, unless it was to defend a child from a bully. And even then, all he did was glower at the oppressor and say "Stop." Never did he resort to force. As for his school work, he tried more than all of them put together. His efforts were really paying off in math, but not in reading. She'd decided to try a different approach. The Orton-Gillingham multi-sensory method was successful with many learning-disabled children. She researched and studied the various techniques that had proven effective with dyslexia and dipped into her banking account for the materials needed. Only one item, the Language-Master, was expensive. A machine that read aloud word cards, it soon became popular with many of the students. The sand trays required only the purchase of cookie sheets and a bucket of sand from the beach. She also cut out sandpaper letters for tracing. She set up a magnetic board with color coded magnetic letters in the classroom. Her plan was to have Zebbie's parents work with him at home using the same techniques. They seemed as determined as she to see him improve, hoping someday he'd be placed in a regular classroom. She'd had to reschedule the conference with his parents because of today's teacher's meeting.

Ugh, teacher's meetings. They were such a waste of time. By the end of the school day, Cassie wanted nothing more than to go home, take a shower, and head to AdaMae's for one of her delicious meals. Then she remembered that Grant would be there. Suddenly her throat was dry and her armpits tingled with perspiration. They'd not spoken since the kiss.

She gulped from the hall water fountain before entering the library. As usual, black teachers were on one side of the room, and white teachers on the other. Somehow, she'd managed to straddle this divide without ruffling feathers by choosing to sit at a back table with Mr. Preston, the physical education teacher. He was black, not far from retirement, and the only male member of the staff other than the principal. Due to his apathy towards everyone and everything, Mr. Preston was a 'safe' tablemate for Cassie. The first time she'd sat at his table, he glanced up briefly and then went back to reading the newspaper, which is what he did during every teacher's meeting.

Mr. Horace droned on for the first few minutes, giving out district news and passing out the forms required for Title 1 funding. Then, as usual, he turned the meeting over to Mrs. Washburn, who labored to stand up before addressing them.

"November is almost here, and I don't have to tell you what that means. Time to start thinking about our annual Fielding School Christmas Show. I'll need you to let me know by the end of next week, what your class will be performing. This year the theme is "Toys from Santa." So try to find songs, presentations or poems that fit. If you have any questions just check in with me or Bethany." She nodded towards the librarian aide.

A show! How exciting! Cassie's mind shifted from the upcoming parent conference to possibilities for the show. As a child, she'd never passed up a chance to be in a school play. It was all great fun; making props, rehearsing, learning new songs, and especially performing on stage. As soon as everyone stood to leave, Cassie hurried over to Mrs. Washburn.

"Mrs. Washburn, could I ask you a few questions?"

"Of course, honey. How are all those little darlins of yours doin? Lot less ruckus comin' from that room lately. Good to see they done quieted down some under your hand. Like I tol' you before, you needs anything, you jes' ask. Now what's your question?"

"The play. I need to know how much time we have on stage. Do we make our own props? Can we get parents to help? And is it all songs, or dances, or skits? I'm new here, as you know, so need a little more information."

Mrs. Washburn pulled a hankie from the pocket of her dress and dabbed the sweat now dripping down her jowl. "Oh, child. I'm sorry. I shoulda' told you. The special kids don't perform. We don't want to embarrass them. No, they jes' come and enjoy the show, that's all. So, you don't have to worry about a thing."

Dazed, Cassie stared at Mrs. Washburn's retreating back. "Wait!"

"Yes?"

Cassie blocked the door. "But I *want* to do the show! It will be fun, and the kids will love it, I'm sure."

Mrs. Washburn shook her head. "No, no. Don't think that will do. Like I said, we know your kids are special. Not right to have them up there bein' laughed at and all."

"But, Mrs. Washburn..." Cassie's pleas were lost in the air as her colleague left the library.

CHAPTER NINETEEN

G rant paced back and forth by the window, dragging his bad leg. "What are you doing off your crutches, young man?" AdaMae walked in from the kitchen, wiping her hands on her apron.

"I'm fine, Grams, honest."

"You're awfully fidgety today. Wouldn't have anything to do with Cassie coming over, would it?"

"Is that tonight?"

AdaMae didn't buy his feigned ignorance. She'd told him earlier that Cassie was expected for dinner. "She'll be here soon enough. I heard her car drive up about a half hour ago."

Grant pulled the curtains aside and spotted Cassie's Toyota in her driveway. He gimped back to the kitchen. "Sure smells good in here."

"Making my famous chicken pot pie, collards with ham hocks, and sweet potato pudding for dessert. Don't fret about Cassie. She never misses my Wednesday dinners." There was a knock on the door. "See, there she is now."

Cassie entered with her usual six-pack in hand along with another small brown bag. "Hi, AdaMae. Got my usual." She held up the beer. "And thought I'd bring some wine too this time, in honor of the occasion."

"Wine? My, aren't we getting fancy. What occasion?"

"Why, your return home, of course." She looked over AdaMae's shoulder to see Grant holding Alice's collar. As soon as he let go, the dog raced toward her, followed by Rufford. Cassie's face was soon covered with dog kisses.

"Whoa there, give her some breathing space, fellas." AdaMae grabbed the dogs' collars and pulled them back.

Cassie smiled, greeted Grant with a brief 'hi', and walked into the kitchen. Sensing his eyes following her, she placed the beer in the refrigerator and wine bottle on the counter before pecking AdaMae on the cheek and asking, "What's that delicious aroma?"

"Chicken pot-pie in the oven. Unless maybe you're smelling the sweet potato pudding that I made a little bit ago."

"I'd say you shouldn't have, but I'd be lying. 'Sides, I know it's not just for me." She glanced back at Grant standing in the kitchen doorway. "And how is the patient, today?" She tried to sound casual.

"Too antsy, if you ask me, especially today. The boy just won't sit still. Been up and down like a cricket. Should be settin' in that living room with his leg up, like I keep tellin' him to. Why don't the two of you go into the living room? I need to start on my collards."

Grant reached for his crutches. "After you."

As her body brushed his in the doorway, heat crept into her cheeks and she cursed her fair skin. It was not the first time she'd experienced an inconvenient blush. Had he seen? Quickly she went into the living room. Crossing her legs, she gripped the edge of the couch cushion, and bit her lip. Would he sit next to her? Instead, he leaned his crutches against the wall and hopped to the corner chair.

Grant was the one to break the awkward silence. "They published my letter in today's paper. Did you see it?"

"You wrote the letter? About the walk-out?"

He nodded. "Paper's on the coffee table in front of you."

She picked up the *Pensacola News Journal* and turned to the editorial page, immediately spotting Grant's letter.

To the Editor:

This paper's recent editorial has criticized the Escambia High School walkout and supported the students' suspension. Published letters to the paper have harshly maligned the students without knowing the facts. As a history teacher at the high school, I would like to share what happened. The students respectfully and appropriately brought their concerns and grievances to the administration without success. They sent a petition to the School Board, which was ignored. The walkout was their last recourse. I know many of these students. They are good students who are eager to right a wrong. Shame on the School Board for upholding the student suspension without listening to them.

Their grievance is a legitimate one. The Confederate flag is the flag of the Confederacy, the confederation of southern states formed to secede from the Union so that the institution of slavery could continue unimpeded. It represents a history of bondage that is extremely offensive to all black Americans. How could it not? The students who engaged in the school walkout should be commended rather than punished for their actions. The Confederate flag does not represent them, and shouldn't represent Escambia High School.

Grant Lee

Cassie nodded a few times as she read.

"Well, what do you think?"

"Well said."

"I hope it's strong enough. It was a lot longer and more forceful originally. I trimmed it down quite a bit, tried not to let my anger spill out onto the page. I also knew they wouldn't print it if it were too long."

"It's well written..." She paused. "It's just..."

"What?"

"You know that I agree with you. Everything you said needed to be said. But, saying you're a history teacher at Escambia. You sure that was wise?"

"I needed to give my credentials, show that I know history and am familiar with the chronology of events with the walkout. Why? Don't you think it was a good idea?"

"Well, your own situation, your suspension. Don't you have to go before the school board soon?"

"Yes, but that has nothing to do with this."

"Doesn't it? I mean no administrators at Escambia High seem to support this walkout. You don't think this letter might tip the scales against you?"

"The students' side of this must be told, and no one is listening to them. I had to do something."

She hesitated to say more. *Had he thought this through?*

"Yes, of course. I hope I'm wrong about its effect on the hearing. When is it?"

"Thursday."

Cassie was happy to have something to talk about other than their last time together. She'd been afraid that everything would have changed with their kiss. Instead, they seemed to be falling right back to the easy conversation of friends catching up. She told him about Sharelle and the exclusion of the special education students from the play.

"I don't know what frustrates me more, getting a child like Sharelle with no information about her, how to help her, or dealing with Mrs. Washburn and her intractability. What I wouldn't give to have my kids up on that stage. I know they can do it."

"Did you try talking to her again?"

"Mrs. Washburn? Of course I did. She just gave me the same answers, smiling all the while like I was some kind of blathering idiot."

"Can you think of anything that would change her mind?"

"I wish I could."

From the way he was looking at her, she knew he was no longer listening. What had she done or said to ignite desire? Standing up, she said, "I best see if your grandmother needs help with dinner."

AdaMae was bent over, potholder in hand, opening the oven door when Cassie came into the kitchen. "Can I do anything to help?"

"Thanks. Maybe get the silverware on the table and see if I have any wineglasses in the top shelf of that cabinet next to the refrigerator."

Grant limped to the table, pulled out a chair, and sat. "Sure is nice to have you back, Grams."

Steam rose from the chicken pot pie as AdaMae placed it on a hotplate. "Hmph. It was your stomach missing me, mostly, I suspect."

Cassie chuckled. "I did my best, AdaMae. But just can't compete with your cooking. He's been spoiled, your grandson has."

Ada Mae cut into the bubbling pot pie and ladled it onto the plates. "Guilty as charged. Why don't you pour that wine, Grant, while I get the collard greens?"

Cassie took a bite of the chicken pot pie. "Oh my, this is heavenly. The crust melts in your mouth."

"Thank you. I do pride myself in my piecrusts. Collards?" AdaMae didn't wait for an answer but went ahead and scooped a large spoonful of collard greens on Cassie's plate and then Grant's.

"So, what were you two talking about in the living room? I thought I heard something about a show at your school, Cassie?"

"Yes, Fielding School has a show at Christmas every year, and each class prepares some kind of song or presentation."

"Sounds like something you'd love."

"I would, but Mrs. Washburn won't allow my class to participate."

"Won't allow it? Why not? And who is Mrs. Washburn?"

Cassie sighed. "She's a kindergarten teacher at our school, but for all intense purposes, she runs the school. Mr. Horace, the principal, defers to her on virtually everything. It appears to be the paradigm they've created over the years, and woe is the teacher who doesn't go along with whatever she says." Cassie set her fork back on the plate. "My kids deserve to be in that show, but I don't see any way …"

AdaMae peered over her wine glass. "You're not giving up, are you?"

"Well, of course I don't want to, but what can I do?"

"Hmm. I worked with someone like that once."

"At the flower shop?"

AdaMae nodded. "Yep. Dina Moore. Tiny little thing, but puffed up with her own self-importance. She insisted on checking every floral arrangement of mine, even when we both knew it was perfect. Always found something wrong with it. Tempted to poke the woman with floral wiring. But I found a better way to handle her. With people like that it's all about letting them *think* your ideas are *theirs*. I'd have my floral arrangement all set and then set out my final selected sprigs alongside something really dastardly, and ask her to choose, knowing that she would pick the one I wanted. She'd tut over the other ghastly selection, and select the one that I wanted all along."

"But didn't you feel belittled?'

AdaMae shrugged. "Not really. I got the arrangement I wanted. That's all that counted."

"So, you're saying that somehow I need to get Mrs. Washburn to think it's *her* idea to have my class in the play."

Grant interjected, "Is that possible?"

AdaMae set down her glass, "It's worth a try, don't' you agree, Cassie?"

Cassie smiled. "Absolutely."

CHAPTER TWENTY

It was Reina who came up with a plan. She marched into Cassie's classroom before school started and plunked a manilla envelope on her desk.

"This will do it."

"Do what?"

"Get your kids into the Fielding School Christmas Show."

Cassie unsealed the envelope and pulled out a newspaper clipping with a grainy photograph of children singing on stage. A wheelchaired child was in the front row. The article, headlined, *Accolades for Integration in the Arts,* told of a nearby school that included special education students in their chorus. Cassie knew of recent court cases mandating education for the disabled as well as increased efforts in mainstreaming. Here was an example of local inclusion.

"Nice, but what does that have to do with getting my kids into the show?"

"Clarice Tinsbury used to teach here at Fielding. She and Mrs. Washburn both applied for the position of principal at that school when it became available. Guess you know who got the job."

"So?"

"So, Mrs. Washburn has never forgiven Clarice, who had far less experience, for taking what she thought was rightfully hers. And she won't be thrilled to see her rival getting media attention."

"I still don't see what that has to do with the school play."

"I'm putting this newspaper clipping on the teacher room bulletin board this morning. Knowing Mrs. Washburn's usual routine, she will have read it before her first morning coffee break. Come to the teacher's room right after you dismiss the kids."

"To do what?"

"You'll see. Just follow my lead, okay?"

Reina was already standing in front of the bulletin board when Cassie walked into the teacher's room. She turned and asked, "Any sign of Mrs. W yet?"

"I just saw her in the corridor talking to Mr. Horace. No doubt she'll be here soon."

"Okay. Remember, follow my lead."

"But what…"

Mrs. Washburn entered the room. Seeing Reina reading the article on the bulletin board, she immediately scowled. She poured herself a cup of coffee from the dregs of the pot, opened the refrigerator, and poured cream into her cup. The chair groaned as she sat down and took her first sip.

Reina tapped the bulletin board. "Mrs. Washburn, have you seen this article? It mentions Clarice Tisbury. Remember her?"

"Of course I remember her."

"Well, this is a really lovely article about what she's doing for the special education class students at her school."

"Hmphf, that's just Clarice, always getting attention."

"True. But this is certainly a good thing that her school is doing. Too bad we don't have a school chorus, or something like that. I'm sure you'd have thought of it, especially given your concern for the children. And our special education classroom is doing so well this year under Cassie. You'd jump at the chance to get your kids into something like this, wouldn't you, Cassie?"

"Oh, yes."

Reina pointed to the byline. "Well, I'll be! I know the reporter who wrote this piece. Adam Richards and I went to school together." She paused, hoping the lightbulb would go on for Mrs. W. When no comment came, she added. "Wasn't he the reporter you called last year to request coverage of the Fielding School Holiday Show? If I recall, he turned you down, saying there needed to be some new angle?"

Now that she'd set the bait, Reina knew it was only a matter of time. Mrs. Washburn's scowl slowly dissipated as she addressed Cassie. "I've been thinking about our conversation the other day, Mrs. Cunningham. I think we may have room for your children in the play after all. Do you think you could prepare something? Our first rehearsal is next week. You don't have much time."

Cassie beamed. "Definitely. The children love to sing. I'll start right away."

"Now, it has to be good, mind you. Especially if this Adam Richards will be there to write about it." She turned toward Reina. "He *will* be there, won't he?"

Reina smiled. "I think I can arrange that. And I'm sure he'll want to interview you, the show's organizer.

Cassie and Reina exchanged a quick victory glance.

***

The following morning, Cassie waited for both the children and Mrs. Hicks to arrive before making the announcement.

"You mean we get to be up on the stage!" Ruby jumped up and squeezed her teacher's waist in delight.

Lewis strutted to the front of the room. "They won't call us 'retards' none after this if we do a good job, right Teacher?"

"No, Lewis, nor should they ever. This is a class of very smart boys and girls. I'm proud of each and every one of you. Now, we need to come up with an idea of a toy-themed song."

Jeff raised his hand. "How b.b.bout that s..s..song you t..t.. taught us about a train, teacher?"

"What song?"

"You know… "And he began to sing. "Down by the station, early in the morning…"

Cassie smiled as she listened to him finish the entire song without stuttering once. She knew how stutterer's anxiety is often calmed through music. Ever since then, she'd been teaching the children songs almost every day, and Jeff loved it!

"What do you think, kids? Does everyone like that song?"

They all nodded.

"We have to do the scenery too. Any ideas?"

"We could make a train," Ruby said.

"Great idea, Ruby! That's exactly what we'll do. But we'll need big boxes."

Zebbie raised his hand. "My dad works at Nick's Appliance Store. He can get us boxes."

"Fantastic! Would you ask him tonight Zebbie, and let me know for sure tomorrow? We don't have much time. I'll get the song on paper for all of you to practice at home as well as in school. We'll start tomorrow."

CHAPTER TWENTY-ONE

Grant's hands shook as he buttoned his freshly ironed white dress shirt. In another hour the School Board would be deciding his fate. Would they uphold his suspension or reinstate him? He had no idea. Slipping on his blue blazer, he walked from the bedroom.

"Which tie looks best with this jacket, Grams?" Clean-shaven with hair combed neatly, he held up three ties.

His grandmother gushed in admiration. "My, don't you look sharp." She inspected the ties. "Best go with the blue and red stripes. Matches the blazer and the red, white, and blue will look patriotic."

He tossed two ties on a kitchen chair and circled the selected tie around his neck. Fumbling with the knot, he said, "Damn it. Never can get it right."

"Let me do it." AdaMae took the ends of the tie, positioning the longer end before looping it around to make the knot. "Just like your father. Always needed my help putting on his ties."

At the mention of his father, Grant swallowed and looked down at his grandmother's white-hair. When his parents died, he was so caught up in his own grief that he rarely thought of his grandparents' loss. Lately, Grams had been recalling memories of his father more often.

As her fingers brushed his Adam's apple, she caught the look in his eye and said, "He'd be so proud of you."

Grant's years without his father now numbered more than the years with him, but the memories were still fresh. His dad had not been a demonstrative man, more bookish than most. Sometimes Grant struggled for his attention, but they had their father-son rituals. Doing the Sunday paper crossword puzzle together was one. Once, Grant sneaked a look at the answers on the back page and his father had lectured him on the value of integrity. He never cheated again. Hearing Grams comment about his father's pride brought back a vivid memory.

"Do you see that, son?"

Grant stared at the New York Times crossword spread on the table in front of them. "What? You mean that we finished it? We always finish it, Dad."

"Yes, WE always finish it. But not this time."

Grant looked again at the letters filling in all the squares. "Nothing's missing, Dad. We finished it."

"No, YOU finished it. Look again. I didn't write or tell you a single answer. Well done."

Grant grinned sheepishly. "I did all of them?"

"Yes, you did. You've just completed an entire New York Times crossword puzzle all by yourself! I'm proud of you, son."

It was the first and last time he'd heard his father express pride in him. Was Grams right? Would he be proud of him tonight?

Grant and AdaMae entered the high school cafeteria, where rows of chairs were filling up quickly. Scanning the crowd for familiar faces, Grant nodded at a couple of colleagues. No black students in the crowd. Good. Leroy had taken Grant's advice to stay home. Unfortunately, Fred and cronies had not. They took up the entire back row. The burly redhead sat with arms crossed over a black t-shirt emblazoned with the confederate flag. As Grant walked by, Fred elbowed a buddy and smirked.

Cassie waved from the front row where she'd saved two seats. Five School Board members sat at a long rectangular table facing the audience. On either side were flag stands, one displaying the American flag, the other the Confederate flag. Grant knew some of the School Board members, but not all. The chairman, Floyd Martin, stepped out from behind the committee table and walked up the side aisle. He was surprised to see him bend down, kiss Amy Nilehouse on the cheek, and then whisper something to her. She nodded before catching Grant's eye from across the room. Why was Floyd Martin kissing Amy on the cheek? And why was she even here? Were they going to ask for character witnesses like in a trial? He couldn't imagine that, but then again, this wasn't a regularly scheduled School Board meeting, but rather a special hearing on his suspension.

Amy got up from her chair and strode over. "Can I talk with you a minute, Grant?"

"Sure." He followed her to the back of the room. "Didn't expect to see you here, Amy. Nice of you to come."

She squeezed his arm. "Of course I'm here for you. And I've already spoken with my uncle about your situation."

"Your uncle?"

"Floyd Martin. He's my mother's brother. Didn't you know?" She didn't wait for a reply.

"I told him what a wonderful teacher you are, and how no one wants to see you leave. So, here's the thing. All you have to do is apologize, and you'll be back at school tomorrow. Suspension over."

Grant grimaced. "Apologize? For what?"

"Come now. You needn't get high and mighty. Just be done with it."

"But I didn't do anything, Amy."

She pursed her lips. "Look, Grant. It's not about what you did or didn't do."

"Of course it is."

There was a static screech from the microphone. "Excuse me. Would everyone please take their seats so this hearing can begin."

"You should be thanking me, but it's your neck, not mine." She turned abruptly, high heels clicking on the parqueted wood floor. Reaching the front table, she whispered something in her uncle's ear; then shot Grant a withering look before returning to her seat.

Floyd Martin lifted a paper and spoke again into the microphone. "This is a public hearing by the Escambia County School Board. We will be addressing the incident that occurred on the night of Oct. 14th, and the subsequent suspension of one of our faculty members, Mr. Grant Lee. The committee will not be taking questions or comments from the public." Turning over the top sheet of paper, he leaned into the microphone again. "The police report recounts that a physical altercation occurred between Mr. Grant Lee, history teacher at the high school, and some of the Escambia students at the game. Oral statements were taken and put on record from Mr. Lee and some of the students present. I will read Mr. Lee's statement first and then two from students involved in the incident."

Grant listened to his rendition of the event. AdaMae squeezed his hand supportively.

"The next statement will be from Mr. Fred Crowley, a senior at Escambia High School."

Me and my buddies came to the game to have a good time, like we always do. We saw Mr. Lee, our teacher, sitting up with some of the niggers...I mean, coloreds, the same ones that walked out. We went to say hi to Mr. Lee, y'know, 'cuz we have him for class. But when we seen them troublemakers, they started calling us "Rebs" and all that. I got a bit mad. Said something back, don't remember just what, and that's when Mr. Lee took a swing at me. But I ducked, and the next thing I know he's falling down the bleachers.

Grant jumped up from his seat, "But that didn't...."

"Mr. Lee, take a seat. We've already read your statement."

A murmur rose from the crowd as Grant sat down.

"Now, we will hear the statement from Mr. Leroy White, also a senior at Escambia High School." Mr. Hyde picked up another sheet of paper and began to read.

I was sitting in the stands with my friends, watching the game. We saw Fred and his gang coming up the bleachers towards us. Fred tried to cause trouble, and Mr. Lee told them to leave. That's when Fred pushed me and took a swing at Mr. Lee, who fell back onto the bleachers. Fred was standing there with a big grin on his face. That's when the fight began.

"I didn't push nobody! Ask my buddies here. It was all those niggers' fault!"

All heads turned at Fred's outburst and then back as the chairman rose, pounding his gavel. "That's enough, Mr. Crowley, or you'll have to leave."

Floyd Martin waited for the room to calm before returning to the microphone. "We have very conflicting reports on the events that occurred on that evening. However, what we do know, is that it triggered a major fracas requiring police intervention and hospitalizations of injured, including Mr. Lee. While there appeared to be many students involved, no arrests were made. Mr. Lee was the only faculty member involved in the incident and the administration and School Board approved a suspension until a more thorough investigation could be made. Principal Frye, and a number of faculty members, have given us written supportive statements of Mr. Lee's character and conduct. Mr. Lee, do you have anything further you wish to say before the School Board makes its decision?"

Grant stepped forward. Brushing hair from his eyes, he cleared his throat.

"As I said in my statement, my actions on that night were an attempt to prevent violence. Fred Crowley's words are false. At no time did I take a swing at him, strike, or threaten anyone. On the contrary, he, or someone with him, struck me, resulting in my fall. The medical reports given to the school show my injuries. My doctor has now given me clearance to return to work, and I'm sure the Board will do the right thing and lift my suspension, allowing me to do the job I was hired to do, teach the students at Escambia High School."

"Mr. Lee, do I take it to understand that you see no action on your part that was inappropriate or showed poor judgement?"

"That's correct, sir. If it were not for Mr. Crowley and friends acting in a belligerent manner, there would have been no incident."

"I see. Mr. Lee, the Board has met prior to this hearing. From all the information that we have been able to gather regarding what took place on the night of Oct. 14th, there is no definitive proof that you broke the law or violated the school's code of ethics. The School Board has met and has decided to recommend lifting your suspension. However, given the conflicting evidence before us, as well as other considerations, we also recommend a probationary period of employment. The Board will now vote on lifting Mr. Lee's suspension, returning him to his position under a six-month probationary period."

Each member's name was called and each responded in the affirmative.

"This hearing is now concluded." Floyd Martin pushed away from the table and stood. The other Board members did the same.

AdaMae hugged her grandson. "Congratulations! Your suspension has been lifted."

Grant scowled. "Probation? Other considerations? What the hell does that mean?"

The Board members began filing out of the room. He hurried to catch Floyd Martin before he could leave, but Frye grabbed his arm, intercepting him.

"Won't do any good, Grant. The decision has been made."

He glared at the principal, shaking off his arm hold.

"Other considerations? Was that *your* doing, Frye?"

"Believe me, Grant. I spoke up for you. Never mentioned any of our issues. But there have been parental complaints. You know that. The Board members have been receiving threatening letters."

"About me?"

Frye nodded. "Your letter to the paper didn't help your cause any. Look, I want you back. But you should know it won't be smooth sailing, at least not for a while. Not 'till this whole thing blows over."

"And when do you suppose that will be?"

Frye shrugged. "That depends. You could be of help in that regard. Talk to Leroy. Get them to back off. Let things calm down, you know?"

"First of all, I don't have that kind of influence, and second, even if I did, I wouldn't get them to back off. Those kids have a legitimate complaint. They have a right to speak out."

"Grant, the kids listen to you. Talk to them. There's a time and place for everything. You know as well as I do, that the community isn't ready for this."

"When will the community be ready, Frye?"

***

At AdaMae's suggestion, they walked to nearby Maxie's Diner to discuss the hearing over coffee and cake. AdaMae ordered a slice of the coconut layer while Grant and Cassie agreed to split a piece of the devil's food. Grant told them of Frye's comments.

"What kind of threats?" AdaMae poured cream into her coffee.

Grant shrugged. "He didn't specify."

Cassie said, "Don't you think you have a right to know?"

"Maybe. Not sure I want to know."

AdaMae patted her grandson's hand. "Yes. Well, the main thing is that your suspension is over."

Grant mumbled in response, "Yeah, but the bad school boy got his slap on the wrist."

Cassie set down her coffee cup, fingering the saucer, "Grant, ah, why did Amy…" She stopped. "Never mind."

"What? What did you want to ask me?"

"Never mind. It's really none of my business."

"You were going to ask me about Amy - what she said to me."

Cassie nodded. "Yes, but like I said, it's really none of my business."

Grant reached across the table for Cassie's hand. "Cassie, you're here, aren't you? You've been with me every step of the way through this ordeal. Of course it's your business." He let go of her hand and tipped his chair back. "She wanted me to apologize to the Board."

AdaMae and Cassie replied in unison, "For what?"

"That's what I said."

Cassie said, "But what does Amy have to do with it? She's not on the School Board."

"No, but her uncle is."

"Her uncle?" AdaMae asked.

"The chairman, Floyd Martin. Guess he told Amy that the suspension would be lifted if I apologized."

"But you didn't apologize, and the suspension still was lifted."

"You're right. I suspect there was some disagreement on the Board and the probation was a compromise. Perhaps an apology would have spared me that. I don't know. But, like I said, there was nothing to apologize for. I'd take the same action again if I was back at that stadium tomorrow under the same circumstances."

AdaMae nodded. "I know you would, because it was the right thing to do. Your father would have been proud of you, Grant."

He looked at his grandmother. The second time tonight she'd told him that his father would have been proud of him. The words brought some comfort.

AdaMae stood. "Well, it's getting late. I best get home and feed Rufford."

Grant started to get up. AdaMae pressed his shoulder. "No, don't get up. It's early yet for you young folks. Why don't you and Cassie stay? Maybe even go someplace to celebrate?

"Not sure if celebration is in order."

"Of course it is, Grant. Your grandmother is right."

"Alice needs feeding too."

AdaMae replied, "I can take care of that."

He looked over at Cassie. "I know of a place across town, over by the Navy base. They make a heck of a Margarita."

"How did you know I love Margaritas?"

AdaMae grabbed her purse. "I'll swing by your place and feed Alice before going home. Have fun, kids!"

CHAPTER TWENTY-TWO

G rant fished the house key from Grams hiding place and quietly inserted it into the lock. The second margarita had left Cassie more than a little tipsy, so he drove her home, leaving his van in Pedro's restaurant parking lot.

He slipped off his shoes and tiptoed to his old bedroom. The walls were still plastered with his posters; basketball idols: Bill Bradley, Walt Frazier, Willis Reed, mixed in with the musicians he loved: Bob Dylan, Simon and Garfunkel. And of course, his fixation in college, Julie Christie. He'd seen Dr. Zhivago three times. No wonder Omar Sharif couldn't resist. Yet tonight he had resisted Cassie. Her kiss on the doorstep had been passionate. He could have taken advantage, wanted to. Hadn't he dreamed of nothing else for weeks? But was she kissing him? She'd talked of Jack for much of the evening. He didn't want to be a 'substitute' in a weak inebriated moment.

When the conversation turned back to the school board hearing, Cassie called him brave for supporting the black students. He knew otherwise. Certainly, he wasn't brave when he deserted his grandmother when she needed him most.

He was in his senior year of college when Gramps died. Grief overtook him. Nothing made sense anymore. Certainly not listening to lectures on ancient civilizations. Yet, dropping out of college could mean getting drafted. His grandfather was a World War II veteran, and Grant liked to think he was every bit as patriotic, but Vietnam? Killing without cause. He couldn't do it. So, he took off during spring break; didn't even call his grandmother until he was on the road. It wasn't right. She was grieving too and needed him. But he was thinking only of himself.

He hitched mostly, slept in pine woods and parks. Rolled joints, and listened to fools who had all the answers. They didn't. His diary entries were full of road adventures, the characters he met, but also questions, excuses, and sometimes just plain rambling, until the final entry. He pulled the diary from his desk drawer and turned to the last page.

March 12, 1966

I'm half asleep in the truck cab when we pass the sign for this shithole town. The driver pulls over and drops me off. Pushing open the diner door, I see their wary eyes, the truckers in the booths and along the diner stools. They see a long-haired guy in tattered jeans enter their territory. I grab one of the empty vinyl-covered stools, drop my backpack to the floor, and glance at the board menu.

"What'll be, son?" Her name tag says Midge. Her eyelids are shaded in fluorescent green and the brassy blond-dyed hair is piled into a beehive do.

"How old is the pie?"

"Yesterday." She sets out a coffee cup and grabs a glass pitcher from the coffee maker. "Want coffee too, I s'pect."

I watch her pour dregs into my cup before slicing the day-old apple pie. The first bite tells me the apples are canned; the crust hard. Grams would be mortified.

I'm tired of Texas, breathing in the red clay dust, and watching out for snakes. Shitting by a scrub brush and walking on hot pavement. I'm tired, period. I must smell ripe. The face bristle is now a beard.

Midge slides the plate in front of me. "Son, y'all look like you've seen better days."

Her voice is soft and kind, like Grams. She's looking at me, really looking, as if I am the only one in the diner. Something in her eyes makes me want to talk. She listens as I spill my guts, about Gramps' death, the crazy war, what's the point of college with the world such a mess, and leaving Grams.

When I finish, she places a liver-spotted hand on my forearm, looks me straight in the eye, and says, "Go home to your grandmother, kid. You're not going to find any answers gallivanting around the country. You can't really plan your life, but you can stand by the ones you love, and somehow it will come out all right."

I followed her advice and Grams welcomed me like the prodigal son that I was. She never admonished me; never questioned me. Would Cassie be so forgiving if she knew of my cowardice? Could she love me?

***

He woke to the smell of coffee brewing. Grams was already up. He splashed some water on his face before going to the kitchen. "Mornin', Grams."

She dropped her spoon. "Grant, what are you doing here?"

"Sorry. I didn't mean to startle you. Slept here last night. Would you mind driving me to Pedro's to pick up my van? And do you have a spare toothbrush I could borrow? I'm going to take a quick shower and change. Should still be spare clothes in my old bedroom, unless you threw them out?"

"No, I didn't. And yes, I can drive you to Pedro's. There's a spare toothbrush in the medicine cabinet. Don't you want breakfast first?"

"Not enough time. Don't want to be late first day back. Just save me some coffee, please."

He gulped the coffee as Grams drove.

"Did you and Cassie have a nice time last night?"

"Yes." He finished off the coffee, hoping she wouldn't ask any more questions. For a full five minutes they rode in silence, but he saw the side glances and the biting of her lips. Knew another question was coming.

"Did you talk about last night's hearing? I know you were upset with the probation, but you know, honey, it could've been a lot worse."

"Yeah. I know. We talked about the hearing some. But more about Jack."

"Jack? Cassie talked about Jack?"

"Why are you so surprised?"

"Because usually she doesn't talk about him."

"Not at all?"

"No. She should, but she doesn't."

"What do you mean she should?"

"Because it helps. You should know that, Grant. Remember how I took you to counseling after your parents died? You wouldn't talk to her, but eventually you did - with me and Gramps. That's when I knew the healing had begun…that you were going to be all right."

"So, you're saying it was a good thing that Cassie talked about Jack?"

"For her, yes. And while I know it might have been hard to listen, you should be flattered."

"Flattered?"

"She chose you to confide in, Grant. You to open up to. That means something. – And Grant?

"What?"

"He wasn't perfect, anymore than the rest of us are."

"I forget sometimes that you knew him. What was he like?"

"Don't get me wrong. He loved Cassie, but he also was committed to his career. Cassie spent a lot of time alone, even before he left for Vietnam. And there was his family."

"What about his family?"

"I met Jack's parents when they came to visit. And while there was never anything directly said, I could tell that in their eyes, Cassie wasn't good enough for their son."

"Cassie not good enough? My God, who could ever think that?"

"I agree, but money can do that to people."

"Jesus. I didn't know."

"Don't repeat what I just said to. I doubt Cassie was aware of their feelings. And Grant?"

"What?"

"It's not a competition, you know. Give her time."

Grant didn't respond. As usual, Grams saw right through him without him saying a word.

CHAPTER TWENTY- THREE

Cassie swallowed two Excedrin with her morning coffee. How many Margaritas had she had last night? Her head was still pounding as she backed the car out of the driveway. What time had she got home? Her memory was fuzzy. Grant hadn't stayed. She knew that. But they had kissed. And this time, she certainly didn't protest.

Pulling into the school parking lot, she grabbed her book bag and rushed into the building. She'd never been this late before. Somehow, she'd have to forget last night and focus on the day ahead. It didn't take long. Mrs. Hicks stood in the classroom doorway with a furrowed brow.

"Sorry I'm late, Mrs. Hicks. I know you have bus duty. I overslept. I know that's not a good excuse, but…"

"That don't bother me none, Mrs. Cunningham. The kids ain't even arrived yet, except for Sharelle. You need to take a look at her." Mrs. Hicks nodded toward the back of the classroom. "Tried to get her to talk, but you know how that is."

"Sharelle? She's here already?" Most mornings, Sharelle arrived well past the morning bell, sometimes as much as an hour late. But today, she sat alone at the puzzle table, head bowed, working on another puzzle. In the short time since her start of school, she'd completed almost all the puzzles, even the

300- piece jigsaw puzzle that none of the other students had even attempted. An encouraging sign of the girl's potential, despite her lack of expressive language. Only twice had she spoken, once to Cassie, and once to Ruby, who responded with a squeal of delight and embrace of her new friend.

"What ..." Before she could ask about Mrs. Hicks concern, Sharelle looked up, smiled at Cassie, and began walking toward her with a pronounced limp. A dark red blotch stained the front of the girl's tattered white skirt.

Cassie hid her alarm. She knew how skittish Sharelle could be. Gently touching her shoulder, she said, "Hi, Sharelle. So nice to see you in school early. Let's see what puzzle you're doing today." As Sharelle worked the puzzle, Cassie pointed to the stain and asked, "Did you hurt your leg?"

Sharelle lifted the long skirt. Matted blood was caked over a deep gash on her right shin. Cassie sucked in her breath. With no school nurse in the building, she needed to wait for Mrs. Hicks to return, who immediately went for the first aid kit, took Sharelle to the bathroom, washed and bandaged the wound.

Holding Mrs. Hicks' hand, Sharelle was all smiles upon their return. She lifted her skirt, proudly displaying the large bandage to Ruby, who proceeded to boast of her many prior injuries.

Cassie saw Sharelle's eyes widen as she listened to her chatterbox friend. How much did she understand? Knowing Ruby was the best model the girl could possibly have, Cassie waited some before telling them to start their morning work. Sharelle was beginning to trace over her name with crayon and repeat the letter names.

Cassie went from desk to desk, checking on each student's progress. Their papers were individually prepared to match their varied levels and skills. She glanced at Tommy, the newest student in class. He was still a mystery, as his transfer file shared minimal information. A nine- year- old boy with a thatch of thick blond hair falling over his sullen eyes, he spoke little and never smiled. At least, she thought, he seemed to be well-behaved. That, however, was about to change. Lewis sauntered up the aisle with his usual swagger, bumping Tommy's desk and knocking pencils and worksheets to the floor. Like a popped cork, Tommy sprung from his chair and shoved Lewis.

Lewis slammed him back. "Don't mess with me, honky!"

Tommy lay on the floor, momentarily dazed. Then, with narrowed eyes, he rose, barreling into Lewis like a raging bull.

"Whoa there, boys!" Mrs. Hicks grabbed Tommy and held him tight as his fists pummeled the air.

Meanwhile, Cassie brought Lewis into the hall.

"Hey, Teach, what's that new kid's problem anyway?"

"I don't know, Lewis, but you shouldn't have shoved and called him a name, especially a racial slur. You know I won't tolerate that in my classroom."

"He started it!"

"Yes, he did. And I will speak with him. But for now, I want you to do your work out here in the hall. Mrs. Hicks will bring out your desk and chair."

Lewis shrugged. "Sure. Anything for you, Teach." He flashed his characteristic Lewis grin. Thank God, Lewis was now more compliant. All eyes were on her as she returned to the classroom. "Fight's over, children. Get back to work." The kids turned around in their chairs, picked up their pencils, and went back to reading and completing their worksheets. She directed Tommy to the classroom couch, sat next to him, and spoke quietly. "Tommy, I want you to take a few more minutes to calm down before getting back to your schoolwork. When you're angry, you can't take it out on your classmates. No hitting, shoving, or yelling. Do you understand?"

He crossed his arms and grunted in response. "I'll take that as a yes. We can talk about this again later, maybe after lunch, okay?" She patted his shoulder and got up to retrieve Lewis. As they re-entered, Tommy grabbed the couch cushions and began throwing them across the room. It wasn't even lunchtime yet. Her headache had returned.

***

Back home, she flipped open the mailbox by the door and scooped up the assorted envelopes. The phone was ringing as she walked in.

"Reina! I was just going to call you. You won't believe the day I had."

"I probably would. But first, tell me how things went for Grant at the School Board meeting last night."

"They lifted the suspension."

"That's great news! I know some of those rednecks on the Board and was afraid they had it in for him."

"I think some of them might have."

"What do you mean?"

"They lifted the suspension but put him on six-month probation."

"What! You gotta' be kidding."

"I wish I were."

"Grant had to be pissed big time."

"Yeah, he kind of was, but by the time we got home, not so much."

"We? Something you're not telling me, girl?"

Cassie smiled into the phone. "We'll talk when you get back. Are your weekend plans with Bill still on?"

"Yep. I don't mind telling you, Cass, I'm a little nervous, first time meeting his folks and all."

"They'll love you, Reina. Look, I hate to bring up work but I was hoping you could make that home visit to Sharelle's when you get back. She's got this terrible gash on her leg. God knows how that happened. And this new kid, Tommy, remember him? He lost it big time today. I need to get to the bottom of what's eating him."

"Okay, Cass. But I took a couple of personal days, so it won't be until mid-week at least."

"I'll be thinking of you, Reina.

Cassie hoped it could wait that long, but decided not to say more. "Have a good time, Reina. I'll be anxious to hear all about it. Say hi to Bill."

Skipping her usual beer, Cassie grabbed a Coke from the refrigerator. Maybe the caffeine would ease her persistent headache. She filled a glass with ice and poured the cola slowly in, watching caramel bubbles fizzle to the top. She took a long drink, kicked off her shoes, and rubbed the back of her neck. The mail sat on the kitchen table. She flipped through the assorted bills and ads until spotting her mother's dainty handwriting. Her mother's infrequent letters were newsier than the hurried phone calls.

Dear Cassie,

We have been busy with your brother's various activities. Basketball season just started and Jeremy is all excited. It's so wonderful that they have this team for the special kids like Jeremy. They play their first game next week. So far, he's only been to practice, but is convinced that he'll be on the starting team. His buddy, Larry, plays too. You know, the one that used to come over after school and shoot hoops in the driveway with him? Got to know his mother some sitting up in the bleachers. Nice woman. She told me that something went wrong at the birth, and there was brain damage. Larry is their only child, a real sweet boy. He's real fond of Jeremy. Kind of follows him around like a puppy dog. Reminds me of how Jeremy always was with you.

Thought I'd crochet you an afghan this year for Christmas, Cassie. Normally I would keep it a surprise, but I know you'd want to pick out the pattern and colors. I'm enclosing the pictures of three designs you might like. Let me know soon, please, as I need to get started on it. The holidays are right around the corner.

Speaking of holidays, your father and I had a conversation after our last phone call. We were so disappointed to hear that you won't be coming home for Thanksgiving. You know how I feel about you choosing to live so far away. You should be with family, especially this year, after all that's happened. So, we decided to come to your place for Thanksgiving! We've already told Jeremy and he is super excited! It will be his first airplane ride. He can't wait! Actually, I can't either. We haven't seen you since the funeral, and I know we talk on the phone and you say that you are doing all right, but I need to see for myself. If only you weren't so far away!

The doctor is pleased with your father's progress since the heart attack. I've thrown away the bacon fat and he only eats ice cream once a week now instead of every evening. He's lost seven pounds!

We can't wait to see you! Only two more weeks.

Love,

Mom

Cassie stared at the letter. Her parents were coming here? In two weeks? She should be pleased, and she was, of course, but she'd already accepted an invitation to spend Thanksgiving at AdaMae's. She hated to disappoint her neighbor. And then there was Grant. Her parents didn't have to know about him, did they? *Stupid thought. Last night's kiss didn't mean anything, couldn't mean anything. She loved Jack.* She folded the letter and put it back in the envelope. Laying it on the table, she spotted dustballs underneath. There was a lot to do before Thanksgiving.

CHAPTER TWENTY- FOUR

All talking stopped when Grant entered the teacher's room before classes. Apparently, word had spread quickly about the board meeting and probation. So, he was to get the cold shoulder? He could handle that, especially after last night with Cassie.

Empty classroom seats were a stark reminder of the continued suspension of black student protesters. He bridled at the injustice of their suspension and the restrictions now put on him. No more deterring from the prescribed curriculum. He was damned if he was going to teach the Civil War, aka The War of Yankee Aggression, using the outdated textbook. But with his job on the line, it was best not to take chances, at least for the next six months. To fill the fifty-minute periods, he asked the students to read their answers to the substitute's assignment. *Christ, they must be as bored as I am. Can I really teach this way for six months?*

He decided to grab a sandwich at the nearby mini-mart rather than brave the stares in the cafeteria or teacher's room. When he returned, a sealed envelope with his name scribbled on it lay on his desk. Enclosed was a clipping of his letter to the paper, with the words BULLSHIT emblazoned in red letters across it. A student? Or more likely a fellow faculty member. He could think of a number of possibilities. He crumpled the paper and tossed it in the basket, trying to calm down.

When the dismissal bell rang, he sat at his desk, staring at the pile of tests yet to be graded. As usual, the halls were filled with the sound of lockers slamming, shouts, laughter, and shoes scuffing on the waxed tile. Finally, the noise subsided and he could concentrate. Relishing the quiet of the deserted building, he reached for the top paper and began reading.

High heels clicking in the hall forewarned him. Shit. Amy was the last person he wanted to talk to right now. After what happened at the School Board meeting, why would she want to talk to him?

She leaned against the doorjamb with mini-skirted legs crossed and a pencil tucked behind her ear. "Got a lot of catching up to do?"

So much for grading papers. Avoidance was the best strategy. He slid the student papers into his briefcase. "Done enough for tonight. Surprised you're still here, Amy."

"Despite what people think, Home Economics teachers work hard too."

He placed his lesson plan book and history text into the briefcase.

"Sorry about the probation."

He clasped the briefcase and looked up, quizzically. "Really?"

She folded her arms. "And what does that mean?"

"You said yourself that you and your uncle had a little chat."

"You don't think *I* had anything to do with your probation, do you?"

"You tell me."

For a moment, she looked like a cobra ready to strike. Her words could be worse than venom. Grant knew that. He'd seen her in action before, ripping into colleagues. So far, he'd been spared, but it looked like he was finally going to be on the receiving end.

Instead, the piercing eyes softened and her face relaxed. "Well, you'll just have to be a very good boy for six months, won't you, Mr. Lee?" She flashed a coy smile, turned on her heels, and left.

Once he was sure the halls were free, he went out to the staff parking lot. He stopped a few feet away from his van and stared. Spray-painted over both sides of his **Can-Do Handyman** in large white letters were the words NIGGER LOVER. He scanned the parking lot but saw no one. He would need to call the police, but the school building had locked behind him at this hour. It would have to wait until he got home. Thank goodness, he was heading back to his own place and not Grams. He would hate for her to see this.

Forty minutes after his call a cop showed up; took five minutes to jot down the information. Tucking the notepad into his pocket, he said, "We'll check the lot for evidence, Mr. Lee, and ask around. Not much we can do, really. Gotta kind of expect things like this, under the circumstances."

Grant watched as the cop hitched up his belt and lumbered back to the patrol car. He was tempted to ask just what was meant by 'circumstances', but decided against it. They wouldn't find out who did this, nor would they try. He needed to remove the graffiti as quickly as possible. He pushed open the front door and took a few minutes to greet Alice before calling the hardware store. They did carry acetone. Not crazy about driving the van back through town, he dialed Cassie.

"Hey, Cassie, it's Grant."

"Aw, the one responsible for my misery today."

"What?"

"My headache hasn't quit yet. How many Margaritas did I have last night, anyway?"

"Three, I think, although I finished the last one for you."

"Thank you for that. I'm sure that saved me."

"But you had a good time, right?"

He caught the hesitation before her response.

"Yes, I did."

Grant smiled into the phone. "Enough to do me a favor?"

"Sure. How can I help?"

He asked for a ride to the hardware store, and told her why.

"That's terrible! You called the police, right?"

"Yeah, but nothing will come of it."

"But they'll investigate? Did they take pictures?"

"Naw. Said it was to be expected under the circumstances."

"Under the circumstances? That's really what he said?"

"Yes."

"You should take pictures then."

"Why?"

"For evidence. They might find who did this."

"Doubt it, but if it will make you happy, I'll take some pictures."

"I'll be right over."

She drove up while he was snapping pictures with his Polaroid. She slammed the car door and shook her head when she saw the van. "Unbelievable."

"Not really. Under the circumstances." They exchanged wry smiles. "Thanks for coming over, Cass." He glanced at her poplin blue skirt and white blouse. "You didn't have to rush over. Could've changed first. It's not like I have any neighbors staring out their windows."

"I know. You live out in the sticks. But you don't want to drive this ..." She pointed to the van. "...into town"

She drove him to the hardware store where he bought the largest container of acetone they carried. "Hope this works. Going to take a heck of a lot of elbow grease. Don't know if I can get it done before dark."

"I'll help."

"You don't have to, Cassie."

"I want to. Just let me stop by my house first so I can change."

As she unlocked her front door Grant asked, "Okay if I step inside?'

"Of course."

Grant watched her toss her keys on the coffee table. "You know, you asked me in last night, but I declined."

"I did?"

He nodded. "I had to pull you off of me."

Cassie blushed. "I... and you didn't come in?"

"No. Didn't want to take advantage. You know, the three Margaritas and all." He stepped towards her. "But I'm here now, at your invitation."

His hands fell to her hips; his mouth found hers. Urgently, they moved toward the couch and tumbled onto it, her head falling back onto the cushion. He began kissing her ear, then her neck. Slowly, he unbuttoned her blouse, fumbling with the last one. His tongue ran along the top of her gold scalloped bra, then pushed closer to her hardening nipple.

As they kissed, he rolled to one side, his leg wrapped around her. Then, she twisted out from under him and sat up, face in her hands.

"What's wrong?"

Tears welled in her eyes. "I'm sorry. It's just…you know."

He brushed back the hair that had fallen into his face. "No, I don't know. What is it, Cassie?"

She wiped her tears with the back her hand. "I'm just not ready yet. It's too soon. He's only been gone for five months."

He wanted to understand, knew this must be hard for her, but damn it, he wanted her. He said nothing.

She leaned forward, dropping her head into her hands. "I know. It probably doesn't make sense to you, but sometimes I feel him here with me still. Like he never really left. There wasn't a body to identify, did I ever tell you that?"

He shook his head. "Do you want to talk about it?" He spoke the words because it seemed the decent thing to say, but a part of him didn't want to hear.

"I don't know. It was all so sudden. He'd only been in 'Nam for a short time, and the next thing I knew they were on my doorstep."

"They?"

"The officers with the news. They said his helicopter crashed, that it went up in flames." She paused. "There was a memorial service in Arlington. It's what his parents wanted, a full military honors ceremony. For me, though, it's all a blur. A dead hero is still dead."

He rubbed her back and then squeezed her neck. "I'm sorry, Cassie."

She wiped her tears, turned, and gave him a weak smile. "I'll go change. We have some scrubbing to do."

Hearing her bedroom door close, Grant inhaled, let out a deep sigh, and mumbled "Oh Cass, when? Ever? Or will it always be Jack?"

CHAPTER TWENTY-FIVE

Hurriedly, she pulled into the school parking lot, annoyed with herself for speeding. She had no excuse to offer the police officer, unless he wanted to hear how distracted she was by thoughts of Grant. All weekend, her mind replayed what had happened on Friday. She'd hoped he understood when she spoke of Jack. But he'd not come by or called. Had she scared him off?

She opened the car trunk to retrieve cans of paint and bagged newspapers. Today they would paint the boxes. Mrs. Hicks dilapidated Chevy station wagon pulled in alongside. She took some of the paint cans from Cassie. "You know you're crazy, right?"

Cassie laughed. "I've been told that before."

"Those kids are going to make one hell of a mess."

Cassie smiled. "I think we can keep it under control."

"Hmph. We'll be lucky if they don't throw the paint at each other."

"It will all be worth it to see them performing on stage with the other schoolchildren."

"I never did find out how you bamboozled Mrs. W into letting them in the play. How are the songs coming along?"

"We've been practicing every day, and once we get the boxes painted and put together to make the train, we can rehearse on stage. Remind me to send out notices to the parents soon. I hope we get a good turnout."

When the children spotted the paint cans, they wanted to get started immediately, but Cassie told them there'd be no painting until their schoolwork was done. With that as an incentive, the children were well-behaved and finished their work quicker than usual.

After lunch, Cassie pried open the paint cans and handed out Jack's old T-shirts for the children to wear. They pushed the desks aside and spread newspapers on the floor. After some discussion about the color design and who would paint what, they got started. Cassie was pleased at their exuberant diligence and cooperation. It probably helped that both Tommy and Sharelle were absent today. But a half hour before the final bell, as the children were cleaning up, Sharelle appeared in the doorway, more unkempt than usual. Her cheeks were flushed. She took a few steps into the classroom and then slumped to the floor.

"Sharelle!" Cassie ran over, pressed her hand to the girl's forehead. "She's burning up."

Suspecting the source, Cassie lifted Sharelle's skirt, removed the tattered leg bandage, and gasped at the sight of yellow pus oozing from the open wound. "Zebbie, help me get her to the back of the room."

Zebbie cradled Sharelle in his arms, gently placing her on the couch. Cassie sat next to Sharelle, letting the girl's head drop to her shoulder. "Ruby, go to the office and tell Mr. Horace that I'd like him to come here immediately. Can you do that?"

"Yes, Ma'am."

The children clustered around Cassie as she stroked Sharelle's damp forehead and waited for Ruby to return.

Natalie, the school secretary, marched into the room. "What's the problem, Mrs. Cunningham?"

"I need to see Mr. Horace. It's about Sharelle."

"Mr. Horace went home early."

Cassie lifted Sharelle's skirt, revealing the infected wound. "Sharelle needs medical attention."

"Did you call her mother?"

"I can't. There is no phone at her house."

"The buses will be here soon. Why don't you write a note to her mother to let her know she's sick?"

"Her mother doesn't read. Besides, Sharelle doesn't ride the bus."

"She should never have come to school in the first place if she's so sick."

"Well, she did, and we must do something."

"We? I don't know what you expect me to do, Mrs. Cunningham. If she's sick, send her home."

"She can't walk home in this condition."

"She walked here. She can walk back." Natalie turned on her heels and headed for the door, almost bumping into Mrs. Hicks.

Seeing Sharelle stretched out on the couch next to Cassie and the children gathered around, Mrs. Hicks asked, "What's the matter?" Then she spotted Sharelle's leg. "Oh my lord, she needs to see a doctor!"

"I know, but Mr. Horace isn't here, and Natalie was no help." Cassie bit her lip. She knew she needed to act. "Reina said I shouldn't be doing home visits any more, but this is urgent. As soon as school is over, I'm going to put her in the car, and drive her home. The mother has to take her to the doctor."

"I wouldn't wait that long if I were you."

"But I have to stay with the kids."

"Don't worry about the kids. I'll handle things here. I'll get Mrs. W to take bus duty for me so I can stay in the classroom."

"You think Mrs. Washburn will do that? I've never seen her do bus duty."

"She owes me a favor. Now go, and make sure her mother takes her to a doctor. That leg is infected."

Cassie gave last minute instructions to the children to be on their best behavior before walking Sharelle to her car and settling her in the front seat. She'd scribbled the address on a piece of paper, 13 Jasper Lane. It had to be nearby, since Sharelle was a walker. She pulled out of the parking lot and looked to the left, then right. "Which way, Sharelle?"

Sharelle's eyes flickered open, and she pointed to the left. She continued to direct Cassie at each turn, until finally they drove down a small dirt road. Sharelle pointed to a wooden shack set on cinder blocks. Cassie had seen many of these small clapboard homes in adjoining neighborhoods but none quite like this. An open-door outhouse stood on one side of the house and an open firepit on the other. A gaping hole punctured the sagging roof.

Cassie held Sharelle tight as they went up the cracked brick steps to an unhinged door. Upon entering, she gagged at the noxious odor of fish and urine. Duct-taped oilcloth covered the windows. Scanning the dim lit room, she saw a fishing rod propped against a corner table. A cloud of houseflies buzzed over a plate of fishbones. A towel and bucket hung from nails on the back wall. No appliances or electricity. A few cans of food were stacked on a shelf.

A squealing sound made Cassie turn. A diapered baby sat on a stained floor mattress. He toddled to his sister, hugged her at the knees, and then raised his arms. Sharelle picked him up and placed him on her hip. "Mama?" she called in a whisper.

From a darkened corner, a voice responded. "Sharelle? Why you's home? You s'posed be in school."

Cautiously, Cassie walked toward a large woman sitting in a caned rocking chair, her blue dress tattered and dirty. The woman stared at Cassie, tilted her head slightly, and said "Who you be?" Not waiting for an answer, she took the baby, pressed him to her bosom and said, "My baby. My Henry."

Squirming in his mother's arms, Henry began to cry and reach again for Sharelle, who took him, placed him on the mattress, unwrapped his soggy diaper and grabbed a fresh one from a nearby bag. Henry pulled on his big sister's hair and giggled as she fastened the safety pins.

Cassie stepped closer to the woman and said, "I'm Mrs. Cunningham, Sharelle's teacher. I brought your daughter home, Mrs. McKnight, because she's very sick. She needs to go to the doctor. Her leg is infected." The woman hummed as she pushed the rocking chair back and forth with her bare feet. "Mrs. McKnight, I think she should go today. Can you take her to the emergency room?" *What was she thinking? There was no car, nor did this woman likely drive.* She glanced over at Sharelle sitting on the urine-stained mattress, her face still flushed and eyes glazed. "Mrs. McKnight, we're taking Sheila to a doctor. Come with me." Grasping the mother's hand, she pulled lightly, and the woman stood.

"We goin' in your car?"

"That's right."

The woman grinned a toothless smile. "I like ridin' in cars."

Walking out into the bright sunshine, Cassie let go of the woman's hand and opened the car doors. Mrs. McKnight sunk into the front seat while Sharelle got in the back, still holding Henry.

Cassie sighed with relief at the sight of Dr. Gooden's car in his driveway. "Wait here Mrs. McKnight, and I'll see if the doctor can see us."

She pressed the doorbell twice and waited. *Please be in, Doctor Gooden.* The door opened.

"Cassie, what a surprise. What brings you here?"

"I have a student who needs to see a doctor. She's in the car with her mother. Can you help?"

"Office hours are over, but sure, bring her in."

Cassie took Henry from Sharelle, who followed her teacher tentatively into the waiting room along with her mother. The girl's eyes grew big at the sight of the brightly painted walls with photographs of children and the large aquarium of tropical fish. Henry wiggled from Cassie's arms and began to crawl across the carpet, pulling himself up to the aquarium to press mouth and fingers against the glass.

Cassie made the introductions. "Dr. Gooden, this is Mrs. McKnight and her daughter, Sharelle."

The doctor smiled at them, but his eyes quickly dropped to the oozing leg wound.

"My, my, we need to take care of that leg of yours, little lady. Follow me." He reached for Sharelle's hand, but she shrunk into the chair, curled into a fetal position, and lowered her head.

Dr. Gooden squatted by the chair and spoke softly. "I need to take a look at that leg, Sharelle. Your mother can come with you. It will be all right. You'll see." Sharelle didn't budge. He turned to the mother, hoping for some help, but saw only a blank stare.

Cassie moved to the seat on the other side of Sharelle. "I know Dr. Gooden, Sharelle. He's a very nice man and a good doctor. You want your leg to get better, don't you?" No answer. Cassie tried again. "If you don't get better, you won't be able to come back to school. I would miss you so much, Sharelle. Everyone would." Sharelle lifted her head. "Do you want me to go with you?"

Sharelle nodded, uncurled her body, and took Cassie's hand. They went into the exam room. Coaxed again by Cassie, she finally allowed Dr. Gooden to lift her onto the exam table. Gently, he spoke to her as he took her temperature, swabbed the drainage, and then thoroughly cleaned and bandaged her wound.

"There, that's much better, isn't it? Just one more thing." He left the room briefly before returning with an injection needle, Sharelle cowered against the wall.

Cassie took Sharelle's hand. "It's all right, dear. It will only pinch a little, but it will make your leg all better, I promise."

Sharelle squeezed Cassie's hand and closed her eyes as the needle pierced her arm.

Dr. Gooden handed the patient a lollipop and lifted her from the table. "Why don't you go tell your mother what a brave girl you were?" As she left the room, he spoke to Cassie.

"It's a good thing you brought her in. That's a serious infection. She could have lost her leg if it hadn't been treated soon. I'll want to see her again in two days. Can her mother bring her in?"

"No. She doesn't drive."

"And the paperwork? I don't suppose she can read or write, can she?"

Cassie shook her head.

"I thought so. Look, I'll talk with her, and see if she can at least answer some of the basic questions for Sharelle's chart. If she can't sign her name, she can mark her X. I have other patients who do that. But I definitely need to see Sharelle again soon. Reina will be home tomorrow. She can bring her in.

CHAPTER TWENTY- SIX

There was a light knock on the classroom door. Grant always kept his door open for students to stop by if they needed help with assignments or just wanted to talk. He was not surprised to see Leroy standing in the doorway. Even though the student suspension was over, tensions remained high. The staff was on full alert, and everyone knew things could boil over at any time. "Leroy, come on in." He closed his plan book. "How can I help you?"

In three long strides, Leroy reached Grant's desk and sat on the edge of a nearby chair.

Grant perused the boy's dark handsome face. "Looks like you might have a scar from the football game fracas."

Leroy touched his forehead. "Yeah. Probably. At least I didn't have to go to the hospital like you."

Grant smiled. "That's true. Still some twinges when I walk but I'm getting there. Have you come about those references I promised? I'm happy to write them as soon as you let me know your college choices."

Leroy shifted his weight in the chair. "That's not why I'm here. I know you said to be careful, that I could get expelled if there's more trouble. But we're not going to give up. Next week we're holding a sit-in. We're going to sit in the main hallway, arms locked, and block classroom doors."

Grant let out a slow whistle. He should have guessed something like this was coming. He met Leroy's eyes, knowing before he even asked the question what the answer would be. "You sure you want to do this?"

"It's all set."

Okay. He should talk him out of this. Keep him from throwing away his future. Instead, he asked, "Do you know how many are going to participate?"

"No. Not for sure. You know how it is, some say they will but then back down. A lot of those suspended were seniors and they don't want to mess up their college chances - the ones planning on going anyway."

"Like you?"

"Like me."

"Leroy, you're a straight A student, a bright kid. I was looking forward to seeing you go to college. Does your mother know about this?"

He nodded. "She wasn't too keen on it, but relented when I explained everything to her. Told her it had to be done."

Grant smiled. He knew how persuasive Leroy could be. "And you came to ask my blessing too?"

The boy leaned forward and gazed intently at his teacher. "More than that, Mr. Lee."

Grant frowned. "Go on."

"We want to get staff to join the sit-in. It will have a lot more impact. We'd get press coverage too. Will you do it?"

"You're serious, aren't you?"

"Yes. I think it will help get more students on board when they hear that teachers are participating. All that history you've taught us - about those who've fought for freedom, the whole Civil War … Dr. King's work, the movement. This is our time now. Yours too, if you'll join us."

"But this isn't about slavery, Leroy."

"Isn't it? We deserve a say in our lives, in our school. We shouldn't have to look at the Confederate flag every day. You know that too, right? I read your piece in the paper. It was great."

"Thanks." *So, it had come to this. Put his money where his mouth is. Did Leroy know about his probation? Did it really matter?* He looked at Leroy's expectant face. "Any other teachers on board?"

"You're the first one we've asked. We've got a few others that we hope will participate."

Grant could think of few that would. Not many sympathized with the cause, let alone want to get involved. "You have to be careful. If word gets out to the administration, I think they'd find a way to prevent it."

"We know how to keep things quiet. It's Monday morning. You in?"

"The police might get called in. You could get arrested."

"We're ready for that. I took a training last summer on non-violent civil disobedience, and I've been teaching others."

This was news to Grant. His admiration for the young man sitting before him grew. Joining the sit-in could mean his job. But the risk and potential consequence was no more than what the students faced. How could he say no? "All right. I'll do it."

Leroy pounded the arm of the chair and jumped up. "I knew we could count on you, Mr. Lee!"

Grant smiled weakly. "If you give me the names of the other teachers, I'll try to persuade them too."

Leroy reached into his pocket and pulled out a small piece of paper. "Here's the list."

There were only three other names besides his own. One was the black assistant football coach, Jefferson Willows. He probably supported the sit-in, but would he risk his job to participate? He'd strained under the yoke of Mel Higgins, a bully of a coach and a racist to boot, despite the fact that half the team was black. The other two names on the list were Eva James, one of the cafeteria workers, also black, and Sam Childers, who taught auto mechanics. Sam rarely left the mechanic shop. His head was usually hidden under the roof or chassis of a car. Grant had never seen him in the teacher's room or hallways. A big, brawny ex-Marine with tattoos on each arm, a man of quiet power with a reputation for not tolerating any nonsense from the kids. He treated them like adults, and expected them all to learn. And they did. Grant didn't see him as the activist type, but maybe the kids knew more than he did. He handed the list back. "Can't say that I know any of these people well."

"We have students that are going to speak with them, so if you don't, that's okay. But your input might tip the scales. Up to you, Mr. Lee. Either way, thanks a million." Before leaving, he added, "By the way, we're going to each bring a small American flag to hold. That's the only flag we want to pledge allegiance to."

Grant met Leroy's eyes. "Got it." He shook his head as Leroy exited the room and mumbled to himself. "That kid is probably going to be in the State House someday. Maybe even the White House."

CHAPTER TWENTY- SEVEN

Only four days left before Thanksgiving break. Cassie glanced around the house, mentally tallying all that was yet to do. She had managed to clean out the guest room, but the rest of the house was a disaster. Living alone meant looking the other way when the clutter piled up, dust collected, or food in the refrigerator soured. Who'd notice?

She needed a to-do list. It was the only way she ever managed to get anything done. But, first things first. She had to decline AdaMae's Thanksgiving invitation. Her time had been so consumed with school problems that she'd not informed her of the change of plans. Reina was back now and had taken the lead with Sharelle, making home visits and getting her to the doctor. After Thanksgiving, they would visit Tommy's house together. His mother had yet to return the permission slip for the school performance, and Cassie wanted answers for the obviously troubled child. At least practicing for the school show brightened his spirits. When he sang, Tommy transformed from a sullen boy with dirty blond hair falling over his eyes, to one with his head held high, as his sweet voice rang out with perfect pitch.

Cassie saw AdaMae already out in the yard raking leaves at eight a.m. Grabbing her sweater, she glanced in the hall mirror, noting the dark circles under her eyes. Sleep eluded her lately.

With the quiet of night came memories of Jack and increasing thoughts of Grant. Added to that was anxiety over the impending family visit, the upcoming play, and the distressed lives of the schoolchildren.

AdaMae stopped raking when she saw Cassie. "Hey there neighbor. Been awhile. I've missed you."

"I know. Sorry I canceled on dinner last Wednesday. Reina was back in town and that was the only night for us to get together."

"That's okay. You'll be coming for Thanksgiving dinner in just a few days."

"Uh-that's what I wanted to talk with you about. I should have told you sooner, but as it turns out my family is flying here for Thanksgiving, so I won't be able to come after all. I'm sorry about that. It was so nice of you to include a neighbor in your family celebration."

AdaMae leaned on her rake and shook her head. "Cassie, Cassie, Cassie."

"I know. You probably already made your plans. I'm sorry. I just thought one less person wouldn't change things much."

"No, of course not. That's not what I meant. I think that's wonderful news."

"Oh." Cassie paused. "But... you seem a little upset with me."

"I am."

Cassie stiffened; brows furrowed. "But...I don't understand."

"Cassie. Don't you get it? I thought you knew by now, you're not just a neighbor to me. You're family."

You're family. Those words released something in Cassie; tears came unbidden.

"Cassie, what is it? I didn't mean to upset you. I'm not mad, you know that, right?"

Cassie nodded. "Of course, it's just what you said, about being family. I mean... I don't know what I would have done without you...after Jack..." She wiped her cheek with the back of her hand.

AdaMae stepped forward and took Cassie in her arms. "You just go ahead and cry now honey. You're long overdue for a good cry."

Cassie wiped her eyes. "I'm sorry. I don't know what came over me."

AdaMae left one arm around Cassie's shoulder. "C'mon. Let's go in for a cup of coffee. Have you had breakfast yet?"

Cassie shook her head.

"I made some cinnamon buns this morning. One has your name on it."

They sat across from each other at the kitchen table, sipping coffee. Cassie took a big bite of the warm cinnamon bun and licked the frosting from her lips. "Is there anything you cook that isn't absolutely scrumptious?"

"Well, if you're going to take the time to cook or bake, might as well make it the best." She set her coffee cup down and stared at Cassie, "I meant what I said - you being like family. I hope you know that."

"I feel that way about you too."

AdaMae patted Cassie's hand. "You must be excited about your parents and brother coming to visit."

Cassie hesitated. "Ah, yes, kind of."

"Kind of? But it's been ages since you've seen them. When was it?"

"Jack's funeral – July."

"Of course. That was a long time ago."

"Uh-huh." Cassie stared out the window, snippets of that day coming back to her. Leaning on her father. The sound of taps. The thick, sultry air. Sweat and tears mixed together, trickling onto her black tailored suit. And words, lots of words. People with words.

AdaMae squeezed Cassie's hand. "You miss him, don't you?"

"Huh?" She did miss him, but something had changed. "I do, but his voice, his touch, his face, ... it's all starting to fade. I... I don't want to lose him... not a second time." She wiped another tear from her cheek. "I guess that sounds crazy."

"Crazy? Not at all. You know that worn out living room recliner, the blue one with the faded armrests?"

Cassie nodded.

"That's Mr. Lee's chair. For a long time after he passed, I'd sit in the living room and talk to that chair, like he was still alive. I'd picture him sitting there, smoking his pipe, stroking Magnolia on his lap. She still prefers sitting in that recliner." As if on cue, the white Persian scampered into the room and jumped onto Cassie's lap.

Cassie stroked the cat's soft fur, comforted by its warmth and steady purr.

"And then one day I realized that I couldn't see him anymore. I stopped talking to the blue chair."

Cassie thought of the shoebox of letters in her closet and realized that she hadn't written to Jack in over a week. "And did you feel like you lost him...again, I mean?"

"In some ways. But now my thoughts of him are pleasant memories of our life and time together. No, I don't feel like I've lost him again. Don't get me wrong. I still miss him, but it doesn't hurt so much."

Cassie understood. Her pain was less intense now too, or at least less consuming.

AdaMae let go of Cassie's hand. "Would you like to see pictures of Mr. Lee?"

"Very much." She started to rise.

"Don't get up. Magnolia's enjoying the attention. I'll be right back."

Cassie finished the last of her coffee. Why did she answer so hesitantly about her parents coming? In some ways she longed to see them, especially Jeremy. Already she could feel his bear hug, see that big grin of his that she missed so much. But she knew that her mother would start in on her again, pestering her to return home. It's what they all seemed to expect her to do.

AdaMae returned with two thick photo albums under her arm. "Let's move to the living room where we can spread out."

Magnolia curled into a ball on the couch, between the two ladies. AdaMae turned the pages slowly, pausing at one of her husband, holding their first born, Grant's father.

Cassie said, "Your husband certainly was a handsome man. Grant favors him."

"He does, doesn't he?"

"Grant has darker hair and eyes, but there is something there."

"Yes. I've always thought so. I'm glad that Mr. Lee had those ten years with Grant before passing away. They spent a lot of time together."

"You never refer to your husband by his given name—Francis. Why is that? I didn't even know what it was until seeing it written here."

"Just a habit we got into. That first night when he carried me over the threshold and said, 'Welcome to my humble abode, Mrs. Lee', I kissed him and said back, 'And welcome to my eternal love, Mr. Lee.' We just kept calling each other that. Corny huh?"

"I think it's sweet." It wasn't until they opened the second album that Cassie saw the first pictures of Grant as a baby and then a boy. Even as a youngster there was something mesmerizing in those dark eyes, as if they could see right through you. "Grant didn't smile much, did he?"

"You noticed, huh? He was a serious boy. At least most of the time."

"Most of the time?"

"When he and Mr. Lee were working in the garage together, I'd sometimes hear laughter through the open door. His grandfather had a knack for making people laugh, especially Grant. When his parents died, I was the one who comforted Grant, but it was his grandfather who helped him to laugh again."

"Grant talks a lot about his grandfather. They seemed very close. You both must have been such a comfort to him after … after the accident."

"Truth is, he was a comfort to us. When our son died, we had a hard time holding it together, but we knew our grandson needed us. What I couldn't have known was how much we needed him. So many times, I felt his arms around me when I needed it the most. And when he started showing an interest in his grandfather's trade, the light came back into my husband's eyes. There's an inner strength and caring in that boy. I've seen it more times than I could mention. Here, I want to show you something." She flipped to the back of the album and pointed to a picture of a tall gangly Grant dressed in a basketball uniform, holding up a trophy with his name on it.

"What was the trophy for?"

"He was awarded the trophy for scoring the most points that year in high school basketball."

"He told me about that."

"Did he tell you that he gave the trophy away?"

"Gave it away? To whom? Why?"

"When Grant went to Escambia High, the school was all-white. Not long after he was given the trophy, he found out that there was a player from Booker T. Washington, the all-black high school, that had scored more points that season than he had. He told his coach about it, who told him he was foolish to want to give it to someone else. He then contacted the Athletic Director, who acted like he was nuts to try to give the trophy to some colored kid. This was never done. Their stats didn't count."

"So, they didn't give the trophy to the player at Washington High School?"

"Pff...I knew that would never happen, and told Grant so. Eventually, Grant tracked down where the kid lived and drove over there. He even had his nameplate removed and put on a new one."

"He doesn't give up, does he?"

"No, not about something he cares about."

Would he give up on her? Did AdaMae know what had transpired between them? Grant probably would not have told his grandmother but she was very intuitive.

As if reading her thoughts, AdaMae stopped turning the pages and looked directly at Cassie. "Have you seen Grant recently? He hasn't been around here much of late. He'll be very disappointed about Thanksgiving. He thinks a lot of you, Cassie."

Cassie blushed. "I know." She looked down and stroked Magnolia repetitively. "He'll be busy catching up with his sister and nephew."

"Unfortunately, no."

"But I thought they were driving here on Thanksgiving."

"My grandson Andrew has mono. Pretty sick, and contagious too. So, they won't be coming after all. My daughter Lisa called yesterday to tell me."

"Oh, I'm so sorry to hear that. I know how much you were looking forward to seeing them."

"Yes, I was. Between Lisa and her husband Mark's jobs, and Andrew's basketball games, they never seem to have time to visit."

"So, it will be just you and Grant for Thanksgiving?"

"Yes. We're going to have a lot of left-over turkey. I bought a sixteen pounder."

"You already bought the turkey?"

"I like to be prepared."

Cassie turned toward AdaMae. "Why don't you and Grant come to my house for Thanksgiving?"

"But your family is coming all this way to be with you."

"I know, but we will have that whole weekend together."

"Are you sure? I don't want to intrude on family time."

Cassie took her friend's hand. "But you are family, remember?"

AdaMae squeezed Cassie's hand in reply. "We'll come on one condition."

"What's that?"

"I bring the turkey and some other dishes. I'll make my usual cornbread stuffing, and cook up some collards and my famous sweet potato and pecan soufflé, make a pecan pie…"

"Hold on. What does that leave for me to cook?"

"Whatever you like, my dear. There must be some family dishes that you'll want to have. But they're coming to the South. They need to sample some of our traditional dishes, right?"

Cassie laughed. "Fine by me. My list of things to do has just been cut in half. But I still best get home and get busy. Lots of cleaning to do." She kissed AdaMae on the cheek.

AdaMae kissed her back. "Grant will be so pleased."

CHAPTER TWENTY- EIGHT

She pushed open the front door, still thinking of AdaMae's last words to her, '*Grant will be so pleased.*' Would he? Or was he still mad at her? She was a widow. Had he forgotten that? Had *she* forgotten that? After all, she had thrown herself at him that night they went out for drinks. She couldn't deny the attraction, even more now that she'd come to know him more. He could have taken advantage of her. Briefly she envisioned them together, was immediately both aroused and guilt-ridden. It had been less than a year. In previous eras, she'd be expected to still wear black.

At what point does mourning end and grief take over? There was a difference between the two. In some ways the first is easier. So many people holding you up. So many things needing to be done. Shock disengages you from reality. She no longer mourned, but she did still grieve. And if she was still grieving, then how could she even think about another man?

Dust particles hovered in the window light. She pushed thoughts of Grant aside, and said, "No more daydreaming, Cassie. This is getting you nowhere. Get to work." It's what she did best, substituting work for introspection.

Determined to do a thorough cleaning, one her mother couldn't possibly criticize, she began in the living room. It didn't take long to sort or discard the assorted school papers, newspapers and magazines. She dusted furniture, wiped away cobwebs, and crawled behind the couch to wash the floorboards. Squeezing her cloth rag in a soapy water-filled washbasin, she began to scrub. As she unplugged the reading lamp and nudged the end table, something slid to the floor. Three envelopes, all postmarked from a few weeks ago. Somehow a day's mail had fallen behind the table. She hoped they weren't overdue bills. The first envelope was a furniture sales advertisement, the next a solicitation from a charity. The third had her name and address scribbled in barely legible blue ink on the front of a small white envelope. The return address read: E. Gifford, 108 Shady Lane, Baton Rouge, Louisiana. Puzzled, she slit open the seal and took out a folded hand-written letter.

Dear Mrs. Cunningham,

We have not met, but Jack talked about you so much, I feel that I know you. I'm sorry that it has taken me so long to write this letter but I was in the hospital for weeks, recovering from the burns. Please forgive the hen scratching. Still hard to hold things. My hands were burnt the worst.

I was Jack's crew chief. We flew sixteen missions together. (The crew chief survived? She was told there were no survivors!) She dropped to the couch, her hand now trembling, as she continued to read the letter). *Jack was a natural pilot. Everyone said so. He made Aircraft Commander faster than most, and I was paired up with him. Assigned to a UH-1. I knew that bird inside and out, made sure she was ready every mission. We took gunfire plenty of times, but Jack was a damn fine pilot; could maneuver our Huey like a pro in NASCAR. But our luck ran out. I was lucky to have survived. Jack and I made a pact that if anything happened to either of us, I'd contact you and he'd contact my girlfriend.*

He left me a couple of things to give to you. Sorry I can't bring them to you but I can't travel that far. No longer have a girlfriend to help out. I can mail them if you like but I don't want them lost in the mail. Could you come here to Baton Rouge? I'd like to meet you. Please write to let me know what you'd like me to do. I send my condolences for your loss. Jack was the best. I still miss him terribly.

Earl Gifford, WO1

She leaned back. How could Jack's crew chief have survived? Why didn't they tell her? She had to talk to him, had to see him. Why didn't he include his phone number? Of course she would go see him. How far away was Baton Rouge? She'd have to get out a map. She wished that she could hop in her car and go now. But first, she'd have to write and tell him she was coming. When could she go? Her parents would be here in just a few days. And they were staying through the weekend. The school show was the following week. It would have to wait until the weekend after that. It would be a long two weeks.

CHAPTER TWENTY- NINE

Grant changed the oil in his van, took Alice for long walks; even fine-tuned his week's lesson plans. Anything to keep his mind off the upcoming sit-in. Principal Frye couldn't do much to stop the School Board from firing him if they decided his participation was a breach of probation. Why did he promise Leroy that he would join them? Because Leroy was right, that's why. He needed a distraction; decided to take a ride over to Grams. Maybe she needed something done around the house.

AdaMae opened her front door. "Grant! So happy you came by. I was just about to give you a call."

He pecked his grandmother on the cheek. "You need something done? I'm at your service."

"No, not really."

"You sure?"

"Well, I suppose I could have you repair the loose slats in the patio fence. Some came loose from last week's storm."

"Great. Let me get my toolbox out of the van."

Before she could stop him, he was lugging his tools to the side yard. She poured a glass of iced tea and went out to keep him company.

The first board creaked as he yanked it away from the fencing with a crowbar. "Some of these needed replacing anyway. I'll visit the lumberyard this week and get started next weekend."

"But that's Thanksgiving weekend. Remember?"

"Yeah, but Thanksgiving is only one day. Lisa isn't staying the whole weekend, is she?"

"Mmm. That's what I was going to call you about. Our Thanksgiving plans have changed."

Grant pulled out another board, tossed it on the grass, and looked at AdaMae. "How so?"

"Turns out Andrew has mono, and Lisa called to say they wouldn't be coming."

"Mono? How the heck did he get that?"

She shrugged. "I don't know. They call it the 'kissing disease', don't they? He's dating now."

Grant chuckled. "Yeah, I suppose that's one way he could've got it. Damn. I was looking forward to seeing the kid, . . . and Lisa and Mark, too, of course." He continued extracting fence slats, hesitant to ask the next question. "Cassie's still coming, right?" It had been a miserable week, but knowing he'd see Cassie for Thanksgiving had kept him going. A thousand times, he went over that evening they'd kissed on her couch, how she'd responded, what she said, and what he should have said. He should have been more sympathetic. After all, he knew all about grief. Maybe if he was patient, he'd get another chance. Perhaps some moments alone at Thanksgiving would provide that chance. Lost in his thoughts, he didn't hear Gram's response at first. "What did you say?"

"I *said,* Yes and no."

"What do you mean, yes and no?"

AdaMae let out a sigh. "I could tell your mind was somewhere else. Didn't you hear a word I said?"

He shook his head. "Sorry. Wasn't paying attention. What's the deal, then?"

"To make a long story short, we're going to Cassie's for Thanksgiving dinner. Her parents and brother will be there too. Flying in on Wednesday."

"Her family is coming here, and she invited us?" Quickly, he tried to absorb this new information. Thanksgiving at Cassie's with her family. "Are you sure she wants me there too?"

"Of course, silly. Why wouldn't she want you to come?"

Grant saw his grandmother's perplexed look. He shrugged. "No reason."

"Naturally, I insisted on bringing the turkey and some of our usual fixings."

"But won't Cassie want to do the cooking for her family?"

AdaMae smiled. "She seemed fine with me bringing most of it. You know I love that girl, but her culinary skills are amateur, to say the least."

Grant remembered the burnt macaroni and cheese that Cassie brought over one evening when he was laid up. "Yeah, I know what you mean. She keeps on trying, though. Gotta give her credit for that."

"Speaking of cooking, are you staying for dinner?"

"Don't have to ask me twice. Let me carry these boards to my van, and I'll be in to wash up."

Grant cut into his chicken fried steak and gravy while AdaMae poured ice tea into his glass.

"Anything new at work?"

He vacillated a moment before deciding it was best she did not know. "Not much. Just getting back into the routine." After all, she'd know soon enough, assuming the sit-in took place. Part of him wanted Leroy to call it off. His job was on the line. Would any other adults join in? He'd talked to the others on the list. Most were reticent to commit. He speared another slab of steak. After all, his next dinner might be in the county jail.

CHAPTER THIRTY

When Cassie appeared not to hear her for the third time, Mrs. Hicks inquired with concern. "Are you okay? Maybe you're catching that bug that's going around."

"No, I'm fine. Thanks, Mrs. Hicks. Sorry about the extra paperwork you had to prepare this morning. I've never left my bag home before."

"I know, not like you at all." Mrs. Hicks placed a hand on Cassie's forehead. "No fever, but you're kind of pale. You're not staying late again today, are you?"

"Not too late. Zebbie's parents are coming in for a conference, remember?"

"Oh, right. That boy is such a sweetheart. Don't tell anyone, but he's my favorite, y'know. 'Jes want to squeeze him like he was a big ole teddy bear."

"I know what you mean. But I'm hoping that he'll be transferred to another class."

"Another class! But why?"

"He's a smart boy, that's why. He never should have been put in special education."

"A lot of them are smart, if you ask me. 'Jes need a little extra help, that's all."

"I agree. But truth is that while this class is supposed to be for children with IQs below a certain level, most of these kids are here for other reasons. Zebbie clearly has a learning disability. Weldon and Lewis are both smart boys who were put in here because of their behavior. With Jeff, it's his speech impediment. I could go on and on. I've tried talking to Mr. Horace and the school-assigned psychologist about it, but they just tell me that I'm doing a fine job and leave things the way they are."

"You *are* doing a fine job. You shoulda' seen the last teacher we had! I did my best to keep things under control but she didn't teach these poor children a thing! She gave 'em coloring pages, and showed silly filmstrips. When there was a ruckus or a fight, she'd take the paddle to them right quick. Now, don't get me wrong, I believe in not sparing the rod, but your honey is working a heck of a lot better than her vinegar. I'd be happy to testify to that anytime."

Cassie smiled. "Thanks. I could never have done it without you though."

"You got that right."

Cassie laughed. "I know that we're helping them, but for some, being in this classroom is a prison."

"What do you mean? They're happier than they've ever been."

"Maybe, but it's still special education. After primary school, if they're still labeled as 'retarded', they won't make it out."

"Out?"

"Yeah —out into a regular class so they can make it in the world."

"I suppose you're right. So that's why you're having this parent conference?"

"Yes. I'm hoping they'll have more luck than I with the administration."

Cassie rubbed her temple and took a deep breath.

"I still say you're coming down with something. You listen to me, now. Soon as this meeting is over, you go home, take two aspirin, and go to bed."

Cassie patted Mrs. Hick's hand. "Thanks, Mrs. Hicks. Maybe I'll do just that."

At the sound of the bell, Mrs. Hicks wagged her finger at Cassie before directing the children into their bus lines and taking them outside. Cassie had been distracted and tired all day. How could she not, after reading Earl's letter? What little sleep she got was filled with distorted dreams, images of Jack screaming as his helicopter plunged out of the sky, or his mouth searching for hers as he pressed against her, the scent of Lifebuoy soap still fresh on his skin.

Last night, she finally gave up all hope of sleeping. When the clock struck two, she threw off the covers, walked to the kitchen, and poured herself a glass of warm milk before turning on the television to watch the tail end of *Casablanca*. The ending always left her mystified. Did Ilsa love Rick or Lazlo? Or perhaps both? Was that possible? As 'The End' flashed on the screen, she turned the TV off and returned to bed, only to be awakened three hours later by the buzzing of the alarm clock.

Sitting at her desk, her eyelids ached with the effort of staying awake. She went to the teacher's room bathroom, splashed some water on her face, and looked into the mirror. Mrs. Hicks was right. She was pale. Pinching her cheeks for color, she inhaled deeply, and stepped back into the hallway.

Zebbie's parents arrived right on time. The father was the adult version of his son. His bulky frame barely fit through the door, his smile so broad and warm, that Cassie immediately relaxed. The mother, too, was tall and broad shouldered. Dressed in a handsome blue suit and white blouse, she fidgeted with her pocketbook as Cassie directed them to two adult-sized chairs. Unlike her husband, Mrs. Wright offered no smile or handshake. But her cool demeanor changed once Cassie shared stories of Zebbie's progress, diligence, and generous nature.

"So, you don't think Zebadiah is retar.... I mean, slow?"

Cassie shook her head. "No, I don't. I think he's a very bright boy."

The father looked at his wife. "See, I told you, Ellie. I always said he was smart. Tried to tell that psychologist too, but he wouldn't listen. Said he was retarded and needed to be in Special Education. Did you know, Mrs. Cunningham, that our son helps at my store sometimes, and that he even checks my accounts book?"

"No, I didn't. But I can't say I'm surprised. He's a real whiz with numbers. It's the reading that's difficult."

The mother leaned forward. "We know that, Mrs. Cunningham. I work with him every evening after supper. For a long time, he just seemed stuck, y'know? But this year, he's finally reading! He loves the books you send home with him. Sometimes, he can get through a whole chapter without much help from me at all!"

Cassie nodded. "I know. He's only one grade level behind now. I've been using some strategies for children with dyslexia. Has anyone ever mentioned that word to you before?"

The parents exchanged looks and shook their heads.

"It's basically a learning disability that affects the child's ability to read, especially with letters and sounds. I've been using a method called Orton-Gillingham with Zebbie. Slowly but surely, he's building up his sight word vocabulary. Fluency is finally taking hold, and he doesn't have to struggle to decode every word."

The mother was nodding. "Yes, you're right. He's not getting stuck on every other word, like he used to. I would tell him to 'sound it out' but he didn't seem to know how to do that."

"That's because the sounds don't come automatically to him."

The father looked confused. "But I thought you said he was smart? Is he always going to need help?"

"Zebbie *is* smart, Mr. Wright. He does need help with reading, and probably will require that for some time, but as you can see, *he can learn.*"

"But he has to stay in special education though, right? I know what that means. My brother was put in special education classes all the way through high school, until he dropped out. Never could find a job. Ended up in prison. Ten years of special education and he still can't read. No disrespect, Mrs. Cunningham, but I don't want that for our son."

"I don't either, Mr. Wright. I've already spoken with Mr. Horace about Zebbie. I'd like to see him move into a regular class."

The father's eyes lit up. "Really?" He looked at his wife. "You hear that, Ellie? Regular class."

The mother frowned. "But won't he just fall behind again? I mean, you just told us how much progress he's making here with you."

"I have those concerns too. So, here's what I would like to propose. Zebbie could move to a regular class and I provide the teacher with some materials. He could get extra help with me either during the day or even after school, if he starts to fall behind."

The father asked, "Sounds good to me. When will this begin?"

Here was the tricky part. How could she tell them that Mr. Horace had already dismissed her idea of moving Zebbie into a regular classroom? But since then, she'd done some back-door finagling. There were three third grade teachers in the building. The best of the lot, hands down, was Stella Fisher. She was the kind of teacher that had high expectations of her students but would modify her instruction to meet the needs of the students. If Cassie could get both the parents and Stella Fisher to agree to her plan, maybe Mr. Horace would also. The problem was that Ms. Fisher stayed to herself, avoiding interacting with the other teachers, especially the white teachers. It took a few well-placed words from Reina to get Stella to agree to meet with Cassie. Turned out it wasn't a hard sell. Stella knew many of Cassie's students and expressed dismay that they'd been 'dumped' in special education. She was more than willing to help one of them if she could.

"Mr. and Mrs. Wright, would you be willing to meet with me again, along with Ms. Fisher, one of our third-grade teachers, and Mr. Horace?"

"Of course," they replied.

"Good. I'll get back with you on the date and time."

Cassie shook their hands and watched them leave the room, muttering to herself, "Let's keep our fingers crossed."

CHAPTER THIRTY-ONE

Grant's palms were sweating before he even reached his classroom. The halls were empty. He had no idea if word had spread about the planned sit-in, or if it was even going to happen. Frye had waved to him briefly when they walked in from the school parking lot simultaneously. Nothing in the principal's demeanor would indicate that he knew.

Skimming through his first period notes, Grant struggled to focus on today's topic of Constitutional history. His mouth was dry. He poured a cup of coffee from his thermos, took a long gulp, and set the cup on the desk blotter. The image of Thurgood Marshall on the coffee mug caught his eye. His quote read: *Truth is more than a mental exercise.* He believed in truth, didn't he? Hadn't his classroom lessons focused on getting out the truth, especially when it came to racism and slavery? How long would his Southern neighbors and friends wave the Confederate flag, blind to its symbolism? He stood, threw his shoulders back to ease the developing tension, and began writing questions on the chalkboard. Each day's lesson began with questions, questions that would make the students think beyond the facts.

What are the criteria written into the Constitution for someone to be President of the United States?

Do you agree with all of these criteria? Why, or why not?

Explain the process of amending the Constitution. Do you think it is it too difficult to amend the Constitution or not difficult enough?

The first bell rang and Grant watched the students enter, looking for some sign. Leroy arrived and locked his eyes on Grant's. The sit-in was on. Grant nodded and then slowly exhaled. He'd been told it would be first period. But when, at the start or perhaps during? The chalk broke in his hand as students took their assigned seats. Grant learned long ago that, just like in society, the classroom would not integrate naturally. Assigned seating was the only way to facilitate inter-racial relations. He sensed tension in the room, at least from the black students. A number of them were absent: George, Mavis, Tyrone, and Priscilla. That left eight black students. Would they all walk out?

The intercom clicked and the familiar voice of the assistant principal began morning announcements. "Coach Higgins would like to remind everyone of the big game on Thanksgiving morning. 11 a.m. kickoff. Come, support our Rebels. The Chess Club meets today in Room 304 after school. The regional tournament is only two weeks away. The Children of the Confederacy will meet after school in Room 201. Their guest speaker will be Mrs. Willoby, the President of the United Daughters of the Confederacy. Now, please stand for the Pledge of Allegiance."

There was the usual shuffling and screeching of chairs as teens rose to their feet. They recited the pledge but as the final words ... 'with liberty and justice for all' were spoken, he saw movement from the corner of his eye. The black students were walking out. As they did, each pulled a miniature American flag from their pocket or backpack. Some stuck their flag into a sweater or jacket buttonhole.

LeRoy nodded at Grant, and then tipped his head toward the door. This was the moment. Grant could either freeze at his desk, gaping at the departing students like their white classmates, or he could keep his promise and join the protest. He followed Leroy.

The hallway filled quickly as black students silently exited. Gathered together, they sat cross-legged on the floor, arms interlocked. Many of the girls tucked under their dresses. Each continued to clutch a small American flag or display it on their clothing. Grant was wedged between Leroy and a young girl he believed was a freshman. He didn't know her name, but doubted he would ever forget her face; the jut of her chin, the beads of sweat forming at her hairline, or the fear in her eyes.

Mr. Frye's door opened. This was not his first go-around with the protesters. The walk-out was still fresh in everyone's minds. But this was a face-to-face confrontation inside the building. How would Frye handle it? Grant scanned the first-floor hallway to see if there were any other staff, any other white faces. The white ex-Marine shop teacher and the tall, skinny black cafeteria lady sat at the other end of the hall. The assistant football coach, not surprisingly, was nowhere to be seen.

"All right, all right, what's this all about?" A frowning Frye walked to the middle of the hallway and crossed his arms. The office door opened again, and the assistant principal, Frank Mead, stepped out to join him. Mead was new, and a bit of a loose cannon. Like most assistant principals, he handled disciplinary problems in the school and prided himself in running a 'tight ship'. Now, he stood behind Frye, hands on hips, glaring at the sit-in protesters. Frye spotted Grant in the crowd and took a step in his direction, and for a moment, Grant thought he'd direct his wrath only at him. But Frye stopped midway, scanned both the crowd of black students on the floor and the gathering crowd of white spectators. He took a deep breath before speaking. "Now look, nobody wants any trouble here. Y'all go back into your classrooms." Then he walked over to Leroy. "Leroy, are you responsible for this?" Leroy didn't answer. He fixed his eyes on Grant. "Or maybe you put them up to this?" Grant clenched his jaw but said nothing. "Leroy, there's no need for this. If you come to my office, we can have a talk, sort this all out."

All eyes were on Leroy, who stared straight ahead, waving his small American flag. The other protesters began to do the same. It seemed to be a signal, as, in unison they began singing "We shall overcome, we shall overcome, ..." As their voices resonated through the halls, Frye ordered the teachers standing in doorways to herd the onlookers back into their classrooms. Some did, but most didn't move. No one wanted to miss this. Frye threw his hands into the air, nodded at Mead, and retreated to his office. Amy stood at her classroom door glaring at Grant and shaking her head.

When Frye left, Mead took over. Grant noted the crimson face, bulging neck, and belligerent stance. He half expected to see steam vent from the man's prominent ears. Mead marched in their direction, stopping in front of Leroy. Kicking Leroy's shoe, he barked, "Get up, boy!"

The singing stopped. Leroy didn't move. "You heard me, get up!" This time he yanked Leroy's arm. Somewhere from a doorway came the cry, "Get the niggers!" Others joined the chant, and in seconds, there were swarms of bodies everywhere, kicking and punching as more cries of "Get the niggers!" were heard.

Grant was shoved to the floor, a heavy weight on top of him. The screams were so loud that he almost didn't hear the sirens until just before the police charged in. The last thing he saw before the police handcuffed him and took him away was the look of horror on Frye's face as the students of his high school were beaten and dragged out the front door.

CHAPTER THIRTY-TWO

Cassie rummaged in her purse for aspirin. The headache had only gotten worse since morning. It was Monday- only two days before her parents' arrival. She had a lot to do, but perhaps she should take Mrs. Hicks' advice and go straight to bed when she got home. Searching for some soothing music, she turned on the car radio, and caught the tail end of the local news. *"A riot broke out at Escambia High School this morning after black students staged a sit-in. Police arrested hundreds of students along with a few staff members. Principal Frye, gave no comment, but the sit-in is believed to be a continuation of demands to remove the school symbols of the Confederate flag, Rebel mascot, and use of the song, Dixie, at school events."*

Did she hear correctly? Did they say staff, as well as students? Was Grant involved? Even before she thought it, she knew. Of course he was.

The phone was ringing as she put her key in the lock. She ran to answer it.

"Cassie? It's Grant."

She exhaled. "Grant! I'm glad it's you. I just heard about the school riot. Are you home now?"

"I'm not home, Cassie. I'm calling from jail."

Cassie gripped the phone. "You're in jail? Are you all right?"

"A little roughed up but okay."

"What happened?"

"Long story. Look, Cassie. I'm sorry to do this to you, but I only get one phone call. Just couldn't bring myself to call Grams. Do you suppose you could post my bail? I'll pay you back."

"Of course. Where's the police station?"

"You'll have to post bail at the courthouse. And… Cassie?"

"Yes?"

"They only take cash. Can you swing five hundred?"

"Yes." She tried to remember the balance on her checking account, probably have to take some from savings too. She jotted down the address as Grant rattled it off. "I'll go to the bank and be there as soon as I can."

Before getting back into the car, she went to the bathroom to splash cool water on her face. It revived her some. She grabbed her purse and a can of Coke from the fridge. Sliding into the driver's seat, she popped open the can and gulped the familiar sugary fizz. The caffeine eased her headache. As the key turned in the ignition, she thought of Grant, sitting in a jail cell. Suddenly, all she wanted was to see him. Her foot pressed the accelerator.

She drove down a number of side streets before spotting an open spot and shakily putting her parallel parking skill to the test. Running up two flights of stairs, she entered the courthouse clerk's office.

"Take a seat," barked a gray-haired bespectacled woman from behind the counter. Every seat was occupied, mostly by black women, their worried faces barely noticing her. She walked to a corner and leaned against the wall. It would be a long wait.

CHAPTER THIRTY- THREE

The cell held only two of them. Sam Childers sat on one of the two bunk beds and looked at Grant staring vacantly into the corridor. "You look a little shaken up. Going to be okay?"

Grant turned around. "Yeah. Got kicked in the gut, but I'll be fine. Did you see where they put the students?"

"Other jail cells. Eva's with them."

"Eva?"

"The cafeteria worker. They're all crammed together at the other end of the station in the remaining cells. Have to keep us segregated, even in jail."

Grant nodded before sitting on the other bunk. He looked over at the muscled ex-Marine, seemingly the least likely candidate for a sit-in.

Sam stood and paced the cell a few times before sitting again. "I'd give anything for a smoke." He glanced at Grant. "You teach history, right?"

"Uh-huh."

"Kids like you, most of 'em anyway. Fred's not a fan, but then he doesn't like me either. I've had to set him straight a bunch of times. Likes to throw around the 'n' word. Don't tolerate that."

"Fred Crowley? I've had my run-ins with him too,"

"So, I've heard." Sam shook his head. "Crazy shit this morning. Kids might have had a chance if Macho Mead hadn't gone berserk. It was all I could do to keep from punching his sorry redneck mug. But Leroy warned me about doing anything violent. I kept my promise." He chuckled. "I see that look, Lee. Wondering how a redneck like me is doing in a black student sit-in, right?"

Grant flinched. "I didn't call you a redneck."

Sam smiled. "Well, I am. Born and raised in Alabama. Spent most of my childhood huntin' and fishin' with my Pappy, and never gave a wit about segregation. Didn't give it much thought, to tell you the truth. They had their school. We had ours. That thinking changed when I went to 'Nam."

"Marines, right?"

"Yep. Proud jarhead."

Grant waited for his cellmate to say more.

"When you're slogging through the jungle trying to stay in one piece it doesn't much matter what color your buddy is, long as he's lookin' out for you like you're lookin' out for him. My sorry ass was saved more than once by Legs, the biggest blackest dude you'd ever want to meet."

"That's a strange name, Legs"

"Real name was Clayton Dobbs, but he had legs like tree stumps. Good thing too, 'cause he was the only one that could've carried me five miles through the jungle."

"Five miles! But you must weigh over two hundred pounds!"

"Two-forty, and I was dead weight. Took a bullet to the side and passed out from bleeding half to death." He lifted his shirt and showed the white scar on his left side. "Legs saved my life. He's also the one that told me to go to college on the GI Bill when I got back. He did the same."

"Do you stay in touch?"

"Naw. Legs is dead."

"But I thought you said he came back and went to college?"

"He did. Wasn't the Cong that got him. He was shot in a bar by some asshole that pulled a gun on him when Legs smiled at a white woman."

Grant shook his head. He'd heard enough similar stories to know that it was all too true. "Don't tell me. The killer walked, right?"

"Yup. His buddies claimed that Legs had a gun, even though no gun was found on him." Sam leaned back against the wall and stared at Grant. "Kids tell me you're a straight shooter. Always talking about how history needs to tell it like it really was, the truth, right?"

"Right. I try, at least."

"Well, teach, you need to tell them that we're fighting the wrong damn enemy. It's not over there in the jungles of 'Nam. It's here. Some of these black kids don't stand a chance. They get called up by Uncle Sam to do their duty, and even if they survive war over there, they face it here when they get back. Ain't right."

"So, that's why you joined the protest."

"When Leroy asked, I hesitated. Knew it could mean losing this job. First real job I've had other than being a Marine. But I'm doing it for Legs and all those other black veterans who deserve better than what this country's giving 'em." He sat back on his bunk, hands resting on his shaved head, fingers interlocked, and asked, "And you? Why are you here?"

Grant had asked himself the same question, and struggled with the answer. He knew what he'd written in the letter to the paper, what he taught the kids. He wanted to believe his actions were totally altruistic, but in honest moments, knew there was more.

"Where are you? You look miles away. Haven't answered my question." Sam stood and leaned against the wall, awaiting an answer.

Why are you here? The question hung in the air as Grant struggled with the memory of deserting his grandmother, his conflicted emotions about his country, himself. He hesitated. His cellmate was a man who'd proved himself. But was a man only measured in war, was courage only tested on the battlefield? He was tempted to tell Sam about his grandfather's death, the grief and confusion that sent him running when his grandmother needed him most. Instead he said, "Have to do more than talk the talk. Need to walk the walk. The kids are right." It sounded corny even as he said it, but it was the truth.

"You know we're both going to be canned, don't you?"

Grant sighed. "Probably."

"You got a family?"

"No wife or kids, if that's what you mean."

"Me neither. Makes it a little easier. No one depending on me."

Grant stretched out on the bunk. "Who's making bond for you?

"No one."

Grant sat up on his elbow and frowned. "You're staying in jail?"

"Yep. Got no place else to go, and sure as hell don't have that kind of cash lying around."

"But if you had it, you'd pay, right?"

"Sure." There was a long pause before Sam spoke again. "When you get out, promise me something."

Grant waited for the cash request, but that's not what came.

"Watch your back."

"Watch my back?"

"Yeah. You've got enemies."

"If you mean the administration, I knew what I was doing when I agreed to join the sit-in."

"So did I. That's not what I mean."

"What *do* you mean?"

"Look, Fred's not the only one who hates your guts. He and his buddies are being egged on and possibly bribed."

"Egged on? By who?"

"Higgins."

"The football coach?"

"The suspensions hurt his team. He may call them 'niggers' behind their backs, but he needs those guys to win the championship. As far as he's concerned, the walkout and suspensions put that at jeopardy."

"I don't see how he can pin that on me."

"Look, I hear Higgins spout off about you plenty. I guess he assumes I'm one of his kind. I keep my mouth shut so I know what he's up to, and I'm jes' sayin'—he sees you as a threat."

"Me? Why the hell, me?"

"You're tight with the blacks, and you're a Yankee, a Damn Yankee at that."

He nodded. "I've heard that before, even though I've lived here sixteen years."

Grant recalled Higgins threatening note. *You'll pay for this, Lee. You're nothing but a Damn Yankee stirring up trouble. Stick to your books and stop putting ideas in the n-kids heads!* He sat up and leaned forward. "You said something about bribery too."

"Fred wants to be on that team. Real bad. And he'll do whatever Higgins wants."

The sound of footsteps coming in their direction brought them to their feet. Grant stood upon seeing his grandmother, still in her gardening clothes, following a police officer.

"Grams, what are you doing here? "You didn't think I was going to stay home when my grandson was in jail, did you?"

"But how did you know I was here?"

"I heard the news reports. Soon as I heard them say 'two teachers were involved in the protest', I knew you had to be one of 'em."

The police officer jiggled the key in the lock and opened the door. "Made bond, Mr. Lee. You're free to go."

Grant reached for his grandmother. "Is Cassie here with you?"

"Cassie? No. Why?"

Grant turned to the officer, "Can I make a call to the courthouse, sir?"

"You're a free man. At least for now. Use the pay phone in the lobby."

"Thanks." Grant hugged his grandmother. "Thanks, Grams, but I have to make a call."

It took a while before Grant connected with the courthouse clerk and with a little bit of persuasion, convince her to put Cassie on the phone.

"Grant, you're not in jail?"

"Grams is here. She took care of bonding me out. Sorry I put you through so much trouble."

"No, no, don't worry about it. I'm just glad to hear you're free. Can I see you? Are you going home?"

"Yeah, but not right away. I want you to do something else for me."

"What?"

He asked that she make bond for Sam, again saying he'd pay her back as soon as possible. He hung up the phone and mumbled under his breath. "A Damn Yankee, huh?"

CHAPTER THIRTY -FOUR

Cassie cut thin apple slices into the pie shell, mounding them high, then dousing generously with sugar and cinnamon, the way her father liked it. Her parents slept soundly in the spare room, while Jeremy snored on the living room couch. She smiled, remembering her brother's excitement as he described his first plane ride. Her mother had secretly told her that he'd been quite scared, but the flight attendant had given him a metal pilot wing's pin, and taken him to the cockpit to meet the pilot. After that, Jeremy relaxed for the remainder of the flight as he rubbed the pilot wings pinned on his jacket.

She hadn't told them yet about AdaMae and Grant coming over. She meant to, but somehow never managed to slip it into last night's conversation. Pinching the rim of the pie crust, she made six slits on top before sliding it into the pre-heated oven.

"No turkey aroma coming out of this kitchen, little girl. We are having turkey today, aren't we?" Her father walked into the kitchen and kissed Cassie's cheek.

"No, Dad, just apple pie. That's your favorite part of the meal, anyway."

"That's true. Top it with two scoops of vanilla ice cream, and I'm all set."

"Did you sleep okay? Is Mom still sleeping?"

"Yes, and yes."

It was good to have her father there in person. Most phone conversations were dominated by Mom. He kept telling her on the phone that he was fine, but she wasn't sure she believed it until she saw him get off the plane. He'd trimmed down some since his heart attack. Mom, however, had put on weight. Her face was drawn and colorless in the car's rear-view mirror last night.

"You look good, Dad."

He patted his stomach. "You noticed, huh? I've been a good boy, following doctor's orders. But today, no special diet. Bring on the pie and ice cream."

She set the timer on the oven. "Ready for some coffee?"

He sat at the kitchen table. "Love some. You remember how I take it?"

"Of course. Black with two sugars." She took two mugs from the cupboard, poured the coffee, putting sugar in one and cream in the other. "What would you like for breakfast, Dad?"

He patted the seat next to him. "Time for that later. Take a seat, little girl."

She did as he asked.

He sipped his coffee. "Not too bad."

She laughed. "I know. I'm not the cook in the family, but I have learned how to make a decent cup of coffee."

"Guess you've had to learn how to do a lot of things on your own." He patted her hand.

He didn't say Jack's name. He didn't have to. Cassie knew what he meant. She straightened in her chair. She wasn't ready to have this conversation. Not now. The past few days had drained her. The letter from Jack's friend, Grant's arrest. Work hadn't been easy either, as she pushed for Zebbie's change of placement and helped the kids practice. And then there was Mrs. Washburn. While she'd agreed to let them participate in the play, she was continually dropping by and making comments as if she were having second thoughts.

"I'm doing okay, Dad."

"Of course you are. You're as strong as they come. I keep telling your mother that."

"She still insisting I should come home?"

Ed McDonald's eyes narrowed as he looked over the rim of his coffee cup. "You know about that?"

"Dad, it's in every letter she writes."

"She's worried about you, that's all."

"And you?"

"Worried? No. Miss you, yes."

"Do you think I should come home?"

"It's not for me to decide. I just want you to be happy, that's all."

"I wish Mom saw it that way."

"Your mother's been through a lot, Cassie."

"You're the one who had the heart attack."

"That's true, but sometimes it's harder on the one watching and taking care. She was still grieving the loss of her own mother when my mother moved in. And then there was… you know… Jack. Your mother was very fond of him."

"I know." *It didn't hurt that his family came from money either.* She couldn't bring herself to say it aloud, but knew it to be true. Mom had been thrilled when Jack's parents had offered their country club for the wedding reception. Cassie would have preferred something simpler, outdoors. She and Jack had argued about it, but he wasn't one to go against his parents' wishes.

The sound of her mother's bedroom slippers scuffing on the hallway floor broke her reverie. Lena MacDonald entered the kitchen, yawning. "Is there coffee left in the pot for me?"

"Of course, Mom. I know what a bear you are in the morning without your coffee, and yes, I know you take it black. Here you go."

Her mother blew on it before taking her first sip and sitting next to her husband. "I can't believe how late I slept."

Cassie leaned against the counter. "Jeremy's still sleeping too."

"Pff. Jeremy will sleep until noon if you let him."

"Want me to scramble up some eggs for you and Dad?"

"No, I'm sure you'll be cooking plenty today. Just let me finish this coffee and I'll get busy helping with all the Thanksgiving preparations."

"There isn't much to do really."

"Isn't much to do? Of course there is. The turkey needs to be stuffed and put in the oven, the pies made, the vegetables prepared." She put her coffee down. "Oh, I almost forgot. I have something for the occasion." Before Cassie could question her,

Lena went to the bedroom and returned with a package. "Here, open it. I made it for you."

Cassie pulled back pale-yellow tissue paper and unfolded an intricately quilted Thanksgiving table runner of autumn colors with appliqued gourds, apples, and pumpkins. "Oh, Mom, it's beautiful!"

"You like it?"

"It must have taken you hours!"

Cassie's father responded. "It did. She started it as soon as we booked the tickets to come."

Cassie walked over to her mother and kissed her on the cheek. "Thank you, Mom."

"You're welcome, dear. Now how about getting that turkey out and I'll work on the bread stuffing? If we don't get it into the oven soon, we'll be eating awfully late."

"That's not necessary. The turkey is all taken care of."

"Don't tell me you ordered one of those store-bought ones? They're so overpriced and really nothing like home cooked."

Cassie shook her head. "No, nothing like that."

Ed said, "Please don't tell me you've become a vegetarian."

Cassie laughed. "No, Dad. I'm not a vegetarian." She might as well just tell them. "AdaMae is bringing the turkey."

"AdaMae?" Her mother frowned.

"Yes. You remember me telling you about her, my neighbor, AdaMae." She waited for a response, but none came. "She's been ever so helpful to me, and you see, before I knew that you were coming, I'd been invited to her house, but then of course my plans changed when you told me of your visit, and I knew that

AdaMae would be disappointed, and like I said, she's been ever so wonderful to me." She was aware that she was babbling, but continued anyway. "And she's a fantastic cook! Wait until you taste her cornbread, collards, and her sweet potato pie."

Her father said, "Collards?"

Her mother followed up with "Sweet potato pie?"

The doorbell saved Cassie from explaining Southern cuisine. She opened the front door, surprised to see Grant holding Alice's collar with one hand, and a pie in the other.

"Grams made this last night, and asked me to bring it over before walking the dog." Alice barked and then lurched forward, slobbering Cassie's hand with kisses.

As she bent down to pet Alice, Cassie was unaware of her family coming from behind.

Freshly awakened Jeremy slapped his knee and called for the dog, "Here, here, girl."

Alice pounced, almost knocking the pajama-clad boy over. Laughing, Jeremy ruffled the thick mottled fur.

"Alice, get down." Grant stepped inside to grab the dog's collar. "Sorry about that. She's super friendly, as you can see."

"Mom, Dad, Jeremy, this is Grant, AdaMae's grandson. And you've already met Alice."

Ed stepped forward and extended his hand. "Nice to meet you. Will we be seeing you later for dinner?"

Grant briefly glanced at Cassie before answering. "Yes, sir. Looking forward to it." He turned back to Cassie. "Grams says everything should be ready by two. Will that be all right or is that too early?"

"No, no, I mean, yes, that will be fine." She felt the warmth creep into her cheeks. "Here, let me take that pie into the kitchen."

Grant pulled a leash out of his pocket and clipped it to the dog's collar. "Oh, by the way, Jeremy. Cassie says you love basketball. You want to shoot some hoops later?"

Jeremy beamed. "You bet!"

"Great. Come on over whenever you're ready."

CHAPTER THIRTY- FIVE

Cassie moved the place cards three times, each time questioning her choice. Finally, she chucked them all. With six people at the table, no one was out of earshot of another. She just had to hope her mother would avoid judgmental comments, her father wouldn't interrogate Grant, and nothing would set Jeremy off on one of his rare tantrums.

Lena had taken over the kitchen to make the family's traditional Waldorf salad, whipped potatoes, stuffed mushrooms, and cranberry chutney. Other than the apple pie, Cassie's only contribution was a squash casserole. She glanced at the clock. Punctuality wasn't one of AdaMae's virtues, and already her mother had commented that the stuffed mushrooms would dry out if kept on warm for too long. The doorbell rang.

AdaMae smiled as she was introduced. "Sorry I can't shake your hands, but I need to get my collards into the oven to keep them warm. Grant will be here soon with the turkey." She hurried to the kitchen and opened the oven door. "Can I take these out?"

Lena answered, "I'll get them. Those are my stuffed mushrooms, our appetizer." She slid the mushrooms onto a serving tray and carried them into the living room where Ed and Jeremy were focused on a football game. "Ed, turn the television off. We have company."

AdaMae found a spot next to Jeremy on the couch. "Don't turn it off on my account. I love football! The Miami Dolphins have a good team this year." She patted the cushion next to her. "Won't you join us, Lena?"

"No, thank you. Never watch the game, but please try some of the mushrooms." Lena pointed to the tray on the coffee table.

AdaMae's nose wrinkled. "Sorry, I'll pass. Never developed a taste for mushrooms."

Lena marched into the kitchen. "Well, *that* was a full two hours of work wasted. You could have told me that your neighbor didn't like mushrooms."

"It never came up, Mom. I don't think mushrooms are used much in Southern cuisine."

"And just when are we going to start eating this *Southern* cuisine? I don't see any turkey yet." Just then, the doorbell rang. It was Grant, holding a large platter with a foil- wrapped turkey. Nodding toward Lena, he said, "Good afternoon, Ma'am."

Lena winced. "Ma'am? I'm nowhere near a rocking chair yet, young man."

"Mom, it's okay. In the South, it's considered polite to call a lady Ma'am, no matter what her age."

"Sorry, Ma'am, ah… Mrs. MacDonald. I didn't mean…"

Lena flipped her hand in the air. "Don't worry about it. Just happy you're here with the turkey. Put it on the counter." She pulled back the foil. "Looks done enough. Cassie, what time were you planning to eat?"

"Guess we can eat now." Cassie called everyone to the table, pleased to see her father turn off the television. As at home, her parents took each end of the table and Cassie sat next to her brother. Her father led them in grace before picking up the carving knife.

"Drumstick goes to Jeremy, right son?"

After the turkey slices were doled onto everyone's plates, AdaMae scooped the cornbread stuffing into a bowl and passed it to Cassie's mother. "Hope you like this, Lena. It's a family recipe."

"I think I'll pass. I never developed a taste for cornbread."

Cassie clenched her jaw. "Mom, you might like it, you know."

AdaMae said, "Oh, I'm sorry, Lena. I probably should have made more than one kind of stuffing. What's traditional in your family?"

"The *usual* kind with bread, onions, celery. I add the cooked organ meat for flavoring and some herbs, of course."

"That sounds delicious. Well, if we ever do a repeat, I'll be sure to ask you to make the stuffing."

"I doubt *that* will happen."

Cassie quickly interjected. "Jeremy, why don't you tell Grant about your basketball?"

The conversation switched from food to Jeremy's love of the game and the trophies he'd won.

At first, no one mentioned Jack at dinner, almost as if his name were taboo. It was AdaMae who spoke of him, as she complimented Cassie's squash casserole. "Delicious casserole, Cassie. Your cooking has improved a heap since you and Jack first arrived. He once told me he sure did look forward to dinners at my place." She gave Cassie a wink and a smile.

"You knew Jack?" Cassie's mother asked.

AdaMae smiled in response. "Yes, fine young man."

Her mother then looked at Grant and asked, "And did you know him, also?"

Grant glanced briefly at Cassie before answering her mother. "No, Ma'am. Never had that pleasure."

"I see."

Cassie frowned. What did that mean? Damn it. What was her mother implying? Her stomach tightened. Why did she have such a hard time deciphering her mother? Did she suspect there was more than friendship between her and Grant? Was there?

She changed the subject. "Daddy, have you done much fishing lately?"

"Naw, been only once since you left home. Just not the same without my fishing buddy."

Grant swallowed the last bite of his turkey meat. "Cassie's mentioned how much she enjoyed fishing with you, Sir."

"Ed, call me Ed." He smiled at his daughter. "Ever since she was a little tike. I'll never forget our first fishing trip. When was that, honey?"

"I think I was maybe seven?"

"Sounds about right. It was hot, I know that. And the fish weren't biting. Only caught one perch by midday, and I was more than ready to call it a day, after getting up at dawn. Couldn't say the same for you though."

Cassie smiled. "I remember I begged to stay. I was determined to catch my first fish, and I did too! A good- sized perch, remember?"

Ed laughed. "Sure do. I knew you would never give up until you snagged a fish. Was afraid I'd die of sunstroke before that happened. That's why I helped you a little."

"Helped me a little? I pulled that fish in all by myself!"

"True enough. But it was a recycled fish."

Cassie frowned. "Recycled fish? What are you talking about?"

"It was mine. I put it on your line when you weren't paying attention. Didn't you ever wonder why we only brought one fish home?" Ed laughed. "You were so damn proud of that fish!"

Cassie joined in the laughter. "Sounds like something you'd do. I guess I can handle the truth now, but good thing I didn't catch you in the act back then!"

Lena looked at her daughter. "That's for sure. Stubborn as you are, you'd have stayed till nightfall trying to catch a fish! Some things never change. You're still stubborn as a mule!"

Grant grinned. "Oh, I don't know, more like determined, don't you think?"

Cassie returned his smile.

***

The turkey had done its thing, filling stomachs and causing sedation. Cassie was the only one still awake. She kissed Jeremy lightly on the forehead and draped an afghan over him. Looking down on her brother, she noted the light stubble on his face, the broadened shoulders. Like most Down's Syndrome children, her brother would never be tall, but puberty had set in. He had held his own on the basketball court today. Grant had even flicked on AdaMae's outside light so they could play after dark in her driveway. Her mother had said her good-nights an hour ago while her father drifted off to sleep in front of the TV, his head slumped against the side wing of Jack's chair. Cassie rarely sat there and had almost stopped her father from doing so, before catching herself. It was only a chair. But it was as if Jack was still there, feet resting on the ottoman, newspaper spread out.

When she switched the TV off, her father grunted but remained asleep. She stared at the ruddy face, thick reddish-brown hair, and emerging double chin. Her mother had often accused her of being a 'Daddy's girl', a title she embraced. Perhaps that is why she never did learn how to cook properly or do all the 'womanly' tasks her mother nagged her to do. She preferred to be digging in the garden with her father, or heading to the lake with him to fish. She smiled, remembering her father's revelation about her first fish.

Today had gone reasonably well. Her mother only badgered twice about returning home, always out of ear shot of AdaMae. The mention of Jack at dinner had thrown her. Over pie, Lena had regaled AdaMae and Grant with wedding stories, how Jack was so handsome in his uniform, how the country club reception was so luxurious. That's when Grant asked Jeremy to join him shooting hoops in AdaMae's driveway.

Last Thanksgiving it had been just the two of them. Jack hadn't complained about the dry turkey or lumpy gravy. He'd dried her tears when she cried over the burned sweet potatoes, and suggested a walk on the beach to cheer her. They parked in the first lot of the Gulf Islands National Seashore. It had been an unusually balmy day, yet the beach was largely uninhabited. They weaved through the sea oat dotted dunes, their feet squeaking in the sugar white sand. Finding a cradled knoll, they spread out a blanket. She still remembered the warm sun on their naked bodies.

Without thinking, she walked to her bedroom and retrieved the box. She sat on the edge of the bed and lifted the lid. Stacked on one side of the box were her letters to Jack and on the other were the ones he'd written. Wedged between was the recent letter from Earl. She'd read it at least a dozen times, but once more she took it from the box. Unfolding the plain white paper, she read it again, stopping at the sentence that was now etched in her brain; *He left me a couple of things for you.* Much as she was enjoying her parent's visit, a part of her wanted it to be over so she could make the trip to Baton Rouge. What did Jack leave for her? Would Earl tell her about his last day, how he died? She needed more than basic facts. Immersed in thought, she didn't hear the footsteps.

"What you got there?" Her father stood in the open doorway.

Startled at the sound of her father's voice, she jumped up, spilling the letters to the floor.

"Daddy! I didn't hear you."

"Sorry I scared you." He stepped closer and bent to the floor. "Let me help you with that."

It took but a moment for him to recognize the handwriting of his daughter and see the return address on Jack's envelopes. Clutching the letters, he dropped a knee to the floor and reached out. "Oh, Cassie."

At the touch of his large calloused hand on the back of her neck, Cassie let her head drop to her father's shoulder and began to cry softly.

He stroked his daughter's soft copper curls. "You know I'd take all this sorrow from you, if I could?"

She nodded, still not ready to talk.

He held her until the tears abated. Together, they gathered the remaining letters from the floor and sat on the edge of the bed.

Ed McDonald looked down at the letter he still held.

"Cassie, this letter is dated *August 31,1972*. That's *after* Jack died."

Cassie bit her lip, and nodded.

Her father frowned. "I...I don't understand."

With puddled eyes, she looked at her father. "I still write to him."

"You still write to him? But Cassie..."

"I know, I know. I guess it sounds crazy, but don't you see? To me, he's still here. It's my way of, of... keeping him with me."

He folded the letter and put it in the box before taking his daughter's hand. "Cassie, he's gone."

She nodded as a tear fell on one of the envelopes. Staring at the smeared ink spot, she said, "He is, isn't he?"

He wrapped an arm around her shoulder as she leaned against him and said, "I haven't written in a while." She waited for his response but there was none. "I'm not sure why."

"It's been months now, Cassie. Maybe you're ready to move on."

She sighed. "Maybe."

He hesitated before asking. "AdaMae's son, Grant. Is he...?"

"Is he what, Daddy?"

"Well, you know. Sounds like you see him a lot."

"He's a friend." She pulled away from her father. Just the conversation she didn't want to have. She tucked Earl Gifford's letter into the box. A moment ago, she almost told her father about it, but no, until she went there and met the man, she wasn't ready to tell anyone about his letter. After all, there wasn't much to tell yet, was there?

CHAPTER THIRTY- SIX

Grant had been fired. The news did not surprise him. He'd known the risk when he agreed to participate in the sit-in and did not regret his decision. Even so, the question remained, now what? He could get a lawyer, appeal the firing, but that would cost money, and he doubted his chances. He was more concerned about the students who'd been arrested, especially Leroy. How could he help? Then he remembered Reina's friend, Bill. Wasn't he a lawyer? He reached for the phone and dialed Cassie's number, his heart racing. They'd not spoken since Thanksgiving.

"Hello?"

"Cassie, it's Grant."

He heard the slight intake of breath on the other end. Was that 'happy to hear your voice' intake, or 'Oh, no, it's him'?

"Grant. I should have called you."

"No, no. You've had company. They left yesterday though, right?"

"Yes. Had to be back on Saturday to pick up my grandmother from my aunt's house. By the way, I meant to thank you for spending all that time with Jeremy. Think you've made a fan for life."

Grant smiled. He suspected as much, but it was good to hear. "No need to thank me. Had a lot of fun with him. He's a great kid."

"Still, you were great, and I wanted to ask, I mean we haven't really talked …"

"About my arrest and jail?"

"Well, yes. What's happening now?"

"Frye called Friday to fire me."

"No!"

"I expected it."

"Oh, Grant. What are you going to do?"

"That's why I'm calling, actually. Isn't Reina's friend Bill a lawyer?"

"You're thinking of hiring a lawyer?"

He fidgeted in his chair. "Yeah."

"That's great! Do you think you can get your job back?"

"Uh- here's the thing, Cass. It's for the kids, not me."

"But what about you?"

Her concern pleased him, but he didn't say that. "What about me?"

"Your job. You shouldn't have been fired. Don't you want it back? You should fight back. Isn't that what you teach the kids."

He sighed. She was right, but how could he even begin to explain to Cassie what that fight would mean, and how slim his chances would be? She'd lived in the south only a little over a year. There was so much she didn't understand. "I'm focused on the kids right now. They should be applying for college, not sitting in jail."

"They're still in jail?"

"Some are; those who had previous arrests, or are over eighteen and can't make bond. The others have been released to their parents."

"So, you're hoping Bill can get them out?"

"Maybe. Can you give me Bill's number?"

"I can do better than that. He and Reina are on their way over. Said they had news. Why don't you come here and talk to Bill yourself?"

"You're sure?"

"Of course I'm sure."

"I'll be right over." He hung up the phone as Alice nuzzled his leg. "Sorry, girl. Your walk will have to wait."

Alice trotted into the bathroom and stared quizzically at Grant as he hurriedly ran an electric shaver over his face. "Crazy, huh? But it's for Cassie. Her husband was as clean-shaven as they come. Gotta at least try, right?" Alice whimpered, raised her paw, and scratched his pants repeatedly. "You wanna come, don't you? Don't know if Reina and Bill are dog lovers. Aw, what the heck. Cassie loves you. C'mon."

Cassie's car was the only one in her driveway. It appeared that Reina and Bill had yet to arrive. As he opened the van door to release Alice, Cassie called out "Alice, it's so good to see you!" Dropping to the ground, she buried her head in the dog's shaggy fur.

"Is that true for me too?" His feet didn't move. He swallowed, trying to push down the rising lump in his throat. Why was he so anxious? They hadn't been alone since the day of the graffiti incident. So much had happened since then.

She responded with a smile. "I'm always glad to see you, Grant."

For a moment, she stood so close that he could smell the lemon scent of her shampoo.

"Come on in. I put on a fresh pot of coffee."

He took a seat on the couch, the same spot where he'd reached for her and she'd kissed him so passionately. Did it mean anything? He wanted, no, needed, to know if she felt anything for him. Instead, he remained quiet as she curled up next to Alice and began stroking the friendly mutt, who growled appreciatively.

"So, how are you, Grant? I'm sorry I didn't get a chance to ask before, but with everyone here it just didn't seem…"

"I understand. Probably didn't want to tell your parents I was a jailbird."

She laughed. "They liked you, you know."

"They said that?"

"Kind of, or at least my dad did. And believe me, if my mother didn't like you, I'd know."

He smiled. "Good to hear. I think I need a little affirmation right about now." He wondered what Ed MacDonald actually said about him, and more importantly, what did Cassie tell them? He didn't dare ask. "I liked them too."

"Grant, I should have said this before, but I think you should be proud of what you did. Losing your job is horrid, but you did what you thought was right."

His arm draped over the sofa back as he looked intently into Cassie's eyes. "Do *you* think what I did was right?"

"You know I do. But I'm kind of ashamed."

"Of me?"

"No, of course not! Of me. I'd never have the courage to do what you did."

"Yes you would." Grant cupped Cassie's chin lightly. "Cassie, you're one of the bravest people I know, not to mention smart and beautiful." He leaned in. The kiss was soft, gentle, just a brush of his lips on hers.

At the sound of the doorbell, Alice barked and jumped off the couch. Cassie followed her to the door. "Reina, Bill. Come in."

Even though he'd met Bill before, the size of the man still startled Grant. He seemed to fill the room. Reina, the tallest woman he knew, only met Bill's shoulder. As they entered, Grant's suspicion of the good news was immediately confirmed when Reina stuck out her left hand to display a diamond ring.

Cassie squealed in delight and grabbed her friend's hand to inspect the ring. The ladies huddled on the couch and began the ritualistic female chatter about romantic gestures, proposals, and weddings.

Bill sat in a nearby chair and obliged Alice's roll-over with a belly-rub.

"You found her favorite spot. She may never leave you." Grant glanced briefly at the remaining chair, the one Cassie referred to as 'Jack's chair', and chose instead to stretch out on the rug a few feet from Alice. His last conversation with Bill had been on the bleachers of the football stadium. Was that really only a few weeks ago?

"You've been a busy man, Bill. Congratulations."

"Thanks. Not as busy as you."

Grant nodded. "Guess you know all about the sit-in and arrest?"

"It's all people are talking about."

Pulling his legs up, Grant clutched his knees, and frowned. "Then you must know about the students?"

"Yes. I even know some of them."

"You do?"

Bill chuckled. "You forget, I grew up here. Pretty tight community."

"Here's the thing, Bill. A lot of the kids are stuck in jail."

"We're aware of that."

"We?"

"NAACP. I've been in touch with them."

Reina jumped into the conversation." Bill interned with the NAACP Legal Defense Team while getting his law degree."

Grant raised his eyebrows. "Really? Are they raising money to make bond?"

"We have to do more than that. They've been charged under Florida statute 877.03: breach of peace and disorderly conduct, just like you."

"I've been charged?"

"They didn't tell you when you made bond?"

"Christ. I should've known." He shook his head. "Breach of peace? The sit-in was peaceful, or started out to be."

"I know, but those are the charges. Only a handful of students have been charged. The others are under legal age. Judge may be sympathetic. They're still kids, still in high school."

Reina scoffed, "Pff- you really think that will make a difference? Bill turned to his fiancé. "Depends on the judge."

Reina shook her head. "Judges here are elected. They know the public sentiment towards 'uppity niggers' – have to put them in their place, make an example of them."

Bill sighed. "Never said it would be easy."

Cassie bit her lip, hesitant to speak. Finally, she asked, "What about Grant? Will his chances be better? I mean he's …"

Reina interrupted. "White. Is that what you were going to say? Look, Cass, there's only one thing people around here despise more than an uppity nigger." She looked directly at Grant. "And that's a Yankee, especially a Damn Yankee."

Confused, Cassie asked, "What's a Damn Yankee?"

Grant answered. "You are, and I'm one too. We both came from the north and then stayed. Okay to visit, but not to live here."

Cassie frowned. "But you've lived here since you were twelve years old."

"Doesn't matter. I qualify. Came down here from north of the Mason-Dixie line."

Bill stood to leave. "I've got some prep work to do before today's meeting, so best go. I'd like you to come if you can, Grant. They'll want to meet you before taking on your case. You free?"

"I'm free as a jailbird."

"Keep that sense of humor. You're going to need it."

CHAPTER THIRTY- SEVEN

Returning to work on Monday, Cassie struggled to focus on the day ahead. During Saturday's trip to the airport, her mother started in once again...*You should come home...It's where you belong...I could use your help with Nana, you know.* Unbidden guilt returned. Was she being unfair to her parents by remaining in Pensacola? It was hard to say goodbye, especially to Jeremy. He cried when she hugged him.

Then there was Grant. She was still processing his arrest, the news about his job, and the kiss on the couch. A part of her wanted to tell him about Earl's letter and her upcoming trip to Baton Rouge. She'd be leaving right after work on Friday. But she'd told no one.

Somehow, she managed to listen to the voice in her head *'Focus on today, Cassie.'* With the school show only days away, the afternoon was spent practicing their songs and painting the appliance boxes Zebbie's father had delivered. After spreading newspapers on the floor, the children got busy with their assigned painting tasks. Lewis and Weldon opened the black paint can for the engine. The three girls, Angie, Ruby, and Sharelle, decided to paint purple polka dots on one box while Trevor and his brother Teddie created a striped pattern of blue and yellow on another. Sitting at a table by himself, Tommy diligently painted cardboard wheels to be attached later.

Cassie watched as Jeff and Dwayne dipped their brushes into a can of red paint for the caboose. They made an interesting pair. Before Dwayne joined the class two weeks ago, Jeff was the smallest member. But seeing this new timid wisp of a child struggle to fit in, Jeff quickly took him under his wing. Bullied himself, Jeff's protective instincts kicked in when he heard some of the children taunt Dwayne with "Hey, nigger, you be darker than a night-coon." For a little guy, Jeff's fists packed a powerful punch. Perplexed by the black children's racist taunts, Cassie got up the courage to ask Reina about it after her second glass of wine one night.

"Cassie, you think centuries of racism haven't infiltrated the black community's consciousness? There's an established societal hierarchy by color; lighter is better. That accounts for all the advertising for skin bleaching and hair straightening products. Some of that is changing with leaders like Huey Newton and Malcolm X."

Cassie asked, "Are you a follower of the Black Panthers?"

Reina threw her head back and laughed. "Me? Good Baptist that I am? Mama would roll over in her grave. Naw, but I've read their books. They're onto something. We need to reclaim our identity. Slavery and racism have stripped us of more than our freedom."

Cassie reflected on that conversation as she watched pale-skinned Jeff and ebony colored Dwayne get ready for dismissal. Dwayne struggled with motor tasks and Jeff was helping to zip up his jacket. As the bus numbers were called, Dwayne lagged behind, hesitant to get in line. Mrs. Hicks had reported she'd been having trouble getting Dwayne to board the bus. Today, Cassie decided to see for herself. She took his hand. "C'mon, Dwayne."

As the line of children moved toward the bus, he hung his head and dragged his feet. She tugged on his arm. "Dwayne, if you don't hurry, you'll miss your bus." She didn't want him to miss his bus. Most households had no phones. With no way to reach the parents, missing the bus meant Cassie driving the child home. Ever since her visit to Weldon's house, Reina had begged Cassie not to make home visits without her, but sometimes it was necessary.

A few feet from the bus, Dwayne stopped. Cassie tried coaxing him again, but he wouldn't move. She knelt in front of the resistant child. "Dwayne, your mother will be worried if you're not on the bus. She doesn't have a phone, does she?"

He shook his head no.

"What's wrong, Dwayne? You can tell me."

His mouth opened, but he didn't speak. Instead, his lips quivered and tears rolled down his cheeks. At the sound of the bus engine starting, she put her arms around him, letting the small shaking body melt into hers. *'What frightens this poor child so?'*

Dwayne remained silent as Cassie drove him home. Swarms of children climbed the playground equipment of the public housing project, The Village. Roads lined with two story concrete buildings stretched out from the central area like spokes of a wheel. Dwayne pointed to the left. "I live at C5, Ma'am."

Cassie had been to other homes in the projects before but not Dwayne's. She'd yet to meet his parents. Parking the car, she inhaled deeply, and looked up hesitantly through the windshield at C5. Dwayne pushed on the car door handle. "Wait, Dwayne. I need to go with you - make sure your mother's home."

Cassie opened the stairwell door and followed Dwayne up to the second-floor apartments.

Dwayne called out, "Mama, I'm home!"

"Dwayne, where you been, child?" A young woman dressed in a maid's black uniform with starched white apron hugged Dwayne as he ran into her arms. She held him tight for a moment before dropping to her knees, grasping his shoulders and scolding, "You scared me, Dwayne. How come's you not on the bus?"

Dwayne hung his head, turned, and pointed to Cassie, standing just outside the doorway. "Teacher brought me home, Mama."

Cassie smiled timidly. "Hello, Mrs. Jackson. I'm Mrs. Cunningham. It's nice to meet you. Sorry for intruding, but I had to bring Dwayne home. He refused to get on the bus."

Taking Dwayne by the hand, she motioned for the teacher to enter. "Please, come in."

The apartment was immaculate, although sparsely furnished. Floral print curtains draped the living room windows and a large framed photo of Dr. Martin Luther King was prominently displayed on the wall.

"Dwayne, go change into your play clothes."

"Yes, Ma'am." Dwayne ran to his bedroom.

"Thank you for bringing my son home. He don't usually cause no trouble, Ma'am. I was worried 'bout him when I seen the other kids comin' off the bus without him."

Cassie nodded. "I'm sure you were. I'm sorry about that, Mrs. Jackson, but Dwayne is having some kind of difficulty on the bus. I tried to find out what it was, but he wouldn't tell me."

The woman uncrossed her arms and said, "I was just about to get myself some coffee. Would you like some?"

"Maybe a glass of water, please."

Dressed in t-shirt and jeans, Dwayne ran back into the living room as his mother returned with the coffee and water.

"Why don't you go out to the playground, Dwayne, while I talk to your teacher?"

"I don't wanna go to the playground. Can't I stay in here with you?"

Mrs. Jackson sighed. "You can play on the porch if you don't want to go to the playground."

Dwayne asked, "Can I take my Matchbox cars out?"

"As long as you bring them in when you're done."

Mrs. Jackson's eyes never left her son as he half-ran down the hall, scooped up his case of mini-cars, then slammed the porch screen door.

Cassie sipped her water, unsure how to begin. "I know you must have panicked when Dwayne didn't get off the bus, but I didn't want to force him."

The mother stared into her coffee cup. "I know. He sometimes gives me a hard time 'bout the bus in the mornin' too, although not if his father is home." She looked up. "Is he doin' all right in school, Ma'am?"

Cassie's fingers rubbed the wet condensation on her glass as she pondered how to respond. "Dwayne is a very sweet boy and tries very hard with all his schoolwork. The written work is a challenge for him, as you probably know, but I bought him some specialized pencils that are easier for him to grip, and lately, he's been doing much better."

The mother smiled. "He likes you. Always says Mrs. Cunningham is nicer than any teacher he's ever had. And lately he's been talking about a boy named Jeff, is it?

256

Cassie smiled. "Yes, he and Jeff have become buddies."

"I'm right pleased about that. Dwayne don't have many friends."

"Mrs. Jackson, I'm not sure about this, but do you think the reason that Dwayne doesn't want to get on the bus is because of the other children?"

"Because they pick on him, you mean?"

"Well, yes. There's been some incidents on the school playground, but fewer since Jeff befriended him. I've tried to stop the teasing, but that's not always possible, and of course, I can't be with him on the bus."

"They done always pick on him. He's so little. Was only four pounds when he was born, did you know that?"

Cassie shook her head.

"I see those kids teasing him, callin' names. He bein' so little, so dark, and wiry. Like his Daddy, that way. And then when his Daddy done left, Dwayne started having nightmares. Thought things would be better when his father returned, but …." Her voice trailed off.

"Returned?"

"From Vietnam. My husband, Raymond, used to be so sweet, just like our little boy. But now, since the war, he done changed. The kids 'round here make fun of him too."

Cassie frowned. "They make fun of his father? Why?"

"Raymond was hurt over there. He…." She stopped mid-sentence at the sound of footsteps on the stairwell, followed by the metal scrape of Matchbox cars being kicked, and the shouts of an angry male voice.

"I told you before, keep those damn cars out of my way!"

Cassie stood as Mrs. Jackson rushed to the door. Dwayne cowered in the porch corner as his father staggered in. Smelling the whiskey on his breath, Cassie froze, trying not to stare at the stump protruding from the man's left cut-off sleeve.

At first, Mr. Jackson seemed not to see her. He held onto the wall with his good hand and stumbled forward.

She looked at Mrs. Jackson, hoping for some signal of what to do. But the woman was too busy clutching Dwayne to her side to note Cassie's plea-full gaze.

Then he spotted her.

In that moment, Cassie knew that she would never forget his angry expression or her immediate fear as he yelled out.

"Who are you?"

Mrs. Jackson stepped in front of him. "This is Dwayne's teacher, Mrs. Cunningham. She brought him home."

He shoved his wife aside, charged towards Cassie, and shouted, "I don't want no honky in my house! You hear me? Get out!" With his arm raised, he lunged forward. But before he could strike, Mrs. Jackson stepped between them. "Raymond, no, please." Cassie saw his rage-filled eyes meet hers but a second. She ran. Dwayne's sobs and the father's angry outburst followed her down the metal stairwell.

***

Her hands shook as she fumbled with the car keys. The ride home was a blur. She hurried to the kitchen, filled a glass with water and gulped. What just happened? This is what it was like to be afraid, truly afraid. She took long deep breaths trying to still her racing heart. She remembered Mrs. Jackson's words...*but now, since the war, he done changed.* She thought of how she longed for her husband's return, the one that never came. Would he too have changed? Sometimes, when she read his letters, something in the words sounded different, almost harsh.

Cassie, I know you keep asking me to tell you more about what I'm doing and what the war is like. It's war, Cassie. What do you want me to say? It's not something I want to write about, not now, anyway. And when I get home, I sure as hell don't want to talk about it. Right now, thinking of you is what keeps me going. So, no more questions about the damn war, okay?

She glanced at the kitchen wall phone, wanting to reach out to someone, someone who would hold and reassure her. But sharing her fears and vulnerabilities was not in her make-up. She needed to reach deep inside and find a way to calm herself. Why couldn't she stop shaking? She startled at the ringing of the phone.

"Hello." Even she could hear the trepidation in her voice.

"Cassie? What's wrong?"

How did Grant know?

"I'll be okay."

"What do you mean, you'll be okay? What happened?"

She tried to answer, but instead released an unintentional whimper.

"I'm coming over." *Click.*

Twenty minutes later, Grant opened the door without knocking and found her still sitting at the kitchen table, staring vacantly. "Tell me what happened, Cassie." He pulled up a chair.

She turned and looked into his concerned dark eyes. "I... I..." she couldn't get it out. Tears came instead as his arms wrapped around her, and she told him in spurts about her close call.

CHAPTER THIRTY-EIGHT

Cassie arrived at the school a full two hours ahead of time. The custodians were setting up rows of chairs in the cafeteria. She'd been told that the community always turned out in large numbers for the annual holiday performance and hoped this was true. Despite her verbal reminders to the children and letters to parents, she was worried that some wouldn't come. She wanted the children to do well, more than well, actually. During their daily practices, Mrs. Washburn often stopped by and Cassie was never sure if her matronly colleague wished them success or failure.

She carried the boxes from the classroom to the back of the stage, lining them up in the correct order. The children's colorful handiwork was evident on each one, with bright purple polka dots on one, blue and yellow stripes on another, and carefully drawn assorted animal figures on the middle box. The engine and wheels were all black, with a handmade cardboard smokestack attached to the front.

Dwayne was the first to arrive, holding tight to his mother's hand. Mrs. Jackson gave Cassie a shy smile that matched that of her son's. Cassie greeted them enthusiastically. "Dwayne, you look so handsome in your dress shirt and tie! Thanks so much for coming Mrs. Jackson. You're early but the other children should be arriving soon."

Mrs. Jackson let go of her son's hand, stepped closer, and whispered, "Mrs. Cunningham, I want to say how sorry I am for …" She hesitated, rubbing her hands against one another.

"No need to apologize, Mrs. Jackson. . . Dwayne did very well today, getting on the bus."

The mother nodded. "I talked to him… Dwayne, I mean. Spoke to the driver this morning too."

"I'm so glad. Seems to have helped."

Just then, Jeff rushed through the door, grinning at the sight of Dwayne.

"Mrs. Jackson, this is Jeff, the friend you've heard so much about."

Cassie noted a brief look of surprise on Mrs. Jackson's face as she looked at the pale freckle-faced boy, already chatting with her son.

"Hi Jeff. I'm Dwayne's mother."

Jeff smiled back sheepishly.

Cassie put her hand on Jeff's shoulder. "Where's your grandfather, Jeff? He brought you, right?"

"Yes, Ma'am. Pappy's g..g..getting seats for my brothers and hisself. He wants to be right up front."

"I guess I'd best go find a seat too." Mrs. Jackson gave Dwayne a brief wave goodbye.

Mrs. Hicks was next to arrive, carrying a white Styrofoam cooler. "Got the dry ice, like I done promised."

"Dry ice?"

"Don't you remember? I told you my idea last week. For the smokestack?"

Cassie frowned. "I don't remember you saying anything about dry ice."

Mrs. Hicks shook her head. "I'm not surprised. You've had your mind someplace else lately. That's for darn sure."

"Are you certain this will work, Mrs. Hicks?"

"Of course. I'll get it set up. Jes' got to keep it closed up until it's our turn. Where are we in the program?"

"Not until the very end."

"Oh, right. My fishing cooler here should keep the block from melting."

The children arrived one by one. Lewis was practically bouncing off the walls with excitement, asking Cassie every two minutes when it was time to go to the cafeteria. Angela sat stoically in her seat, nervously biting her nails, while Ruby fiddled with the pink bow in her freshly washed hair. Cassie had never seen Ruby's hair combed, let alone so clean with a bow! The hallways were abuzz with children arriving. It was almost 6:15, the appointed time for everyone to file into the cafeteria.

At the sight of Grant, the children rushed to the door. By now, they all knew him, having piled into his van for Saturday field trips to the fair, pumpkin farm, and petting zoo. He gently pried Ruby's arms from his waist, easing his way through the clutching children to get to Cassie. "All present and accounted for?"

"All but Tommy."

"Isn't he the one with the solo?"

She nodded. "I reminded him so many times. When Reina and I made the home visit, his mother reassured me that she'd bring him." Cassie thought back to the woman who had met them at the door, pale and haggard, her yellow-tinged fingers holding a cigarette in one hand and a baby bottle in the other. A diaper-clad baby stood in a corner playpen, chewing on the wooden railing. Both she and Reina had expressed their concerns about Tommy's bursts of anger; the chair throwing, the ripped-up papers, the kicking of others, but all the woman kept saying was "He's just like his father." The father, they discovered, had been jailed for assault and battery four months ago.

The children were getting antsy to go on stage. "Everyone, take your seat. Just a few more minutes." She turned to Grant. "I'm not sure what to do. No one else knows Tommy's singing part." She bit her lip. "Maybe his mother is having car trouble. The one in the driveway was quite a junk, and she told me that it sometimes wouldn't start."

"Where does she live? I'll get them."

"Are you sure?"

"It's worth a try. You told me yourself that he's the star of the show."

She wrote down the address and handed the paper to him. "Good luck." She followed him to the door and touched his arm as he turned to go. "Thank you, Grant."

He winked back at her.

***

Grant thought of Cassie as he tried not to speed on the way to Tommy's house. After comforting her a few nights ago, they'd talked just like those days when he was recuperating and she'd bring over those barely edible meals. It felt good to be the one helping her after all she'd done for him.

The small paint-chipped house stood on a patch of dirt and weeds. A tire swing hung from the giant oak tree in front. No car in the driveway. *Maybe the mother is on her way after all.* Then the living room curtain moved and he saw Tommy's face peeking out the window. Grant knocked on the front door and waited. No answer. He knocked again. Finally, the door opened. "Hi Tommy. Is your mother here?"

"Naw. Ma ain't here."

"Mrs. Cunningham sent me here. Did your mother forget about the school performance tonight?"

"She ain't forget. Took my baby brother and went to visit my Pa."

"Oh, I see. You didn't want to go with your mother?"

"Naw. I wanted to go to school but Ma said she didn't have time to take me. Is Teacher real mad at me?"

"No, of course not, Tommy. She just wants you to come, if you can. She told me you're the star of the show."

"Teacher said that?"

"She sure did."

"Can you take me, Mr. Lee?"

"Well, I don't know, Tommy. I expected to take you *with* your mother. Not sure what she'd think of me taking you alone."

"She won't care none. She said she'd be gone a long time. Can you take me, *please*?"

"All right, but we best leave a note for her."

Tommy grinned and opened the door. "C'mon in. I'll look for paper."

Grant stepped inside and followed Tommy to the kitchen. The stench of garbage, soiled diapers, and stale tobacco permeated the air. Dirty dishes filled the sink and cockroaches scurried across the countertops.

Tommy opened a kitchen drawer. "Ma sometimes has paper in here." He pulled out packs of cigarettes, rubber bands, jar tops, and gum sticks before finding an old paper receipt. "Here. You can write on this."

Grant took a pen from his shirt pocket. "I think you should write it."

"But I don't write so good."

"I'll help you." Taking a seat at the kitchen table, Grant spelled each word as Tommy gripped the pen and labored over each letter. "Where do you think your mother's sure to see it?"

"By her cigarettes next to the TV."

Grant set the paper by the pack of Kools, then looked down at the grinning child, suddenly realizing that it wasn't just the garbage that was rank. "When's the last time you took a bath, Tommy?"

The boy shrugged.

"Hmm." He took Tommy's hand and led him to the hall bathroom. Filling the sink with water, he grabbed a washcloth and bar of soap. "Take your shirt off. Let's give you a good scrubbing."

Grant had to repeatedly wash out the cloth as he scrubbed layers of dirt off Tommy's neck and chest. He handed Tommy the wash cloth. "Here, wash the rest of your body, while I go find you some clean clothes... and don't forget to use soap!" After a few minutes of searching Tommy's closet to find something presentable, he returned to the bathroom with a pair of brown pants and a pullover striped shirt. Once Tommy was dressed, he combed the boy's unruly hair, then turned him around to face the mirror. "There, what do you think?"

Tommy grinned at the rosy-faced boy in the mirror.

"Now, better get moving. We're already late."

***

When they arrived, the audience was applauding a performance while Cassie's class prepared to climb the stage steps. As Grant walked up the side aisle and positioned Tommy at the end of the line, Cassie beamed in relief and mouthed a silent 'Thank you.' Smiling at Tommy, she reached into a bag and handed him a black and white striped engineer's hat. "This is for you. I'm so glad that you're here and that everyone will get to hear your wonderful voice." She gave him a quick squeeze before leading the children onto the stage.

The children paired up in the boxes as they'd rehearsed, with Tommy standing in the engine. Cassie took her place on the side stage. When the curtain rose, the children's eyes widened at the sight of the large audience. For a moment, she feared the children might freeze, but then Tommy's voice rang out loud and clear.

I've Been Working on the Railroad

All the live long day.

I've been working on the railroad

Just to pass the time away

Don't you hear the whistle blowin'

Rise up so early in the morn

Can't you hear the captain shouting

Dinah, blow your horn.

The last line was the cue for the other children to join in the chorus. There was brief silence before Cassie whispered from the side. "Sing, children!" Slowly, the other children's voices joined Tommy's in the chorus. Cassie beamed with pride. Just one more train song. She saw the children all look over at her, and she signaled for them to begin. Again, the voices rose,

Down by the station

Early in the morning

See the little pufferbellies

All in a row.

Mrs. Hicks was on the other side of the stage. At the cue of 'pufferbellies' she crept behind the engine box, and lifted the cooler lid. Her plan was to lift and close the lid to create the smoky 'pufferbellies'. As the first puff of smoke rose the audience gasped in appreciation. The children continued to sing.

See the station master

Turn the little handle

Chug, chug, puff, puff

Off we go.

Another puff of smoke, and then another. Mrs. Hicks coughed as she inhaled the steamy air. With the onset of a coughing spasm, she tried to cover her mouth, but as she did so, the cooler lid slipped from her grasp. Blindly, she fumbled for it, only to inadvertently tip over the cooler. Tommy jumped as the block of ice crashed into the engine box. The box wobbled a few seconds and then fell forward, spilling Tommy onto the stage floor. As smoke billowed from the dry ice, the children's voices trailed off. Sputtering and coughing, they clambered out of their boxes. In their eagerness to escape, they tripped and fell or tore at the boxes.

Cassie gasped in horror at the sight of children sprawled on the floor. Soon, the entire stage was engulfed with smoke, and a gray haze began to seep over the audience. Mrs. Hicks finally regained her footing, found the cooler lid, and used it to push the block of dry ice back inside. Panicked, Cassie ran up to the stage where Mrs. Washburn was attempting to close the stage curtain without success. With the dry ice now enclosed, the air began to clear. The children cloistered around their teacher, unsure what to do next. Cassie looked them over, saw no one injured, and quickly positioned them in a line facing the audience. "Finish the performance, children." Tentatively, they began singing, their clear voices growing stronger as they completed the last verse, and then glanced at their teacher behind the curtain, who whispered, "Take your bows, children."

Hesitantly, the children bowed, just as they had rehearsed. The audience stood, cheered, and applauded. Some whistled and yelled *Bravo*. Smiles crept over the children's faces. But no one beamed more than Cassie.

CHAPTER THIRTY- NINE

With the children tired and exhilarated from last night's school performance, Friday was a calm day. Given the dry ice fiasco, Cassie expected an angry Mrs. Washburn to storm into the room at any moment. Exhausted herself from the evening, she was not in the mood for any attacks. She would counter attack, if necessary. But Mrs. W never came. At the end of the day, Cassie expressed her surprise to Mrs. Hicks.

"Don't you worry 'bout it none, Cassie. Spoke with Maisie already."

"Maisie?"

"Mrs. Washburn."

"I didn't know you two were on a first-name basis."

"Maisie and I go way back. Her brother done work on my uncle's farm long time ago. When I seen her gettin' into her usual fit over the 'incident' last night, I told her it was all my fault, and don't she dare blame those poor children. Reminded her that she kind of owes me one. That cooled her down some."

Cassie's eyebrows raised. "She owes you one?"

"Well, not me, really. Her brother got hisself in some trouble back in '57, I think it was. KKK was ready to lynch him. Woulda' done it too, but my uncle stopped them. My family never threw in with them sheet-heads, especially my uncle. He always called them a bunch of no-good cowards."

Cassie's jaw dropped as she fell back into her desk chair. "Oh my God, Mrs. Washburn's brother was almost lynched? Why?"

"Who knows? They never needed much of a reason. After he stopped the lynching, my uncle got her brother a job at some warehouse up north. Had to get him outta here fast, or they'd try again, fo' sure. You all right? You look as white as a Kluxer sheet yourself."

Cassie tried to process this new information. She'd read about these things, but it hadn't seemed real before. When she and Jack first drove down to Florida, they were shocked by the monstrous billboard on the side of Rte. 3 as they crossed into North Carolina. An image of a white robed Klansman holding a flaming torch astride a rearing horse. Beneath the image were the words, *Welcome to Ku Klux Klan country. We fight Integration, Communism, and Catholicism.* She and Jack rode on in silence.

And now, that same sense of shock gripped her. She tried to imagine a lynching happening to someone she loved. She shook her head. "It's just so awful to think about -that happening to Mrs. Washburn's brother. God, 1957 - That was only fifteen years ago."

"Yeah, happened more than most want to talk about, that's fo' sure." Mrs. Hicks frowned. "Ya'all right? Want me to stay with you for a bit?"

"No, no. You go on home. I'm fine."

Mrs. Hicks turned at the door. "I know I done told you this already, but I'm real sorry about last night. Thought the dry ice would add that 'special touch'."

Cassie laughed. "Well, it was a special touch, all right. I'm sure we'll laugh about it down the way."

Mrs. Hicks smiled. "I suppose so. You take care now. See you on Monday."

The weekend she'd been both anxiously awaiting and dreading lay before her. She needed to hurry home to pack for her trip to Baton Rouge. Instead, she remained seated, still shaken by Mrs. Hicks story. Finally, she pushed back her desk chair, grabbed her purse, and stepped outside. Before going to her car, she strolled to a nearby live oak tree, where she often took the children for outdoor reading time. Its significant circumference would indicate a tree well over a hundred years, maybe even two hundred. AdaMae had once taught her how to gauge the age of these majestic trees. But she'd forgotten exactly how to do so. She leaned against the sturdy trunk, inhaling the earthy smell of its bark and hanging Spanish moss. Looking up, she envisioned a noose hanging over the tree's stretched out limb. She shuddered. Had this tree ever witnessed such horror? As she stepped away, her foot rubbed against something. Small honey-colored mushrooms had popped up at the base of the tree. Honey fungus. That's what AdaMae had called it. Pretty, but if not eradicated, potentially deadly to the tree. It was like that here, this land of such beauty and charm. An ugly fungus, one of hatred and racism, had taken root long ago. Would it ever be eradicated or would this place be strangled by its poison?

At times, it seemed she'd traveled to a different country and was experiencing a foreign culture. Was this still America? The American flag could be seen flying in front of schools, banks, and ballparks, just like back home. The difference was that the

Confederate flag flew alongside it, with many residences flying only the latter. AdaMae phrased it best. "Cassie, you're a Yankee girl in Dixie, you got a lot to learn."

A sudden breeze blew a wisp of Spanish moss across her face. As she brushed it aside, she spotted the two school's flags flapping in front of the school building flap: one American and one Confederate.

CHAPTER FORTY

She hadn't taken a road trip by herself since college days. Her plan was to arrive in Baton Rouge Friday evening and find a cheap motel for the night before driving to Earl's house Saturday morning. She purchased maps for Alabama, Mississippi, and Louisiana, but hoped that following the road signs would be sufficient. It would be Interstate 10 most of the way.

No one knew of her trip. She should be back in time to make the weekly Sunday evening phone call to her parents, yet was a little uneasy leaving without telling anyone where she was. More than once, she'd been tempted to tell someone, AdaMae or Grant, or perhaps Reina, but she didn't know how to tell them about the letter, about what she was seeking or expecting. She didn't know herself.

Driving out of Pensacola, the road became less traveled. Scrub pines dotted the sparse landscape. The occasional businesses alongside the road; One Spot Gas and Grub, Auntie Jane's Antiques, Tried and Treasured Thrift Shop. Periodically, a ramshackle home appeared, its front yards littered with old appliances and assorted household furniture. She'd seen this before in the Southern countryside, and often wondered if there was any furniture left inside. As she drove south of Cantonment, the noxious smell emanating from the International Paper Mill made her gag. Even though the paper mill was a few miles north, thick white smoke blanketed the sky. At times, it was like a white-out from a Northern blizzard. She could barely see the road ahead.

When she crossed into Alabama a large Welcome sign with a picture of George Wallace greeted her. The popular Governor, who'd made his reputation by fighting integration, was a household name in both Alabama and the panhandle of Florida. His 1968 presidential campaign for the Democratic nomination was successful in many of the Southern states, including Florida, where he won every single county. Cassie had voted for the first black female candidate ever to run for President, Shirley Chisholm. Neither Chisholm nor Wallace won the nomination. That honor went to George McGovern, who lost to Nixon by a landslide.

Alabama scenery was much like northern Florida, and she grew bored with its flatness and scrappy pines. She fiddled with the car radio's dial, but as usual, found only country music. The growling of her stomach was a reminder that she'd not eaten in hours. Hoping to find food and gas, she turned off at the next exit. Relieved to see the familiar yellow and red Stuckey's sign, she pulled into the adjoining Texaco station for a fill-up. Bells jingled as she opened Stuckey's front door and inhaled the sweet aroma of pecans, honey, and other delectables. Grabbing two pecan logs, she walked up to the counter. A portly man sporting a Nascar cap and t-shirt eased off his stool. He rang up the total for the gas and pecan logs. "Will that be all, Ma'am?"

Cassie spotted the nearby cooler, reached in and grabbed an orange Fanta. "Add this please." She tapped on the counter, spying the various folded roadmaps displayed. "How's the traffic going through Mobile this time of day? Should I expect any delays?"

"Y'all going into the city?"

She nodded.

He shook his head. "Ain't no good time these days, Ma'am. They're building a new tunnel, George Wallace Tunnel. Was supposed to already be open but you know how gov'ment works. Costing a mint too."

"So, what's my route?"

"You gotta take US 90, go through the Bankhead Tunnel, and then onto the Causeway. It's always a mess, but bein' Friday, it'll be a damn mess."

The Stuckey's cashier was right. Backup at the tunnel meant thirty minutes of sitting still in traffic. When she finally got onto the Causeway going over Mobile Bay, traffic began to move but at a crawl. The drive had taken longer than expected. As Cassie reached the end of the bridge, the coral sun set like a giant conch shell over the USS Alabama, the WWII decommissioned battleship anchored in the bay. Jack had wanted to visit it someday, and Cassie suggested combining it with a trip to Bellingrath Gardens, just south of Mobile. She'd heard about the acres of azaleas, rhododendrons, and oleander bushes. They never made the trip. So much of what they had planned together never happened.

Why was she letting melancholy slip in? Tomorrow, when she met Earl, what would he share about her husband that she didn't already know? Why had he survived when Jack had not? Questions circled through her mind like a revolving door as she drove into the night, finally stopping at a Motel 6 just outside Baton Rouge.

***

At the front desk, Cassie asked for a Baton Rouge city map and a nearby breakfast place. The clerk directed her to a gas station and Krispy Kreme donut shop up the street. She stopped at both. Spreading the city map on the donut shop table, she smoothed out its creases as she licked the thick glaze on her donut. Its syrupy sweetness made her think of Grant and his proclaimed sweet tooth. She found herself smiling at the thought of him and briefly wished he were here.

Pulling a pen from her purse, she traced the route to Earl's street. Still on the outskirts of the city, it would take a half hour or more to get there. She wished she could call, but he had no phone. Finishing her coffee and donut, she went to the rest room before getting back in the car. The scratched mirror above the sink reflected an image of a pale face with darkened circles under the eyes. She pinched her cheeks for color, applied some lipstick, and said, "Be strong, girl. Whatever is coming, be strong."

She pulled up in front of 92 Beauregard St. a small white house with neatly trimmed hedges. Latticed slats framed the front porch. Six-foot oleander bushes stood like pink sentries at the corners. It was only 9:15 in the morning; no sign of life inside. Perhaps he was still sleeping. She took a deep breath, exhaled slowly, and started to step from the car, but then paused, immobilized. Why was she wavering? She felt a soft tickle. A tabby, softly mewing, rubbed against her ankle, raised a paw and scratched her pants leg. The feline's eyes were ice blue, like Jack's eyes. Cassie shivered. *It's time.* She got out, shut the car door, and started up the brick walkway. With each step, her heart beat faster. As she stood on the front step and raised her fist to knock, the front door opened. She could not make out his face in the shadows, but was comforted by the welcoming tone of voice.

"You're Cassie? Please come in. I've been expecting you."

She stepped inside and stood hesitantly in the dark front foyer.

"I just put on a fresh pot of coffee. Why don't you join me?"

She followed Earl, who walked with a limp, down the hall and into the kitchen. With the basic appliances, mini-counter, and one cupboard, it accommodated two people at best. A table and two chairs set against the wall. An open window overlooked a patch of grass and small vegetable garden.

Cassie watched Earl pour two cups of coffee, take a can of evaporated milk from the refrigerator and two spoons from a drawer. She noted the taut mottled skin on the left arm and both hands. One finger was missing and another was stubbed at the knuckle. She recalled his letter, which spoke of burns, and saw that the left side of his face was scarred and discolored. Of average height in a sleeveless t-shirt and army fatigue pants, his upper body was pure muscle, what her father would have called a 'bull-dog build.'

"I'm glad you were able to make the trip. Right now, I can only handle short drives. Still got shrapnel in my hip, and it gets to aching if I sit too long."

"Do you have a lot of pain?" Cassie poured milk into her coffee and took a sip.

"Enough." He took the seat across from her and blew on the hot black coffee. "My sister made some coffee cake. Want some?"

She waved her hand. "No, that's fine."

"Are you sure? She made it special for you."

Cassie smiled. "Maybe a small piece."

He reached for the cake platter and sliced a wedge. "She's a fine cook, my sister. Sorry you couldn't meet her. She's working today. Cleans houses every day 'cept Sunday."

"Oh, so you don't live alone, then?"

"No, Ma'am. Been living here with Junie ever since I got back from 'Nam. Not sure what I'd a done without her, what with all my surgeries and doctor visits."

"I wish I'd have known, Earl. Maybe I could have helped somehow."

"Nice of you to say, Ma'am. But you had your own problems, losing Jack and all. Kind of surprised you got my letter. Was sure you'd have gone back to Connecticut. Sounded like that's where Jack hoped to return eventually."

"Yes, some day. But we bought a home in Pensacola, and I got a teaching job, but I imagine Jack told you all that." She looked into his eyes, wishing he could telepathically share what he knew but knowing words were necessary. "Earl, they never told me how Jack died. I mean I know about the crash. That's why I was shocked to get your letter. Thought everyone had perished." She saw his jaw tighten as he gripped his coffee mug.

"But you want to know more, don't you?"

She pressed her lips together and nodded, feeling hot tears welling up.

His barrel chest swelled as he took a deep breath and began to tell the story, the deep timber of his voice so compelling in narration that Cassie was transported in time. She could hear the voices, see her Jack.

I'm just outside the alert shack when the Company Commander's voice comes over the compound. Pop my head in the door to tell Jack, "Get the lead out! Dustoff orders!"

He's on his bunk, scribbling on a pad, writing to you, no doubt.

"Yeah. Be there in a minute."

Shows up as I'm removing the tie-down strap from the main rotor-blade and securing the cargo door. He climbs into the pilot's seat and starts going over the panel instruments. Paul, our co-pilot, arrives, hands out the bulletproof vests, and tosses in the M-16's. The new medic, Carlos, is loading up the stretchers.

Jack yells over to me, "What's the situation report from the evac zone?"

"Light casualties so far, Up in the Central Highlands, tight LZ."

"How tight? Do we need the hoist?"

"Don't know. Carlos and I will load it just in case."

"Enemy sighting?"

"In the area, but no official force evaluation."

Our bird, Gigi, lifts into the humid air. It's rainy season, hot and muggy. My flight suit's already damp. There are only 2 Hueys in the slick. We lead the way, flying just over the treetops, following the coordinates radioed in. The smell of gunpowder is everywhere but the firing is intermittent, and we can't discern the NVA's location. We see our guys huddled in a thicket. The medic is signaling us. Jack points to an opening just east of him. I hear Paul shout something about not enough of a clearing, but Jack ignores him, moves our bird in for the landing, and sets it down perfectly. I undo my monkey strap, jump out with Carlos, and run toward the wounded. With the medic's help, we load the three worst on stretchers while the other three climb aboard. We had our max. The other Huey hovers not far behind, still above the trees, ready to land. Jack throws some juice in the bird and we depart with a backward takeoff and pedal turn to the right to avoid the enemy fire coming from the left. As Gigi rises, I say a quick prayer that the second Huey manages to land.

Carlos is wrapping a tourniquet on one guy's leg. I grab one of the M-16's to return enemy fire, hoping to give the second Huey some cover as it lands. I kneel in a puddle of blood by the door and fire my weapon. Through the treetops, I can see the medic below, frantically loading the rest of the wounded. Carlos yells for me to unwrap a unit of blood and set it up for the guy with a plugged-up bullet hole in his abdomen. I ask the guy his name, but he just stares blankly ahead.

A burst of enemy fire hits the fuselage. Jack swerves our chopper further right while I pick up my M-16 to give cover for the second Huey, now lifting from the ground. I see it rise twenty, thirty, maybe fifty feet. But the rounds come fast, one constant barrage of fire after another. The Huey swings to the right, but suddenly begins to lose lift. It's spinning in circles, and we realize she's been hit. We hover high above, staying out of range, and watch as the bird hits the ground, falling off to one side. Paul radios in our sitrep, asking for another Dustoff.

Jack holds our position, waiting for a response. He calls to Paul, "What they'd say?"

"Negative. Not for at least another hour or more."

"Hour or more? Shit!" He yells back at me. "Earl, can you make out the situation down there?"

I grip the door frame, and lean out. "It's down but in one piece. Some wounded on the ground. Medic is waving at us."

"And the NVA?"

"Still firing, but less."

"Can you make out the enemy location?"

"Negative."

"Carlos, can our wounded hold on for another twenty minutes?"

Carlos glances at the listless men. "I think so, sir."

I knew those men on the ground wouldn't last another hour. Jack knew it too. They would die from their wounds or be captured. Jack yells from the cockpit.

"We're going down, Earl. Pass Paul one of those M-16's. Both of you get ready to fire."

He takes us down fast. When we're a few feet from the ground, I jump out, crouch under the blades, and run toward the downed bird. Its rotor blades are still spinning, and I wince as bits of dirt and twigs slap my face. I spot the medic lying on the ground, a bone protruding from his left arm. I'm surprised he's still conscious. I hear moans from inside the mangled chopper. Ducking inside, I see a jumble of bloodied bodies. The pilot's head presses against the shattered cockpit window. Dark red blood oozes from the hole in his temple. I turn away and Paul and I look for life, load them on our chopper.

The enemy fire sounds closer now. We shove them in. A Huey holds 6-8 men, depending on size. We now have eleven wounded and our crew. I look at each of them as Jack revs the motor for lift-off. None of them are light-weights. I know the engine like the back of my hand. The payload is 2200 pounds max. I hear the 'whup-whup' of the blades and hold my breath. The bird rocks from side to side. Jack is giving it all its got. I know we won't make it.

"Lower it, Jack. I'm getting out."

"What?"

"Put this damn bird down. You've got a chance without me."

"You're crazy!" He torques the engine again, but the chopper doesn't rise.

I point to the ground and glare at him. "Damn it Jack. No way in hell we'll make it unless we lighten the load. Down, now!"

He nods. I grab my rifle and when the chopper lowers within a few feet of the ground, I jump out the door and look up to see our bird lift slowly. I smile, sure it will make it with less poundage. Jack is the best there is.

Cassie wasn't aware of her shallow breathing, tightness of chest, or fingernails cutting into the palms of her hands. She didn't know what was coming, and yet she did.

Earl noted her puddled tears, clenched brow. "Are you sure you want to hear the rest?"

She gulped, bit her lip, and nodded.

Earl closed his eyes, took a deep breath, and retreated back to Vietnam.

All I want to see is Gigi rise into the sky and clear those trees, be home free. I make the sign of the cross and watch her rise. She dips and rocks like a wild bronco at first. But then, ... I see her rise... just enough. Her tail scrapes the trees and I hold my breath. ... exhaling, as she keeps on rising. I say a silent prayer - Jack will bring her home!

But then I hear that sound, 'BOOM –BOOM.'. I see the white smoke. An RPG has hit the tail rotor blade. Gigi pitches forward, violently yawing in the sky. I run fast through the thickets. I don't' know how far I run or how long it takes. "Please God, Please God" I say it over and over. I hear the distant sputter as it descends. Then I see it...our bird...crumpled... branches all around. I draw closer - see Jack slumped forward in the cockpit, unmoving. Is he dead or alive? Is anyone alive? I rush forward, my hand just inches away. Inches! Then the fireball erupts, throws me back. I try again to get to him, but there's too much heat, too much fire. I tried... I tried...

Dropping his head, Earl slid his fingers over his head.

Cassie saw his shoulders shake and realized that he was crying. Why wasn't she crying too? Instead, she sat staring into the distance, unconsciously twisting her wedding ring.

CHAPTER FORTY-ONE

They sat in the living room, each holding a glass of whiskey. Cassie took a sip of hers. "I don't think I've ever drank hard liquor this early in the morning."

"There are times it's necessary."

Cassie nodded and swirled the ice with her finger. She wondered how often whiskey had been necessary for Earl these past few months. "I know now how you got the burns, but your leg?"

He patted his right leg. "That came later, when I was shot."

"Shot?"

"I wasn't the only one that made it to the crash site. NVA arrived moments after. Took a round in the hip and leg. Some shrapnel's still in there."

"How'd you get away?"

"When I got hit, I fell backward, tumbled into a ravine."

"And that stopped them?"

"Naw, but I spotted this overhang and rolled under it. Covered with mud, I lie still, barely breathing. They were looking for me. I could hear them, just a few feet away. *Nhin, nhin.* They were telling each other to keep on looking. Then the rains came, sheets of it, like a wall of water. After awhile, they stopped looking, but I knew they'd be back."

"So you started walking out?"

He shook his head. "Negative. I couldn't walk. My leg had stiffened up. But the rain let up during the night, and at first light, I heard one of our birds overhead and flagged it down."

"And then?"

Earl finished his whiskey before answering. "Now—I live with the memories and this." He touched his face and patted his leg, before standing up. "I'm getting a refill. You want one?"

"No, thank you."

Cassie watched him leave the room. Is this what she came for? To hear how Jack died, to meet the man who saw it? Did it make his death any more or less real? Jack was not coming back to her, no matter how many letters she wrote. Why *did* she come?

Earl returned with his refill in one hand and an envelope in the other. "Jack made me promise to give this to you if anything happened to him. Told me to give it to you in person."

Cassie slowly opened the envelope. A photo fell onto her lap. It was one he'd taken their last full day together. She was wearing the yellow sundress that he liked so much, and was looking over her shoulder, smiling into the camera. She unfolded the letter inside and read.

My dearest Cassie,

If you are reading this letter, it means that I didn't make it. The war took me, this damn war. I saw a lot of men die, Cass. Too many. For a long time, I was sure that I'd be one of the lucky ones. How could I not be? Look who I had waiting for me. I had one picture of you in the

*cockpit, and this one in my footlocker. Not a day went by
that I didn't look at both of them. Your love DID keep me
alive, inside, anyway, when all I was seeing was death.
I want you to know that. You kept me believing that the
world was still a good place because you were in it.*

*I know you, Cass. You'll keep me alive in your heart
and in your memory, but Cassie, please don't hang on too
long. Remember me but don't just love a ghost. If you want
to honor me, then live! Open that big heart of yours and
love again. Just make sure it's for someone who deserves
you! Get married. Have babies. Be happy, and know that
loving you was the best thing I ever did.*

Always,

Jack

CHAPTER FORTY-TWO

He'd expected her to call, wanted her to call. Stopped by her place on Friday evening, but she wasn't home. Where was she? She hadn't called to talk about the play, as he'd hoped. And then there was the visit to Tommy's house. The poor kid was living in a rat's nest with a negligent mother. He should probably call Reina about Tommy. Then he could ask after Cassie. Maybe she'd spent the night at Reina's. He dialed her number.

"Reina. It's Grant."

"Hi Grant."

He caught the hesitancy. *Was Cassie there? Had they talked about him?*

"I suspect you're calling about the article in the paper. Don't know how they got that information. Believe me, it wasn't Bill who gave it to them."

"What article?"

"You don't know? Do you get the *Journal*?"

"Yeah, it should be on my front lawn right now. I sleep in on Saturdays."

"You'd best read it first, Grant. I think Bill plans to call you."

"Ok. I'll do that."

Reina waited a moment before asking, "If it wasn't about the article, what did you call about?"

"Huh? Oh yeah, right. It can wait. No, wait a minute. Is Cassie there?"

"Cassie? No. I haven't seen her since Thursday, the night of the play. Isn't she home?"

"Aw, probably now. Just checking. Thanks."

Alice barked as he stepped onto the lawn. She was ready to be fed. He patted her, picked up the newspaper, and went into the house. Filling the dog dish, he poured a cup of coffee and unfolded the paper, quickly perusing the front- page headlines: '*Giant Alabama Sinkhole Collapses*'; '*FBI Watergate Investigation Continues*'. No mention of Escambia High School. He turned the page. There it was. '*Escambia High Teacher Colludes with NAACP*'.

Colludes? What in the world? He sat at the kitchen table and spread the paper out to read the full article. First, there was the explanation of the lawsuit brought by the NAACP, giving Bill's name as the legal representative for the plaintiffs. In the second paragraph the background of the walkout, subsequent suspensions, and sit-in protest, including his involvement. Then came the kicker.

In response to inquiries about Mr. Lee, two faculty members commented on their colleague's involvement in the school sit-in. Amy Nilehouse, Home Economics Teacher at the high school, said, "I wasn't surprised at Mr. Lee's participation. He has the reputation of being a troublemaker. It's all so very sad." Coach Higgins, who has been Escambia High's head football coach for eighteen years, also spoke of Lee. "There's no doubt in my mind that Lee was the instigator of the whole thing. The colored kids listen to him. Our school was doing just fine until he stirred things up. I think the NAACP put him up to it from the very beginning. We all know that it's those damn Yankees coming down here that cause all the trouble. Our football team was on track for the state championship before this all happened."

No doubt his grandmother and Cassie had both read the paper by now. He was livid. When the phone rang, he hoped it was Cassie. It was Bill.

"Grant, I just spoke with Reina. Have you read the paper yet?"

"Yeah. What the hell, Bill? I thought you promised to keep my name out of this until the preliminary hearings at least."

"I'm not their source, Grant. I'll talk with the other lawyers and folks at NAACP headquarters. Maybe one of them spilled the beans, but I doubt it. Did you tell anyone else about working with us on this?"

"Not that I recollect."

***

Sitting up in bed, Amy grabbed her emerald silk blouse from the floor and slipped it on. She looked over her shoulder. Mel Higgins lay sprawled across the sheets naked and snoring. She was beginning to have regrets about this hook-up. Mel wasn't bad looking and had muscles in all the right places, but his love-making was of the slam-bam-thank you-ma'am variety and a little rough, as the bruises on her arm evidenced. She attributed it to his anger over the student suspensions, which he blamed on Grant. Thank goodness he was unaware of their brief dating past. She sighed, remembering Grant's gentle touch and tender kisses. But chasing the handsome history teacher hadn't gone anywhere.

Mel awoke and gripped the back of her neck. "Where you goin'? You're not leaving already, are you?"

She tried to shake him off, but his hand slid into Amy's thick black hair, pulling her backward. He leaned over, pressed his lips on hers, forcing her mouth open with his tongue. It tasted of stale gin. She wiggled free. "Not now. I'm not in the mood."

"Not in the mood? That wasn't the case last night."

"Well, that was last night. This is this morning. I've got to get going." She stood up and finished buttoning her blouse.

"What's so important?"

"I've got things to do, that's all."

"Like what? It's Saturday. I thought we'd spend the morning together at least. No game this weekend and practice isn't until two. C'mon, I bet your cunt tastes even better in the morning." He was off the bed now, coming toward her.

Why was she hesitating? He was right about last night. She was eager enough. But that was before things got rough, before he spouted off about Grant. It made her uneasy. Not sure why. After all, wasn't she mad at Grant too? He was stupid to get involved in that sit-in. When she'd heard about his arrest, she could have slapped him. Mel said that someone should teach him a lesson. Maybe he was right.

He pressed against her, already excited. She tried to pull away. "C'mon, baby. You don't want to leave."

How was she going to play this? She'd been with rough men before. Resistance didn't usually end well. She needed to distract him. Do or say something to dampen his mood. "I promised my nephew I'd help him with his college applications today."

"Your nephew? You mean Fred?"

"Yeah."

Mel snorted. "Fred's not going to college."

"If you'd given him more of a chance on the team, maybe he could have gotten a football scholarship."

"My job is to put the best out on the field. Leroy was the best. I may hate the nigger kid's guts off the field, but I want that championship. I told Fred I'd give him another shot. Did he tell you that?"

"You did? But it's too late for scholarship offers."

"Who says? I've got some pull you know."

"You mean you'd help him get a scholarship?"

"Depends. You stayin' or goin'?"

She unbuttoned her blouse.

Mel grinned as his hand cupped her bottom. He wouldn't tell her that the favor he'd be asking was not from her, but from Fred.

CHAPTER FORTY- THREE

The clock chiming two awakened her. Cassie opened her eyes, disoriented. Where was she? She was lying on a faded slipcovered couch. The curtains were pulled in the sparsely furnished living room. Earl sat in the corner chair, an empty whiskey bottle on the end table. His head leaned against the wingback, mouth open, emitting a raspy snore.

Then it came back to her, all of it. What happened to Jack, what happened to Earl. She had listened. She'd read Jack's letter, and finally she had cried. She cried for Jack, for all he was to her, and what might have been. She cried for the loss of him, for the tragedy of war, and she took that second glass of whiskey, Earl's only way to comfort. How long had she been asleep? She sat up and immediately grabbed her head, feeling a dull throb. She found her way back into the kitchen, rummaged for the coffee, and began a fresh pot. Waiting for the percolation, she took a seat at the table and pulled Jack's letter from her pocket to reread. When did he write the letter? There was no date. Certainly, it was after he'd seen death, plenty of it, enough to know he might not make it. And yet he thought of her and her future. Wanted her to be happy. Quiet tears rolled down her cheeks. He was saying goodbye, but he was also giving her permission to live, to love again. But how could there ever be another Jack? *Open that big heart of yours and love again. Just make sure it's for someone who deserves you.* Suddenly, Grant's face flashed before her. Jack would approve. It didn't matter that Grant was not a soldier or that he didn't support the war. He was a man of quiet courage, integrity and kindness, a man who she suspected was falling in love with her. Was she in love with him? She folded the letter and put it back into her pocket. Some questions would have to wait.

Earl was awake when she came back into the living room carrying two cups of coffee. "How do you take your coffee?"

He straightened in the chair. "You made coffee?"

"I thought we could both use it. How do you like yours?"

"Black." He reached for the cup she offered. "Thanks. I should be waiting on you."

"You have already." She sat back on the couch and took the first sip, and then another, letting the caffeine ease her headache. Unsure what to say, she gazed at Earl and stammered, "I don't know how to thank you."

"Thank me? For what?"

"For telling me his story, your story. For the letter, and for... well, this may seem strange, but for giving me Jack back, the Jack I knew."

"But he's gone, Cassie."

"Not in here." She pointed to her heart. "And he's told me what I must do. I have to move on. It's what he would want. I should have known that. But until I read that letter, I didn't. In many ways I think I was stuck. I couldn't get past the grief."

He nodded.

"You feel it too, don't you?"

"Being stuck, you mean? Sure. My sister tells me every day that I have to stop blaming myself, let it go, move on. I know she's right, but somehow, ... I don't know." His voice rose. "I was right there. I saw him, ...so close. If I'd been there just a few minutes sooner."

She set down the coffee cup, walked across the room, and squatted next to his chair. She rubbed his arm. "Survivor's guilt. I've felt that too. Not like you, of course. I wasn't there when he died. Jack would have wanted you to move on too, Earl. You know that."

He squeezed her hand and nodded. "I suppose. I wish I could have gotten the letter to you sooner. Should have."

She squeezed back. "No. I probably wasn't ready yet, ... to really hear, to understand his words. I am now."

"Maybe I am too. When Junie gets home, I think I'll tell her that I'll go to AA, like she's been pushing me to do."

Cassie smiled. "I think that would be a good start, Earl."

***

It was dark when she got back on the road. Earl had begged her to stay for supper. He wanted her to meet Junie, who didn't get home from work until 5, yet still was able to create a Southern perfection of collards with ham hocks, macaroni and cheese, and candied sweet potato. Cassie left stuffed and despite her earlier nap, was already drowsy. She'd have to stop for coffee periodically to make the long drive home.

Emotionally spent, she found it difficult to focus on the road signs, almost missing an exit. Strangely, despite the initial horror of hearing the details of Jack's helicopter crash, her mind no longer fixated on the story of his death.

Jack's penned words reverberated in her mind–... *love again. Get married. Have babies...*

CHAPTER FORTY- FOUR

Grant grabbed a jacket from the hook by the door, whistled for Alice, and stepped onto the back porch. A cold front had pushed through earlier and now, a crisp evening breeze pushed lead-gray clouds across a sky streaked with pink. Zipping up his jacket, he walked briskly through the yard and into the woods. He'd bought his house in part for the surrounding expansive pine forest. Solitude suited him. Grams had begun to chide him for his bachelor ways, accusing him of being too picky when it came to female companionship. There had been a few ladies in his life, although none for too long. Amy was the last, but the attraction was purely physical, and he'd quickly regretted it. Now, at age twenty-eight, he wanted more than a lustful body in his bed. Lately, he found that he couldn't stop thinking of Cassie. Did that mean he was in love? Whenever he arrived home, he wished she were there. When he was at school, he was constantly distracted with thoughts of her. And when they were together, he wanted her to never leave. *Why couldn't she be free?* She wasn't. He was increasingly aware of that. Her heart still belonged to Jack. Would the loss of him forever haunt her? Could she love again? Should he give up trying?

He thrust his hands into his pockets, shuffling the carpet of pine needles beneath his feet. Hoping the cold front had killed all the chiggers, he plodded through the underbrush and shifted his thoughts from Cassie to today's earlier meeting, where Bill had shared the latest.

The hearing was scheduled for Dec. 20th. Grant faced charges of disorderly conduct and breach of peace. At eighteen, LeRoy would be charged as an adult. Most of the other students were juveniles and would not face criminal charges. There would, however, be school disciplinary action. He asked about Vice-principal Mead and the students who attacked the protesters, only to find out that no charges were filed against them. The NAACP would be providing legal guidance with Bill and another lead attorney. Grant listened as Bill patiently explained the legal jargon for the upcoming fight.

"It won't be easy, Grant."

"I never thought it would be. But do you think we have a chance?"

"A chance, yes, although the community is biased against us."

Grant exhaled. "I'm aware of that." He saw Bill shift in the chair, lean forward, and frown. "What? Is there something more?"

"I'm concerned about your safety."

"My safety? Why?"

"Shots were fired at Leroy's house yesterday."

"Oh my God! Is he okay?"

"No one was hurt, fortunately. But that's not all. I've been receiving threatening phone calls and letters. Your name was mentioned in a couple of the calls. You haven't got any such mail or calls?"

Grant shook his head. "My phone number is unlisted. And not too many people know where I live."

"Well, just letting you know. Best stay aware. It's only going to get uglier, I'm afraid."

"Do you own a gun?"

"A gun? God, no."

Bill raised an eyebrow. "A southern boy like you without a gun? That's a first."

"I'm a pacifist."

"Just be alert is all I'm saying."

It wasn't the first time Grant heard such remarks. Friends had mocked him for his pacifism and refusal to own or shoot a gun. Even Grams told him that he needed a gun. She had one in her bedroom drawer and said she knew how to use it. He finally got her to at least put a lock on the drawer. His mother would have approved of his reluctance to give in to social pressure. Her lessons on non-violence had taken root in him as a boy. To use a gun would be defiling her memory. It had taken a long time to get over his grief and anger at losing his parents. But the memories, the lessons they'd tried to instill, were very much a part of him.

He often thought of how different his life would have been if his parents hadn't died. Manhattan was worlds apart from Pensacola. Would he have embraced the academic and cultural world of his mother? Or would he have rejected it in adolescent rebellion? At twelve, he had begun to be rebellious, choosing the neighborhood basketball court over museums visits with his mom.

Alice bounded ahead, barking at squirrels and any other creatures she encountered. Grant paid her little mind. He saw the first star appear in the darkening sky and decided he'd best turn back. As he whistled for Alice, he once more thought of Cassie.

She hadn't answered her phone in two days. Where could she be? He should take a drive over there.

At the sound of barking in the distance, he walked in that direction. The barking grew louder and more frequent. And there was the distinct sound of chopping. Were those voices he heard as well? Male voices. He could hear them distinctly now.

"Shut up, mutt." More barking. "I said, shut up!"

Through the trees he could make out three figures; one hovering over Alice. He saw the kick, heard a responsive whimper, and immediately shouted "Hey, cut it out! That's my dog." Sprinting as fast as he could, Grant brushed aside low-lying branches and jumped over deadwood. Finding Alice motionless amid the pine needles, he crouched down and stroked the thick mottled fur. The dog lifted her head and whimpered once more.

"Are you okay, girl?" Grant turned to look at the dog's attacker. "What the hell is wrong with you?" .... He stopped and stared. "Fred? Fred Crowley?" The high school student stood above him, dressed in a white robe, axe in hand. Grant didn't hear the footsteps behind him, or the crack of skull when the log struck.

Fred glared at his friend, as Grant slumped to the ground. "Jesus Christ, Howie, you didn't have to hit him so hard!" He kneeled and put his ear to Grant's chest. "He's still breathing."

Howie dropped the log. "Coach said to make sure we weren't seen."

"I know what the coach said! C'mon, you and Duff better finish stripping those pines. We still have to lash them together and get out of here before he comes to. We've got two stops to make, remember?"

Howie and Duff stared at Grant's motionless body. Fred walked to the fallen pine trees, stood one on end, and methodically slashed at the branches. He turned around. "Well? What the hell you waiting for?"

Howie lifted up another tree and began chopping. Duff took a step toward Fred. "Do we have to go to both places? Couldn't we just strike Lee's house?"

Fred scowled in the darkness. "What's your problem, Duff? You sceered?"

"No, it's just I have shop with Childers. He's a good guy. I mean, he's helped me …"

"I don't give a rat's ass about how Childers has helped you. He's a nigger-lover, just like Lee and besides, the coach ain't goin' to keep his promise if we don't finish the job. You want to be back on the team or not? Start chopping. We'll hit Lee's house first, cuz he ain't got no neighbors to see us. By the time we get the cross burning and get over to Childers house way over in Cantonment, it will be well past midnight and everyone in the neighborhood should be asleep."

CHAPTER FORTY- FIVE

Cassie's hands encircled the styrofoam cup. She blew on the coffee before taking a sip. Pressed into the corner of an orange plastic booth, she leaned against the window and closed her eyes. The emotion of the last twenty- four hours along with the long drive was taking a toll. Fortunately, the coffee shop was empty except for the clerk, who was too absorbed in her teen magazine to pay the sole patron much mind. Mobile to Pensacola was the home stretch. With any luck, she'd be back before midnight.

Had anyone noticed that she was gone? She hoped her parents hadn't phoned. Not likely, as they'd never wavered from Sunday evening's designated time, except when Dad had his heart attack. What if there had been some kind of emergency? She probably should have at least told AdaMae of her trip, or maybe Grant. She'd not talked with him since the play. Delivering Tommy to school had saved the performance, yet she hadn't even thanked him. There was a lot she hadn't done when it came to Grant. In these past few months, she'd shared so much with him, her grief, her frustrations at work. He'd been the shoulder to cry on after the Dwayne home visit debacle, the chauffeur and chaperone for field trips, and the friend she'd talked to for hours, especially when he was recuperating. Ever since that first kiss, she couldn't stop thinking of him and couldn't stop feeling guilty. But now, after reading Jack's letter, she no longer felt guilt. Was she now ready to admit that she was in love with another man? And was he in love with her?

She swigged the rest of her coffee and stepped from the coffee shop. As the key turned in the ignition, she knew what she needed to do - drive straight to Grant's house- now- while she was certain what to say, before needless doubts crept in. She'd tell him that she was ready, ready to love again, and it was him that she wanted. That decision, as much as the coffee, recharged her, and it was all she could do not to barrel down the interstate in her eagerness. Perhaps the only thing that kept her from speeding was the increasing wind buffeting the car as she drove over Mobile's causeway.

It was just shy of midnight when she turned onto the back road that would take her to Grant's house. Without street lights or moon to light the way, she proceeded cautiously, knowing that a deer might jump out from the surrounding loblolly pines. She'd been to his place only once, but was sure that she would recognize it, as there weren't any other houses for miles. A few minutes down the road, she saw an amber glow in the sky. Someone camping with a bonfire, maybe? Grant had said that sometimes kids did that, although they weren't allowed. As she drove further, there was a distinct smell of smoke. Car tires spun on the gravel road as she pressed the gas pedal, causing the car to swerve on the final bend before Grant's house.

She stopped the car and gaped in horror at the sight of an eight-foot blazing cross on Grant's front lawn. Wind whipped the flames as sparks rose high into the sky. Tongues of fire danced atop the roof and sides of the wood-shingled house. There was no sign of Grant, but his van stood in the driveway. He must be inside! She jumped out of the car, frantically calling his name, but heard only the belch of new flames erupting in the gusty air. She ran toward the house, yelling, "Grant, Grant!" A blast of heat struck her as she stepped onto the front porch. The metal doorknob seared her fingers. She jumped back. Using her sweater sleeve, she tried again, this time kicking the door wide as soon as it opened. She coughed as acrid smoke seeped into her lungs. Fumbling in the gray haze, she searched without success for Grant. Could he be sleeping? She hesitated at the foot of the stairs. Here, the smoke was even thicker, with near zero visibility. But he could be up there, unconscious maybe? She had to try to reach him! She grabbed a kitchen towel, doused it with water from the faucet, and placed it over her mouth before running up the stairs.

CHAPTER FORTY- SIX

Grant wakened with Alice licking his face. He strained to focus in the darkness of the dense forest and then reached up to muss Alice's fur. "You're all right, girl. Thank God." He sat up slowly, clutching the back of his head, where he could feel a huge lump. "Those bastards!" Sam Childer's cautionary words came back to him – "Watch your back." What were those delinquents up to? Were they really after him? Or was it just a case of guys having a few beers and his catching them unexpected? Then he remembered the white robes.

Rising, he wobbled some before taking his first steps. How far from home was he? It took a few minutes before his night vision kicked in and he could make out the trees. Alice had now recovered and was running ahead repeatedly barking and returning to her master, urging him forward. He quickened his pace despite the lingering dizziness. He could judge neither time nor distance. Each step made his head throb more, but he didn't stop.

First, he smelled it. Then he saw it – gray smoke wafting high into the sky, coming from the location of his house! He ran, weaving around the silhouetted trees, the branches slapping his face as he strained to see ahead. Alice was no longer beside him. She sped toward home, her deep bark growing ever more distant and within seconds she was no longer visible. By the time he exited the pine woods, he was breathing heavily. He lowered his head and grasped his knees, trying to catch his breath. When he entered the clearing near his home, he gasped at the sight of a flaming cross on his front lawn!

He'd seen the KKK signature only once before. Not long after he'd moved in with his grandparents, Gramps got a call from Old Rolly, the black handyman who lived on the edges of Cantonment, where the old sharecropper shacks stood. Rolly sometimes called on Gramps to help with plumbing jobs. On this one occasion, Grant tagged along. They arrived at dusk, and Grant never forgot the shock of seeing the burning cross and finding Rolly fearfully huddled inside a closet of his home. The old man had seen them coming, at least a dozen or more, torches lit, white hoods stark in the darkness. The calling card accomplished its task. Rolly withdrew his application for a business license and became a recluse. It was Grant's first introduction to the Ku Klux Klan.

Now, he stood staring at their hallmark symbol, once again horrified. Within seconds he realized that there was more than the cross on fire. At the sight of flames and smoke swallowing his house, he ran the final twenty yards before spotting Cassie's Toyota parked in the road. Cassie, here? It took him only minutes to check the car and the yard. She wasn't there. Oh my God! Was she inside?

The front door stood open, but entry was impossible. The draft fed the fire, engulfing the entire entranceway. He ran to the back door, where Alice stood, incessantly barking. Cautiously, he pushed open the door, and thankfully no flames greeted him, only thick smoke, precipitating a coughing spasm. Between the searing heat and abundant smoke, he probably had but minutes to find her. The dog barked again and then bound up the stairs.

Grant followed, calling Cassie's name. Eyes smarting and laboring to breathe, he crawled along the floor boards, silently praying that he'd find her alive. Alice bolted into the bedroom, ran out barking repeatedly, and then retreated into the bedroom once more. As Grant crawled toward the bedroom door, Alice appeared, this time with her head lowered and backing up slowly, dragging something. "Cassie!" Grant lifted the limp body and cradled her against his chest. He sprinted down the precariously charred stairs and out the back door, collapsing on the grass with Cassie in his arms.

"You all right?" Sam Childers stood above him.

Grant coughed in response and Sam bent down, lifted Cassie from his arms, and carried her away. With a hoarse voice Grant yelled after him, "Is she alive?" Sam didn't answer. He continued to cough, then retched on the grass. Nauseous and dizzy, he tried to stand. He could hear voices coming from the front of the house. Finally, he gathered his strength, stood, and staggered toward them. Firetruck lights flashed as firefighters dragged out thickly coiled black hoses. Grant bent over, clutched his thighs, and watched a gush of water spray his house as Sam laid Cassie on an ambulance stretcher.

CHAPTER FORTY- SEVEN

It was a full twenty-four hours before Grant saw Cassie. The doctors insisted his chest be x-rayed, oxygen delivered, and blood tested before he was released. He didn't tell them about the blow to his head. A concussion diagnosis would delay his visit to Cassie.

He took the elevator to the third floor and followed the numbers to Room 312. He walked around the curtain, unsure what to expect. Hooked up to oxygen with IV fluids dripping into her veins, Cassie sat in a hospital bed, eyes closed. Softly, he stepped to the bedside, brushed back her damp curls, and kissed her on the forehead.

How long had she laid on his bedroom floor and how long had she searched the house for him? She was alive, at least for now. The doctor that he spoke with briefly was reluctant to give a prognosis. A lot depended on the next few days. Fluids and oxygen were the primary treatment. Later, she might need hyperbaric therapy if the lungs were severely damaged. He pulled over a chair to begin his vigil, grateful that the young duty nurse let him stay after visiting hours.

He took Cassie's hand in his. "Can you hear me, Cassie? It's Grant." No response. How could he not feel guilty? If he hadn't gone for that walk, or if he hadn't joined in the sit-in. No, he didn't regret that choice. Cassie had told him she was proud of his actions. Even so, it had its consequences. He was prepared for the arrest, the termination. But he hadn't bargained for this. Despite all his years living here, he still underestimated the power of hate.

Sam had filled him in on what had happened. Fred was not only a racist, but stupid as well. The kids hadn't banked on Sam Childers being a night owl and catching them in their cross-burning act on his front lawn. Three punk teenagers were no match for the brawny ex-Marine. By the time the police arrived, all three kids were splayed on the ground groaning. Duffy had already begun to spill the beans. Fred yelled at him to shut up, but when they arrived at the police station and were shoved into a jail cell, he too was willing to talk. They told how it was all Coach Higgins idea. He even gave them the white robes. After the arrest, Childers told the cops to check out Grant's place, suspecting that he might be a target. What Grant couldn't figure out was how the kids knew where he lived. He had an unlisted phone number and few visitors. Then he remembered that Amy had been to his place a couple of times. She must have told either her nephew Fred or Higgins. Damn her. Damn them all.

He looked into Cassie's face, willing those beautiful gray eyes to open. His mind reeled with questions. Where had she been these past two days? And why had she come to his house? "Cassie, please wake up. I need to tell you what I should have told you before. I love you, Cass. Can you hear me?" He laid her hand back on the bed, resting his head beside it. Silent tears fell on the bedsheet as he said her name repeatedly, "Cassie, Cassie, Cassie, *please* come back to me." At three in the morning, the second shift nurse came into the room and tapped him on the shoulder. "Time to go home. No visitors."

***

She is flying high above in the sky. Someone is calling her name way off in the distance. Who is it? The sky is what pilots call 'severe clear', and she can see for miles. The landscape looks familiar; rolling hills dotted with lush green maple trees, and then a town. She knows this place, the small cape and ranch homes on quarter acre grass plots, streets lined with shops, churches, and gas stations. Like a homing pigeon, she follows the streets and landmarks of her Connecticut home town to find her way to 93 Alling Avenue. Jeremy is bouncing and shooting a basketball in the driveway. Her father, dressed in his usual baggy jeans and sweatshirt, is bent in his garden, oblivious to her passing. Then, she spots her mother, pinning wet sheets on the clothesline. She calls out to her, at first with no response. Dipping lower to the ground, yet still in flight, Cassie yells, "Mom, it's me, Cassie". With hand shading her eyes from the bright sun, Lena MacDonald looks up. "Cassie, is that you? Come home, dear, come home." Cassie hovers for a moment, but then that other voice, a man's, calls her name again. She waves to her mother before flying higher, following the voice that summons.

Her home is far behind now. She takes extended deep breaths, savoring the inhaled air like long swigs of ice water.

"Cassie, come back to me." Is that Jack calling?

I'm coming. Then she sees him in his flight uniform, slowly walking through a green meadow as the mournful lament of taps trumpets in the distance. She cries out,

"Jack!", but he keeps on walking. Where is he going? And why is he no longer calling for her? Instead, he strides purposefully through the meadow, reaching miles of perfectly aligned white crosses. Attired in crisply creased whites and caps, a Navy honor guard stands erect by an open grave. Another man stands nearby, head bowed. Cassie flies closer. As Jack approaches, the man looks up and salutes. Earl! Cassie is confused. An open casket lies on the ground. Who is being buried? Why are Jack and Earl both there? When she sees her husband step into the silk lined casket, she screams, "Jack! No!" She calls his name once more, and finally his eyes meet hers, and he says, "Goodbye, Cass." As she watches the sailors close and lower the casket, a distant voice beckons, "Cassie, come back to me." This time she knows it isn't Jack calling for her.

CHAPTER FORTY- EIGHT

AdaMae waited at the gate. Lena MacDonald's plane was twenty minutes late. At Grant's request, she had called Cassie's parents and told what she knew, which wasn't much. Grant had come in too late for any conversation, and headed back to the hospital as soon as he'd showered and dressed. The news of the housefire, Grant's own close to death experience, and Cassie's hospitalization had been shocking events that she was still trying to process. Lena called back later to say she was catching the next flight to Pensacola.

The woman that walked off the plane was not the one she'd met at Thanksgiving. Her round-cheeked face was now haggard with dark circles under bloodshot eyes. The fastidious brunette coif was now mussed.

"Lena! Over here!" AdaMae waved while stepping away from the gathered crowd. Lena waved back and ambled toward AdaMae, who immediately embraced her as if they were old friends.

"How is my daughter?"

"I haven't seen her, but we can go there now. Visiting hours are almost over."

"Yes, I'd like that. And thank you for picking me up. Ed wanted to come too, of course, but there's Jeremy to think of. This would be too much for him."

After retrieving Lena's suitcase, they rode in silence to the hospital. AdaMae glanced frequently at Lena, who clinched her gingham housedress while staring out the car window. She strained to think of some words of comfort but all she could do was drive through the drizzling rain to bring this distraught woman to her daughter.

AdaMae was not surprised to see her grandson sitting at Cassie's bedside. A young man in a white coat stood holding a clipboard at the foot of the bed. He looked up as Lena rushed toward him.

"Are you my daughter's doctor?" Lena didn't wait for a reply. "Is she going to be all right?"

The doctor set the clipboard back on its hook and took a step back. AdaMae had a better look at him now, and saw the forehead creases, the gray speckled hairs around the ears. He was not that young. How would he answer Lena? She'd known doctors who had a gift for giving medical news with compassion and honesty, and others who, wrapped in cloaks of vain superiority, retreated from their patients. Which was he?

"It's too early to tell, I'm afraid, especially since she's still unconscious. Now, if you'll excuse me, I have to finish my rounds."

Grant leaped from his chair and grabbed the doctor's sleeve. "Wait, Doctor."

The doctor stared at the hand clutching his white coat. "What is it?"

"That's all you can tell us? What did the tests show? Do you expect her to come around soon? What's typical in cases like this? You must know more than you're telling us. Please. Her mother has just flown in all the way from Connecticut." He realized that he was squeezing the doctor's arm.

"And you are?"

"Grant Lee, a friend... a good friend."

"Well, Mr. Lee, there are no 'typical' cases. Without knowing the duration of exposure or possible inhaled toxins, it is difficult to give a correct prognosis. She is breathing on her own but is being supplemented with oxygen through the nasal cannula. Once she becomes conscious, we can more definitively assess her lung function with the use of spirometry. Multiple tests of her pulmonary function value will tell us whether the damage to her lungs is reversible or not. Her heart rate is normal with no apparent cardiac complications. We are continuing to do blood tests and an EKG has been scheduled."

"But shouldn't she be conscious? When will she wake up?"

"We don't know. We have noted some response to stimuli, so we hope it will be soon."

Grant turned back to find Lena bent over Cassie, stroking her daughter's hair. He looked at his grandmother. "Did her mother hear all that?"

"I'm not sure. She hasn't taken her eyes off Cassie."

CHAPTER FORTY- NINE

She blinked repeatedly in the glare of the bright lights and immediately wanted to scratch everywhere, but couldn't lift her arms. Spotting the needle taped to her forearm, Cassie followed the attached tube and watched clear liquid drip rhythmically into her veins. She wiggled her nose, aware of some kind of nasal intrusion. As she took a deep breath, oxygen filled her expanding lungs, causing both a burning sensation and slight light-headedness. With parched lips, she whispered, "Water." Someone squeezed her hand and called her name. It was the voice from her dream. Was she still dreaming?

"Cassie, thank God, you're awake!"

It took a couple of minutes for her eyes to focus, for her mind to clear. "Grant?"

He bent over her, his brows furrowed, dark eyes intent on hers.

"Here. Have some water."

She leaned forward, lips pursing the bent straw, and sipped. A quick scan of the room – the blank beige walls, the guard-railed raised bed, the white sheets and gurney gown tightened at the neck – all told her where she was. It took only a moment to remember - the fire, the smoke, crawling on her knees, searching for him – for Grant. "You're okay? I thought... I mean I was looking for you ..." Her voice was strained, her throat sore with each word. She coughed, which only made it worse.

"I know, Cassie. We found you, or rather Alice found you. I'm fine. ... And you will be too. Here, take another sip."

She did as she was told, this time taking a long draught before falling back on the pillow. "How long have I been here?"

He glanced at his watch. "Not quite thirty hours. Seems a lot longer." He stroked her cheek with his thumb. "Oh, Cassie, I have so much to tell you. I...."

The sound of footsteps stopped him mid-sentence.

"Cassie! Oh my God! You're awake!" Lena MacDonald ran to her daughter and burst into tears. Once composed, she took the tissue Grant offered and wiped her eyes. "You have no idea how worried I've been."

Cassie glanced from her mother to AdaMae, who stood at the foot of the bed holding a beautifully arranged potted plant. They exchanged brief smiles before AdaMae set the plant on the window ledge and took the chair offered by her grandson.

"Good morning, neighbor." Her fingers brushed Cassie's. "I thought we'd see those beautiful eyes open today. How are you feeling?"

"Tired." She coughed again. "Hurts some to talk."

"Of course it does." AdaMae patted her hand and then turned to Grant. "Does the doctor know that she's awake?"

"No. It's only been a couple minutes. I'll go to the nurse's station and let them know."

Lena folded down her daughter's sheet, fluffed her pillow and pulled a chair to the bedside. "I find this totally unacceptable, that no doctor has been in to see you! What kind of hospital is this? As soon as they release you, you're coming home with me, Cassie. We're only thirty minutes from Yale Hospital, where you can get top-notch medical care. I've already called your father about it and he agrees. We'll get you the best doctor."

Squeaky cart wheels announced the arrival of a nurse. Even without the starched cap and white uniform, the woman who entered would have commanded respect. AdaMae stepped aside to allow the broad-hipped woman passage as she drew the cart next to the bed. "The doctor has ordered some blood samples, Mrs. Cunningham." Cassie watched man-like hands strap tubing around her upper arm and then insert the needle into one of her veins, filling a vial with dark red blood. Grant had now re-entered the room, and Cassie wished with all her heart that he was the one next to her bedside, instead of this stern-faced woman folding her arm.

"Why hasn't the doctor come yet?" Lena asked.

"If we had been informed as soon as the patient was alert, when he was doing his morning rounds, I'm sure he would've been in. It might be some time now, however. He's extremely busy, you know."

Lena pressed, "But surely, he knows now."

"He's been informed of Mrs. Cunningham's condition." She turned to Cassie. "Is there anything you need, Mrs. Cunningham?" The brow softened, and the voice was now gentle, compassionate, and for a fleeting moment, Cassie wanted to say, *Yes, hold me.* In those massive arms and bosom, she might find refuge, retreat from physical and emotional exhaustion. Instead, she shook her head, and the nurse plus squeaky cart left the room.

Lena shook her head. "Cassie, as soon as you're well enough to travel, you're going home with me."

"Mom, I live here. This is my home."

"There you go again. Same old stubborn Cassie. Well, I've held my tongue long enough. Now you're listening to me. You're coming home, where you *should* have been all along. This crazy place practically killed you!"

Held her tongue? Hardly. But Cassie was too tired to argue.

***

All she wanted was a few minutes alone with Grant, a few precious moments to tell him why she drove that night to his house. But the next few days were filled with doctors and nurses coming in and out of her room. They ran tests, poked and prodded, asked questions constantly. And even when there weren't medical personnel doing their thing, other visitors were ever present. Her mother came daily with AdaMae. There was a visit from Mrs. Hicks, Reina and her father, Dr. Gooden, and most surprisingly, Mrs. Washburn, who reassured her that she was 'keeping an eye on her 'chilluns and would make sure that the substitute did her job.'

The shades had been drawn, her breakfast delivered, and bed raised. The scrambled eggs were soft and runny, the toast dry. No wonder people lost weight in hospitals. It wasn't the illness. It was the food. She managed a few bites, and then shoved the tray aside. The doctor said she was making remarkable progress. Tests indicated no permanent lung damage, and with lung function now up to 85%, the oxygen was withdrawn yesterday. Deep breaths were still difficult but it felt good to be free of those plastic nasal prongs. What did the doctor call them- oh, right - a nasal cannula. She turned to the window, basking in the radiant sunshine. It was

December but she'd lost track of the exact date. Mrs. Hicks had delivered beautiful home-made cards from each of the children. She'd read them all multiple times, picturing their faces, missing them terribly. Reina had arranged for her aunt, who'd taught special education in the past, to substitute.

"Hey there, girl. How you doing this morning?"

Reina entered the room with Bill and Grant right behind her. Grant slid over a chair for Reina and took a seat on the other side of the bed. Standing behind his fiancé, Bill blocked the incoming rays of sunlight. She'd almost forgotten the immense size of the man. His fingers tapped nervously as his eyes drifted about the room. She tried to put him at ease.

"It's nice of you to visit, Bill. Reina tells me that you've been very busy with the NAACP lawsuit."

Bill refocused on Cassie. "Yes, very. Leroy is our main plaintiff, but now many of the other jailed students have signed on. And then there's Grant's upcoming hearing."

Grant's hearing? They'd yet to speak about his situation. She knew nothing about a hearing. "When is it?"

Grant answered. "Tomorrow. That's when preliminary evidence will be presented and a trial date set."

Bill chimed in, "There may not be a trial. We're asking for the case to be dismissed."

Cassie responded, her voice still hoarse and raspy, "Grant, that's wonderful! Does that mean you'd get your job back?"

He frowned, "Not likely. Very much a long shot for the case to be dismissed, but Bill said we should shoot for the moon, see what happens."

She looked at Bill, "Is it a long shot?"

"Probably, but nothing ventured, nothing gained."

Reina piped in. "I think Bill underestimates the racism here. He's been away too long."

"I haven't forgotten anything. Mort, the NAACP trial lawyer assigned to the case is experienced and will argue the motion for dismissal. Then too, there's been a lot of press coverage on these latest attacks. A real hornet's nest has been stirred up, and some are anxious to put a lid on it. Dismissing the case and avoiding a trial might help in that regard."

"You mean the attacks on Grant and Sam, right?" Cassie asked.

"Those and more."

"More attacks?"

"Unfortunately, yes." Bill answered. "Mrs. Hunt was lured from her home by a telephone call asking her to a non-existent meeting, only to come home to her house in flames."

Cassie's face went white. "Oh my God! Who's Mrs. Hunt?"

"She's a member of the Pensacola-Escambia Human Relations Committee who expressed sympathy toward the student protesters."

Reina heard the distress in Cassie's voice. "Didn't you say you and Grant had to leave early for a meeting with one of the NAACP lawyers?"

"Ah, right." Bill stepped from behind the chair. "Good to see you, Cassie. Hope you'll be home, soon." He gave a quick wave goodbye. "You ready to go, Grant?"

"Give me a minute. I'll be right there." He squeezed Cassie's hand. "If I can, I'll try to get back here later." Cassie's eyes followed him out the door.

Reina tucked the bedsheets under the mattress. "Are they taking good care of you, Cassie?"

"The nurses are wonderful, or at least most of them. Food is nothing to rave about."

"I hear that Mrs. W was in to visit. I bet that was a shock!"

Cassie laughed, triggering a coughing spasm. "You can say that again. But she reassured me that all is well with the kids. Is that true?"

"Appears so. I haven't heard of any incidents. I pop in from time to time. Did have some news regarding Sharelle, though."

"She's okay, isn't she?"

"Yes, yes, but you've been to the home. You saw the conditions. After visiting three times, I was obliged to call Child and Family Services."

"But the mother loves Sharelle and Henry. I'm sure of it."

Reina sighed. "I know. But Cassie, the woman is not capable of taking care of those children. Sharelle is doing everything, including fishing for their food."

"They must have more than fish to eat!"

"Not much more. A kindly neighbor drops off milk and cereal every week, and diapers for the baby. That's it."

"She could apply for food stamps, welfare. Couldn't you get her signed up?"

"Yes. But there are other concerns. The neighbor has found Henry toddling in the street or wandering in the nearby woods. The stove was left on, causing a small kitchen fire. And then Sharelle was found by the police one night in downtown Pensacola. I shudder to think what might have happened."

"So, they're going to take the children away, probably separate them? Sharelle loves Henry and she was just opening up, talking more. This could set her back."

"I know. And I'm doing everything I can for the mother and the children. We have an unexpected helper in that regard."

"Who?"

"Aunt Barbara, my mother's sister."

"The one substituting?"

"She's become quite fond of Sharelle. Went with me on one home visit, and fell in love with Henry too. She and her husband offered to foster the children long term. They never had children of their own. Barbara grew up poor in Mississippi, and when she went into the hospital for her endometriosis problems, she was sterilized."

"Sterilized? But why?"

"Cassie, there were lots of such incidents, and not just in the South. Poor black women were seen as a burden on society. Doctors thought sterilization meant fewer black mouths to feed. In my aunt's case, she was only twenty and consequently never had the chance to have children."

"Oh my God. I had no idea."

"Cassie, are you all right? You're crying. I know you're worried about Sharelle but Barbara has a heart of gold and would love those children as her own. ..."

Cassie shook her head. "No, I'm sure that's true. It's just everything."

"Everything?"

"You know, all you've told me, what's happened to your family. My God, Reina."

"It's not just our family."

"I know. That's the point. I've been so blind to it all. Before I moved here, that is. And you're right. It's not just here. But until I started teaching and met you, learned of all the humiliations, the way Blacks are treated, left out... and then the cross burning, the fire, Grant and those students being arrested, just for standing up for what's right. So much I didn't know and should have."

Reina patted Cassie's hand. "It's okay, Cass. You have a good heart and an open mind. That's enough."

Cassie grabbed a tissue from the bedside table and wiped her eyes. "Is it?"

"Cass, get some sleep. You need your rest." Reina blew a kiss and started to leave.

"Wait!" Cassie straightened up in the bed.

"What about Sharelle's mother? They're not going to institutionalize her, are they? I've been to those institutions for the retarded. My parents were told to put Jeremy in one. They're horrid!"

"I know. I don't want that for Sharelle's mother either. I'm trying to work out arrangements for her. Barbara wants her to be able to visit the children regularly." Reina waved from the door. "Stop worrying, Cass. I've got this. Rest up. Your mother will be in soon."

Her mother would be here soon. Cassie was beginning to feel too weak to resist her mother's insistent pleas to come home. Maybe it was time to give in. According to Reina, the children in her classroom were doing fine. Grant had his hands full with legal problems. Why complicate life further? Maybe going home was the right choice. She rolled over, pressed her face into the pillow, and whispered "Grant, please come. I need you"

CHAPTER FIFTY

The rattling of lunch carts and persistent patient call signals kept Cassie from drifting back to sleep. Where was her mother? She'd been in every morning right after breakfast. It was a pleasant respite for Cassie, yet that realization brought familiar guilt. Her mother loved her, came all this way to be by her side. So, why did she find every visit from her mother so exhausting? Had it always been that way? As a tomboy, Cassie spent most of her time outdoors, much to the annoyance of her mother, whose frequent admonishments for not helping out were largely ignored by Cassie. Instead, she chose to play with Jeremy, talk with Nana, or sneak off to tend her garden.

Almost as if the reflections conjured up her presence, Lena charged into the room toting a small satchel. "Cassie, you're going home! Doctor called this morning with the news you're being discharged." She set the satchel onto the bed, unzipped it, and pulled out a blue blouse, jeans, bra and underwear. "These should work. Chose blue. You always look so nice in blue. Don't know how you can be comfortable in this skimpy bikini underwear. Here, let me help you get changed."

"Mom, I can get myself dressed, but I think I should wait and see what the doctor says. He hasn't been in yet."

Lena shook her head. "Really? Don't know what's taking him so long. All the more reason why we need to get you home to get better medical care. Must be the southern way of doing things. Everyone takes their sweet time around here, don't they?"

Cassie ignored the comment, and looked to the door as the doctor entered.

"Good morning, Mrs. Cunningham, we're discharging you today. I have a few things to go over with you beforehand." Cassie listened as the doctor rattled off test results, wishing she had someone here to interpret the medical jargon.

"Of course, you'll need follow-up appointments. Included with your discharge papers is my office number. I want to see you again in two weeks."

"She won't be here then, Doctor. I'm taking her home."

The doctor raised his eyebrows. "She'll need follow-up care, Mrs. ..."

"MacDonald. Of course she'll need follow-up care. I'll have her medical records sent to our doctor."

The doctor looked to Cassie. "Do you have any questions for me, Mrs. Cunningham?"

Cassie glanced at her mother. "How soon can I resume normal activities, Doctor?"

"Use your own body's response as a measure. If you start to fatigue or breathing is labored, slow down. You should be able to do most things, maybe at a slower pace at first. I wouldn't run any marathons or engage in heavy exertion just yet. Do you need me to write a medical report for work dispensation? I think a couple more weeks of rest is advised before returning to work."

Lena retorted, "That won't be necessary, Doctor. As I said, she's going *home!*"

***

Cassie slid into the car's passenger seat; her stomach tight. What could she say that would change her mother's plans? Everything already seemed in place. As usual, her mother didn't ask for her daughter's opinion.

"It was nice of AdaMae to loan me her car. She's been a godsend. We'll have to send her a nice gift once we get home. Do you know what she might like, other than plants, that is? She seems to have plenty of those, and I'd have no idea what to get her." Cassie stared out the window, not replying. Lena rattled on. "Maybe a cookbook, or something for the kitchen. She seems to enjoy cooking. All those meals she cooked for you and Jack. Although, I must say, she could afford to spend a little more time cleaning. I swear, hard to find a thing with all the clutter in her house." She patted her daughter's hand as she changed the subject. "The Cunninghams are quite anxious to see you, my dear. They've been asking after you. Even offered to take you to their country club. You remember how Jack wanted to teach you to play golf. His father said he was a natural. But then, Jack was good at everything, wasn't he?"

Jack. Was it really only a week ago that she visited Earl? She clutched her purse, remembering the letter folded inside, the one that led her to rush home to Grant, only to find his home in flames.

"So, what do you suggest?"

"Huh?" Cassie looked at her mother.

"The gift for AdaMae?"

"Oh, I don't know, Mom. Maybe we can pick out something together this week."

"There won't be time for that. We're booked on a Tuesday evening flight. I've already packed a lot of your things, but there's still more to do. That leaves us only the rest of today and tomorrow. Are you all right, Cassie? Tired?"

Cassie grit her teeth. Tuesday! Once again, her mother was taking charge. She wanted to scream, 'I have a life, Mom!' but instead just mumbled. "Just very tired."

"Well, then, I'll do most of the packing. You can rest when we get to your place."

Cassie nodded and again stared out the window.

***

It was late afternoon before Grant finished up with preparations for tomorrow's hearing. He strained to focus as Mort and Bill explained court proceedings and their strategy. The legal jargon was difficult to follow and his mind was elsewhere. All he wanted was to see Cassie, to finally tell her what he'd put off for so long. He loved her, wanted her. Was she ready to hear that? Put her grief behind her? The hospital elevator wait was too long. He raced up the stairwell to the third floor, strode into the room, only to find a candy striper stripping sheets from Cassie's hospital bed.

"Where's Cassie, Cassie Cunningham?"

The dimpled teenager smiled in reply, "She's been discharged, sir. We're expecting another patient soon."

"Discharged?" *That was good news, wasn't it?* Even so, it meant delay. More ruminating, finding just the right words. *Cassie, I love you, I've always loved you...* And it meant going to her house, where her mother would sure to be standing guard.

***

Lena answered the door. "Grant? You must be here to see Cassie. I'm afraid she's quite busy right now."

"Excuse me, Mrs. MacDonald, but I *must* see her now. Please."

"Well, if you insist." She opened the door and Grant spotted the suitcases in the corner.

"Are you flying home today, Mrs. MacDonald?"

"*We're* leaving – Tuesday."

"We?"

"Cassie and I. Your grandmother has offered to drive us to the airport, which is awfully nice...."

"Where is she?"

"Your grandmother is at home, of course."

"No, Cassie." *The woman could be so exasperating*! He stepped around her and into the living room.

"She's in the bedroom, packing."

He took a deep breath before rounding the corner leading to the master bedroom. The door was slightly ajar. He saw an open suitcase on the bed. Cassie sat next to it, her back turned to the door. She was holding her wedding photograph, choking back tears.

"Oh, Jack. You know that I'll always love you..."

He didn't wait to hear the rest. His practiced declaration of love evaporated as he turned and walked out the house door, out of earshot.

Cassie sniffed and brushed the tears from her cheeks. "But it's time to finally say goodbye. No more letters to you. No more living in the past." She kissed the glass and set the framed photo face down in the suitcase.

CHAPTER FIFTY-ONE

Grant chose the same blue blazer and striped tie that he'd worn at the School Board meeting. At his grandmother's insistence, he made an early morning barber appointment and reviewed the notes from yesterday's meeting as the barber combed and clipped. He even opted for the shave.

Bill and Mort, his NAACP colleague, were already at the courthouse by the time Grant arrived. He took a seat on the corridor bench alongside them. With elbows on outspread knees and hand under his chin, he leaned forward, watching the comings and goings of dark-suited lawyers with their assorted clients. He was not in the best frame of mind to face a judge today. He knew that. Yesterday's marathon prep session with Bill and Mort followed by his unsuccessful visit to Cassie left him drained. Did he have any chance with her? As for the hearing, he was beginning to wonder if he shouldn't have offered a nolo contendere at the arraignment, plea bargained, and hoped for a fine rather than jail time. The only thing that stopped him was the fact that if, by some chance, they were successful in getting the case dismissed, the same legal arguments could be used going forward with Leroy and the other students.

He slid back onto the bench seat and began tapping his right foot on the polished wood floor. "How much longer, Bill?"

"The bailiff should be calling us in soon."

"What are our chances?"

"A lot depends on the judge."

"Who is?"

"Just got word this morning. It's Judge Ralston, fairly new on the bench, so not much of a record yet. Younger than most. Elected by a slim margin a year ago. The prosecuting attorney, however, is well known; Wilt Emerson; elected four years ago, sharp cookie, but definitely politically connected. You can guarantee he's getting direction from higher up."

Mort opened his briefcase and retrieved a stack of papers. He would be the lead attorney, as Bill was not only a novice, but black. Given the racially charged nature of the case, having a black lawyer for representation might bode poorly. Mort Goldman was from Atlanta, an experienced civil rights lawyer. Taciturn and all business, he offered no opinion on Grant's chances.

The courtroom doors opened and they took their designated seats in front. Grant surveyed the crowd, not seeing any familiar faces. Grams wanted to come, but Rufford had an emergency vet visit.

Mort nodded at the prosecuting attorney across the aisle. Tall and slim, Wilt Emerson was what Grams would call 'distinguished-looking' with gray hair at the temples and erect bearing. He returned the nod.

"All rise." The judge entered the courtroom. Pressed between towering Bill on his left and five-foot six Mort on his right, Grant tried to assess the man taking the bench. He was indeed young for a judge but hefty, with a protruding stomach beneath the black robes. Bushy eyebrows framed deep-set eyes that seemed to take in the entire courtroom in one glance.

The judge announced the case and then looked over at the defense. "The defendant has entered a plea of not guilty. Is that correct?"

Mort's baritone voice belied his diminutive frame. "Yes, that is correct, Your Honor."

"This is a preliminary hearing. Before we proceed, are there any motions that the defense would like to make to the court? "Yes, Your Honor. The defense would at this time like to make a motion for dismissal."

The judge frowned. "On what grounds, Counselor?"

"On the grounds that the county has violated Mr. Lee's First Amendment rights and those of the students arrested at the Escambia High School sit-in. Should we proceed to trial, the defense will refer the court to prior rulings by the Supreme Court in similar cases. I'm sure the judge is familiar with Edwards v. South Carolina and Garner v. Louisiana."

"I am, but this hearing pertains to Mr. Lee, Counselor, not the students also charged with disturbing the peace."

"I'm aware of that, Your Honor. But, as you may already know, my firm has been retained for the defense of all those charged at the sit-in."

Across the aisle, Emerson stood. "The prosecution objects to this dismissal motion, Your Honor. We intend to call witnesses to testify to the violence that occurred as a result of this sit-in."

Mort responded. "Should we go to trial, the defense will prove that neither Mr. Lee, the defendant, nor the other sit-in participants, ever engaged in violence. In fact, we are prepared to bring forward witnesses stating that county employees initiated the violence, resulting in various injuries."

All heads in the courtroom turned at the sound of the back door opening. A smartly dressed woman walked quietly down the side aisle to the prosecutor, bent over, and whispered something in Emerson's ear. He frowned.

Judge Ralston said, "Is there a problem, Counselor?"

Emerson replied, "May I approach the bench, Your Honor?"

The judge raised an eyebrow. "Does it relate to the motion made by the defense, Counselor?

"It does, Your Honor."

"Come forward, then."

Mort joined the prosecutor in front of the bench as Bill and Grant strained to hear the muffled conversation a few feet away.

After a few minutes, the judge banged his gavel. "The court will take a thirty-minute recess."

Grant and Bill exchanged perplexed looks as Emerson made a beeline for the exit while Mort stuffed papers back into his suitcase.

"What the hell was that all about, Mort?" Bill asked.

"Prosecutor has to follow up on some additional information just received."

"You have any idea what it might be?"

"No. Not a clue." He grabbed his briefcase, then paused and looked directly at Grant. "Is there anyone you may have neglected to tell us about? Any unknown witness who would testify against you?"

"It's just like you said, Mort. The violence came from others. All the sit-in participants were peaceful."

"Anyone who might say otherwise, lie under oath?"

A flash of Amy shaking her head at him from her classroom doorway. *Would she do such a thing?*

He responded in the negative. "No, I don't think so."

They followed Mort, who headed to a standing ashtray in the corridor, lit up a cigarette, and took his first drag. Grant approached him as Bill left for the men's room. "No sign of Emerson."

Mort exhaled a stream of smoke. "I'm sure he's in an office somewhere making his phone call."

"That's what he said? - he had to make a call?"

Mort nodded.

"So now what do we do?"

"We wait, and hope this 'additional information' doesn't hurt our case."

***

Grant's underarms itched from perspiration as he re-entered the courtroom. He spotted Emerson and tried to discern from the prosecutor's expression what might be coming. He decided that lawyers' faces, like those of good poker players, could not be read. Again, they all rose when the judge entered and then took their seats.

Judge Ralston looked at the prosecuting attorney. "Counselor, we have a motion from the defense for dismissal. The state has objected to that motion. Is there anything you have to say before we proceed?"

Emerson stood. "Yes, your Honor. The State of Florida would like to drop all charges against Mr. Grant Lee and others so charged." An audible gasp went up from the crowd.

"Counselors, approach the bench please." The judge shifted in his chair and waited for the lawyers to come forward. "Emerson, you have some explaining to do."

"I'd like to do so in private, Your Honor."

Judge Ralston stood and banged his gavel. "The court will take another short recess. Counselors, in my chambers now."

***

Bill was experiencing mixed emotions as he entered the judge's chambers with Mort and Emerson. They'd done their homework. They were prepared for a fight, but this latest announcement was a welcome but unexpected twist. He remained uneasy. What had precipitated the prosecutor's announcement?

Judge Ralston unzipped his robe, hung it on a coatrack hook, and took a seat behind a massive oak desk. "Take a seat, gentlemen."

All three sat on the edge of their chairs, waiting for the judge to speak.

"Normally, when charges are dropped in a second-degree misdemeanor case, I wouldn't ask for an explanation. But as you know, gentlemen, this is not a normal case. Whatever is decided in this courtroom today will be on tomorrow's front page. Emotions in the community are high. I need answers." He looked at Emerson. "You objected to the defense motion asking for dismissal. Now, after a short recess, you say the state wants all charges dropped. You want to explain the change of heart?"

Emerson cleared his throat. "I'm not sure how much I'm at liberty to say, Your Honor."

"Let me help you with that. Does it have anything to do with Representative Beasley and what happened at his residence this morning?"

Emerson blanched. "How'd you know about that? I just found out."

"I have my sources."

Mort interjected. "Your Honor, the defense is unaware of what's being referenced."

Judge Ralston tilted back his chair. "The additional information that Counselor Emerson received was from Representative Beasley, am I right Counselor?"

Emerson nodded. "His home was set fire in the middle of the night."

Mort interjected. "Let me guess. KKK?"

Emerson replied. "There are no suspects at this time."

Mort looked at the judge. "I don't get it. From what I know, Representative Beasley wasn't a supporter of the sit-in, or the Confederate flag removal. Why would he be a target of the KKK?"

The judge smiled. "Counselor Goldman, you're not from here. You may not be aware of the Representative's public statement condemning the recent attacks by the KKK and calling for peaceful resolution of the symbol controversy. I imagine that caught certain people's attention." He looked at Emerson. "What I don't understand is how the arson precipitated dropping charges in this case."

Emerson squirmed in his chair. "Your Honor, may my response be kept confidential?"

The judge looked at Mort and Bill. They nodded in reply.

"He's had further threats. And then there's the publicity, Your Honor. AP wires have picked up the story. It's hurting Pensacola's image."

"Dropping the charges may not help your re-election prospects, Counselor, …or mine."

Emerson replied, "I'm aware of that, Your Honor."

"Hmm. You'll need to complete the required form for dismissal charges, Counselor. And that should be done for all defendants."

"Yes, Your Honor."

Judge Ralston turned toward Mort and Bill. "For the record, Counselors. I was impressed with the precedents cited in the courtroom and would have liked to hear your arguments should we have gone to trial. Looks like that won't be happening." He stood and reached for his robe. "That will be all, Counselors. I'll see you in the courtroom."

***

Bill was able to give Grant the basics before they again rose for the judge's entrance. It took only minutes for the judge to address the courtroom.

"At this time, the state is dropping all charges against Mr. Grant Lee. Is the prosecution's dismissal request with or without prejudice?"

Emerson stood. "With, Your Honor."

The judge nodded. "The clerk will so note that the state will not press charges against Mr. Lee at a later date. It should also be noted that the court understands that the state has its reasons for dismissal; but the court's granting of the state's motion should not be taken as the court's concurrence in this action. Understanding this, does the Prosecuting Attorney's Office continue to insist on a dismissal of charges against Mr. Lee?"

"Yes, Your Honor."

"I'll expect those forms in my office by tomorrow, Counselor."

CHAPTER FIFTY-TWO

Cassie opened the bedroom closet, pushed clothes aside, and reached for her suitcase. As she pulled it out, she spotted a large shopping bag. The kids' Christmas gifts! What day was this? She'd lost all track of time in the hospital. She checked the wall calendar. Christmas vacation would start tomorrow. How could she leave without delivering the gifts and saying goodbye? Ignoring her mother's angry cries of 'Where are you going?', she grabbed car keys, slammed the door, and sped toward Fielding School.

The children greeted her with shrieks of joy and hugs so tight she could barely breathe! They ripped open the presents, tossing ribbons and colored tissue paper into the air. She'd selected books to match each child's interest and reading level. Another gift bag included packs of Santa pencils and boxed raisins.

Delighting in the moment, she didn't see Reina come in. "I see you're back where you belong, my friend."

Cassie smiled. "I've missed them so much."

"I thought you'd be at the hearing. I would have gone, but couldn't take the time off. Bill was pretty anxious about it."

"Oh my God! That's today?" She hugged the kids one last time, wished them all a Merry Christmas, and hurried to her car.

She had to parallel park three blocks from the courthouse. Her lungs complained when she started to half-run through Lee Square before reaching the corner of Palafox and Government Street, where the four- story Escambia County Courthouse stood. A news van was parked nearby. She stepped onto the brick walkway and then climbed the concrete steps leading to the entrance. Pushing open the heavy double doors, she immediately heard loud voices in the corridor. A throng of people came toward her. She saw Grant and Bill headed to the exit, followed by a newsman with a hefty camera on his shoulder. Ignoring the shouts and commotion, she pushed her way through the crowd. *Did the judge dismiss the case?* Grant's face revealed nothing. Bill, however, had a wide grin.

She wanted to run into Grant's arms but her feet were frozen to the floor. Then he spotted her; immediately stepped in her direction. "You're here." Words she'd held in for so long wouldn't come. All she could say was, "Yes, I'm here."

Bill tapped Grant's shoulder. "C'mon. Let's get out of here. Mort will handle the press, then meet us over at the office."

Grant glanced at Cassie, and turned back to Bill, "Can it wait? I can come by later."

Bill clapped Grant's shoulder. "Sure. I'll let Mort know you're detained." He grinned at Cassie.

Grant and Cassie left through the back door of the building.

"You have to get home?"

Cassie shook her head.

"Let's go for a drive."

She didn't know where they were going, nor did she care. Finally, she was no longer in a hospital bed, but alone with Grant.

When they left downtown Pensacola and headed toward the outlying area, she knew. The Can-Do Handyman van drove onto the familiar dirt road winding through the pines.

There still was a whiff of smoke in the air. Grant parked the van and opened the driver door. She got out and together they stood staring at the charred house and blackened grass.

He reached for her hand. "This is where it all happened, and I knew."

"Knew what?"

He turned toward her. "Knew that I couldn't live without you. When I saw you being taken away by ambulance, not knowing whether you were dead or alive, nothing else mattered." He brushed back her hair, ran his thumb along her cheek. "I love you, Cassie."

She pressed against him and looked up into his eyes. "It's why I came here that night. I knew too."

"Knew what?"

"That I'm in love with you. And it's time to tell you that. Jack *sent* me to tell you."

Grant flinched at hearing her husband's name. "Jack? But he's ,,,"

"Dead. I know. I know that more than ever, but I got a letter from him."

She saw his puzzled expression, then tugged on his hand to join her as she sat cross-legged on the grass. "I've got a lot to tell you." She told him about Earl's letter, her visit to Baton Rouge, the recounting of Jack's death, and finally the message her husband left behind. "I know who I want, who I love. It's you, Grant."

Their kiss was long and sweet and this time no one said stop.

EPILOGUE

May, 1973

C assie wiggled her toes in the fine white sand of Pensacola Beach as children ran with abandon chasing seagulls, collecting shells, and frolicking at the water's edge. Mrs. Hicks, swathed in a long-sleeve shirt and wide brimmed hat, collected their lunch trash to deposit in the nearest waste can. Grant, on his hands and knees, was helping Weldon and Lewis build a sand castle. Sharelle and Ruby scurried back and forth dumping buckets of water into the castle moat. She watched Grant digging, his arms and legs bronzed from the daily construction of the new house. He'd petitioned the School Board for reinstatement, but between the extensive time he was spending on his book and the high school still experiencing unrest, he wasn't anxious to return. He was, however, very much looking forward to attending Leroy's graduation tomorrow.

This was the field trip Cassie had looked forward to the most. None of the children had ever been to Pensacola Beach. When sharing that incredulous fact with Reina, the response was, "Cassie, you forget that everything was segregated, including the beaches, well into the '60's. The one beach designated for blacks was polluted. Most of us still feel uncomfortable going to Pensacola Beach—afraid of being harassed."

The sun was brutal. Mrs. Hicks, having lathered the children, informed Cassie that yes, black children also burned in this blazing sun. She smiled, recalling AdaMae's comment about how much her Yankee neighbor still had to learn about living in Dixie. She stripped to her bathing suit, generously applied sunscreen, and rose from the beach blanket.

Seeing their teacher at the water's edge, the children clustered around her, clinging to Cassie's arms like tentacles as they entered the water. One by one, she coaxed them deeper into the water for their first swimming lesson. As expected, Ruby was fearless, immediately put her face under, and followed Cassie's instructions. Next, came Lewis. Grant strained to hold the hefty child, yelling, "Kick, Lewis!" Cassie added, "And put your face in!" Briefly, Lewis dipped his face in the water, came up sputtering, "Yuck, it tastes like salt!" Cassie and Grant both laughed before calling out, "Who's next?"

Mrs. Hicks rolled up her pant legs and lifted Angie, now without her brace, into the water. "I've got another candidate for you." Grant passed Angie to Cassie, who wrapped her arms around the girl's slim body. Not to be outdone by her friend, Ruby, Angie took a breath, put her face in, and kicked and pulled, as instructed. Everyone clapped as Angie took a few strokes by herself before reaching for her teacher's arm once again.

Cassie helped her back into the shallows. "Angie, wow! You're a natural!"

The girl beamed at Cassie's praise. "Teacher, I like swimming!"

Cassie hated for the day to end. With only two weeks left of school, she cherished every moment with these children she'd grown to love. Swimming lessons complete, she encouraged the children to walk on the beach to dry off before returning to the van.

"Can we run, instead, Teacher?" Weldon asked.

Upon her permission, most took off in a dash. Angie and Teddie joined Mrs. Hicks on the beach blanket. Grant toweled off before jogging to catch up with Cassie and asking, "A penny for your thoughts?"

She sighed. "I hate to see the school year end."

"You have a couple of weeks. Don't forget Field Day coming up."

"The kids are looking forward to that. Who would have ever thought the P.E. teacher, Mr. Preston, would organize such a thing?"

"Another feather in your cap. Reina told me how it was you who first approached him with the idea."

"It was the pressure from Mrs. Washburn that did it. She's become quite the kids champion since the play. Speaking of Field Day—look at Sharelle run! I bet she wins one of the races on Field Day."

"And to think she almost lost that leg."

Cassie smiled. "I know. It's been quite a year. But it's coming to an end. So many of them are moving on."

"That's a good thing, isn't it? Thanks to you, many of them will be in regular classrooms, or doing well enough to move up a grade. And I think that heart of yours is big enough to embrace another batch next year."

She leaned into his shoulder. "Thank you, Mr. Lee."

"You're welcome, Mrs. Lee."

ADDENDUM

The fictional story in this book takes place in Pensacola, Florida in the early 70's, a time when this city and much of the southern states were transitioning from a segregated society to a court ordered integrated one. There was resistance to this integration on the part of many, as well as resistance to the push by African Americans and civil rights advocates for both equal opportunity and recognition of the injustice and transgressions of the past.

Escambia High School in Pensacola reflected the racial tension and attitudes of the community in that time period. Formerly an all-white school, Escambia High School was forcefully desegregated in 1969. Black students protested the use of the Confederate flag, the school mascot of a Rebel (Confederate soldier), and the school song, Dixie. They voiced their objections on the grounds that these images represented the Confederacy and were insensitive to black people. In the fall of 1972, a riot erupted at a home football game when the school band played "Dixie", the official school song, and the mascot "Rebel" (Confederate soldier), came onto the field.

After the 1972 football incident, some of the parents of the black students were plaintiffs in the case brought before a United States District Court to prohibit the use of these images at the school. The court ruled in their favor but the Escambia County School District appealed the decision and the injunction was overturned in January of 1975. Racial tensions increased after the school board victory with varying forms of demonstrations, both non-violent and violent, occurring in the years from 1972 until the worst riot on Feb. 4, 1976, in which close to two thousand students were involved, four students were shot, and twenty-six students were injured by rocks and debris. The community experienced violence also. Crosses were burned on some school board member yards with one member, who was black, specifically targeted with gunshots fired through his home window. A human relations board member, Teresa Hunt, as well as a state legislator, R.W. Peaden also had their homes torched. The Florida National Guard was called in to patrol the school. The Ku Klux Klan held an eighty-vehicle caravan with 450 participants in the nearby town of Milton.

The school needed to be patrolled by the Florida Highway Patrol and numerous local law enforcement agencies for the remainder of that school year. In 1977, after a court ruled that "Rebels' was not to be reinstated, the students chose "Gators" as the permanent nickname. The Ku Klux Klan, upset with this change, petitioned the School Board to hold a meeting at the school, but the petition was rejected.

As recent as 2018, Escambia High School administrators removed and rewrote a page about the history of the school's past regarding the riot and racial tension. The student editor who wrote it objected, but was overruled by the principal.

In my book, I have not followed the exact timeline of historical events, but instead used them as the backdrop for the story of Cassie and Grant's lives amid the social-political climate of this time and place.

About the Author

Yankee Girl in Dixie is Theresa Schimmel's second novel and sixth book. Her other novel, ***Braided Secrets*** is a family drama placed in a New England town in the '60's. She has written four children's books, ***The Carousel Adventure, Sunny, David's War/ David's Peace,*** and ***The Circus Song.*** A life-long writer, her published works also include numerous short stories and poems. For further information about the author and her works, go to her website: www.tamstales.net.

Her career as a classroom teacher and educational consultant has provided insight and inspiration in her writings. She lives in Rhode Island with her husband Steve and is the mother of two sons and grandmother of three children.

Made in the USA
Middletown, DE
11 October 2022

12305668R00210